BASED ON A TRUE STORY

SARAH VAUGHAN

SIMON & SCHUSTER

London · New York · Amsterdam/Antwerp · Sydney/Melbourne · Toronto · New Delhi

First published in Great Britain by Simon & Schuster UK Ltd, 2026

This paperback edition published in Great Britain by Simon & Schuster UK Ltd, 2026

1 3 5 7 9 10 8 6 4 2

Simon & Schuster UK Ltd, 7th Floor,
199 Bishopsgate, London EC2M 3TY

Simon & Schuster Australia, Sydney
Simon & Schuster India, New Delhi

www.simonandschuster.co.uk
www.simonandschuster.com.au
www.simonandschuster.co.in

The authorised representative in the EEA is Simon & Schuster Netherlands BV, Herculesplein 96, 3584 AA Utrecht, Netherlands. info@simonandschuster.nl

A CIP catalogue record for this book is available from the British Library

Paperback ISBN: 978-1-3985-0212-3
eBook ISBN: 978-1-3985-0210-9
Audio ISBN: 978-1-3985-0211-6

Typeset in Bembo by M Rules
Printed and Bound in the UK using 100% Renewable Electricity at CPI Group (UK) Ltd

MIX
Paper | Supporting responsible forestry
FSC® C013604
www.fsc.org

'Sarah Vaughan is the queen of psychological thrillers. *Based on a True Story* is another twisty, breathtaking banger that held me captive until the dying moments' **STEPH McGOVERN**

'A timely and compelling study of family guilt. Sarah Vaughan's finest novel yet' **MICK HERRON**

'Vaughan's cool, careful prose is a pleasure to read' ***TELEGRAPH***

'Expertly plotted and crackling with tension, this is dysfunctional family psychodrama at its unputdownable best' ***GUARDIAN***

'Cements her place as one of our finest thriller writers' ***DAILY MAIL***

'The gap between public image and private life is the theme of this clever novel . . . Intriguing' ***THE TIMES***

'A notably well-written, thoughtful thriller, strong on family dynamics' ***MAIL ON SUNDAY***

'A flawlessly constructed thriller, perfectly paced and filled with smart reveals. This is a read-in-one-sitting delight of a novel!' **LUCY CLARKE**

'A rich, intoxicating brew. I loved it' **LOUISE CANDLISH**

'This is a compelling story . . . It manages that rare trick of being both addictive and thoughtful' **ARAMINTA HALL**

'A deliciously twisty page-turner that also packs a real emotional punch. Vaughan is simply a genius at immersing you in simmering tensions and turning up the heat' **ELLERY LLOYD**

'An immersive, vivid, escapist story . . . this is Sarah Vaughan at the height of her powers' **LUCY ATKINS**

'Smartly plotted and wickedly fun' **CLARE FULLER**

'A juicy, atmospheric and unpredictable family thriller' **ERIN KELLY**

'Wholly absorbing and utterly addictive . . . One of my favourite books of the year' **ANDREA MARA**

Also by Sarah Vaughan

The Art of Baking Blind
The Farm at the Edge of the World
Anatomy of a Scandal
Little Disasters
Reputation

To my sister, Laura –
who, thankfully, is like none of these women.
With so much love.

One

Sunday: the day after the party

Rachel

Later, after the body is found, the police will ask Rachel why she left the party. Why venture out into the storm, braving the cliffs and the unlit coast path, to race down to the beach?

She hadn't heard the cry by then. The shriek that pierced the air, as shrill as a vixen, though she knew, in a heartbeat, it was human. *That* came as she hurtled across the wet sand, heart staccato-ing so fast she had to stop and fight a wave of dizziness that threatened to bowl her over. And, as she stood, listening to the sound coming in from the shore, she sensed more than one other person, in the darkness.

Not that she shared any of this with the police.

So no, it wasn't the cry that drove her from the noise and celebration of her mother's seventieth birthday. Because, by then, the party had settled into a good rhythm, the conversation flowing naturally as more than a hundred guests drank enough to be merry. To be properly at ease. Her mother's

North Cornwall home was magical. Fairy lights strung around the marquee; jasmine over the porch; and braziers along the path adding a frisson of Celtic danger: a reminder that this wasn't a quintessential English manor, but something a little wilder, more elemental, particularly as the wind picked up and the flames flared.

Elsewhere, glasses were chinked, wine was poured, canapés offered. On the lawn, a string quartet segued from Mozart to light jazz, and continued valiantly even when their music, attached to stands with clothes pegs, was blown over by the wind. Rain stopped play – a rumble of thunder and a flurry of fat drops – but the musicians rushed to the marquee with the guests, now shrieking with hilarity at the raging of the elements. A fierce crack of lightning and the screams turned hysterical – and it was at this point that Rachel's fear for her mother properly kicked in.

After all, it was more than an hour since she'd last seen her. Nothing unusual in that: Dame Eleanor Kingman had all these people to talk to and hardly needed any of her three daughters alongside her, but she suddenly seemed vulnerable, this seventy-year-old out alone in the wind and the rain.

Or more terrifyingly, not.

Because that was Rachel's real fear, wasn't it? That instead of being alone, out in the storm, her mother had met her nemesis. Her stalker. Someone Rachel had only just discovered, who was threatening to bring her carefully constructed world crashing down like a giant Jenga puzzle of bricks.

And it was *this* that forced Rachel out into the storm,

silk midi-dress clinging to her wet legs and hampering her movement; that drove her to run through the heath with its tufty scrubland, seemingly designed to make her trip. It was this fear – that her mother was in danger – that compelled her down the cliff path, toes digging into the compacted sand, hands clutching at the odd rock or shrub as she trusted that she wouldn't slip. And it was this that spurred her towards the shoreline and the tide, now rolling in in fury, driven by a hunch that the cry had originated from here.

Under a crescent moon that barely spilled light, she whirled around, straining to peer in every direction. 'Muu-um?' she called, into an air filled with the keening of the wind and the churn of the sea.

Because, at that moment, she wasn't Dame Eleanor Kingman: bestselling author, Labour peer for services to children's literature, stalwart of literary festivals, and the broadcasters' cultural darling. She was just a seventy-year-old mother and grandmother who, for all her complicated spikiness, was loved.

The wind gulped down her cry, and any response. Nothing. There was nothing. She tried to see through the velvety blackness. Was there someone, merging with the darkness? If she used a torch, then at least she might see. With trembling fingers, she fumbled with the clutch bag she still somehow gripped, found her phone, and swiped to the setting. And, as the pure white light puddled on the sand, she saw it: a mound of sodden clothes, she thought at first, and then, something very different indeed.

She crept a little closer, the tide no longer lapping at her toes but swilling around her ankles; her trepidation growing with every step.

'Oh my god,' she said, in a whisper, and then because that couldn't come close to capturing her shock, 'Oh my god, oh my god, oh my god.'

Because sometimes, you can recognise that something has happened and still refuse to accept it. That was how Rachel felt when she saw it.

The body.

Lying flat on its back; head against a rock; eyes firmly closed.

She bent and shone the light at a face that was usually so expressive; that indicated a fierce intelligence.

But that now would do so no more.

THURSDAY

Two Days Before The Party

Two

Eleanor

Dame Eleanor Kingman takes her place on a stage and looks out across the packed audience. More than two hundred fans have filled this open-sided tent on a Cornish clifftop to hear her speak as the literary festival's headline event.

'All set?' the moderator asks, gesturing to the microphone that whirrs in front of Eleanor's face like an insistent fly.

Rearranging the discreet ripple of diamonds on her wrist, Eleanor sits ramrod straight. Frances Pearson might be on the board of the festival, but Dame Eleanor, fresh from her million-selling sequel to her classic *Jess the Detective* – is the unashamed talent.

'Absolutely,' she says.

And her audience is rapt. Even before she begins, their excitement is palpable, and once she starts, well . . . if she'd suggested joining a cult, they would have signed up immediately. All these people who want to listen to her speak! It still gives her a quiet thrill, over thirty-five years since her first children's book was published. And when that stops? Well, then, she'll retire from public speaking. Give up the gig.

She feels her audience's appreciation most acutely, as she always does, when she gives a reading.

'Would you like me to read you a little?' she says, as if they alone, and not all the other audiences she will be seeing – two in Devon next month; then Oxford; then Cheltenham – are being offered this most delicious treat.

A frisson of excitement. She scans the sea of upturned faces, but her audience is benign (not a given these days).

'Well,' she pauses, and then, with a smile that fills her voice, so that she sounds as if she is reading the most enchanting bedtime story. 'Let me begin . . .'

She keeps her readings short. Even though there are just as many parents in the audience, she knows it's the children she needs to appeal to. Seven-to-nine-year-olds get bored so very easily, and the more entitled will roll their eyes or yawn extravagantly. Best to keep it under two minutes, and to make it dramatic.

'"Why was *that* there?"' she reads, hamming it up so they audibly gasp.

A hundred children watch, entranced. Or perhaps it's ninety-nine because her attention snags on a boy of around eight who stares, unsmiling, a distinct coldness to his pale, plump face. The nape of her neck prickles and she makes herself sound jolly as she brings the reading to an end. There! That's better! She's only feeling jittery because of the emails, in particular the latest which arrived yesterday. But this boy can't have anything to do with that.

'I think that went rather well!' Frances says, as soon as they've finished. Her ringlets, piled messily on top of her head, quiver as she nods, and her cleavage shudders.

'Yes, I think so, too.' Gathering her marked-up copy of *Jess the Detective*, and detaching her microphone, she follows Frances to the signing tent. 'Now. How quickly can we get through these?'

Because, as ever, there is a lengthy queue of over a hundred people snaking from the signing table back through the tent and into the separate tented bookshop. A takeaway cappuccino has been placed in her spot, thanks to Gilly, her eldest daughter and right-hand woman, and she sips it, eager to warm herself – and get on.

'So, who shall I dedicate this to?' she asks the first child, while glancing at a Post-it on the cover. 'Ah, Tilly!' And she is off.

And it's all fine. Despite the queue being even longer than she had calculated, she can do this, can even enjoy it because meeting readers, and hearing of their connection to her stories, is what writing is all about. There are always several early fans, and there is often one who says something like 'your female characters really don't like male authority figures, do they?' as if they fancy themselves as academics. She tends to tilt her chin up, look them in the eye and reply, 'Now what in the world makes you say that?'

But there are no spiky readers today, and she has just

turned to Gilly and remarked that it has been a good – by which she means easy – audience, when she realises she might have spoken too soon.

Because the boy, that unnerving boy, is standing in front of her, and he's looking antagonistic rather than bored.

'Do you have a book to sign?' she asks, glancing at his father whose hands are empty.

The man shuffles his feet. 'Jake just had a question, didn't you, Jakey?' And he nudges his son.

'Hello, Jake!' She makes herself smile. 'What was it?'

But the boy merely glowers.

'I suppose it's more of an observation,' his father helps him out.

Jake clenches his small fists and puts them deliberately on the table.

'You make everything up,' he mumbles, at last.

'I'm sorry, Jake. I didn't quite catch that?'

He raises his eyes and frowns at her; then repeats it. A clear accusation.

'You. Make. Everything. Up.'

'Well, yes, that's rather the point. That's kind of my job!' She pulls a bemused smile and turns to his father to enlist his help, but he is chuckling, along with those behind him.

'I mean, my books are filled with truths but they're the products of my imagination.' She smiles, trying to soften the edges of her speech.

'But that's lying. You're lying. You're not meant to *lie*.'

'Well,' she begins, glancing at his father because surely

the man will step in and soothe his son; tell him that fiction is a game in which everyone is complicit. But the man is unwilling to help and stands back, upper lip curled; arms folded across his chest.

'It's not really lying—' she continues.

'And lying's naughty,' Jake interrupts. 'You're not meant to do it. People who lie are mean and no one likes them. They just pretend.'

'OK!' she says, blowing the air from her cheeks. 'Well, we don't call it lying. We call it telling stories, and it's done for good reasons: to entertain people and help them emotionally connect with others.' A pause. She doesn't believe in talking down to children. 'Do you understand?'

'No.' He's starting to go red, and he looks to his father for confirmation. 'Telling stories is lying! And liars are bad, Daddy says so.'

The man tries to calm him, but Jake bats his soothing hands off.

'Right, well, thank you for your time.' His father's tone is clipped. 'Come on, Jake!' and, refusing to meet her eye, he manages to drag his son away.

'Well, that's one interpretation!' she says to the mother and daughter who've been waiting patiently behind them. The woman gives a little tut and shakes her head as if *her* child would never behave like this.

'Now, who am I signing this for?' Eleanor directs her attention to the little girl. And yet, as she goes through the motions of writing her name and discussing which character the child likes best, she watches the boy, looking fearfully over his shoulder.

You make everything up. You're lying. You're not meant to lie. Lying's naughty.

And it's hard to shake the feeling that he has seen right through her.

Three

Eleanor

It was the emails that started it. That made Eleanor feel as if exposure was imminent.

Not that there have been that many: just the four, from the first, six months ago, to the latest, yesterday morning. Sufficiently infrequent for her not to bother her daughters. Sufficiently frequent to keep her on her toes.

At first, she tried to convince herself they were the work of a crank. After all, every female writer of any stature experienced abuse. But two things cut against this: one, they had been sent to her personal email address, not the public one, which Gilly vetted; and two, there was a specificity to that first message which suggested it wasn't from some random reader, but from someone who knew a cold, hard truth.

By the time she received the second email, this suspicion had sharpened into a certainty. This was someone who knew something concrete about her. This was someone who, quite probably, *she* knew.

And though she had enemies – you didn't get to be a

highly successful septuagenarian author without incurring envy – this was next level stuff. She would have to tread rather carefully now.

So, although the party was conceived as an extravagant celebration of her seventy years on the planet and her extraordinary luck, as she still saw it, in becoming a 40-million-copy bestselling author, it quickly evolved into an exercise in unearthing her accuser. In coaxing him – she was sure it was a 'him' – out. Because while there were certain people from her past she would *not* be inviting, she could widen the guest list to include any acquaintance who might hold a grudge. What was that proverb about keeping your friends close and your enemies closer? She would kill off these allegations with kindness, and, if not, weasel out her critic. If there was one thing she had learned during her long and successful life, it was that she couldn't sit back and absorb the slings and arrows of fortune, outrageous or otherwise.

Eleanor considers all this as she sits on the terrace of her new Cornish home and reminds herself of the guests who will be arriving this afternoon ahead of Saturday's party: joining Gilly will be her two other daughters, Rachel and Delia, plus Rachel's two children, and Carole, her agent. Her core group – or inner sanctum – if you will. Then Rachel's husband, Tom, Eleanor's former agent, Peter, and her illustrator, Aiysha, will arrive tomorrow, together with a television crew documenting her life for a BBC retrospective. The bulk of the one hundred guests will turn up for the party on Saturday night.

Most of the partygoers will lodge elsewhere but these early arrivals will stay in her home: both in the main house and, in the case of the documentary crew, the renovated coach house beyond the kitchen garden. She needs some distance; was irritated that Gilly suggested they stay on site.

'I could do without them all descending on me, couldn't I, really?' she addresses Edith, her golden spaniel, who is sitting at her feet, alert, as always, to the need to guard her. The dog turns and rests her head on Eleanor's lap, nudging her hand so that her mistress strokes her brow and caresses the silky threads of fur behind her ears. The girls joke that she is her favourite child, and there is something in this: Edith is so *uncomplicated*. All that unconditional love; no sense of time beyond the present (and certainly no bringing up the past). Eleanor doesn't believe in mindfulness – who on earth has the *time*? – but there is something in the truism about learning from a dog's mindset, she thinks, as she closes her eyes for the briefest of moments and allows the sun to kiss her forehead; to ease her lines.

'Your coffee, Dame Eleanor.'

Her eyes snap open. Beside her, Natalie, one of the girls Gilly has hired from the village, places a fine ceramic coffee pot beside her, a matching cup and saucer, and a jug of hot milk.

'Thank you.' Eleanor is careful to sound gracious, and the girl bobs her head and scurries away.

She shifts in her seat, not liking having been caught unawares. *Do calm down*, she tells herself, as she sips her coffee and looks across the bay, enjoying the light on the sea. The waves roil then crash, the surfers riding their crests before flitting away; black specks that duck and dive while daring the elements to do their worst. Not that any squall looks likely today. The morning's chill has lifted, and the sky is a bolt of azure; the cliffs ablaze with mustard gorse and pink thrift and that wonderful earthy green. Above her, a pair of choughs rise on a thermal, crying out in delight just as she did when she first saw this spot, half a century ago. She hadn't known a place like this existed (though, at twenty, there was so much she was unaware of: the world was unspooling at a frenetic pace). And, as she stood on this cliff, basking in the warm, salt-scented breeze, she made herself a promise: that she would live here, one day.

Well, she has only gone and done it. For a moment, she allows herself to feel smug. All this is hers. This view, which gets better still at sunset, when the sun dips into the sea and turns it molten; this terrace, with its Delabole slate wrapped around the west-facing side of the property; the house, with its eight bedrooms, and another four in the outbuildings, its outdoor pool, where she swims each morning if the weather's fine and which she imagines her grandchildren enjoying; the walled kitchen garden and the lengthy drive from the B road, just in case she needs to signal her tasteful yet high-wealth status even more clearly, or her desire for privacy because it's perfectly possible to shut herself off from the world here. The heath behind the house – a reminder that Cornwall can only ever be partly tamed, and that it would be foolhardy to try this. The ramshackle summer house that a team of builders has nearly finished renovating and where she intends to write.

She loves this place. And she loves it not just for what it signifies – the resolution of a promise she made herself all those years ago, and a demonstration of all she has achieved – but because it is so coveted. A Michelin-starred celebrity chef was keen to buy it, and she took an intense delight in telling the estate agent to slap another £100,000 on her £4.15 million offer and beating him there and then. She cried when the estate agent rang to say she had been successful; felt uncharacteristically sentimental. What would Lea Savage think? Because that's who she was when she first stood on those cliffs all those years ago: a twenty-year-old student whose knowledge of the sea was based on Whitby – visited once – and *Five on a Treasure Island*. Not bad for someone who'd grown up in a back-to-back with a shared outside loo!

And now she is going to show it off to everyone who is important to her. Her older daughters have already seen it of course. (Rachel, who works as her accountant, had queried if she needed to spend quite so much; she has, after all, an Arts and Crafts mansion on the banks of the Thames, a Covent Garden flat and a cottage near Agatha Christie's Greenway in Devon, which, liking her wealth in bricks and mortar, she is reluctant to sell.) But her colleagues and Delia haven't, and it will provide a stunning backdrop for the documentary crew. She takes another sip. That's another thing that's bothering her. When she agreed to take part, she hadn't realised there would be *quite* so many talking heads with colleagues and members of her family. Much of *Eleanor Kingman at Seventy* will consist of an extended set-piece interview with her, but she still can't control what others will say.

Her heart gives a little stutter. It's been happening more frequently: perhaps she's been drinking too much caffeine, though it's inevitable that she should feel on edge. And not just because of the emails but because of the hundred-plus guests due in a couple of days. She strokes the dog, who rewards her with a typically loving look. What could possibly go wrong in a world in which she inspires such unflinching devotion? Well, quite a lot. Though the sky remains clear, she's unfathomably cold, her skin goose-pimpling, a ghost walking over her grave. For all her strength, the invincibility her ex-husband once accused her of wearing as a carapace, she is prickly with apprehension, as if that stolid boy's words have brushed against her and provoked an allergic reaction; a rash she can't scratch away.

You make everything up. Surely it was a coincidence that he echoed the thrust of the latest email. She reaches for her iPad, eager to check for any parallels. To see if that boy, backed by his father, is connected in any way.

Her fingers tremble a little as she swipes the screen. But here it is. A long email address – ineverythingillegitimate@yahoo.com – with literary pretensions, mirrored by the clichéd Shakespearean references in the text. The tone is uneven, the allusions asserting themselves too vigorously alongside a voice that veers from over-familiarity to waspishness to outright aggression. A quick skim reassures her that the phrase, 'you make everything up', doesn't appear, but the boy – she hopes by coincidence – had pithily summarised the email's gist.

And her memory is right. There's no explicit threat of blackmail in the message. This, and the three that came before, merely set down a marker. That someone knows something explosive about her: a secret that would destroy her career – and her life.

Well, she isn't having it.

She needs to be on high alert over the next couple of days. To channel the guile of her anthropomorphised vixen, and the perceptiveness of her neurodivergent child detective to get inside the psyche of her tormenter and determine who they are.

Which means she needs to scrutinise this newest email, and the ones before, as forensically as any set text.

Cursing her new vulnerability, she jabs the screen and starts to read.

From: ineverythingillegitimate@yahoo.com
To: freida@eleanorkingman.co.uk

How's the imposter syndrome going? I suspect it's raging, three days before your party. Or maybe you've managed to quieten it. After all, you've always been so good at pretending to be something you're not.

It's so easy to believe the blurb. To fall for the hype. Publishing loves a winner. (Until, of course, it doesn't.) But change can happen so easily. Because no one's immune to a scandal. Yep. Not even you.

It's entirely possible your brand could turn so toxic your publisher immediately drops you. No more printed copies and the existing ones pulped. Netflix pulls the animated *Jess*. Broadcasters ghost you, the *Culture Show* and *Question Time* embarrassed that they championed you as their arts pundit. Dame Eleanor Kingman cancelled. Wouldn't it be something for this to happen to such an established national treasure? It's happened to men who've done far, far less.

But as the kids say: you keep doing you. You keep on telling yourself your stories. You keep spinning those yarns, filched, in some cases, from others. As long as you remember that's all they are. Words signifying nothing. Full of sound and fury. As meaningless as a blogger's paid review, or an Influencer post on the gram. Yes, even one by your daughter. (And do you ever think what a waste of her talent? What an imagination, and such a good turn of phrase.)

Anyway, must let you get on. It must be exhausting continuing with the narrative you've created; your mind always wheeling; conscious you can never slip.

You should be congratulated, really, for your success in maintaining it all these years.

Perhaps it's time, though, that the truth came out.

Perhaps that would be a relief?

A party would be a great time for that to happen.

Because while you've been sustaining your greatest fiction, do remember . . .

That some of us know the truth.

Four

Rachel

'Can you. Just. Stop. Bickering.'

Rachel grips the steering wheel as her car soars over the River Avon, leaving the docks of Avonmouth behind them. They are on the M5 now. Over halfway there.

In the back seat, her children are momentarily silenced, Maisie glowering at her brother, Charlie staring fixedly at his iPad. Rachel watches them in the rear-view mirror, disarmed by her daughter's pout, the stubborn jut of her son's jaw. The journey has been fraught and, three hours in, she is finding it hard to remember quite how much she loves them. She doesn't even recognise her youngest, this child she adores with her dandelion clock of hair, her fierce self-belief. Why is that pout – a new, unnerving mannerism – so familiar? With a shudder, she realises that she reminds her of Delia.

Her tyres judder as the Audi veers towards the inside lane. A long blare of a lorry's horn. *Fuck.* She mustn't get distracted. Wouldn't do to get the three of them killed on the way to her mother's milestone birthday, a long weekend that should be absolutely glorious – Cornwall, late August, a country estate – but about which she is trying hard not to feel apprehensive. (Her younger sister is returning, after all.) *OK! OK!* She holds a hand up to the car behind her, indicates and nips from the middle lane to the slip-road, risking the rage of the trucker behind her, who flashes his lights and blares his horn at her again. *Think! Don't Drive When Tired!* The warning is splayed on signs along the route. Sound advice, but these days tiredness is her loyal companion, and she would never go anywhere if she did that.

'Why are we stopping?' A call from the back seat. Maisie. (Charlie's attention is fixed on the screen, his Beats making him oblivious to everything.)

Rachel shifts forwards in her seat, craning to find a space in the service station car park as they snake up and down.

Because, sometimes, my darling, you just have to. Because sometimes you can't go on.

She darts into a space, confounding an old gent who has driven up the wrong way and is waiting patiently for the slot.

'Because,' she says, more prosaically, as she flashes him a compensatory smile and ignores his grimace, 'we all need a wee.'

The service station is heaving with families making the exodus to the West Country. The air is stuffy, thick with the meaty stench of pasties, the grease of fries, the balm of milky coffee.

'Strawberries and cream Frappuccino,' Maisie states, as the Starbucks queue inches forwards, 'and a blueberry muffin.'

'No, Maisie. No, the Frappuccino's quite enough.' Rachel gives her youngest a smile which she hopes conveys she's vetoing this because it's financially excessive. Are her children spoiled? Yes, indeed they are. Despite her best efforts. Despite the fact they go to state primary schools and that little of their grandmother's wealth has trickled down, Eleanor believing that her children and grandchildren should *graft* (although this rule doesn't seem to apply to Delia). Despite all this, Rachel has managed to produce an eight-year-old who asks a barista for the most expensive item on the menu without even saying 'please' or 'thank you'. The temptation to sing 'change of mind' and march them to M&S to buy them a bottle of water each is acute, but she can't face a meltdown. It's a long journey and she needs to present her children at their best.

Because, if they don't somehow win their grandmother over, their days of buying Frappuccinos, not to mention all the trappings of their comfortable, middle-class lifestyle, are well and truly over.

Back in the car, Rachel tries to think more positively about the party. Eleanor absolutely deserves to be celebrated. What her mother has achieved is quite incredible: a multimillion-pound business that stemmed from a bedtime story she made up for her and Gilly when they were tiny, because the £20 million worth of sales for the *Fox Hole* books, and the Netflix series, and the various merchandising spin-offs – the plushies, and the stationery, and the children's melamine bowls and plates – all sprang from this. The *Jess the Detective* series, inspired by Delia and published twelve years later, compounded her success and paid for the Thames-side home and a lifestyle far removed from the humble upbringing Eleanor rarely mentions. Still, it's this background, or the fear she will never be financially secure, that drives her. It's completely irrational. Or, as Tom would say: utter bollocks.

Her mother is, frankly, filthy rich. Her latest bestseller, *Tyler the Detective's Daughter* – a sequel to *Jess* that was the overall Christmas number one and has sold a million copies in the ten months since publication – has paid for half the Cornish house, if you include agent's fees, tax and stamp duty; and she can justify a £25,000 party for a hundred guests in the same way Rachel might justify a takeaway cup of tea. Aside from her habit of acquiring properties, understandable for someone who knew to hide from the landlord as a child, she has grown accustomed to money, buying clothes or jewellery for herself; employing an interior designer for her main home; and giving each of her daughters a £100,000 lump sum at Delia's twenty-first birthday, ten years ago. To all appearances, Dame Eleanor Kingman is a woman who is intensely relaxed about her wealth.

And yet, in other ways, her mother is extremely frugal – insisting heels of parmesan are kept, or bread eaten past its best-before date; paying her middle daughter way below the market rate; gifting her grandchildren free paperbacks as their Christmas presents, and, of course, numerous *Fox Hole* plushies, of which they have long become bored. The truth is – and Rachel feels guilty even considering this – Eleanor can be extravagant with herself but, bar those £100,000 bequests, isn't always with others.

Which brings her back to the subject she has been trying to avoid thinking about. Her husband, Tom.

Oh, bloody *hell*! Her thoughts are spiralling so fast she almost drives up the back of a red Fiat Uno plodding along in the middle lane. *Get a move on, grandpa!* Accelerating into the outside lane, she speeds up to ninety, quietly thrilled. A blast and a flash of bright lights and a black Porsche is sitting on her tail. Watching the driver in her rear-view mirror, she refuses to go any faster, resenting his bullying insistence that she nip back in. How dare he assume she'll submit as a woman driver. Everyone always expects that of her: that she'll just roll over and forgive.

'Mum-meee. Why are we going so fast?' In the back seat, Maisie cranes behind her, fingers reaching to unclasp her seat belt.

'Don't undo your seat belt, darling. All fine! We're not.' She slips back into the middle lane and cuts her speed. As the needle drops back to seventy, the need to keep her children safe overrides her frustration, though it returns within minutes: a hard ball of fury, like heartburn, lodged in her chest.

She is so tired of being the person who always forgives. Who smiles serenely as she holds everyone together. Who says 'No worries!' and 'Of course, I understand.'

She'll continue to be the responsible one, particularly given her husband's recent behaviour. To be good and calm and kind.

But inside she is so furious, she feels as if she is going to combust.

And she fears that, at some point very soon, she'll no longer be able to suppress her rage.

Five

Delia

As arrivals go, it is pretty spectacular.

Delia, a connoisseur of long-haul travel, has seen more than her fair share of white beaches. You could even say she is jaded. But the Cornish coastline, glimpsed from a four-seater Cessna light aircraft, takes some beating. So much so that she can't help but grin.

The sea, where it is shallow, is as turquoise as the Med but the fields are apple green after a particularly wet summer, and these, and the granite farmhouses and odd ruined tin mine, are both quintessentially British and deliciously novel: a breath of fresh air after her extensive travels – quite literally. And then she spots a Georgian manor house: confident in its own good looks, exuding understated wealth, much like Delia.

It has to be her mother's new pad.

'Is that it? Could we circle over again?' she asks the pilot, a friend of a friend; she is adept at cadging favours.

The guy – Marcus, that's his name; early forties; pudgy and florid-faced; his Cessna an obvious expression of a midlife crisis – obliges, and she looks down at the house with its outdoor pool and tennis court and kitchen garden; its proximity to the cliff and its way of asserting itself, looking westward. Will her mother or sisters see her, looping high above them, drawing circles in the blue?

'Pity we can't land in her fields.' Marcus flashes her a grin. 'Would make quite the entrance. Then again, I guess you're used to making those.'

She smiles back, less warmly this time. He's been making similar insinuations throughout the flight and if she'd realised what a creep he was, she would have made different arrangements.

'Oh, occasionally,' she says, with a shrug of her shoulders and a dose of faux modesty. Just the descent to go, and then, with a vague promise to give him a call and the instant blocking of his number, she'll be on her way.

He is right, though, because making an entrance is something Delia does automatically, and not just because of her looks, which she has long realised are her currency. If you are brought up in the limelight, you soon learn the importance of making a strong first impression. And if, during those formative years of eight, nine and ten, you have to perform, even if it isn't expressed that vulgarly, then it's just what you do.

Yes, Delia is used to making an entrance because that's what she was taught to do when she was little. All those press interviews when *Jess the Detective* proved such a hit! The posing for adoring photographs with her mother; the 'at home' features for glossy magazines; even the odd appearance on a BBC sofa until she began to rebel at thirteen. For much of her childhood, she lived two parallel lives: part Delia, part Jess, the fan mail conflating both; the books' illustrations, too. 'I grew up with her, or she with me.' That was her line at parties, and then to disarm her questioner: 'Of course, Jess could never rebel, so I had to do it for both of us.'

But though she rebelled, and oh *how* she rebelled, against the constraints imposed upon her, the expectations she felt shackled by, she still acted as she had been schooled.

She made an entrance because she had been brought up to do so, and because she liked the power it gave her.

The power to wrongfoot people.

Take her arrival. No one knows she is coming by plane. No one knows what time she is arriving. Not the hour; not even the day.

'A free spirit' is how her mother puts it. ('Selfish,' say her sisters.) 'She likes being spontaneous, just like me.'

And it's amazing that her mother can spin this fiction because Eleanor is never allowed to be spontaneous. One of the things Delia most admires about her is that she is such a hard worker: a borderline workaholic who sticks doggedly to a writing routine. In contrast, Delia is enjoying a prolonged adolescence. At thirty-one, she has a huge platform – 689,000 Instagram followers; 830,000 YouTube subscribers – but no responsibilities beyond producing content. (And staying sober: more of a problem. A continual reckoning.) Sometimes, she wishes her mother would call her out on this.

'Ready for the descent?'

She smiles at Magnus – *that's* his name – who has whisked her further down the coast.

'Could we do another loop?'

'Bit of a thrill-seeker, aren't you?'

She shrugs. 'More like power crazed. You could get a God complex up here.'

'Why do you think I love it so much?' he says, pulling out the throttle and soaring upwards until – yes! – they are rising into a circle, and she hears herself whooping with exhilaration and delight and, for the briefest of moments, considers not blocking this guy's number because this is as thrilling as good sex and she could do it again and again!

'Once more?' he asks.

'No, no,' she says, laughing, but there's a slight edge to her voice because she can only cope with so much danger. Or rather, though she embraces danger, she needs to remain in control. Talking of which, she should film this: capture it for a reel she can post later. Though Gilly has stressed the need for privacy, a view from on high is hardly going to be problematic. She touches the screen to start filming, imagining the copy she'll write underneath and the possible music – All Saints' 'Pure Shores'?; Morcheeba's 'The Sea'? – as Magnus obliges by flying back over the bay and around.

'Time to begin our descent,' he says, and they head towards Newquay airport. She is untouchable, here in the blue; looking down at the specks of people bombing down the Cornish lanes below: her sisters; her mother; the guests and the TV crew arriving for the party. All these people descending on this isolated spot on this peninsula for one spectacular, celebratory night.

She shivers with excitement, and a touch of apprehension.

It's going to be a party to remember. And she wouldn't miss it for the world.

Six

Rachel

Well, if it isn't the blooming prodigal!

Her resentment grows as Rachel watches her younger sister crunch across the gravel drive to their mother's house, having been driven there by a man in an MG. The man hauls Delia's Louis Vuitton luggage from the boot and carries it to the door, giving it a little pat as he puts it down as if to tell himself that he has done his duty, or to reassure Delia that everything will be OK.

Watching from the sash window of her first-floor bedroom, Rachel sees him kiss her sister on both cheeks, then step back and laugh, apparently flattered. Delia touches his forearm lightly and smiles in response, her lithe body curving away. Whoever he is, and Delia collects and discards men with the careless abandon of someone for whom the supply will never dry up, he will be even more intrigued by this and by the peal of laughter that follows: a throaty cackle. Men love it. Even Tom. Her dirty laugh: loud, indulgent, replete with the promise of a good time.

And then she looks up at the house and Rachel feels a complicated mix of emotions that no one else prompts: a lift of excitement, because look how cool she is! Look how gorgeous! – and something darker: a jealousy that fills her with shame.

Always the golden girl, her younger sister is taking it to ridiculous lengths now. Her naturally blonde hair has a wave to it, and this and her white-blonde highlights mark her out as every inch the surfer chick she has recently become. Her face is tanned and her body sculpted, not just from her yoga, but from all the surfing and water-skiing and stand-up paddle-boarding if you believe her Instagram feed.

According to her socials, she has just been in the South of France or possibly holidaying on someone's yacht. The amount of freebies that girl is offered still baffles Rachel. Before that, she has been creating content in LA or Australia: the girl knows to chase the sun. And before that, of course, she was on what her mother euphemistically describes as her 'detox retreat'. Rachel, preoccupied with her kids, with Tom, with her own career as her mother's accountant, sometimes glances at her sister's grid, a colour-coordinated carousel of her travels in calming shades of blue and gold, and finds herself seduced despite knowing how carefully it's curated. Recently, she unfollowed her and felt intense relief.

The problem – or part of the problem – is that Delia makes Rachel feel so physically inadequate. So humdrum. So – she hates to admit it – prematurely *middle-aged*. Even now, fresh from a journey, her sister looks good: her yoga pants the right shade of charcoal, a white cropped vest revealing a slice of stomach neither of her sisters would dream of showing; an ear cuff and neck-mess of delicate gold suggesting both a nod to fashion and an understated wealth. Just above her trainers, a tattoo of briars circles her left ankle: sufficiently discreet to be hidden; sufficiently visible to suggest an edge. Rachel looks down at her feet. She has had a pedicure: bright red gels that now look too garish, as does her Greek-inspired maxi-dress, chosen because she thought it was vaguely hip, though she sees now that it's too voluminous; too mumsy; too obviously the dress of an almost thirty-eight-year-old hurtling towards forty. There are only six and a half years between them but the gap between early and late thirties feels extreme. Motherhood makes her feel closer to being part of Gen X, while Delia is clearly a Millennial babe.

The bell rings. A firm, bright sound: direct and authoritative. Rachel doesn't want to answer it, needing time to give herself a pep talk; to plaster a smile on her face. Besides, she assumes Natalie or one of the other staff will help. Instead, she hears Eleanor race for it, the dog at her heels, barking excessively and clattering across the slate hallway. From the landing, Rachel watches her fling open the heavy oak door, the afternoon sun flooding the cool hall and bathing her mother in a golden light.

'*Dar*-ling. Oh my darling!' Eleanor cries, her voice cracking with emotion.

And Rachel feels a sting of envy mixed with tenderness at the pure, uncomplicated relief of a mother whose youngest, most cherished daughter is finally home.

If Delia is aware of Rachel's resentment, she gives no indication.

Everything is *heavenly*. The French Riviera on her most immediate recent trip; LA and Australia, of course – 'you have no *idea* of the space; the quality of the light and the intensity of the sunsets' – though Rachel has been to LA with their mother, and Eleanor has visited several times to discuss adaptations; and indeed this Cornish spot, which she remembers as a child.

'You're so clever! The sunsets from here will be stunning – and a writing room in the summer house? Are you sure you shouldn't be showing that off on Insta, Gilly?'

'I think Eleanor's sufficiently famous not to require a social media presence,' their elder sister says.

Their mother gives a regal smile and delivers as close to a putdown as she will allow her youngest daughter. 'Really, darling, it's not my thing.'

There's a pause before Gilly tries to sound more conciliatory. 'Your Influencing's going well. Have you put the acting on hold, while you focus on this?' Because, after a spate of modelling, their youngest sister did a drama course in New York and was an extra in a *Hobbit*-type spin-off movie.

'Oh, I think so,' Delia says, a distinct edge to her voice.

'The beauty of social media is that it's so transportable. I could do it from here for a while: spend some time with Eleanor; reconnect. And it's something that, to an extent, I could just allow to happen.' She gives a little shrug. 'After a certain point, the business grows organically.'

Rachel glances at her mother: the hardest-working person she knows, someone who, for all her considerable faults, could never be accused of sitting back and letting things happen. But Eleanor isn't snorting with derision, as she would if either of her elder daughters came out with this hippy shit.

'Well, this is a form of acting, isn't it? Or of storytelling! All those little films – and you play acting to a certain extent? Because it isn't really you, is it? It's a brand.' Much like Dame Eleanor Kingman, Rachel thinks, because the twinkly-eyed children's author isn't the same as the sometimes-acerbic woman they all know, though no one mentions this.

And Eleanor gives her youngest daughter an indulgent smile.

Standing in front of the kitchen sink, Rachel unfurls her fists and concentrates on the view across the lavishly stocked kitchen garden, towards the grounds and Bodmin moor in the distance.

She would love her children to have a space like this. She was fifteen, and Gilly, seventeen, when her mother bought her Edwardian mansion on the Thames, and though they both benefitted, it was eight-year-old Delia who grew up believing this sort of upbringing was her right.

Delia was the one who learned to play tennis on the pristine court; who had a Fox Hole built for her, though it was dark and dank, and she never really enjoyed it; and who played in the old orchard, making fairy dresses from rose petals confetti-ing the grass.

Rachel and Gilly had a taste of their mother's wealth, but for a long time it felt precarious, not to be trusted, because the bulk of their childhood was spent in a very different home. A modest, three-bedroomed Victorian terrace, where they shared a bedroom, a handkerchief of a garden, and the sense of too many people jostling – teens and their annoying, adored little sister – while being told to *keep quiet*.

The *Fox Hole* books brought Eleanor financial success, but she was extremely cautious, only buying the larger house when *Jess the Detective* became a runaway hit. Even then, it took her a few years to get used to the feeling that this money wouldn't be spirited away. And, while Delia was brought up to be more relaxed, Eleanor was determined her older girls wouldn't take it for granted. Her greatest fear, she once confided, was that they would lose the fierce work ethic that had driven her to achieve all this.

Fat chance of that! Both Rachel and Gilly are grafters, working for the family firm out of loyalty to their mother and a need to feel connected to her books just as much as the muse-like Delia. Gilly, as the person who gets everything done, is properly compensated; Rachel, for reasons she has never quite understood, not so much. And she should work elsewhere, she knows she should; perhaps will have to, given Tom's fuck-up. But she doesn't want to. Her mother is concerned with her legacy; and Rachel is concerned that her mother isn't exploited and, less nobly, that she secures bequests for her children. If Eleanor is preoccupied with control, then so is her middle child.

She pours herself a glass of water, noticing that her hand quivers as she brings it to her lips. She needs to get a grip: her fear and rage feel all-consuming, as is her jealousy, because that's what's driven her from the room. This overwhelming sense of her mother's favouritism towards Delia, and the contrast between the way she treats her and Rachel's kids. She thinks of Maisie, who Eleanor practically ignores despite her displaying her stubbornness and resilience, and her rage builds like a fire, the embers stoked. Recently, she asked her mother to look after her daughter for an afternoon, hoping they'd bond. Maisie, ever energetic, had burst into her study, scattering papers and clamouring for a story, and had spent the rest of the time in the kitchen with Marta, the housekeeper.

Footsteps. She turns as Gilly joins her.

'OK?'

She nods.

'Got to let that green-eyed monster go, you know.' She says it with a wry smile; an awareness that she's aping their younger sister.

'Stop it! You sound like her. So fucking Zen.'

Gilly gives a hollow laugh. 'Far from it.' She leans against her sister and gives a quick shoulder bump of solidarity.

'Why does she indulge her? Can you imagine if we came out with all that? It's not even true, is it? She clearly works at her brand: not work as we know it, but nothing's left to chance. It's so scripted. So curated. She's completely *on* it.'

'I think there's probably a fair bit of guilt.'

Rachel snorts at the idea. It's a well-worn conversation, and it's hard to remain angry while Gilly is so calm. God knows how she does it. She glances at her sister, who, like Delia, looks like their father: sandy-haired, blue-eyed, high-cheekboned, while she is dark like their mother (or as Eleanor was as a young woman, because her gamine crop is now an expensive ash blonde). Perhaps that's part of the problem? When her mother frustrates her, Rachel feels as if she is raging at herself.

'Come on. We'd better get back.' And yet she delays leaving, enjoying this moment of quiet. For a moment, she toys with telling her older sister about Tom, but shame and a dogged loyalty stops her. Gilly hasn't been in a relationship for years and, though fond of her brother-in-law, would judge him. Rachel might criticise her husband, but others can't.

'Yeah, we should,' Gilly agrees, equally reluctantly, it feels, because it's relatively peaceful in the kitchen: no one's demanding attention or sparking up resentment in a way only Delia knows how. Life felt calmer and gentler before their younger sister was born. It was a time of creative energy and excitement – Eleanor was rattling through the *Fox Hole* books; her parents were collaborating on projects – but tiny Rachel felt safe. Unchallenged in that six-year period of being the youngest, before another contender came along.

'Can we have something to eat?'

A flurry of movement, and Maisie hurtles in from the garden.

'Tea with Eleanor?' Gilly teases, because their mother is never Granny, and the idea of sitting inside listening to the adults, even with the prospect of chocolate brownies, isn't one that will appeal.

'Not likely.'

'Tell it as it is, Maisie,' says Gilly, with affection, and Rachel is torn between telling her daughter to treat her grandmother with more respect and colluding in her laughter because her daughter's is infectious, and Gilly is suppressing a snort.

'Milk, an apple, or one of Marta's many cakes?' Rachel ticks the choices off on her fingers.

'Cake!'

'Please.'

'Please *and* thank you,' says Maisie, already racing off to find her grandmother's housekeeper.

'She'll go far,' says Gilly, a touch of wistfulness in her voice.

'Remind you of anyone?'

'You?'

'Not Delia?'

'No! Well, maybe the charming everyone bit . . .'

'Hmm.' Rachel shovels teaspoonfuls of Earl Grey into the white ceramic teapot and fills it with boiling water, feeling conflicted because, while charm might be appealing, it does make it easier to be spoiled.

They make their way back to the sitting room, where Delia is sitting at their mother's feet, listening intently; one tanned hand resting in Eleanor's, the other tucked under her chin. She looks just as she did as a little girl desperate for her mother's attention. But she's thirty-one now, and it's time to grow up.

'I have missed you all *so* much,' her sister enthuses, as she catches Rachel looking at her. Her left hand remains tight in Eleanor's, and their mother gives it a squeeze. Eleanor looks positively giddy: a dot of pink high on each cheekbone; something approaching contentment on her face. *I am being mean*, thinks Rachel. *Look how happy Delia makes her.* But a smaller part of her thinks: easy to be the good daughter if you've been away for the past twenty months; easy if you're the favourite child.

'Tea, Delia?'

'Do you have any lemon? No dairy. Sorry – herbal's good, or fresh mint? I can ask someone?' Delia springs up and gestures towards the door as she makes as if to move towards it. Her toenails are soft pink shells.

But Eleanor is determined not to lose her audience.

'Rachel can go, can't you, darling?'

She nods, her lips a thinned line. It's far easier not to offer resistance.

'Of course,' she says. 'That's absolutely fine.'

Seven

Eleanor

'Darling!'

Carole Jenkins, Eleanor's agent of forty years, rushes towards her, arms outstretched, a jangle of silver bangles clanking from her wrists.

'What a place! What a find! You said it was glorious, but you completely undersold it!'

At five foot three, Carole is several inches shorter than her client, but she still manages to clutch her to her breasts. Eleanor stands rigid as she endures the hug for the couple of seconds Carole always seems to demand, then relaxes as she is released. The bodily contact isn't over yet, though, because Carole is holding on to Eleanor's forearms as she squints up at her, her heavily kohled eyes as beady as a robin's beneath her shaggy fringe. The two of them met back in the late Seventies, and while Eleanor's style has evolved – sharp tailoring and clean lines; a classic palette – Carole's still references her hippy past. As she speaks, she rearranges a tasselled silk scarf entangled with an Indian necklace, then pats her cleavage, where another pendant dangles, with a hand studded with large silver rings.

'I didn't want to over-hype it,' Eleanor says, gesturing behind her to the sea that glints obligingly in the late summer sunlight. Even the waves are picturesque; little eddies and flurries, capped with spume, which dance their way to the beach.

'I'd never accuse you of that. Not your style. You're the epitome of quiet luxury now.' There's a pause. No need for either of them to mention that this hasn't always been the case.

Her agent divests herself of a large tote bag and they sit down in Eleanor's drawing room. It is early evening: that dead-end time between afternoon tea and dinner, and the French windows are wide open so that the scent of tamarisk and sea salt and the sound of seabirds float in on the breeze.

'Well!' Carole says, settling into a duck egg blue linen armchair and batting away Edith, who is sniffing at her legs. 'This is all quite marvellous.'

'It is, isn't it?' Eleanor says, and she feels a wave of what must be *contentment* as she lets herself relax at the end of the day. She is surrounded by four women who have her best interests at heart, and, just for this evening, she is going to put any nagging anxieties, about that creepy child, about the party, and particularly about the emails, aside.

Except Carole has other ideas.

'So,' she says, once they have toasted her latest sales figures – 'extraordinary'; the latest picture book remaining high in the charts after topping them at Christmas – and the efficacy, or not, of a particular marketing strategy. 'What's bugging you?'

'Bugging me?'

'Oh, come on, Eleanor. You should be looking like the cat who's got the cream, not least because of this rather excellent Pol Roger we're drinking in your exquisite drawing room.' She gestures with her champagne coupe at the eighteenth-century marble fireplace. 'But you're not commanding this glorious space. You're sitting on the edge of your chair, as if there's something you want to spit out, and that's not like you.' She takes a sip of her drink and studies Eleanor, deliberately. 'I know you, remember!'

Which is interesting, thinks Eleanor, because there are certain key things that her agent has no idea of, in the least. Carole doesn't know, for instance, about the extent of her ex-husband Michael's indiscretions (though she may have a clue); she doesn't know the extent of her childhood poverty, nor the reason she turned her back on her family so emphatically at eighteen. She doesn't even know that Eleanor has recently been wondering how much longer she will be able to write because her ability to spin a story, which has always been relatively effortless, is proving difficult for the first time.

And if Carole is clueless about all this, then Eleanor is hardly going to tell her about the recent emails with their implicit threat of exposure, is she? Her agent will want to know what they are about! And Eleanor has absolutely no intention of opening that can of worms. What would she say? *There's a chance I'm going to be found out, after all this time – and I'm scared.*

It's preposterous, and so she brings up something that has been quietly needling her, but that until this point has felt rather irrelevant.

'I'm having slight concerns about this documentary. I can't bear the thought of the "team"' – she makes quotation marks in the air with her hands – 'having free rein at the party. Mingling with my family and friends.'

'I thought you were all in favour?' says Carole, who has been less enthusiastic about the idea.

'It's the lack of control that bothers me,' Eleanor continues. 'I'm not used to it, and I don't like it. The idea that someone else gets to tell *my* story.'

Her agent gives a wry smile.

'Oh, I wouldn't worry about that,' she says, finishing her glass and reaching for the bottle in the ice bucket beside her. 'You know Humph,' she says, referring to the controller of the BBC. 'He won't agree to anything being transmitted that's disturbing unless,' and here there is a glimmer of interest in her shrewd eyes, which makes Eleanor's scalp shrink, 'they get a real scoop.' Carole shifts in her seat, then remains very still, like a leopard stalking its prey. 'There aren't any skeletons in your closet, are there? Any secrets you're not telling me?'

'Why would you think that?' Eleanor concentrates on keeping her expression blank.

Carole gives her a long, hard look, punctuated by a quick shrug as if to say, *well, you tell me.*

Around them, the air seems to still. The light has shifted, and with it, the birds have quietened. Eleanor ponders her agent's implicit invitation, wondering if this is the point at which to share something that has weighed her down for half a century. Then, as quickly as the thought occurs, it disappears. She has spent more than fifty years creating a specific narrative: one that has allowed her to flourish, to succeed, to get away with – well, she can't even articulate it. And so, very deliberately, she lifts her champagne glass, and holds Carole's gaze, challenging her to spill whatever she's suspected; gambling on neither of them wanting to risk it.

'I don't think there's anything you need worry about,' she says.

Carole decides to go up to her room shortly after this, and Eleanor, for a quick stroll. The need to clear the air is overwhelming, and she stands abruptly, eager to be away.

Besides, Edith has heard something: her ears prick and she gives a deep growl of warning. Eleanor puts her fingers to the dog's neck, as she murmurs some reassurance, but the dog remains unconvinced. Her body's rigid, the muscles in her flanks stapling her to the floor as she stares fixedly through the French windows and across the grounds, before barking, the sound insistent and high-pitched.

'There's nothing over there,' Eleanor says, more sharply than she intends. The dog barks again, which isn't like her – she's not neurotic – and Eleanor peers to spot what she has seen. The light has changed, the sky no longer a periwinkle blue but a bleached-out navy that will soon be lightened with peach, and, at first, there seems to be nothing – until there is, and her apprehension distils into a cool, sharp fear.

Because of course someone is there.

At the other side of the lawn, where it meets the shrubland, a figure – she can't make out the gender – seems to be crouching.

'OK! Let's go!' she says, softening her tone so that she talks to the dog in a way she wishes she had managed with her kids. The spaniel sticks obediently to her heels as they start across the lawn, Eleanor's calmness belying the fact her heart has started to race. One of the reasons she coveted this house was because it was so private, the Atlantic acting as a natural barrier to intruders, and the private stretch of coast path meaning no one would stumble this way. Eleanor isn't the suspicious type; has never worried about fans turning sinister, or ghosts from the past tipping up, until, that is, she started to receive these emails. Now, she realises she has been rather naïve.

It doesn't help that the dog is increasingly agitated, trotting a little faster and barking in a way that indicates her intense anxiety, until she starts running towards the person, who isn't staring at the house, Eleanor now realises, but facing out towards the sea.

'OK, OK!' she calls, because Edith's barks are suddenly

joyful as she races around the figure, rounding her up before burrowing her way into her lap.

'Hello, Ma!' Delia turns from her cross-legged position and waves at her across the lawn. With her other hand, she strokes Edith, who has rolled onto her back, panting and yelping, and demanding that her tummy be rubbed.

Stupid dog! Eleanor is flooded with exasperation at Edith's behaviour, and sweet relief that her half-formed fear – of what? An obsessive out to stalk her? – is unfounded, after all.

Her youngest child – the only person permitted to call her anything but Eleanor – unfurls like a snake.

'Darling,' she says, as Delia bounces towards her and places a soft kiss on her left cheek.

'What was that for?' She is hijacked by tenderness, and a small, hard ache in her chest.

'Does there have to be a reason?' Delia asks, her tone amused. Then, with a smile, she turns towards the view, her phone gripped in her hand, the camera framing the marshmallow pink sky.

'Selfie for my grid?' she says, with a sly smile because, of course, she knows the answer will be no.

'Certainly not,' Eleanor says, a little more briskly than she intended, but the emails have rattled her, and she wants no technological footprint of her home. 'Delete it now, will you?'

'It's fine. I haven't taken one.'

'You know I can't bear that sort of thing.'

'Well, it's my bread and butter,' Delia says with a mournful little shrug, then to demonstrate, turns so that the sunset and sea are behind her. Phone held high, she tilts her head to one side, looks up from beneath her lashes and smiles beatifically, holding her expression just long enough to capture the image. 'Done! See?'

It's all rather superficial, Eleanor can't help thinking, and simultaneously: does everything *really* have to be captured? *Come on, let's get inside*, she's about to say, when her daughter performs a perfect handstand. Eleanor waits. And waits. It is all *slightly* unsettling. Is her youngest intending to continue her yoga routine while they carry out this conversation? And then until the sun sets? The plan had been to regroup for a kitchen supper at eight.

Just as she is about to turn away, Delia rights herself, one long leg angling backwards and then the other. Her hair, far lighter than it was as a child, is scraped back into a messy bun and a couple of tendrils have escaped, which Delia blows from her face.

It is impossible to be irritated, and Eleanor watches with a mix of admiration and envy. Though she has practised Pilates for thirty years, she has never had her daughter's suppleness or strength. *Strong not skinny; brave and bold; faith not fear*: the creeds she trots out on Instagram, a platform Eleanor neither understands nor rates but which she believes still demands exacting copy, are most dreadfully *trite*. And yet Delia epitomises them. (Though, if not skeletal anymore, she is very slender. *Strong and slender* is a better description than *strong not skinny*. More positive, too. Eleanor isn't one to interfere in another's copy – no, *really* – but she might suggest her daughter tweak it. No need to *constantly* define herself through opposition.)

'Hey – so how are you?' Delia asks, her blue eyes searching hers with a disarming frankness that suggests she is genuinely interested.

'Oh, pretty good!' And again, there it is: that temptation to mention the email, to confide in someone, uncharacteristic though this is. But how on earth can she admit this? It would mean confessing to the thing she barely thinks about, but which is always there in her subconscious; the most formative event of her life; intrinsic to who she has become, fundamental on a granular level to her story, though something she can never share.

And so, she tells the same half-lie she told Carole: that she is just the tiniest bit apprehensive about the documentary team's arrival.

'Well, you don't have to do it, do you?' says Delia, rolling up a yoga mat and tucking it under her arm. 'You could just send them away or tell them you're no longer cooperating.'

'I think that would guarantee a less than effusive take.'

'Or you could refuse to do the interview if that's what's bothering you. It's not as if you need the publicity. Couldn't you just pull the whole thing?'

'I *could*,' she says, her tone indicating that the moment has passed, and the conversation is over, 'but it's rather too late.'

'I wouldn't worry.' Delia starts walking back to the house.

'Everyone will be falling over themselves to praise you. Who's been interviewed, apart from the three of us?'

'The usual suspects.' She reels off a list of publishing types, including her agent, editor and a clutch of fellow authors.

'Not Dad?'

And there he is again: mentioned not long after Carole made her think about him. Bloody Michael! Eleanor's heart factors in an extra beat. She waits a couple of seconds before trusting herself to speak. 'Not your father, no. Why on earth would he be involved?'

Her daughter bends to fuss over the dog, and Eleanor is grateful that Delia can't see her expression. Why bring him up? He is usually blocked from conversations: the older girls know not to refer to him and she can't remember a single reference the entire time Delia has been away. But her youngest has now lobbed him in. Is Eleanor triggered because she's been considering how much she kept from Carole – and here she can't help thinking about that particularly horrid business with that girl; the point at which their marriage was always going to fail, though it limped along for a further decade – or because he has the knowledge to ruin everything?

Delia stands back up and gives her a guileless smile. 'No reason!' She tucks her arm into hers, and Eleanor tells herself to relax. 'Honestly, you've got absolutely nothing to worry about. This isn't like you!' Delia gives her a friendly nudge. 'You're always telling us to seize the day. What would Delightfully Delia say?' she continues, referencing her Insta handle. '"Better to regret the things you've done than those you haven't?"'

'Well, perhaps not.' She never knows how to take her daughter's inspirational quotes, which are *surely* meant tongue-in-cheek?

'"Move forward with hope", then?' Delia gives a grin as if to say that of course she is in on the joke. That she doesn't buy into the guff she parrots; that she knows it's a game.

And the relief that her daughter has somehow retained a sense of humour allows Eleanor to relegate the emails – and all the complicated emotions they provoke – to the back of her mind.

She has her girls. She has her work. She has this exquisite house. She even has – and Edith is leaning into her right calf as if to reassure her that she is still her favourite, despite her slavish adoration to Delia – this ridiculous dog.

A malicious emailer, even a persistent malicious emailer, need not be a threat.

They are crunching across the circular gravel drive now, to reach the porch with its Palladian pillars. She pulls open the original oak door and shuts it against the dusk, giving a heavy sigh. The hall smells of woodsmoke and melted butter. Dinner is sea bass, samphire and mash: food that conjures the warmth of an idealised childhood and showcases the wildness of the north Cornish coast.

All will be well; all manner of things will be well, she tells herself, as she crosses the hallway towards the high-ceilinged corridor which leads to the west-facing dining room. By day, a fanlight casts a shaft of sunshine onto the floor's worn slate, and she tries to imagine – manifest, Delia would say – being encased in its gentle glow.

But the hall is uncharacteristically gloomy: the lamps haven't yet been switched on and dusk has properly fallen. From further down the corridor, a gong sounds, as ominous as a tolling bell. And with it she hears that child's voice: his mounting distress as he pinpointed the artifice of her work, and of this life she has built around her: *You make everything up. Telling stories is lying. You're not meant to lie.*

And then that threat from the email: *Perhaps it's time, though, that the truth came out . . . A party would be a great time for that to happen . . .*

'Let's get some lights on in here, shall we? Goodness, where is everyone?' She fumbles her way to the switch, an uncharacteristic wave of panic tightening her chest.

'You OK?' Delia looks at her, quizzically, as light streams down and Eleanor feels relief course through her.

'Yes, darling.' Her tone is brisk. 'Perfectly OK.'

She gives her youngest a tight smile, then consciously tries to make it more heartfelt. It is rare for Dame Eleanor Kingman to relax, but surrounded by her daughters, she is going to have to try.

FRIDAY

Eight

Rachel

It isn't even seven a.m. and Delia is already being performatively beautiful.

Rachel pulls her zip-up hoodie closer around her as she spots her younger sister mastering a firefly pose at the edge of the cliff against a backdrop of a flaming sunrise and limpid sea.

How on earth does she *do* it?

It must be not having kids that allows for a core so strong she can hold her body weight on two straight arms while her legs shoot out in front of her. That, and having the time to practise. She waits for Delia's arms to give way, but her sister's strength is formidable and her concentration, unflinching. After what feels like a couple of minutes, she shifts position and executes some kind of complicated headstand, her endless legs crossed in a lotus position and neatly packed away.

Will she be OK with being disturbed? Rachel hovers, conscious of intruding on her sister's morning ritual. Is this part of her mindfulness? Ever since Delia's 'problem', as their mother delicately refers to it, they're all aware that she's far more fragile than she might appear.

Be kind, Rachel reminds herself, except that it is hard not to be cynical when you spot a camera on a tripod and realise that this isn't an intimate communing with nature, but something choreographed and curated. Because everything, from Delia's yoga kit to her dewy make-up to the camera angle, has been chosen for the 'gram.

Realising that Delia is preoccupied with the recording, Rachel heads for the beach, intent on calling her husband. With both children still asleep, this is the only time she can guarantee their talking uninterrupted, and there is so much she needs to say. The path requires concentration, but she is soon kicking off her Birkenstocks and jumping onto the fine sand. For a moment, she enjoys the sensation of sinking her toes into the silky coolness, remembering childhood holidays and their mother's fascination with this stretch of the coast. But any rose-tinted memories are brief as she anticipates a call that will be difficult.

Because what can they say that hasn't been discussed, far from calmly, on Tuesday evening, when she confronted Tom about the phone call – then watched a wrecking ball swing into their marriage? Just the thought makes her stomach hollow with pain. But they can't regurgitate it this weekend. For two days they need to keep it together; to make sure that nothing threatens her mother's happiness; and that their fear doesn't seep into their expressions or body language, let alone those little asides they're bound to make when they think no one is listening.

'Hi.' She keeps her voice cool.

'Hi!' Surprise and delight and a recognition that he needs to make things up to her pretty damn quick fill his simple greeting.

'Just thought I'd check when you'll be down.'

'Early afternoon? I'm leaving in a sec.'

'Oh.' She had thought he might suggest not coming, which would be easier, in a way.

'I didn't want to risk offending your mother by being late.'

'Yep.'

'Particularly since I thought we could ask her about, you know . . .' His voice trails off and she waits, hardly believing he is saying this. 'You know. About what we discussed the other day?'

'Oh no,' she says. 'Oh no, no, no.' Her anger, which she has been trying to keep under control, starts to bubble up. 'You will *not* be discussing that with her.'

'Or *you* could.'

The suggestion makes her catch her breath.

'You know I won't be doing that, and I explained why,' she says, at last. She sinks one foot into a patch of quicksand and watches the gloopy mixture cling as she draws it out, still waiting for his reaction.

'Rach. It's the only way.'

He is wheedling, and she wonders if this is the point at which she stops loving him, because there is no hint of the husband she knows. That decisive, *confident* man, who isn't particularly complicated, and who provides her with the emotional ballast with which to counter her family.

'It is not the only way, and I won't be doing it.'

'It would be nothing to her . . .'

But that isn't the point. 'It would be *everything* to me.'

There is a pause while she hears him suck air through his teeth. He'll be pacing the kitchen of their London home, and she mirrors that pacing, until she comes to a partly submerged granite rock and kicks it, quite deliberately. *Ohnononononono.* Pain stymies her speech. Her big toe has slashed on a barnacle, and she watches, mesmerised, as blood swirls in the rock pool and she waits for him to speak.

'I'll text when I'm at Bristol.'

'Yes. Fine,' she manages.

'We'll talk properly when I'm down.'

She nods.

'Rachel?'

She kicks out at a puddle, craving the salt's sting.

'Yes,' she says, her voice shrunk with pain.

'I'm so sorry. You do know that, don't you?' His voice cracks, as if he's only just holding it together. 'I'm so very sorry for what I've done.'

'Yes, well, OK.' She thinks she might start crying. 'OK. Yes, O*K*. I'll speak to you later.'

Because what can he possibly say?

She thinks back to her discovery, just three days ago. That call from the mortgage company, informing her they were terribly sorry but their application for an additional mortgage had been rejected.

'But we're not applying for an additional mortgage.'

The too-long pause at the end of the line.

'You're Mrs Quinn? Rachel Quinn?'

'Yes.'

'You signed the application, with your husband, for an additional five hundred thousand pounds to enable building work?' the young woman says perkily, as if the figure of half a million pounds is something that might have slipped Rachel's mind.

'Err, I'm sorry, I don't—'

'Perhaps I could speak to your husband?' the woman continued, her tone now more hesitant.

'He's at work. You can speak to me.' She smarted, knowing that she sounded like her mother, but she needed to counter this idea she knew nothing about it.

'Well, we'll be writing to explain, but I'm very sorry: we can't underwrite this. Your repayments would be just too high.'

And Rachel couldn't bear it. The fact the woman knew she was lying; her palpable sympathy; perhaps her suspicion that Tom had another family; that Rachel was just another highly credulous woman and not an accountant on top of her family finances, as she wants to insist she is.

'Of course!' she tried to rescue her. 'The building work! I thought we'd agreed not to apply for that amount after I signed the documents. The plans were just too ambitious.'

'Well, it *is* a substantial sum of money on top of the existing mortgage,' said the woman, eager to get this conversation over.

'It is, isn't it,' she agreed.

She managed to hold it together until the end of the call, then waited until Tom came home.

It had all started with the odd online flutter to distract himself from the stress of work. As an anaesthetist, he needed to remain calm and measured. But patients sometimes died, on-calls could be punishing, and the increased workload, relentless. One night an eight-year-old boy died on the operating table, the victim of a hit and run. Back home he'd poured himself a drink and opened an app; anything to prevent himself from thinking about the horror of the evening. It was mindless. Little thought. No calculation. The antithesis of everything required of him, professionally. To his surprise, he'd won.

He'd chased that emotion again. Of course, he lost the next bet, and so he obsessively repeated the process; emptying their savings; acquiring extra credit cards, and, fatally, borrowing from a loan shark he met via a hospital porter. (The guy was his cousin.) And all the time, the debt rocketed as he gambled higher and higher in the hope of that one big win that would put everything right.

By the time he'd put in the mortgage application, the amount he owed the loan shark had spiralled to £280,000 – due today, the day before her mother's party – with the sum set to double to £560,000 if he can't make that deadline. The

£500,000 mortgage – madly; incredibly! – was an attempt to consolidate the debt and provide a tidy sum with which to gamble, in the hope of swiftly paying it back.

That discovery had been on Tuesday, and Rachel has barely slept since, those terrible hours from four a.m. onwards spent trying to think of a solution and willing the dawn to arrive. How to magic up £280,000 within three days? It's beyond them – because there is no magic money tree.

Except, as Tom was quick to point out, there potentially is. According to her husband, she should ask Eleanor for help, his rationale being that £280,000 is nothing to a woman who has just spent more than £4 million on a fourth home.

But Rachel can't ask her mother to clear her husband's debts. Dame Eleanor Kingman knows what it is like to have to support a husband financially and she'll be appalled that Rachel has got herself in her position. Nor will she have any sympathy for his addiction. Eleanor has seen the devastation this wreaks and is vigilant in distancing herself from it.

Besides, while he's been gambling away, she has grafted to achieve her massive success and, at seventy, still hawks herself to literary festivals, gives lectures to students, meets deadlines and keeps generating new ideas. To ask her to write a cheque for this amount without the hope of being repaid is insulting. The only possible solution is to see if she would consider offering them a loan.

And even that isn't something that Rachel can ask. It

would mean admitting to her husband's weakness, her marital ignorance and her financial ineptitude, and she can't risk her mother's, at best, *disappointment* that the daughter who is supposed to be financially savvy has found herself in a situation like this. Then there's the added complication that she oversees Eleanor Kingman Limited's accounts. The fear that she will jeopardise her career. All the goodwill she has earned by working for the family firm, all the emotional collateral, will be squandered. She'll be the least favourite daughter, again.

She shoves her phone inside her pocket and looks out to sea. There's a mound on the sand that doesn't look like a rock. Something left by the tide in the night. She stomps over, seeking distraction, her cut throbbing as it fills with sand.

It's a beached dolphin. Around six feet long, a pristine midnight blue and white, as solid as fibreglass, its jaws revealing many tiny teeth. It's perfect. Unmarked, unscathed, no sign of blood. Such a beautiful creature, dead for no apparent reason, and, even now, beginning to decay.

Well, this is morbid! The thinking of someone who feels trapped like this beast. She'd better get back to her kids and her mother and sisters; to all the incremental problems that make up her day. High above her, up on the cliff, Delia stands, her arms raised as if poised to dive. She has the world at her feet, that girl; has absolutely no idea how much she is blessed.

And Rachel? Somehow, she needs to find £280,000 within the day to prevent the sum doubling to an inconceivable

£560,000; to stop her family falling apart and her home being repossessed.

But, as she traces her steps back to the house, she has no idea of how to avoid it.

Nine

Eleanor

The noise startles Eleanor.

A brusque *rat-a-tat-tat* on her office door. Unusual because her daughters and staff all know to knock gently.

For once, she is immersed in her work, getting the words down and getting them *right.* The knocking, which Edith greets with her usual frenetic bark, feels like an affront. Everyone knows a closed door and no response means she mustn't be disturbed. Except, it appears, this person. She waits, determined to ignore it. Hoping whoever it is gets the hint and slinks away.

Rat-a-tat-tat. Oh, for goodness' sake! Another volley of barks from the dog as Edith trots to the door, nose quivering, tail wagging, alert and expectant.

'OK, OK!' Irritation makes her voice grate. 'You'd better come in.'

'Just thought I'd say hello!' The door opens, and Ned Simpson pops his head around.

'Oh, how lovely.' Her bad temper disperses at the sight of

the documentary maker, in part because he is an outsider, and she knows the importance of charming those outside her inner circle, but also because Ned Simpson is the sort of breathtakingly beautiful young man Eleanor has never been able to resist. Six foot three with the bone structure of a leading man and eyes that hold hers a millisecond too long, as if he can't help but find her intriguing. The dog, meanwhile, is making Ned's attractiveness known less subtly by nuzzling his groin.

'Good girl, what a good girl.' Ned bends to ruffle her back and move her snout, then strides towards her owner, his hand outstretched. Eleanor grips it, enjoying the warmth and breadth of his palm; the length of his fingers; his customary firm handshake.

'Lovely to see you again.'

He looks at her intently. Not many people have genuinely green eyes: she has only known one other person, and she wasn't a fan. But she has warmed to Ned, not just because of his looks – 'gorgeous' is the adjective usually applied: 'The Gorgeous Ned Simpson', and it amuses her that he is objectified like this – but because he conducts himself in such a confident and decisive way. Like her, he is a go-getter, and it is partly because she could see herself in him that she agreed to this documentary.

'So, are we all set?' he asks, after she has checked that he is happy with his accommodation – 'charming; so generous' – and that he is aware of the best spots from which to capture the sunset. ('I know it's not as simple as shooting to the west.')

'I think so,' she says, as she gestures that he should sit. 'We've our final interview tomorrow morning, isn't that right?'

He nods.

'And you're doing one with Delia?'

Eleanor's youngest daughter has had such a hectic travel schedule she hasn't yet been interviewed on camera. Plus, given her issues, Eleanor has wanted to protect her.

'Yes, indeed.'

'And it sounds as if you've a lot of material?' she fishes, though she told herself she wouldn't pry.

'I have, yes.'

'You should have an easy couple of days, then?' She doesn't mean to sound combative, but she is used to wheedling stories out of others.

'There are a couple more interviewees I'm hoping to squeeze in.'

'Oh?'

'It's such a unique opportunity: having your family and your friends amassed like this.'

'Well, hopefully there'll be a consensus?'

She delivers it as a question, but he merely gives a shrug, his generous mouth curving into a smile.

'If you'll excuse me one second?' Drawing out his phone, he rattles out a text, perhaps to one of his interviewees or his crew. It's rather rude. 'Sorry about that,' he says, and his smile is so beguiling, she can't help but feel charmed. It was like that with that other green-eyed individual, too. 'Oh – just one thing. Delia? I know there were specific reasons we couldn't interview her before, but is there anything else I should know?'

It's an elegant way of alluding to her youngest's alcoholism – Eleanor doesn't acknowledge the former coke problem – and her two-month rehab at the luxurious Clinic Les Alpes, eighteen months ago. Delia has made no secret of it; indeed, it's been critical to Delightfully Delia's success. Still, Eleanor would prefer it if they skirted around the whole episode. Moved on. Not so much pretended it hadn't happened but refused to allow it to become part of the story. How to convey this, while impressing upon Ned that of course it has made a mark? That it's made Delia particularly vulnerable?

Her throat tightens and she turns away to fuss with the dog, wanting to mention her youngest's fragility without undermining Delia's credibility. Perhaps she should just appeal to his better nature, something she has never found easy because she never likes to ask favours. Can only really trust herself.

'I realise she looks very "sorted", but appearances can be deceptive. Be gentle with her, please.'

He has been gentle with Eleanor, up until now, at least. (There have been three interviews so far, with various email exchanges.) And, as he heads off to meet his colleagues, she thinks back to the first interview, around ten months ago.

There was so much *faffing* involved: the 'soundie', Glen,

fiddling with a boom, and the cameraman, Adam, moving tripods and suggesting she sit so she benefitted from the most flattering natural light. They had wanted some footage of her writing (or pretending to write). And while she was going along with this masquerade, Ned began his questions, asking about her 'process' – a load of twaddle – and then about the origins of her success.

'If I could take you back to the beginning . . .'

'The beginning?'

'When you started to write?'

'Do you mean when I decided I needed to get published?'

Because she had always written. Lengthy stories as a young girl, then poetry as a student in London, and an unpublishable, coming-of-age novel.

'When was that?' Ned leaned forwards, willing to be led wherever she took him. And so, she started her narrative where it best fitted the Eleanor Kingman story: the mother of two, crafting stories with which to entertain her preschool girls.

Even now – some thirty-six years later – it is easy to teleport herself back there, to their freezing Chiswick terrace. Michael, his thick fringe falling in his eyes, hammering away at his typewriter near the wood burner, while she wrote, longhand, at the kitchen table: a colder, decidedly more domestic, place.

The fierce joy of working as the girls slept; the two of them fuelled by mugs of tea, or cheap red wine; by optimism and the sharp focus of competition: her prose sculpted in the unspoken knowledge that she needed to be *better* than her husband, with his clear head start in life.

Because Michael had it all: upper-middle-class parents; a public-school education; the sort of Rupert Brooke looks that silenced her when she first met him; the First from Cambridge; the gigs reviewing fiction for *The Observer* and *The London Review of Books*. He would never be an Angry Young Man, a writer of kitchen sink dramas (his class – he was a judge's son – precluded this), but he had a breezy self-belief he would make a career through writing. Everyone knew he was an emerging talent. One who would be heralded as a Best Young British Novelist within the next five years.

Lea, as she was then, held no such ambitions; was too busy dashing off short stories for women's magazines: tear-jerkers about salt-of-the-earth mothers, and girls who might rebel but came good at the end. They couldn't have been more different from her stream-of-consciousness debut, but she learned about character arcs and pacing and plot. Unburdened by the need to display her intellect, she learned how to write.

And as she did, late at night, or while Rachel napped and Gilly drew with fat wax crayons beside her, she considered what sort of stories she could produce that would fit with the children, since Michael, for all his vocal support of feminism, had never once considered a role at home with the kids. Ruthlessly self-critical, she was also pragmatic: she needed to write something that would sell and that she could fit in with the demands of mothering. She had tiny children to whom she read each night: why not write the sort of stories *she* wanted to read?

Because for women like her who had come of age in the late Sixties and Seventies, Blyton didn't cut it; and though she rated Dahl's imagination, she recoiled from his misogynist view of the world. Instead of making the women weak or villainous – she shuddered at the aunts in *James and the Giant Peach* – why not put them front and centre? She considered this as she made yet another meal with red lentils (Rose Elliott was her saviour); as she filled buckets with Napisan and ploughed her way through the seemingly limitless mounds of washing two small children created; as she tried to fit her writing around the edges of looking after them and this stultifying, domestic work. She considered it as she tried not to resent Michael for having his ring-fenced time to write, the reviewing meaning an office and a means of escape, and as she experienced an envy so intense that, in her most sleep-deprived moments, she imagined stabbing him with a vegetable knife.

Of course, she told Ned none of this. Instead, she offered a sanitised version in which the couple wrote side by side to provide for their family.

'You felt a need to provide financially?'

She looked at him. 'Have you ever been chronically hungry, Ned?'

He gave her a rueful look because, really, there was no need to ask. Beautiful young men who worked in arts broadcasting came from a rarefied world. Besides, she was good at detecting fellow escapees from poverty, just as she instinctively recognised eldest siblings, and specifically eldest daughters. There was an alertness to them; a drive that persisted long after their physical hunger was satisfied.

'It's not something I could ever risk my children experiencing,' she replied, smoothing down her skirt and taking a moment to think of her own, very different childhood. 'Of course, that was unlikely with their father and his family, but it was still something I feared.' She wrenched herself firmly back into the present. She is *not* going to go there. 'But I was lucky. I had a little skill to prevent that from happening.'

'More than a little,' he said. '*The Fox Hole* was a huge success as soon as it was published, wasn't it? So from 1986 . . .'

'Well, perhaps 1987. It took a few months. I didn't have a vast marketing budget, like some debuts have now. But it seemed to resonate with mothers from the very beginning. Freida Fox was a hunter; a provider; and a lone vixen. A vulpine single parent. And though the children liked the cubs' stories, their mothers seemed to respond to her resilience: what I suppose would now be dubbed, horrible word, her "feistiness". Freida was a fighter – quite literally – and women recognised her ferocity and tenaciousness.'

'And yet, these were very much books for children?'

'Oh yes. The feminism wasn't explicit: no child would want that rammed down their throats. Obviously, character always comes first, but children need plot. They need good stories: a strong narrative – whether that concerns the danger inherent in catching chickens or in stealing from the farmer's kitchen. Anything that involves enough jeopardy to scare them a bit.'

'The books are unapologetic in their willingness to scare children?'

'They allow children to scare themselves – or perhaps *thrill* themselves is a better way of putting it. It's a controlled sort of jeopardy, like the kind experienced by adults when they devour thrillers. But ultimately children know they're reading from a book and so, ultimately, they're safe.'

'It's a gentle jeopardy?'

'If you like.' She knew her daughters had been properly scared at key moments, and she didn't like him diminishing their emotions, but she wouldn't quibble each point.

'One might say the books are cosy?'

'Cosy?' She could hear the tremor in her voice. 'Do you mean because of the setting?' The fox hole was in a copse at the top of a hill in farmland: she'd imagined the Cookworthy Knapp beech trees as you crossed into Cornwall from Devon. But it was reductive to think that because the setting was rural, the stories lacked menace. The first draft – the one her first agent, Peter, had dismissed as being too dark – had featured the fox cubs ripping the weakest of their litter apart. And while she accepted that was a step too far, she had insisted on keeping the cubs' fighting. All siblings bickered, as her young readers – and daughters – knew.

'They're not urban foxes. If you'd set it in inner city London, you'd have a very different type of book, perhaps?'

She knew all about urban foxes. It was while they were living in Chiswick that she saw the vixen who inspired Freida. She was ripping apart a bin bag; had stopped and stared at Eleanor, her eyes phosphorescent. *This is my manor; now back off.*

'I toyed with setting it in London,' she explained. 'But I thought children would prefer to read about other animals. It didn't occur to me that there would be less jeopardy because, as children and their mothers know only too well, danger is everywhere.'

Ned nodded, as if to concede that she made a good point, and, despite her best intentions, she found herself being drawn further back into the past. Beyond those cherished days of writing the book to the unspeakable events that had informed her rejected debut and the first, far-too-bleak draft of *The Fox Hole*.

Too bloody right that danger was everywhere . . .

Of course, it is hard to believe that today, with the guillemots dive-bombing into the ocean, and the sky a cloudless, cornflower blue. The sea is a strip of teal. All apparently serene, though the darker patches of water indicate the lurking currents, the rip tides around the jagged rocks beneath.

And, as Ned walks across the lawn to find his colleagues, Eleanor feels a wave of dissatisfaction, as if this tranquil setting is deceptive, and the extreme beauty has worn a little thin.

Ten

Tom

Tick tock. Tick tock.

Even though Tom deleted the message, which landed just as Rachel put the phone down on him this morning, he can't shake off the warning.

Tick tock. Tick tock. The words nag as he snakes along the M4 towards Wiltshire, having mistimed quite how early he would need to flee.

It's not the first message of the day. Though he muted his phone, he failed to switch off his notifications, and the WhatsApps from Ralph – the guy's so confident no one will report him to the police, he spurns Snapchat – have been typically relentless. A hundred and fifty received yesterday, and it looks as if he'll top that today. As his sat-nav screen flashes with yet another message, Tom fumbles with his handset, trying to stop them, but he's driving too fast, and doesn't have a death wish. Not yet. He has to keep reminding himself of this.

There's another. Flick. And another.

Fuck.

His left hand's quivering as he fumbles with the phone again, and, defeated, drops it back into the central console. The pressure's mounting because, *tick tock*, today's payday. Five months ago, that meant something very different: flowers for Rach, a more expensive bottle of wine, and yes, invariably placing some online bets (because who is he kidding: his gambling was already a problem). But he hadn't met Ralph then. Now, rather than a cause for relief, the last Friday of each month is something to be viewed through barely opened fingers; approached with a coruscating sense of dread.

Because the monthly repayments to Ralph, the initially charming businessman from whom he borrowed £10,000 four months ago, are due the day on which his NHS salary hits his bank account. £280,000, that's the sum he needs to pay by the end of today.

And, having been too ambitious in that remortgage application – thinking he might as well apply for more so that he could have a flutter and repay the full amount – he has absolutely no means of paying it.

A flicker on his satnav screen. Another WhatsApp. Ralph just making himself felt. Piling on the pressure. Yes, he knows today's the day. That the *parasite* wants to be paid.

How the hell has it come to this? He slams the steering wheel in frustration, inadvertently striking the horn so that the driver in the inside lane shoots him a foul look. Raising a hand in apology, he ducks his head as if to say he's a good man, then finds himself repeating it like a mantra. *I'm a good man, a good man, a good man. I didn't mean it. I didn't mean it. Honest to god, I didn't mean it, Rach . . .*

He needs to get a grip. He just didn't see this coming. Double trouble, that's what Ralph called his interest rate. And it had sounded so innocuous, and the prospect so unlikely – of *course* this wasn't going to happen; of *course* he'd win back the stakes he was gambling – that he didn't interrogate the obscene mark-up as he should.

Really? So if he missed the repayment at the end of the month, the sum just doubled? That was nursery rhyme maths: the kind even Maisie could do. But yes, the initial £10,000 and an extra £5,000 – because he'd lost the initial loan – became £30,000 at the end of the first month; £60,000, at the end of month two. That doubled, with a further £10,000 loan, meant £140,000 at the end of month three. And today, four months after he believed he would never miss a payment, he owes a massive, inconceivable, but apparently very real £280,000.

And Ralph is letting him know.

Tick tock. Tick tock.

Payday, Mr Quinn.

Perhaps the Trust should be told?

Perhaps the GMC should be told?

Does your hospital know you're taking these risks?

Does the hospital know you're selling methadone and ketamine from the pharmacy? Want some Special K? Quinn's your man.

Tom Quinn: gambling addict and dealer.

Tick tock.

Tick tock.

As payday has loomed, the threat of exposure has become more intense. And, though the drug dealing allegation is as much a fiction as anything that Eleanor has ever written, that doesn't matter. All Ralph needs is a credible story that will take root. A rumour that will heap shame on Tom and his family and will lead to his suspension pending an investigation, from which point he may as well kiss goodbye to his career.

No smoke without fire. It makes sense, doesn't it? He has access to the drugs, and he's already shown he's a risk taker. That's how his patients and colleagues will view him, and it will make little difference if he's cleared. Who'd trust an anaesthetist who's an addict? Who'd want them to be involved in an operation? *Perhaps the GMC should be told?* And every five or six messages, *Tick tock. Tick tock.*

He looks in his rear-view mirror. For the past five minutes, a black Range Rover Sport with tinted windows has been playing cat and mouse, hovering two cars back but shadowing his every move. The game is starting to get on his nerves. He indicates and joins the outside lane, in part to check this out; in part to try to put some distance between them. There's a BMW immediately behind him, but the Range Rover takes the bait and pulls out behind it so that it retains its two-space gap. Tom slips back into the middle lane, then watches as the Beamer surges past with a full-throttled roar. In the outside lane, the Range Rover hovers, not in his blind spot but further back: a strategic decision – *I have my eye on you* – or is he just a bad driver? The longer this continues, the more he fears it's something sinister. That it's somehow connected to the text.

Come on, though: he sounds paranoid. The driver could just as easily be incensed by some imagined slight, miles back. Pulling into the inside lane, he watches the Range Rover slip into the middle, where it has to remain uncomfortably at sixty to keep him in its sights.

Tom shifts in his seat. He doesn't like this. He *really* doesn't like this. He might look physically strong – he's six one; runs a bit – but he's uncomfortable with this incipient aggression. Even the choice of car feels menacing. New money, but with its tinted windows, alloyed chrome and ripped-off badges, it feels like a drug dealer's – or loan shark's – car. Does Ralph drive a car like this? He's met the guy once. Late thirties; younger than he'd assumed; smooth; a bit flash – open-necked white shirt and well-cut navy suit: he could have been a Mayfair estate agent or upmarket car dealer – supremely self-confident: the sort of guy Tom, and he hates himself for this, wanted to impress. But though the psychological warfare has been intense, would he really chase him down here?

Remaining in the inside lane, he watches as the Range Rover continues to languish in the middle lane, where it sits at sixty to remain in his rear-view mirror. By now, Tom has petered down to a crawl as he sits behind a vast articulated lorry. Let's see how that makes him respond.

Within seconds the Range Rover has had to sweep ahead. Good. Tom feels himself physically lighten as the car hares away. But his mind goes back to the stream of messages. *Perhaps Rachel should be told? Tick tock. Tick tock.* His heart races. *He needs to just chill out.* He tries to slow his breath, *in for four, out for six*, and manages to ward off a looming panic attack. Twenty minutes later, when he finds himself two cars behind a black Range Rover with tinted windows, he kills his speed and hangs back.

It may not be the same car, but he isn't going to take any risks.

He checks his notifications at the service station after Bristol. Forty-eight in the three hours since he left London, all piling on the shame; all suggesting he'll be exposed in some way or alluding to the timeframe. Midnight. That's the deadline he's been given. Not that he's ever managed to meet it and not that he's going to achieve it this time either, unless he can work on Rach.

Perhaps that's possible. She's understandably livid, but she loves him, or before Tuesday, he was sure she loved him, and that must count for something, mustn't it? Maybe he should tell her about the WhatsApps? He hasn't because he wanted to protect her, and because, well, he's just so bloody ashamed. *Does the hospital know you're selling methadone and ketamine from the pharmacy? Want some Special K? Tom Quinn's your man.* I mean, Jesus. In sickness and in health but she really didn't sign up to this.

He should tell her, though, because then she might finally ask her mother. If he's honest, he can't quite understand her reluctance. Sure, it's embarrassing, and he gets Eleanor's revulsion towards addiction, but his mother-in-law is fond of him, and she'll hardly want her daughter and grandchildren to be threatened in any way. And now he is experiencing this new level of intimidation, she'll surely agree to a loan? A loan that doesn't need to be paid off any time soon, or only at a minimal interest rate, ideally, but a loan, nevertheless. He wouldn't be asking unless he knew she'd barely notice; the sum is one that could be withdrawn without causing much financial harm.

With the notifications silenced, he tries to convince himself that Eleanor, harsh though she can be, will be persuaded; and by the time he peels off the A30 and is heading through the heart of Cornwall, he tells himself this can be achieved. The road is a single-track ribbon of grey weaving between high hedgerows, and at the peak of a hill, he spies the sea. His mother-in-law loves it here, and perhaps the setting, and the fact it's her birthday, will mean she softens? Just the thought of her saying yes – the relief! – makes his eyes burn, and he rubs them brusquely, dislodging a tear.

He glances in his rear-view mirror and his momentary lightness vanishes as he spies a hulking black mass behind him. *Shiiiit.* A black Range Rover with tinted windows. He can't see the driver through the windscreen, but that's academic because this driver seems intent on forcing him off the road. *OK, you wanker.* He tries to remain calm, but the four-by-four is far too close now: not just pushing him to drive faster – and he's going over sixty down a lane normally populated by holiday traffic and tractors – but almost nudging him, its registration plate obscured because its grille's that close.

Putting his foot down, he surges beyond seventy, knowing this is insane, that if someone comes around a bend, it would be fatal, but desperate to flee this pimped-up car, which has to be the one he saw four hours ago. A junction is coming up: he needs to go to the left; will have to stop so that traffic from the right doesn't plough into his side. But his pursuer will ram into his back if he slams on the brakes, they're driving so fast. He slows a little, the Range Rover sending his parking sensors wild. There's something about the menace of that blank windscreen; the fact that his faceless antagonist is still nudging, still pushing at him, still maintaining the pressure, that's chilling. He's seen the consequence of a road rage incident – a fatal stabbing he's had to attend to at work – and he has no intention of experiencing this himself.

The junction looms up ahead and, stomach clenched, he refuses to stop; darts to the left, just missing a trundling tractor, which admonishes him with a blast of its horn. Miraculously, it blocks the Range Rover off, as does the stream of traffic that's been crawling behind it for miles and has no intention of letting the black beast in. To Tom's amazement, he finds he's protected; realises the Range Rover driver won't notice him take the lane to Trecarrow. He can't contemplate that anyone pursuing him might already know he's heading there. He drives fast and unaccompanied, and when he finally pulls up the oak-canopied drive leading to the house, he reminds himself to keep it together: any emotion needs to be attributed to the sheer joy of seeing his family, or to exhaustion, not fear.

He parks and gets out of the car, marvelling at the beauty of this place: the bright sunlight making the soft stone of the old house glow gold against the intense blue of the sky; the lavender, thick with bees, its purple and sage fringing the gravel; the chamomile lawn leading to wilder scrubland, windswept tamarisk and blackthorn trees. High above, a skylark sings: joyful; carefree; oblivious. It's Tom's second trip down here and he's struck by its otherworldliness: the fact that somewhere so tranquil exists. He takes a couple of deep breaths, savouring the purity of the sea air, feeling his shoulders ease as a Red Admiral butterfly lands on his car's metallic grey bonnet then flutters away.

But the reprieve's momentary, broken by his switching on his notifications. A flurry of them. *Did you think you'd escape me?* He goes very cold. A lucky guess? Or is Ralph connected to the Range Rover that tried to run him off that lane? He bends over, wanting to retch; waiting for the sensation to pass. He is sweating, he notices, and his heart is ricocheting: all the physiological tells of someone seized by panic. *Get a grip, man.*

No one need know that he fears someone has trailed him down here.

That he exists in a state of near-constant threat.

*

'God, it's good to see you.'

When Rachel comes to meet him, he is close to crying. He puts his arms around her, but drops them when she stands, stiff and unyielding.

'Still cross, huh?'

She looks at him as if he is a cretin. *I'm not cross, I'm livid*, the look says.

'You look ill. Grey.'

'Thanks a lot,' he tries to joke, but the look she gives him shows she is being serious. 'Yeah. Just a bit knackered.'

'Did you manage to sleep last night?' Her expression softens.

'A bit, yeah.' He shrugs, knowing she's also been sleeping badly. 'It was more that it was a bad drive down.'

With a spray of gravel, her mother's dog runs out and his wife bends to stroke its head. Both her mother and her elder sister do that when they're thinking, or when they want to avoid confrontation. Eventually she looks up.

'We can't fight this weekend. It's not fair on Eleanor, or the kids.'

'Agreed,' he says, and risks a smile. Theirs is a good marriage. At least it was a good marriage before these past few months when he's been so secretive; so deceptive.

She smiles back but it's a tight, wan smile that says, *we'll call a truce for everyone's sake and because I'm so exhausted. But I can't forgive you. Not yet.* Perhaps he'll never be forgiven. His skin itches, as if uncomfortable at cladding his body, and he wants to rip it. He seems to be going completely insane.

'I'm feeling a bit stiff after my drive down, actually.' He scratches the back of his neck; looks at her enquiringly. 'Do you mind if I go for a quick run?'

'Yes, sure.' She hesitates, perhaps irritated by him taking yet more time to himself, rather than spending it with her or the kids.

'I could take the dog?' He gestures to the spaniel.

'That would be good, actually. She can never have enough exercise.'

'Great. I'll just get my kit.' He grabs his bags and they walk inside together, Edith trotting at his heels. At least he might endear himself to Eleanor if he takes her beloved pet on the cliffs, and he could do with being buffeted by the Atlantic's breeze. A run is about the only thing that momentarily drives his anxiety from his mind.

What harm could possibly come of it?

Eleven

Eleanor

Eleanor shoves back her chair and stretches up on each side before pacing her study. She'd wanted to get her usual five hundred words down this morning, but Ned's interruption has rather blasted her concentration. Now she's thinking again of those emails, and her apprehension about Peter's arrival later today.

Her thoughts will keep circling around their past. All those hopes and dreams her former agent encouraged before seeing her fly higher than he could have envisaged; his ensuing bitterness; the court case; and her and Carole's jubilation at their victory. And, all the while, certain choice lines from those emails beat a vicious tattoo inside her head. *Do remember, won't you, that it's all a fiction.* Then that silly little boy intrudes: *You make everything up.*

Like hell, she does.

Standing by her French windows, she sees a taxi sweep up the drive and circle around the turning point. Well, that's just typical. Peter arriving half an hour earlier than he suggested:

keeping her on her toes; trying to put her in her place. No chance of writing now! For a moment, she considers playing his game: allowing one of the staff to answer the door and only emerging when it suits her, though that will mean keeping him waiting. But the instinct to charm is strong. And, besides, she won't stoop to his behaviour. Far better to be gracious; to play the lady of the manor and greet him, as she ought. Backing away from the window, in case he catches a glimpse of her, she crosses over to the cool hallway – and prepares to welcome her most unwanted guest.

It is amazing that he's still alive, she thinks, as she watches him climb out of his taxi and make his way towards her.

Well, there's a lot to be said for a financially comfortable childhood. If you were born in Chelsea, your life expectancy is always going to be better than if you were born in Leeds.

How she wished he would pop his clogs, though! He's eighty-eight, for goodness' sake! Still, as she watches him crunch over the gravel, his posture as ramrod straight as ever, his expression as jaunty, with that crooked smile and dark brown eyes which at best invite gossip and at worst, malevolence, it seems as if her former agent, who only recently stopped working, might continue forever.

'Peter, how glorious to see you!' She forces herself to go and greet him as Josh, the young lad who helps with driving and gardening and general dogs-bodying, carries his leather luggage from the car and into the house.

'Darling.' Peter leans towards her to give her two air kisses, his hands resting lightly on her shoulders and holding her in place as his paper-thin skin brushes her cheek. 'Well, this is a surprise,' he continues, drawing back without removing his hands so that they remain in closer proximity than feels comfortable. 'I never imagined I'd count as part of your inner circle. One of the select few with whom you would want to celebrate your birthday.'

'Oh well, that's the thing about milestone birthdays, isn't it?' she says, stepping back and slipping from his touch. 'You start to appreciate quite who's important.'

'Is that so?' He looks at her beneath heavy-lidded eyes. 'Or perhaps those you want to keep sweet?'

'I always want to keep you sweet, Peter,' she says. 'That's how one should feel about one's oldest friends and most esteemed colleagues.'

'Which of those am I, I wonder?' he asks, head tilted to one side.

For a moment, she is silenced, not having expected his verbal parrying to begin quite so soon. She takes a deep breath and reminds herself that she will not be needled by him.

'I think you're both,' she says, in what she hopes is a conciliatory tone.

'Well, I'm flattered.' He places his right hand flat against his chest and gives a little nod. 'And I think it's wonderful,' he adds, as he rights himself and holds her gaze, 'that we can . . . evolve like this.'

'Absolutely,' she says. 'As I said: milestone birthdays can be moments of contemplation. Now, talking of friends and colleagues, you do know that Carole is here?' She had mentioned this in his invitation, but it wouldn't harm to remind him.

'Yes. You told me.'

She waits, hoping he will indicate that there is no residual animosity, but he refuses to oblige. It's hardly Eleanor's fault that, after Peter palmed her off on Carole, *The Fox Hole* did far better than any of them could have imagined; only natural that she would follow Carole when she set up as a literary agent on her own. That decision led to a lengthy legal action and a pay-off for Peter, but it was all water under the bridge, or so Eleanor thought until she discovered that Peter was being interviewed for the documentary. Once she heard that, she knew she had to invite him. It was only by doing so that she could try to determine what he might remember, and what he has chosen to reveal.

'Tea?' she suggests.

'Perfect.'

They sit and she obsesses over what he has divulged as they gossip about which author is doing particularly well; who justifies their seven-figure advance (no one, in Eleanor's opinion); and which celebrity author has failed to read the children's book he has purportedly written, which is now riding predictably high in the charts. They don't venture into the thickets of the past, but Peter is a sly old fox and is giving absolutely no indication that his memory is fading. Her fear is that he can still recall a crucial conversation when he rejected her debut, and one particular scene that stood out.

Let's face it, she thinks, as he pours Lapsang Souchong from the pot, her even greater fear beyond him remembering this and revealing it, is that he has lied about no longer possessing the manuscript. There has only ever been one version of her unpublishable first novel, hammered out on a Remington Idol typewriter, because she didn't have the resources to make a second: the thought seems unimaginable, but it was perfectly normal in those pre-digital times. When he rejected it, she was so grief-stricken, she refused to take it back. And then he claimed it was lost. It didn't matter, she told herself: it was unreadable; a 'baggy mass of pretension'; more of a confessional than a novel, and not entirely honest. Based on a true story: her first attempt at rewriting her life. Besides, it was all her fault: she knew his office was notoriously disorganised and chaotic. Only, during the legal action she became convinced he had retained it as a form of collateral. That he was intent on playing the long game . . .

And then the emails began. Could they have been written by Peter? He is one of the very few people who knew her as Lea Savage: a completely different person to Dame Eleanor Kingman. Raw, vulnerable, rough around the edges: not a child – she had needed to grow up fast – but someone who had not yet learned to filter the most revealing parts of her life.

It was this Eleanor who Peter knew, and who that first novel betrayed. Lea, straight out of university, with a fresh narrative and a backstory that needed to be buried firmly in the past. And the loss of the manuscript – the fact it hasn't been burned or isn't in a lawyer's safe – wouldn't matter were it not for those poisonous emails: too inelegantly written to be obviously his, but quite possibly penned by him. Take the first one, fresh in her mind after she reread it earlier. *Hello Eleanor. Well, this has been a long time coming.* Is that an allusion to events more than fifty years ago, or to their acrimonious court case?

Or take a line from the second: an allusion from *Macbeth* she can hardly bear to think of. *Who would have thought the old man to have had so much blood in him.*

She is considering all this as they sit on the terrace, Eleanor half-listening as Edith rests her chin on her lap and looks up at her adoringly. She strokes the dog's forehead, grounding herself in the present, enjoying the velvet softness of her fur.

'I believe you've contributed to the documentary?' she says, as she spies Ned sauntering from the direction of the coach house.

'Indeed.' He blinks like a lizard.

She refuses to rise to the bait.

'And here's the man himself!' Peter adds as Ned raises a hand in greeting and makes his way towards them.

The dog shifts her head and looks intrigued, then bounds towards this newcomer, her tail wagging frenetically.

'Hello, lovely girl.' Ned pats her as she sniffs at his legs then rolls on her back. She really is the most incorrigible flirt.

'Eleanor,' he says, once he's finished attending to the needy dog, 'and Peter.' He gives him a nod. 'Good to see you.'

'Ned.' Peter looks up at him almost coquettishly, his

neat chin pulled back into his cravat. 'I hoped you'd be here early.'

'Oh, yes?'

'There was something we discussed. Something I wanted to clarify.' He shoots Eleanor a rather furtive glance.

'We discussed various things.' Ned smiles at Eleanor as if to reassure her that he's not amused by this puerile cloak-and-dagger stuff. 'Shall we catch up later? I need to find my assistant, who seems to have gone missing.'

'Will do.'

'Pleasure seeing you.' And he sets off in the direction of the house, walking with a brisk, decisive tread.

'Very impressive chap,' her old agent notes, as he watches him appreciatively. '*Highly* impressive, and excellent at his job, yes?'

'Well, one hopes so.' Eleanor pauses. 'I certainly found him personable.'

'And thorough.'

She waits, not wanting to betray anything that might convey her anxiety. 'I do hope so,' she says.

'Oh yes,' he goes on. 'I should think it will be an excellent documentary: balanced, informative, revealing. Isn't that what one wants? No whitewashing affair.'

Edith has run back to her now, and Eleanor resumes her ear-stroking.

'I must say,' Peter continues, managing to sound both sly and smug, 'I had the *most* interesting chat with him.'

Twelve

Gilly

Oh god. The guests have started arriving, thinks Gilly as she spies Peter's car drawing up while she's leaving the walled kitchen garden. Her arms are laden with freshly picked flowers, but she needs to crack on: these should be in the bedrooms by now.

Then she has to double-check that the staff have dressed the guest rooms, and see if Eleanor needs rescuing, given that Peter has a particularly prickly reputation and he and her mother, a rocky past. As Gilly runs through her mental to-do list, she imagines herself standing on the deck of a swaying fishing trawler, only just maintaining her balance. There is so much she still hasn't a handle on.

Just another couple of days. By Sunday afternoon, the guests will have gone and this celebration of her mother's milestone birthday – the biggest but the first of several – will be over, as well as the documentary filming which seems to be adding an extra level of stress.

Two more days – probably three; she's not brutal – and she can finally tell her mother she needs a sabbatical. Or rather, and here she corrects herself because she needs to stand firm on this, she can tell her she wants to resign.

Placing her bundle of flowers – scabious, pink sea thrift and Michaelmas daisies, together with fronds of tamarisk and sprigs of lavender and rosemary; delicate blooms don't survive here – down in the flower room, Gilly starts stripping the lower leaves from the stems, her movements practised and efficient. The very thought of the conversation fills her with a bubbling excitement, like a teen preparing to sneak out to a party or anticipating a first kiss.

It's not that she doesn't love her mother, or that she resents working for her, or that she begrudges her this celebration. How on earth can she, when Eleanor has achieved far more and works far harder than anyone else Gilly knows? But there is nothing like organising someone else's milestone birthday to bring into sharp relief your failure to celebrate yours properly. And there is nothing like observing someone else's big life – several beautiful homes, a highly successful and rewarding career, three daughters, and the confidence not to settle for, still less require, a man – to make you conscious of the smallness of your own.

Forty.

Bloody hell, she thinks, as she fills hand-blown posy vases with water, then studs them with smaller sprigs of rosemary, lavender and thyme. Isn't forty the critical landmark? The midpoint. The *turning* point. The birthday at which you're forced to assess quite where you are in life?

By forty, her mother had three daughters, was apparently

happily married, and was so well established as a children's author, she was the family's breadwinner, earning far more than her husband. And Gilly? Divorced after a disastrous early marriage, she is childless, has a career entirely dependent on her mother, and has done little about her own secret desire to write. As her father learned, there was only room for one writer in a family and Gilly has never shown Eleanor her no-doubt risible attempts, wary of her judgement and conscious she sees everything as potential copy. It isn't malicious, or even deliberate, but her mother magpies others' stories, pouncing on snippets, anecdotes and even fully fleshed-out plot lines, then guilelessly weaving them into her work as if this just makes sense.

So, yes. Gilly has a small life, and she had a suitably modest fortieth birthday celebration one wet Saturday night in February. She hadn't wanted a fuss made, she insisted, but still, it had felt too obviously lacking. So very, *very* small. A perfectly lovely dinner in central London with Rachel and two of her oldest girlfriends; great food and company; but all very grown up and civilised and age appropriate. No secrets shared, or drunken dancing, as she had hoped.

By midnight, everyone had gone back to their families, and she had returned to her beautifully renovated house, where everything was just as she'd left it that morning, and her king-sized bed felt too pristine and vast. She'd cocooned herself in her duvet, drunk a fresh mint tea, broken into a bar of Green & Black's chocolate, logged into Netflix – all the clichés – and had begun to cry.

Anyway, that was that. Watching Delia's latest reel the next morning – her sister surfing in Bali; then tasting rambutan, and laughing with someone off camera as the juice dripped down her chin – she wondered why she had never properly travelled, let alone had an extended gap year as Delia seemed to be doing; why she had never taken such risks. Why had she never put herself first; or, as Rachel had challenged her the previous night, embraced new opportunities – they'd been talking about online dating – with an unequivocal 'yes'?

She hasn't booked a ticket, but while she's been organising her mother's caterers, and musicians, and deliberating over cake, Gilly has been considering her adventure. Her escape. And something has shifted. In the six months since her birthday, and increasingly these past three months since she's been to-ing and fro-ing to Cornwall, she *has* been open to new opportunities. Stripping the rosemary a little more vigorously and enjoying the scented oil that clings to her fingers, she smiles at quite how her life has recently changed.

Two more days.

Well, three: she's not brutal.

And then she will put herself first for once.

'There you are!'

She looks up from clearing away the leaves to see Rachel standing in the doorway.

'OK?' her sister asks, the line between her eyebrows deepening.

'Yes. Just lots to do . . . Tom arrived safely?'

'Yep.'

Gilly looks at her more closely. 'Good to have him down?' It's an odd question, given that they always seem such a happy couple, but her sister's clipped response is puzzling, as is her whole manner, as if she's just containing a simmering anger. Gilly had planned to confide in her this weekend. Though they talk on the phone or Zoom each day, it's usually about their mother or work. This needs a proper, face to face conversation. But she can't share her excitement when her sister clearly has other concerns.

'Yeah.' Rachel sounds equivocal, then shrugs as Gilly looks at her enquiringly. 'It's nothing. Well, nothing important.'

'*Re*ally?'

'Yes, really.'

'Well, OK then.' If her sister doesn't want to talk, she mustn't push. Rachel can be stubborn: will only dig her heels in if she pries. Wiping her hands on her apron, Gilly takes the secateurs to the thicker daisy stalks, and gives a satisfying, 45-degree snip. 'I'd better see if Delia's at her interview,' she continues, her mind running back to her to-do list.

'Oh!' Rachel slaps the palm of her hand to her forehead. 'That was what I meant to say. I've just seen her walking towards the cliffs.'

'But she's supposed to be being interviewed!'

'Didn't look dressed for filming . . .'

Gilly's chest tightens. This is *exactly* what she should have predicted. 'That's just typical. She *knew* her interview was at two p.m.'

The two share a look that says their youngest sister always does this: risks letting Eleanor down in one of her apparently negligible but endlessly frustrating ways.

'I could take her slot, if that helped?'

'Could you?'

'Of course.' Rachel smiles, and it's a genuine smile: one not strained by whatever it is that's been causing a muscle at the side of her mouth to twitch.

'Thank you.' Gilly feels her anxiety ease like a slip knot yielding. The need to confide in her sister tugs at her again. But there are more immediate concerns, namely finding Delia and working out why she's scuppered the interview, and whether she's just uncharacteristically nervous about being questioned for TV. Impossible not to notice her nerviness yesterday when they'd hugged. *You'll be brilliant*, she'd wanted to whisper, as she had when Delia was eight and first faced with the tsunami of *Jess*-related publicity. But seventeen-year-old Gilly failed to protect her then and, on some level, Delia hasn't forgiven her. Perhaps because of this, she refuses to accept her advice these days.

As Rachel prepares to leave for the interview, Gilly bins the discarded leaves, her movements jagged, as if she's junking this documentary idea. When pitched, an Eleanor Kingman retrospective had sounded superb: an exploration of why her work deserved to be part of the canon of children's literature, and Eleanor part of a tradition of writers who were working mothers, stretching from E. Nesbit through to Enid Blyton and J.K. Rowling, but it's clearly put her mother on edge. Take yesterday morning when she was thrown by that little boy, who clearly meant no harm. And look at her behaviour – coquettish, skittish, *flirtatious*? – around Ned, who no longer seems to be creating a puff piece masquerading as arts journalism, as Gilly had anticipated, but something more serious as the process has continued and he's become more invested and involved.

Yes, the whole thing is unsettling. She's not uneasy – that's too strong a word, though she's edging towards it – but she's conscious that a spotlight is being shone on her mother in a way that, because she's been so distracted, she hadn't fully taken on board.

'I'll go and look for her. No – I'll find her,' she says, and she wonders if the slip is subconscious.

Because, while Delia is unlikely to have gone very far geographically, she's long been resistant to being truly found.

Thirteen

Rachel

'So how can I help?' Rachel asks Ned, some twenty minutes later as she settles herself in the drawing room, where they've set up for filming.

'If you could just turn – that's perfect.' Ned gives her the full benefit of a smile that could be properly described as radiant. 'Excellent. The light's not in your eyes?'

'No, no, it's fine.'

'Wonderful,' he goes on, as she forces herself to focus because his smile is so distracting: both dazzling and weirdly familiar. It must be because she's seen him on TV. 'It's so good of you to agree to doing this early. Now, there are just a few issues from your initial interview to tidy up. For continuity reasons, it might look as if we're covering some old ground, but we need to film it all, so apologies if it feels like we're wasting your time.'

'Fine, fine.' She takes a deep breath and counts for seven seconds as she exhales, then repeats the sequence.

Ned looks at her intently. 'Are you sure you're feeling OK?'

'Absolutely.' She gives him a bright smile because it's a relief to be briefly distracted from worrying about Tom and their debt. Satisfying, too, to know that she's the daughter who's willing to be flexible. Who, unlike Delia, is only too willing to prioritise her mother, and this documentary.

'So, in our previous interview, you spoke about the *Fox Hole* books: your very early memory of your mother telling you these stories as she put you to bed each night.'

'Yes.' She smiles. This part is easy. She has told this story so many times, she barely has to think about it at all.

'You must have been pretty tiny? I think you were three when the first book came out?'

'I was. I remember our mother taking us to see it in a bookshop. Standing there – barely as tall as the table on which they were piled – and, on some level, understanding that our bedtime story had been packaged into a distinct thing. A book for other children to enjoy.'

'You must have been a precocious child.' He looks amused, his eyes – those incredible green eyes – glinting with mischief as if to say it's OK: she can confide in him.

'Oh, I wouldn't say that. Academically, Gilly was the bright one. I was the one who struggled to read.' She frowns, remembering Eleanor's impatience: it would be decades before her dyslexia was diagnosed. 'But I think I was quite intuitive, and I remember my mother's excitement. She was wearing a new Laura Ashley dress. I remember clutching her floral skirt – I was a shy little girl – and watching her hands fluttering above me; and knowing her book was the reason for this. And it was clear that she wasn't just our mother. She had a life separate from us.'

'I meant that children don't typically remember things before the age of three, but you have a clear memory of her creating these characters, as she tucked you up each night?'

'Ye-ees. I mean yes.' She gives a bright laugh.

'Could you tell us a little more?'

'More?'

'About her "process". How the stories evolved?'

'Well.' She rifles through her memory and settles on the long-established version. 'She would sit on one of our beds, typically Gilly's, and ask us where she'd got up to and then the story would just flow.'

'And how long would she spend doing this each night? Can you remember?'

'Oh, goodness! Well, I mean we didn't time it. Ten or fifteen minutes? The length of a chapter because she always ended with a cliffhanger. It was in telling these stories that she learned about suspense.'

'And where was your father while this was going on?'

'My father?' The words feel like cotton wool; it's hard to enunciate properly; to bite down on their meaning. She never thinks of her father these days; doesn't even consider that she has one.

'Oh, I'm not sure he's part of the story, is he?' She tries to soften her words with a smile because of course he was present; was part of the stories in a very literal sense. 'I expect he was writing, himself. I doubt he was cooking! It was our mother who did everything domestic.'

'I only ask because Gilly said something that suggested he might sometimes contribute to the story?'

'Contribute to the story? Do you mean sit and listen?' Blood rushes to her cheeks; she feels herself going red. 'I mean, I suppose it's possible he was there, but I can't remember.' She blinks. 'Look,' she glances at Adam behind the camera, then back at Ned, a silent appeal in her eyes. 'Do you mind stopping filming, or me answering that question again? It's rather taken me by surprise, and I've lost my thread.' She winces as she hears herself floundering. 'My father's not relevant to my mother's story – and he's certainly not relevant to her success.'

'Of course.' Ned is soothing but there's that mischievous glint in his eyes again: she has reacted as he wanted.

'Just to clarify, please can you cut that question and my response? As I understood it, my father was off limits. Not someone we would discuss?'

And there it is: the steel in her voice; her clipped, autocratic tone, so mortifying because she isn't like her mother; and an undertone of spiralling panic, as her voice becomes shrill.

'He was part of your mother's life for over twenty-five years,' Ned replies, with that same steady smile. 'But of course, we'll edit it out.' He nods to his assistant Katie.

'Thank you.'

'Absolutely not a problem. I only wanted to clarify something Gilly said—'

'And what was that, specifically?' She hates herself for asking but she can't let this go.

'She gave the impression that the *Fox Hole* stories were a collaboration. That your parents created them together. It was such a sweet story: both sitting on your beds; each taking turns, on alternate nights, to provide the next chapter?'

'That's not my recollection at all.' Her voice is cold, and her throat, tight. 'And I'm quite sure it's not Gilly's. I think you must be mistaken. You'll have to check again.'

'OK, we will.' He smiles that infuriating, familiar smile, and now it's as if he doesn't believe her. 'I guess that's the thing about memory, isn't it? It's so subjective. We all have a different take on what happened, and siblings can have very different recollections of the same childhood. But I'm adamant she said it for the tape.'

Fourteen

Delia

Delia stands at the edge of the cliff, her iPhone outstretched, smiling for the camera. 'Wild, isn't it?' she says as she films a video for Insta. The breeze lifts the tendrils around her face to form a halo and she gives her dirty cackle of a laugh.

'I'm here in beautiful Cornwall, feeling as wild as the ocean,' she begins. 'And I know I always talk about the need to be serene, but it's also important to be at one with the elements. To give into nature's energy. Allowing the wildness to infuse you. To be stirred and buffeted and churned.

'To push. To test. To be as dangerous, as brutal and as damaging as the waves' – and here she moves the phone to capture the white horses racing behind her, before bringing it back to frame a smile that will be dissected on Tattle Life and Reddit at length.

'And then you can relax,' she continues, her tone deepening as if sharing something sacred. 'When you realise that you've tested yourself to the brink. Now you can be buoyed by the water. Be lifted as you feel the stress easing from you. Now you can allow yourself to breathe.'

With her smile turned up to its full wattage – 'Is she doing coke?' the faux fans will ask – she presses the screen to stop filming, then turns towards the sea, where the waves are rolling in at quite a pace. How far before the ground falls away? she wonders, as she takes a step closer to the edge and transfers her weight onto her front foot. The length of a ruler? Thirty small centimetres? Perhaps this is as far as she should go.

It probably *is* her limit. She has a head for heights and a taste for danger. She hasn't needed any of her numerous therapists to confirm this. It's as intrinsic as her forget-me-not-blue eyes, the mole on her right cheekbone, the kink in her hair. And so, she leans forwards, focusing on the spume crashing against the rocks; mesmerised by the churn of the grey-green waves. It wouldn't take much to propel her forwards. The slightest noise from behind her; a switch in mood. She's capricious – she loves that word – and a tiny part of her could just imagine doing it. Disappearing. In one small step.

She's on the edge of a precipice, and not just literally. Each of her thirty-one years has been building to this moment. All the little rebellions: the drink, the drugs, the reckless sex; those early dawns when she woke not knowing how she got somewhere, or who she was with. All the ways in which she had spent her late teens and twenties kicking against the good little Delia, barely disguised in those pen and line drawings as a prepubescent Jess.

'You feel stuck?' the therapists would say as they tilted their heads in sympathy. 'Trapped,' she always replied. Forever a little girl in jeans and a T shirt; with a shaggy fringe and unbrushed hair, and a tendency to suck the tip of her thumb when she thinks. (And how bored she is of those men, those oh-so-liberal, book-loving, fuckboy feminists, who ask her to do that as she straddles them; who fail to see that it's problematic; who think it's *cute*, for fuck's sake.)

She peaked at eight and, just like A.A. Milne's Christopher Robin, she has been preserved at that age, not just in the books, but, she feels, in the eyes of her mother, who displays the original illustrations on her study wall.

And now? Well, now she is toying with the most potent act of self-destruction. Poised to take a mallet and swing it at Delightfully Delia to kill Jess, that fictitious imp she can't escape.

Wouldn't there be easier ways to rebel? She flirted with this idea last night, considering inviting in Josh, the handsome twenty-year-old who carried her bag to her room. But no. Sleeping with inappropriate men was a classic way in which she rebelled in her teens and twenties, but she's moved beyond that – just as she's moved on from the coke and the booze. She won't think of the cellar, where countless boxes of champagne are waiting to be uncorked. She's been sober for 556 days, ever since she set foot in the Swiss clinic, virtually frog-marched by her mother after The Awful Incident, the event they don't talk about, at a family dinner in Mayfair, and her sobriety's not something she's rushing to give up.

'Delia! Deels . . .'

She turns to see her eldest sister running along the cliff path, gesticulating wildly. *Oh my god!* She feels like laughing, surprised by the look of terror on her face and the ferocity of her panic. Gilly *actually thinks* she is going to jump.

'Stop stressing!' she calls, as she looks back at the sea. Let Gilly think that a little longer; let her consider the impact of appropriating someone's life; of fixing them in a moment of time and expecting them to be grateful for it. Let her eldest sister gain some insight into what it is like to be compared with your fictional alter ego, and to never live up to her.

Her older sisters have *no idea* how blessed they are to have had the luxury of an unremarkable childhood; that it's the lack of this that makes Delia rage. There are nine years between her and Gilly but there might as well be a generation, so different are their experiences, the older sisters untainted by, and Delia intrinsic to, their mother's success. Neither Gilly nor Rachel has ever understood. They've just joked about her being the prodigal, the favourite child, with no awareness of the added level of expectation – or the fact that Delia would have liked to have been both emotionally closer to and more like them. And it's this, she realises in a moment of pin-sharp clarity, that is all she has ever wanted: for her sisters to acknowledge that she hasn't enjoyed being different – that she would have far preferred their kind of childhood! – and that their mother has wreaked damage in the most casual way.

She takes a step back and starts walking towards Gilly.

'Keep walking. Just keep walking.' Her sister, lovely, caring, ever-so-slightly-anxious Gilly, still thinks she is talking her down from a suicide attempt. Which is clearly ludicrous because it's something she's never contemplated, not even after The Awful Incident when she marinated herself in so much vodka she lost control of what she was saying (and has only the haziest memory of the following days).

'*Oh. My. God.* I had no intention of jumping.'

'Then what were you doing? Why aren't you being interviewed?' Gilly looks uncharacteristically furious. 'Why do you have to be so anarchic?'

'I just needed to think. I'm not sure I want to do the interview, OK?'

'But you said! You agreed to it. And it's kind of key to the whole thing.'

'Of course it is.' She takes a deep breath. *Of course it fucking is.* 'I know, I know. I just . . . I know I'm meant to be doing it, but right now, it all feels a bit intense.'

'Oh, Deels.' The old childhood nickname, which their mother hates – and there's something about this that makes Delia want to confess to her vulnerability; that claws at her chest so that for a tiny moment she wants to be eight, and Gilly seventeen, again.

'I'm just a bit nervous, you know? Of saying the wrong thing. I want to be honest, but I'm also conscious there's so much Eleanor wouldn't want us to say.'

'Oh, lovely.' Gilly puts her arms around her, and Delia fights the instinct to recoil, her automatic defence, because what would happen if she accepted this support and rowed back from what she plans to do? She shivers and, as she pulls away, Gilly grabs hold of her upper arms and looks at her with a ferocious intensity. 'Please go easy on her, yes? Remember how amazing she is, despite everything – all her spikiness; the difficult aspects; and that this is meant to be a celebration of her. Can you do that for me?'

For fuck's sake. She isn't a child – and her desire to regress vanishes in an instant. How *dare* they all think she is.

Time to sound compliant. She lowers her lashes, bats them and looks up, just as she does for her Insta reels.

'I guess.'

It seems to do the trick.

'Good. Thank you.' Gilly's expression softens; melts; the anxiety that's been etched across her face ever since her youngest sister arrived, easing.

And there's another pang of guilt. Is she really going to go ahead with this?

'Well, he-*llo* there.'

Delia is two hours late for her interview with Ned, but she knows he won't hold it against her, and so she gives no hint of an apology. She's made her decision, she's here now, and she'll make it worth his while.

Ned beams back. Delia just refrains from giving a flirtatious wink. After all, she wants to be taken seriously. Most of the documentary's viewers will have grown up with Jess; may have remembered identifying with her and be curious to learn more about the woman who was her inspiration. Whatever Delia says, they'll pay attention, and if she manages to sound credible, she'll be the one they believe.

She sits in the armchair positioned in front of the bookcase, her left leg crossed, her hands loosely in her lap, though she knows she'll gesticulate and recross her legs repeatedly: she never likes to feel constrained. Gilly has suggested she look smart, but she is wearing an outfit designed to signal her distance from the character she inspired: an oversized white shirt, opened to reveal a neck-mess of gold chains dipping into her small cleavage, and French-tucked into stonewashed jeans.

They exchange some pleasantries but Ned's keen to crack on. The interview's been rearranged several times, Delia invariably cancelling at the last minute, and citing unavoidable PR trips. But they've established the parameters on Zoom before this meeting, so there should be no unexpected questions to throw her off course. And he's so familiar: all those chats and poring over his Insta. (Someone needs to take him in hand: he's a sporadic poster, but with his looks could really build his followers.) In *theory*, nothing should go wrong.

'I thought we'd go straight into what it's been like to grow up as a muse,' he says, as Adam adjusts a light. She nods and shifts so that she is at the desired angle and sits a little straighter. 'Can we discuss what it was like to grow up as the inspiration for a book read by millions of your peers?'

'I think muse is a little grand. I wasn't put on a pedestal. I was just Eleanor's little girl and if she plundered my speech or asked how I might react to things; if she described my mannerisms – well, that was just what writers did. You could say the relationship was symbiotic – I benefitted materially from her success, of course I did – although, ultimately, it was parasitic.' She shrugs, her mouth forming into a resigned moue. 'All writers are parasites.'

Ned's eyes gleam with a spark that tells her she has provided him with a terrific soundbite. In the last couple of minutes, Gilly has sidled into the room, and Delia can sense, without glancing in her direction, her profound unease.

'Perhaps that sounds a little harsh. But I think it partly accounts for my mother's success, and that of any successful author. The ruthlessness with which they are willing to draw on others' lives; to use aspects of others' experience and make it their own.'

'And you've been honest about your own mental health,' Ned presses. 'On your YouTube channel and on Instagram in particular, you've talked about your previous addictions. Do you believe your issues are connected to your need to rebel against being perceived as Jess?'

'Yes,' she admits as her eyes begin to prick. She wasn't going to cry but it's self-pity that always gets her. 'I mean, obviously, I can't blame my parents for my being an addict, although there is a strong genetic element. But my excessive drinking was a rebellion against the bright, sparky, *fictitious* eight-year-old I was still confused with, and who my mother so clearly wanted me to be. The publicity didn't help. All those photos accompanying the interviews. The replies to the fan letters. At the start, I didn't know any different. I even found it exciting. But I quickly grew to hate having to perform. To behave as if I was Jess.'

Ned waits, and watches, and this silent encouragement is all she needs to continue.

'Can you imagine how embarrassing it was to pretend I was ten, when I was thirteen? I was going through puberty and yet my mother wanted me to look like a pre-teen. People ask why I rebelled so spectacularly, but why wouldn't I? To become myself, it was psychologically necessary.

'I suppose the thing I found so difficult is that, as a child, I had little sense of my own identity. I felt as if *she* – Jess – had taken ownership of *me*. And the problem with inspiring or being so closely entwined with a fictional character is that they are always going to be more interesting. A Platonic ideal. My mother loves me, of course she loves me, anyone can see that – but she wasn't particularly demonstrative, and she could be distracted: was immersed in her work, to be fair. I was a lonely little girl with far older sisters preoccupied with their own lives, and I feared I was wanting. As if Jess was the better version of me.'

She gives a laugh that teeters on the edge of bitterness before just managing to pull back: she hadn't intended to be *quite* this open, but the words have spilled from her as if she's in therapy. In the corner of the room, Gilly's mouth is set in a line, but Delia is unstoppable. More reckless than she was on that cliff.

'It's so hard failing to live up to an ideal, fearing that

your mother, the only parent in our lives by that time, would always prefer the fiction – because why wouldn't she? In print, she could shape her ideal daughter: write her words; manipulate her behaviour; ensure she was never bad-tempered but witty, engaging, smart. Jess didn't exist independently. But unfortunately, I did.'

She takes a deep breath. Is she going to go there? Well, yes, she is.

'In many ways, my mother robbed me of my potential. Jess, the perfect daughter, was – and is – a huge success, but she existed to the detriment of Eleanor's real daughter. She existed to the detriment of me.'

'And cut.'

There is a silence of perhaps five seconds after Delia delivers this speech (and yes, it does feel like a speech). She watches Ned, sees his mouth curl into a slow smile.

'Would this be a good point at which to take a break?' Gilly's voice is ice as she walks towards Ned with a quiet determination. She stops beside him. 'I wondered if we could clarify a few things?'

Ned looks mildly irritated. Delia doubts he is happy with having his interview process interrupted, but he gives a quick nod.

'I'll just be five minutes,' says Gilly.

'I'll pop outside,' Delia offers. 'I'll be on the terrace. Don't worry. I'm not going anywhere. We're on a roll, aren't we?'

She perches on a teak recliner and stares at the strip of the sea. She can see why her mother loves this place. Just watching the different shades of blue is relaxing. She feels her breath slow, her exhilaration ease.

Has she said too much? She gets up and starts to pace. She may have told her followers to be as dangerous, as brutal and as damaging as those waves, but doing so is unsettling, and the complete reverse of her usual advice. *Calm and clear. Still and serene.*

Acting Zen is all such an affectation, though. As much of a fiction as one of her mother's novels. It has never come easily. She is always hankering after the next thrill. Talking of which, she pulls out her phone and switches off airplane mode. A flurry of notifications. Twenty, thirty. She skims through them, dismissing most without glancing at their contents; searching for one, from a number named in her contacts as D.

And there it is. Sparse. To the point. Five words that cement what she has helped set in motion.

Arrived. See you tomorrow night.

Fifteen

Aiysha

It was a mistake to come.

Aiysha Johnstone knows this from the moment the 8.43 leaves Paddington. At first, she manages to distract herself: to listen to a podcast and do some sketching as the train rattles through the Home Counties. To remind herself this is an amazing opportunity, and that it will All. Be. OK.

But as the scenery becomes more rural, it is hard not to be aware that she is journeying a very long way from anywhere familiar. Both literally and metaphorically, this is uncharted territory.

The feeling builds as the train pushes through Devon, the stops becoming more frequent and the scenery quainter. It is all so much emptier, greener, and, as the track hugs the coastline, more . . . is the word *elemental*? Sunlight blasts through the window but a squall slaps it, minutes later, and the carriage is buffeted by wind.

The sensation intensifies once she arrives at her station, and finds she is in a sun-dappled forest. It is all so otherworldly, like the setting for a fairy-tale she would like to draw. And as her taxi driver pulls off the B road and heads down a two-mile wooded private lane, fringed with old oak trees and maples, she feels divorced from reality. She had been anticipating the quiet luxury of Eleanor's Thames-side home, but everything about the approach to Trecarrow Manor is next level: from the grounds, with this sweep of a drive, to the elegant façade, with its classically symmetrical windows and six chimney stacks, to the sea, stretching out to the horizon, the deep turquoise sparkling with diamonds of light.

There is nothing about this that makes Aiysha feel remotely comfortable. At twenty-six, she has spent her entire life in London, and though she has learned to hold her own in publishing meetings, she is well aware that she is the expendable part of this deal. Of course, she is hugely grateful. The collaboration with Dame Eleanor has changed her life, but that isn't the whole story because there's a *massive* imbalance between what they earn. And the greater the sales for *Tyler the Detective's Daughter* (or *TTDD*, publishing loving an acronym), the more that imbalance rankles – so that now, as she approaches this exquisite manor, she is both in awe and seriously pissed off.

If only she had been sharper. She wasn't brought up on Eleanor Kingman's books and so she didn't realise there was such a hunger for Jess, her fearless, quirky protagonist. That there was a wealth of fan fiction written by grown-up women so obsessed they would buy themselves the plushy toys. Hadn't realised, either, that in creating Tyler, Jess's bi-racial, unashamedly neurodivergent daughter, Eleanor would both appeal to her original readership and cast her net so much wider. Signing a young woman of colour as an illustrator was a brainwave of her publisher's, who correctly speculated it would make an ageing national treasure appear relevant to a new generation of readers. A sequel that reflected a more diverse world, and that appealed to its audience's sense of kindness, was, in a risk-averse industry, the safest of bets

And its success was insane. BookTokkers embraced it; book groups pounced on it; and Bookstagrammers relayed its pithy aphorisms in Helvetica Neue and Comic Sans. 'Who wants to be ordinary?' asked Tyler. 'What *is* normal?' And one of several lines since seen on mugs on Etsy (something Eleanor Kingman Limited is pursuing legal action over), 'If you're on the outside, you can see what's wrong within.'

But if the text was endlessly quoted, the drawings were a huge part of its popularity, Tyler's scrutiny, joy and humour conveyed with a few deft strokes of a brush. Aiysha had loved working on it: spending months on the drawings and contributing several lines and even a key plot twist when Dame Eleanor was stumped. And when she accepted the £18,000 flat fee, she never questioned the lack of royalties: it was by far the largest sum she had ever earned, but it was obvious that Dame Eleanor should receive a higher cut.

Besides, as her agent, Charlotte, advised, it was brilliant exposure and would lead to several new commissions. Only, once it became a roaring bestseller, Aiysha wondered if Charlotte had realised it would do so well. In her mid-twenties, her agent had never previously been involved with such a success. The contract didn't allow for a retrospective readjustment, though they would work to improve her cut for any subsequent deals. The bottom line was that Aiysha just wanted to be published, and, at first, it had been more than enough to see the queues at signings; to receive the overwhelming number of DMs from people telling her Tyler had changed their lives; even to discover – and this was unnerving – that they had had her drawings inked on their skin.

But then her sister, Amber, calculated what Eleanor would have earned compared to Aiysha's £18,000. A cool £2.6 million – and she became obsessed. The disparity clouded her imagination; stopped her creating; stole her joy. 'You're not just going to accept this, are you?' Amber asked. 'In any other business, you'd ask for a review; lay out the evidence; challenge her for an increase. This sort of opportunity only happens once. You can't just take this lying down.'

'But how can I challenge her? I've hardly seen her since publication, and it's not as if we socialise.'

'You said you were invited to her birthday?'

'Only for PR reasons. I'm not sure that I'll go.'

'Don't be ridiculous. You go; you hold your own; and you win her over. If the publishers won't change the contract retrospectively, then you ask her for compensation as a goodwill gesture,' Amber said. 'Or you find something to hold over her.'

*

The taxi circles around the gravel drive, like a big cat prowling on shingle.

'All right, my love?' asks the cabbie.

Aiysha nods though her stomach tilts.

'You getting out, then?' His eyes meet hers in the rear-view mirror: shrewd, dark, concerned. Does he know something she doesn't? She glances at the manor, its ancient stone basking in the mellow afternoon sunshine, and wants to stay in this small, safe space, staring out of the window. But she's being ridiculous. Besides, she can't back out now.

'Yeah. I guess I'd better.'

'Come on then.' He hauls himself out of his seat, opens her door and retrieves her bag from the boot. And then he is off, and there is no turning back. She is trapped; about to spend the next two days with a woman who she knows she needs to confront, but who terrifies her.

The door swings open before she knocks and a dog bounds out and skitters round her, chased by two young children.

'Woah! Woah there!' she calls, as it puts its front paws on her knees, overwhelmed with enthusiasm, and tugs at the rip in her jeans. Never having had a dog, she is thrown by its tongue and the way it keeps leaping up at her, and she backs away, hands in the air.

'Aiysha?' And here she is. Dame Eleanor Kingman, rather than a housekeeper or maid, is standing in the doorway. 'You're a little earlier than I expected?'

'Yes, yes, sorry.' *Shit, shit, shit. Why hadn't she texted on the way?* She'd been so apprehensive that she'd arrived at

Paddington too early; then did that London thing of racing for a train. 'I caught an earlier train and there were no delays. I should have let you know . . .' Her voice peters out because of course she should have done so, and there's a short pause, during which her host doesn't contradict her, which manages to underline this.

'Oh! Well . . . great!' She watches Dame Eleanor recalibrate and suppress her irritation as she steps forwards to kiss her on both cheeks. 'Come on in. We have so much to celebrate, don't we?' she adds, as her generous mouth curls into a smile.

'Yes, we do, don't we?' Instinctively, she smiles back because it's been an exhilarating ten months, and how could she not be thrilled?

She will ride this wave, bide her time, and hope Dame Eleanor, in this expansive, welcoming mood, will agree with her.

Sixteen

Eleanor

Eleanor stares at her inbox.

Oh no. Oh no, no, no, no, no. Even though she feared this, surely it can't be happening?

But here it is. Another email from ineverythingillegitimate@yahoo.com.

She's not sure she can face it. She only popped into her study to try to make up her word count, shortly after Aiysha's arrival. Had checked her emails as a nervous tick. And here it is. Brazenly sitting at the top of her inbox with a heading that gives her a shock, just as its sender intended:

Do they know what you did?

Dare she open it? Stupid question. She doesn't have a choice. Eleanor Kingman has never shied away from danger, and these are just words, the currency in which she deals. They might be vicious but, unless they're being posted for others to see; unless they impact on her sales and her reputation; unless her emailer makes good their threat – *Perhaps it's time, though, that the truth came out . . . A party would be a great time for that to happen* – they signify nothing. As she knows from experience, they're far less painful than the blow of a fist, or the sting of betrayal.

She moves her fingers over her mouse and clicks. It's a shorter missive. Good. The first few could have done with some editing! That's better. Black humour, that's the way. She gives it a quick skim: thank god they've dropped the laboured literary allusions and cut to the chase. But her chest is tight; her physiology undermining her bravado because her body is stronger than her mind, and she can't help but feel a little panicked. *Pull yourself together! You can work out who has sent this.*

She makes herself read it again:

From: ineverythingillegitimate@yahoo.com
To: freida@eleanorkingman.co.uk

Well! Less than 36 hours now before your big event and I'm wondering if you're getting nervous? Perfectly understandable. You're usually calm under pressure, but the stakes are pretty high!

All your nearest and dearest gathered to celebrate you and your many achievements. To toast your sales; your status; to applaud your professional longevity, and to covet your new home. All those you still speak to, I should say.

Those closest to you know your public persona's just that.

That, away from the cameras, you can be spiky. Defensive. That you push back against those you love.

But do they know what you're capable of doing? Do they know what you did?

Less than 36 hours.

Perhaps it's time they found out.

She gets up from her desk and moves around her study: action always helping with thinking. Whoever sent this knew her as Lea or is connected to people who did. Peter, and Michael, her ex-husband, fall into the first category; but the second could be absolutely anyone. Is too unknowable and vast.

What can she detect from the tone? It's as snide as the previous emails, but more direct: the writer is keen not to waste time. And it's clear she's about to be exposed.

Less than thirty-six hours? The party is due to start at seven thirty p.m., to allow people to enjoy the sunset, and her emailer obviously knows this. It makes sense that they're one of the hundred guests. But several other people are also aware of the arrangements: the catering company; the members of the string quartet; her staff, recruited from nearby villages, and their families.

It's no good. The sea, that's what she needs: to calm herself and focus. A glimpse of the sea, and, ideally, a walk along the cliffs. She stands at the window, feasting on her usual dopamine hit: the green of the cliffs, the pale blue of the horizon, the teal of the bay. But those words have crept under her skin and it's going to take proper exercise to rid herself of this deep sense of unease.

She steps through her French doors and starts off over the chamomile lawn. *That's better. Now, think of something else.* Scanning the horizon, her eyes snag on the old summer house, in the process of being renovated: she bought this place to write with an uninterrupted sea view. The apprehension she's been trying to stifle returns as she spies someone – no, a couple of people – at the edge of her garden who've clearly not understood that this is part of a private estate and the public coast path detours around the nearby golf course.

Except, is it a genuine mistake?

Her heart races a little faster so that she feels unsteady. She wishes she had Edith. Though hardly a guard dog, she's hugely protective and her barks, sharp and penetrating, would summon help. But she continues to stride on. From this distance, they look harmless. Late middle-aged; overweight; the man with a pork-pie hat shoved on his head and bandy legs protruding from shorts – why do British men dress like that? – the woman lumbering, her handbag slipping from her shoulder; her gait rolling; her plodding laboured as if it's a physical effort for her to walk fast.

It's no good. However much she tries to reassure herself, her body is firing clear fight-or-flight signals. She has to get away, *right now.* And so, she turns, no longer intent on confrontation but on racing back to the safety of her house.

Almost jogging, she slips into her study, pulling the French windows shut and struck by the flimsiness of her security. There's just a small key, and the doors could easily be forced. Still, as she stands in the familiar space, letting the quiet embrace her, she tries to relax. It helps to focus on the reassuring cool of the flagstones beneath the antique kilim rug; on the desk where she writes each day; on the elegant mantelpiece with its photo of her three daughters; and on her many shelves of books, forty of which she has written. *This is who I am*, she tells herself. *This is who I am now.*

'Natalie?' she calls. She needs someone to get these trespassers off her property. And it must be a member of her staff, not one of her daughters. 'Marta? Josh?' She goes to the door of her study and calls across the corridor, before striding to the kitchen to convey her request.

She has always trusted her intuition, and it is telling her very strongly that neither she nor anyone from her family should go anywhere near those individuals.

Because there is something far too familiar about them.

Seventeen

Tom

These cliffs are bloody high. But it feels so good to have reached the top of one, thinks Tom, as he powers along the coast path.

The wind is pretty brisk, too. It buffets him along, ushering him towards the edge where the path erodes and the track veers to a halt. He peers down. The drop is sheer, and any fall would be brutal: the rocks, spikes of slate capped with spume, would skewer you.

For a moment, he makes himself stand there, heart pounding with adrenalin and the effort of running. That's much better. Scaring himself, rather than allowing himself to be scared. Or exhausting himself, he thinks as he sets off again; flooding himself with endorphins to achieve a runner's high. And, despite tonight's deadline, he's getting there. Not having his phone helps. He's left it back at the house: doesn't need a pocketful of threats. What he does need is some sort of reprieve while he gets his head around how he's going to persuade Rachel to talk to her mother. Or if not, how he'll talk to Eleanor himself.

He ups his pace, focusing on the here and now, but the worst threats keep looping through his mind – *Perhaps the Trust should be told? Perhaps the GMC should be told?* – and he keeps returning to the Range Rover. The one on the lanes. Is he being paranoid in imagining it's linked to Ralph? *Did you think you'd escape me?* A generalised threat, or something sent by someone who knows he's in Cornwall; who's tailed him here; who's absolutely incandescent – and dangerous – because he gave him the slip?

The dog circles around his feet. At least *she's* enjoying this: scampering along, occasionally distracted by a scent that sees her career in a different direction, but generally intent on running as far and fast as she can. Ears flying, head up, ever alert, she hurtles back. *It must be so lovely being a dog,* he thinks, as she tries to herd him up, and for the slimmest of seconds he shares her exhilaration, because what could be better than bounding along a clifftop with the sea glittering to his right and the sun beating down?

His chest burns, and then a sob stops him in his tracks. For god's sake. He can't succumb to self-pity. It's his wife and children who deserve all the compassion, not him. But here, on the clifftop, with no one watching, he is ambushed by a roar of fear, and the most intense distress at having brought this upon himself and his family. The sound – primeval, visceral, alien to someone whose job demands he is calm and in control – rings out across the bay and the dog starts yapping and jumping up at him, perturbed by this startling display.

'It's OK, Edith,' he reassures her, because she reminds him of his children when they were small. 'What am I going to do?' He ruffles the dog's neck as she tilts her head and whimpers. *Christ. I'm losing it*, he thinks, *or becoming like Eleanor who shows this dog more affection than her older girls.* 'Never mind,' he adds, because she's a dog; she's not going to be able to help him solve this situation. He resumes jogging, wiping his eyes with his forearm, while she stops and stares at him, uncomprehending. 'Come on.'

They carry on towards the nearest village, Trecarrow. It's almost 5k there and he's in his stride now, convincing himself that, with some flattery and reassurance, Eleanor *might* be won around. His calves are burning, and he drives himself faster, ashamed of that guttural outburst on the cliff. *Man up; pull yourself together; don't be such a tit*: he draws on all the clichés, and whether it's this pep talk or the endorphins, but his mood starts to turn.

Or perhaps it's the surroundings. The cliffs are particularly lovely and, though the breeze is picking up, he welcomes the blast of cold on his cheeks. The path is empty and he's relieved because he's not as fit as he assumed he was, or rather this terrain is far more taxing, and his forehead is dripping with sweat. He wipes his brow with the bottom of his running top as the dog scampers ahead and disappears into a thicket of brambles leading to a kissing gate. He ought to put her on a lead because they're nearing the village and people who might not welcome an exuberant spaniel, but he doesn't call her: she's so needy, he knows she'll come bounding straight back.

Except she doesn't.

'Edith?' he calls, after a while. Feeling faintly ridiculous, he peers through the bush for a flash of a feathery tail, but there's nothing to be seen. Has she hurtled through the hedge and run back in the direction they've come, or has she raced on ahead? Ducking through the kissing gate, he picks up the pace as he scans the path for a sight of a golden spaniel. But there's no sign of the dog in the distance. It's as if she's vanished into thin air.

'Edith? Edith!' His tone is more assertive now, then, as he repeats her name, more jocular. He's nowhere close to panicking, but this dog *is* his mother-in-law's pride and joy. He passes through another gate and into a field. There's a group of static caravans on the cliffs. ('An eyesore,' according to Eleanor, although they've been pimped and, in peak season, are rented for thousands a week.) Could she have run into one of those?

He makes his way over the neatly cropped grass between the first two of them, feeling very much as if he's trespassing, particularly when a man in his late fifties glowers at him from a deck chair tucked between his car and his property.

'Can I help you?'

'You haven't seen a dog, have you? A cocker spaniel?'

Mouth downturned into a crescent, the man gives an emphatic shake of his head.

'Well – thanks.'

The man continues to watch Tom keenly, offering no small talk; giving him the distinct impression he really shouldn't be there. Conscious of being judged, he scurries along, glancing from side to side, bending to peer beneath the parked cars.

'Edith,' he repeats. 'Eee-dith, Ee-dith?' and then – thank god – he hears a whimper of delight.

'Looking for this little cutie?' A man – shaved head, waxed Barbour jacket, broad physique and pristine white trainers – calls from another of the static homes. He's bent down, stroking Edith, who's basking in the attention.

'There you are!' Tom gives the man a brief, grateful nod as he's flooded with relief.

She turns and starts chirruping at the sound of his voice. But, despite her obvious pleasure – tail thudding as she wags it enthusiastically – she doesn't run to him, remaining welded to the ground.

'Come on, Edith,' he calls, bemused.

More manic ground-thudding but then he sees that the man has a fat forefinger hooked through her collar while his palm rests on the scruff of her neck, firmly holding her in place.

'You don't mind, do you?' he asks, indicating a dog treat in his other hand. 'Energetic girl like this, racing on the cliffs, needs plenty of sustenance.' He gives her the treat, and she sniffs at his fist for another, ferreting away.

'Err, fine.' Tom does that peculiarly English thing of saying the opposite of what he thinks because he doesn't want to cause offence. 'She's probably had enough, though?' he adds in what he hopes is a jokey tone, though what he wants to say is: *What the hell are you doing?* Because this is really *odd*, isn't it? You don't just feed another person's dog. It's like feeding their kids, he thinks as the man posts another treat in her mouth. Supposing she's allergic and it gives her the shits, or it's poisoned? The thought's melodramatic, but there's a possessiveness about this man. That assumption that he can feed someone else's dog; that he can assume temporary ownership; that – and this is what is making him increasingly uncomfortable – he could hook a finger in her collar to prevent her from running away.

Why the *hell* is he putting up with this?

'Well, thanks so much but we'd better get off now.' He takes a step closer, the clip of her lead in his hand and reaches down to attach it to her collar. The man doesn't move, and as Tom bends, they're suddenly face to face.

'In a rush?'

And there is something about the glint in his eye, and the mention of time that reminds Tom of his warning. *Tick tock. Tick tock.* For a couple of seconds, he seems to freeze. Then he breaks the man's gaze and reaches for Edith's collar. There's perhaps a second – too long to feel comfortable – when they both have their hands on it before the man relinquishes his grip.

'What did you say?' Tom manages at last, as they both straighten up, because perhaps he was imagining that glint and is reading malevolence into a misjudged joke? Although he's not imagining the green inked tentacle curling above the man's white T shirt up the side of his neck. Nor the biceps straining beneath the waxed jacket; or the thighs that look as if they could crush you with one brutal squeeze.

'I asked if you were in a rush.'

Each word feels sliced with menace. A local psycho? Or someone socially inept but perfectly innocuous?

'Yeah, yeah,' he gabbles. 'We need to get on.'

'Well, look after the dog, won't you? Lovely little princess like this: wouldn't want any harm to come to her.' His tone jacknifes back to pseudo-friendliness as he holds another dog treat over Edith's nose.

'Yeah. Come on, Edith.' The dog is pirouetting on her hind legs, but Tom tugs her towards him to start walking back towards the cliff. And, as he does, he catches a glimpse of a black Range Rover Sport with tinted windows parked just ten metres away.

And now the fear that has simmered throughout this conversation peaks so dramatically that he jerks Edith's lead, absolutely desperate to flee. Every cell in his body is telling him to break into a run even as he reminds himself that Range Rover Sports aren't uncommon in north Cornwall in peak season, and that this isn't necessarily connected to any pursuer; that it's just his anxiety, which has reached a crescendo this week as he's realised he cannot possibly repay £280,000, that is making him react so illogically.

He starts walking comically fast as the man watches: feet planted wide; head up; arms crossed against that barrel of a chest.

Eager to be conciliatory, Tom half-raises a hand as if to thank him, as he backs away in the direction of the cliffs.

But, his gaze unflinching, the man just stares after him.

Eighteen

Eleanor

Eleanor smells of power.

At least, that's what her custom-made Parisian perfume is supposed to say about her. *La Puissance*, the besuited perfumier had murmured in her throaty, Gallic way, in that tiny atelier in the 1st arrondissement, and Eleanor had sniffed at the crystal, modern deco bottle, enjoying the hints of sandalwood and golden roasted almond, with top notes of jasmine and vanilla, and thought: *Yes. That's what this will convey.*

Of course, she knows this is bilge. Brilliantly marketed and ludicrously expensive bilge. A six-thousand-euro bottle of golden liquid can no more denote power than a Max Mara coat or a Hermès Kelly bag, or the Aston Martin parked in her garage. But layered up, each detail lending texture and depth, as with any good fiction, and power is the inescapable effect.

She reminds herself of this every morning, as she dabs the amber potion on her neck and wrists, and she reminds herself of it now, as she reapplies it in the sanctuary of her bedroom, trying to calm herself; to reiterate that, yes, she is a strong woman; a woman who, professionally and as the head of her family, enjoys a certain power. *La Puissance*, she mutters, and it's more like an incantation or a spell than the usual decadent relishing of the sibilant S's. *La Puissance.* She repeats it again and again.

But it's no good. Despite Josh searching the grounds and reporting that there's no one to be seen, she can't shake the idea that he has somehow missed the intruders. That she is vulnerable because those ghosts from her past *were* there. Darlings she's killed: that's how she would describe them if she were writing a book. Characters no longer relevant who need to be ruthlessly edited. Except this isn't a book. It's real life.

She shivers, thinking of Michael. Someone else she cast out; and someone else who knew her as Lea Savage. Who fell in love with her former self in her final year at University College, London; who saw past her accent, and gaucheness, and recognised a kindred spirit – another writer; someone with whom to spark ideas because they'd (briefly) been enemies-to-lovers: a Beatrice and Benedick who'd thrilled at sparring, before tumbling into bed.

Michael had detected the writerly splinter of ice in her heart, but he never knew the extent of it; what she had done for a happier ending. Or at least, she has always hoped that he never guessed. There was just that one instance when she risked confiding in him. She forces herself to consider it now: those three words that had slipped out, in an unguarded moment, as she lay in his arms after sex. She had stayed still, hoping he hadn't heard; knowing he had; telling herself it had all happened two years before they met, and he had no way of unearthing any details; no way of discovering what she had done.

She must stop obsessing. It's the emails – *Do they know what you did?* – and Delia's question about him being interviewed that has made her think of her ex-husband. She needs to pull herself together. Enough of the past. Backstory slows the pace. Clutters the text. Her unpublished adult novel was riddled with it. No wonder she writes children's fiction, which largely focuses on the present. Like a compulsion, she reaches for the laptop she keeps in her bedroom and navigates to her emails. She just needs to check that there hasn't been another. Unlikely, she knows, but she can't bear to think of one festering. When she sees that there's nothing sinister – nothing from ineverythingillegitimate@yahoo.com – she is woozy with relief.

Time to get *on* because she can't keep hiding up here in her bedroom. She pulls a soft cashmere cardigan over her shoulders; fiddles with her necklace: a five-carat emerald that glints against the tan of her chest. Despite being cinched in with a leather belt, her black linen dress feels more appropriate to the heat of Tuscany, not a Cornish cliff, and she changes into slim jeans and a blouse, cursing the fact she still wobbles as she stands on one leg. Seventy later this week – like so much else in life, the party date has been a bit of a fudge; impossible to hold it on her actual birthdate – and my *god*, she feels every one of those years.

It's those bloody emails that have done this. That have given her a glimpse of what it must be like to be a frightened old lady. They've made her see her ghosts everywhere. Or is she reminiscing because it's a milestone birthday? Was she like this before her sixtieth: suddenly conscious that she mustn't leave it too late if she wants to make amends? *The past is a foreign country: they do things differently there* and all that – and how she wishes that her head wouldn't fill with other writers' thoughts on the passing of time. It's bad enough having her own phrases coursing through her head!

Only *the past keeps pricking at her.* (Thank you, L.P. Hartley.) Michael wouldn't dare to turn up, but she feels haunted by those figures: the tubby man with the pork-pie hat, the woman with her roiling gait. Mid-sixties. Sixty-three and sixty-four? Yes. They would be the right age.

Perhaps they're there now? Her bedroom is at the edge of the house, with three large sash windows: two facing the sea and one overlooking the Victorian walled garden, and she looks out of each of them. A 270-degree view, and there's nothing amiss. Just Maisie cartwheeling on the front lawn and Charlie doing a handstand that turns into a crab. She was never any good at gymnastics, but the others were. Had loved skipping too, while she'd cooked or done the washing. *The past is not a package one can lay away.* Well, that's all well and good, Emily Dickinson, but she has done so perfectly successfully for over half a century.

And she isn't about to change that now: she is *not* going to permit those packaged memories to come crashing down. *The past is never dead. It's not even past.* Stop it, William Faulkner! *La Puissance.* That's what she needs. Moving erratically, she reaches for the bottle and gives herself a heavy-handed spritz – and, with that, she is back in that perfumier's, casually handing over her Gold Amex, barely glancing at the amount; and feeling the thrill of picking up the bag, with its froth of tissue and beribboned box, and stepping out into the sunshine of the Parisian street.

Just think of how far you have come, she reminds herself, as she recalls her quiver of delight in that shop, of knowing her economic and social status was unchallenged. *And look at this glorious home: refined, elegant, resolutely old-moneyed. A lady novelist's* – she uses the phrase ironically – *exquisite retreat.*

Nothing can touch her. The couple on the cliff were either a projection of her fears or entirely innocent. Life isn't a Thomas Hardy novel, for goodness' sake!

She tries to laugh, but the sound is strained. Perhaps she should check if they could get some last-minute security? When Gilly had suggested bouncers, she had rejected the idea as over-the-top, discourteous, excessive. Now, she wonders if she's been woefully naïve.

Perhaps it's time, though, that the truth came out.

A party would be a great time for that to happen.

Because while you've been sustaining your greatest fiction . . . some of us know the truth.

Everyone has their secrets. And she has absolutely no intention of hers spilling out, or turning up and, for all the wrong reasons, making this a far more memorable occasion than she ever intended it to be.

Nineteen

Tom

Tom runs like the wind on the way back, despite battling against it. Edith is kept on a short lead and keeps shooting concerned looks as she trots beside him. But there's no way he is letting her out of his sight.

Rachel is in the kitchen with the children when he bursts in, and there is something so wholesome about the three of them having a snack and chatting that he can't bear to interrupt them. Nor can he physically do so. His chest heaves as he fights to catch his breath.

'Dad!'

'Edie!'

The kids make a fuss of the dog, now slurping water dramatically, while his wife does a good job of pretending their previous disagreement never happened and he concentrates on trying not to die.

Eventually he manages to cough out a few words.

'What was that?' Rachel blinks, as if she's been thinking about something entirely different.

'We need to talk,' he repeats.

'Absolutely,' she says, and if her tone was conciliatory before, it is now distinctly cool as if there are several things they need to discuss and none of them will be pleasant.

The kids, always alert to the slightest dog whistle in the atmosphere, pick up on it immediately.

'What's wrong?' asks Charlie.

'Nothing,' his parents chorus.

There is a pause while Maisie juts out her bottom lip, and Tom wonders if she will blow a derisory raspberry, or cry.

'Daddy and I do need to chat about something to do with Eleanor's birthday, though. Why don't you take Edith out?'

'No, no. It's better that she stays with us.' Tom pats the spaniel's flank.

Rachel looks at him, one eyebrow raised. He's never been a dog person. Thankfully, Edith is exhausted from her 10k sprint and barely manages to raise her head. The children, ignoring their father, try to rouse her and she wags her tail half-heartedly, but they quickly realise she's no fun.

'The dog gets it,' he hisses, as soon as the children have run out, then, as Rachel looks bemused, he elaborates: 'If I don't pay back some of the money by tonight, something will happen to the dog.'

'What are you talking about?' She looks at him as if he's insane.

'I met this bruiser of a guy on the cliffs. Edith ran off and I found him making a fuss of her. Said she was a lovely girl, and it would be a shame if anything happened to her.' He looks at Edith, luxuriating in the cool of the slate floor and oblivious to her probable imminent demise.

'Oh, some people are just a bit odd,' his wife says, but her tone is no longer quite so irate; a reminder that, just three days ago, she apparently loved him. 'She *is* a lovely girl.' On the floor, Edith's tail gives an appreciative thud. 'But I'm sure he was perfectly harmless. Do you remember when that old woman told us Charlie was just the sort of baby she'd want to abduct?'

'Yeah. No. It was a bit more than that.' But even as he says this, Tom wonders if he's overreacted. If the guy was just a tad possessive and he's been seeing his eccentric behaviour through a prism of fear.

There was no mistaking the incident on the lanes, though, or the messages on his phone. He left the latter switched off in their bedroom before he went for his run. 'Wait a minute. I'll show you something,' he says, sprinting from the kitchen and racing up the stairs to grab it from the room. As he powers it on, he sees that there are several fresh WhatsApp notifications, and though he almost can't bear to look at them, he also knows this is how he'll convince her that the threat is real.

'Look!' Back in the kitchen, he brandishes the phone at her, opening the app and revealing the slew of messages, which cascade in a list of malevolent instructions and questions.

Time's running out.

Time to tell the Trust what their consultant anaesthetist sells.

Special K from the pharmacy? Quinn's your man.

Does your wife know?

Tick tock. Tick tock.

You can run, Quinn, but you can't hide.

'Just look at them,' he repeats, his voice cracking as he explains that though the previous days' messages have disappeared, this isn't a one-off occurrence; that the WhatsApps have been relentless: she can see that from the reams received earlier today.

'There's something else,' and he fills her in on the incident in the lanes, that souped-up Range Rover on his tail.

'But why would they be connected?' she asks, her tone calm and frustratingly logical. 'Had you cut him up by mistake? Could he be a boy racer?'

'I don't know.' He stops, wary of developing the idea he could have inadvertently led Ralph or an associate to her mother's home. But his wife's not listening; is too preoccupied with reading through the messages, her eyes widening as she takes them in.

'And these – they don't make sense. The drug claim's not right, is it? You're not dealing, are you?'

It's as if he's been winded. *How the hell could she think that, and if she does, what will others think?* 'Of course not,' he eventually says.

'And these have come before today?'

He nods. 'More this week, but it's been pretty relentless.'

'Why didn't you tell me?'

He wrinkles his nose, incapable of explaining the maelstrom of emotions that consumes him. 'I guess, well, shame.'

'Oh, Tom.'

And there it sits. Her disappointment, polluting the space between them. Not much he can say to counter that, really. *Tick tock. Tick tock.* The deadline's midnight tonight and time is ticking on. Regardless of how she views him, he needs to push her on this.

'Look – he's stepping up the pressure because today's payday, so please can you ask Eleanor before he follows through on these threats? Before he contacts the Trust. Or the GMC. Or puts allegations on Facebook. And I need to pay something before the debt doubles again.'

'I can't see how I can. Not after Delia.'

'But that was different. A different addiction. Different behaviour. This is just a stupid decision on my part: I'm not harming anyone, least of all her.' He scrubs at his forehead. That's not quite true. He's harming her daughter and grandchildren and putting Eleanor out. He may even have lured one of Ralph's flunkies to her cliffs. Still. He thinks back to Delia's behaviour, eighteen months ago. The Awful Incident, as her sisters dubbed it: Delia getting so drunk at a Mayfair restaurant she'd swiped their mother's purse from her bag and stormed out into the night. It was after that drink-and-drug-fuelled bender that Tom was conscripted into talking her into rehab – something you'd have thought would have given him brownie points – and Eleanor paid for the stint at Les Alpes.

'Fine,' he continues, because time is running out and fear is making him abrupt. 'I'll ask her myself.'

Rachel makes an irritated *tch* as if his suggestion doesn't merit a response. He waits. She's chewing her bottom lip, and he tries not to let his desperation show. And though he only has himself to blame, he's so very tired of it all. The entire day – the long drive down from London; the road rage pursuit; the showdown on the cliffs – seems surreal. So divorced from his life as a doctor and family man – everything he tells himself he is, or everything he was – that it seems unbelievable. More far-fetched than one of Eleanor's stories. Except, of course, it's not. *In a rush? Tick tock. Tick tock.*

He itches for her to say yes, and as he waits, his phone, on the island between them, obligingly swooshes with a fresh WhatsApp.

Does your mother-in-law know? Nice birthday present for her.

Rachel looks from it to him. 'Did you do that?'

'Don't be ridiculous.' He holds his hands up.

'I'm sorry. I'm sorry. My *god.* This is serious. He knows about Eleanor? Does he know about the party, this *Ralph*?'

'I don't know. How would he? I mean, I guess he could Google?' Because there'd been a casual reference to Tom's name and profession in an interview, and it's widely known her daughters work for her.

'But he knows it's her birthday? OK.' Her lips press together in a fine line of determination. Ralph's knowledge has incontrovertibly changed things. 'OK. I'll do it. I'll ask her. I'll go and find her now.'

'Thank you,' he says, and his heart aches with relief. 'Thank you. Thank you. *Thank* you.'

She closes her eyes and rubs them. 'She's not going to like it.'

'I know.'

'I won't tell her about the WhatsApps. They might freak her. And I won't mention the guy with Edith, or the car on the lanes. After all, they're probably just coincidences, right?'

'I don't know.' He's not sure of her rationale: surely Eleanor will understand their urgency if she understands the level of threat? 'I mean, she's your mother – you know her best – but OK . . .'

'I can't tell her anything that would scare her. It's her birthday party. Her big event, and she's preoccupied with her interview. Trust me. There's just no need.'

At least she's no longer antagonistic, and he trusts her to know how to handle her mother. Still, time is ticking. *Tick tock. Tick tock.*

'I have to pay a deposit by tonight.'

'I know. You said.' Her tone is tense, and she starts pacing around the kitchen, her shoulders stiff, her movements quick.

He's such a shit for putting her in this position. Perhaps an appeal to Eleanor's better nature will be enough? Apart from that £100,000 windfall ten years ago, she's been historically tough on her older girls (while subsidising Delia). Still, Tom tries to think the best of her. Could her most recent successes – the latest bestseller; the new Netflix deal;

the Channel 4 Christmas show; all these incredible sources of income – have made her mellow?

They will just have to hope so.

Tick tock. Tick tock.

Twenty

Aiysha

'You wanted to see me?'

Aiysha feels horribly, desperately nervous as she stands in front of Eleanor. She has asked for this meeting, blurting out the request just minutes after her arrival when she should have been making small talk, but now that she is in her study, it seems like a terrible idea.

Eleanor looks up from the typing. The interruption has been unwelcome, she's making that clear. And yet, there is something performative about her tapping away at the keyboard. While Aiysha blathers an ineffective answer, she seems only too ready to spring from her chair.

'Shall we walk?' she asks, grabbing a pair of Jackie O shades and shoving them on her head, and it's more of a statement than a question. 'Such a glorious day and you must want to stretch your legs.'

Aiysha doesn't. Not really. She'd been looking forward to having a drink; perhaps to taking afternoon tea, imagining a pot of Earl Grey might help to smooth things over. Plus, she has changed into something smart for this meeting: is wearing delicate sandals and a skirt, not her jeans and trainers. She's not equipped for a walk on the cliffs.

But Eleanor is off and leading her into the hall and out of the front door, then across the lawn towards the coast path, walking at quite a pace. As she strides along, she gives a running commentary on various plants – *sea thrift, lichen, wild foxgloves, late heather, cow parsley, fronds of the stuff* – all while scanning the area, head switching from left to right. *The end of the honeysuckle; blackberries – unripe; no, don't try one*, she says as Aiysha reaches to pluck a garnet berry. It pricks her finger, the blood beading, as sharp as a sting.

They carry on, Aiysha prising the thorn out then sucking the blood, not really concentrating, but distracted by the nip of pain and the rub of her new sandals, when Eleanor stops abruptly.

'What was it you wanted to say?'

Her glasses are down now, and her expression, impenetrable. Aiysha can't raise the question of pay when she can't see her eyes and she doesn't want to blurt it out, on the top of the cliff. The wind has picked up, the mid-afternoon sun tempered by a breeze that makes her feel chilled – though that could be down to the turn of Eleanor's mouth, as if she is about to laugh derisively.

Aiysha stutters, and murmurs something about it not being important.

'Well, it must have been?' The older woman is insistent. She pushes the glasses back like an Alice band and gives what a feature writer once described as her 'Paddington Bear stare'.

'I wanted to ask if you could lobby the publishers on my behalf,' Aiysha manages at last. 'I was paid eighteen thousand pounds for the illustrations. And that was amazing and I'm truly grateful, honest – but it doesn't seem quite fair given how successful the book has been.'

There. It is out. Expelled like a particularly explosive sneeze.

Eleanor recoils, just as if the full force of a sneeze has hit her.

'Oh, I don't think so, Aiysha. Oh no, I couldn't do that. I'm sorry but that's just not how these things work once a contract's been signed.' She gives a little sigh and continues, not unkindly, but as if this is quite outside her gift. 'I'm so sorry, but if I were you, I'd be looking at changing my agent? She really should have thought this through properly . . .'

'But could you, I mean *would* you, help?'

'Me?' Eleanor's eyes narrow, and she shoves the glasses back down.

'I mean . . .' Aiysha continues – and what is *wrong* with her for sounding so weak? – 'It's been hugely profitable, and it feels a bit unjust that there's such a disparity in what we've been paid. After all, the *Guardian* praised the illustrations, and *The Times*. I've had so many parents messaging me, saying how they love Tyler, and grown-up Jess . . . I worked so hard on the illustrations, you know I did . . .' There were various revisions; Eleanor had been *extremely* exacting.

'And I helped with some of the story, didn't I, and some lines . . . That one about not being ordinary, and the riddle at the end . . .' She *had* been useful; had pointed out that a solution Eleanor had written didn't quite make sense (and had done this diplomatically, obviously), before the two of them thrashed out how to put it right. 'I just . . . Eighteen thousand pounds isn't masses . . .' She hears her voice spiral into a whine, and cringes as the words trip out and yet she can't stop this flood of injustice. 'I mean. Compared to what you've earned—'

'And do you think this would have sold were it not for my name? Were it not for my brand, and the fact it was a sequel to a huge bestseller? You'll build a career off the back of illustrating this. You'll get far more work. I bet that's already happening?'

'I guess . . . No, yeah, it is. Yes.'

'Well, there you are. And if there's another book in the series you would obviously illustrate that? And your agent should negotiate a better deal for that. You needn't get the flat fee.'

It all sounds so reasonable, and yet there are no guarantees there will be another book – Eleanor hasn't committed to it; unsure if she has the time – and even this won't help with her current bills or recoup the hundreds of thousands of pounds she could have made. The polite thing is to be pacified, but she resents Eleanor's tone: assertive, powerful, patronising.

I could shove her from the path right now.

The thought pops into her head. Eleanor is notably shorter

than her, and Aiysha, fitter and stronger: the result of cycling around London, and of being twenty-six to Eleanor's seventy.

It wouldn't take much effort to push her now. She must stop. Her sister reminded her to keep her temper, known to flare despite her best attempts to suppress it through exercise, daily gratitudes and journalling. Hard though, when Eleanor is behaving like a typical Boomer with absolutely no concept of how financially precarious life can be for a Gen Z.

What a selfish old woman. What a nasty bitch.

For a delicious moment, she imagines saying this. Seeing the shock on Eleanor's face because she always has the upper hand. Everything about the older woman exudes this, from her twitch of a smile to the fact she has turned her back and is striding down the cliff. Just as Eleanor casually incorporated Aiysha's ideas, scooping them up and weaving them into her text, so it doesn't occur to her that Aiysha might be resentful. As far as she's concerned, *she* is the *only* reason for the book's success.

And she has no *idea* how charmed her life is, or how much Aiysha would benefit from that money. To own one house seems impossible, at any point in the future, let alone a ridiculous four!

Anger, red and molten, flushes up her neck. And then the impulse returns – and she sees herself shoving Eleanor so hard that she skids from the path, her white leather trainers providing no resistance as she falls like a rag doll to the sea. The tide is in, but there are rocks below: Aiysha can see their dark shadows lurking beneath the water. The landing would be far from pretty.

She shakes her head, surprised by her strength of feeling. Ahead of her, Eleanor continues, unaware that her young colleague is trying to contain her rage. Aiysha watches her neat, ash-blonde head bobbing along, and she wonders if the idea that someone might resent her would even cross her mind.

And then she realises that Eleanor knows. Aiysha could hardly have made it plainer. What was it she said? *It's just, eighteen thousand pounds isn't a lot compared to what you've earned.* Dame Eleanor is fully aware of Aiysha's resentment: she just isn't letting it bother her, and there is something about this that is admirable. She's one tough old bird, and her ruthlessness partly accounts for her success.

Shame cloaks Aiysha's anger like a blanket smothering a flame, and yet, she needs more money. How on earth can she press her case? *If there's another book in the series, you would illustrate it.* That's something to cling on to. Something to hope for. Perhaps she had better act compliant.

Because what choice does she have when faced with someone this formidable?

'Of course it wouldn't have sold without you,' she says.

Twenty-one

Rachel

With hindsight, it's particularly unfortunate that Rachel asks for money moments after Eleanor returns from her clifftop walk with Aiysha.

She should have realised something had happened given that Eleanor appears irritated: walking rapidly, shutting doors too firmly and rolling her eyes when asked if she's had an enjoyable walk.

Still, it's not as if this can wait. *Does your mother-in-law know? Nice birthday present for her.* Those text messages, the weight of them, their cumulative sense of threat, have got under her skin.

'You're asking me to what?' Her mother's eyes widen as Rachel corners her in the boot room.

'I'm asking if you could lend us three hundred thousand pounds.' Rachel winces as she makes herself repeat her request, rounded up because a precise figure will only raise more questions.

'It would be a *loan*?'

'Yes, of course.'

'But for what?' Her mother is uncomprehending. 'You can't need anything else done to your house?'

'No, not the house,' Rachel agrees, and it's true: her Edwardian semi has stretched upwards and outwards as her family has grown, and there is no room to build any further, even if it was something they could afford.

'Then what?' Her mother's dark eyes are pools that mesmerise her daughter, who avoids answering the question. But Eleanor isn't having this. 'Rachel!' she snaps.

'I can't say. I'm sorry. But I wouldn't ask if I wasn't absolutely desperate.'

'Hmmm.' Eleanor remains unimpressed.

Rachel waits, wondering if she should tell her mother the whole sorry story of the loans and the threats. But she would like to avoid, or at least delay, her disapproval.

'We can't talk about this here. Let's do this properly,' her mother says.

They move to her study, where she takes the rather formal, wing-backed chair, leaving Rachel the antique chaise longue, with its firm upholstery and elegant mahogany legs. Not for the first time, Rachel wonders if her mother has picked the seating to give herself a psychological advantage: while Eleanor sits upright, Rachel can't help but squirm and shift.

'Well, I can't possibly lend you money without knowing what it's for. As my accountant, you'd advise me that doing so would be quite stupid . . . Aiysha asked me for money a moment ago. It's as though I'm being mistaken for a high street bank!'

'Eleanor. That's not how we see you at all—'

Her mother dismisses the claim with a wave of her hand. 'Of course, I can understand why Aiysha's fed up. But none of us knew Tyler – and a grown-up Jess – would resonate so strongly, nor that the sequel would be such a success.'

Rachel bites her lip. Everyone knew they had a certain bestseller on their hands, given the plethora of Jess fan fiction, even if no one predicted it would top the charts for so long. But her mother tends to rewrite history. It suits her to tell herself she never intended to hoodwink her young illustrator, although she and her publishers knew exactly what was going on. And none of them – not Carole, nor Gilly, nor herself – had ever suggested that Aiysha should have a bigger share.

'Of course, I told her that my lobbying on her behalf, as she suggested I ought, was impossible.'

'Yes?' Rachel tries to appear interested.

'Her agent will secure a much better deal next time.'

Rachel shifts on the sofa. Her mother is doing this on purpose: filling the air with something of little interest to her daughter while she waits for her to tell her why she needs such a sum. If Rachel is to have any hope of securing it, she is going to have to tell her more.

'Tom got himself into a spot of trouble,' she says at last.

'Trouble?'

'He owes some money.'

Eleanor takes her time to consider this. 'Is it drugs?' she says eventually.

'No, of course not.'

'There's no "of course not" about it. Look at your sister.'

Rachel smarts in surprise. Her mother rarely acknowledges Delia's problem, once snapping, 'It's hardly something to boast about,' when Rachel raised it, and using euphemisms – her 'problem', her 'detox' – if she ever has to refer to that period.

'I promise it's not drugs,' she says, and wants to add, *he's a doctor,* as if this might excuse him. For a second, she even doubts her denial. *Of* course *he doesn't gamble*, she would have said a week ago; *he's an anaesthetist: not someone who can afford to take risks, and of course he doesn't lie to me; of course he isn't trying to defraud me; of course he wouldn't be so stupid as to borrow money from a loan shark – and he'd have no idea how to find one.* Now, it seems she barely knows him at all.

'Well, it must be an addiction of sorts, or you wouldn't need a sum like this, and you wouldn't be so cagey.'

Rachel closes her eyes to shut her mother out for a moment. Damn her for always being so sharp! Then again, she's been hurt by other's addictions, not just Delia's but her ex-husband's, if you accept his philandering was a form of compulsion, and, though Eleanor never mentions him, her own father's. Telling her about Tom must be like pressing a bruise.

'Well?' Her mother is waiting. 'It doesn't involve another woman – or man – does it?'

'No. It's not sex.' From somewhere, she manages to muster a dry laugh. Tom has never given any hint he would be unfaithful. If only it were that simple: sex might be destructive, but there wouldn't be this level of threat. And then, because, perhaps, she hopes for her mother's support, she finally admits to the thing that shames them. 'He's been online gambling.'

'Oh no,' Eleanor says. 'Oh no, my darling. Oh no, no, no, no, no, *no*.' She sighs as if it pains her to consider this. 'Haven't I taught you anything? You can't bail a man out like this. You need to keep your finances separate. You need to protect yourself, and I need to protect you. You can't be tied up in this.'

But I already am, Rachel wants to say. *We already are. Even if I wanted to extricate myself* – and now that she has seen his fear and despair, she knows she can't – *that's not an option because he's my children's father, I still love him, and he's involved all of us in this.* She shivers at the thought of that latest WhatsApp: 'Does your mother-in-law know?' And what if she's deluding herself? What if he was followed? What if he's brought the problem right down here?

But she can't tell her mother any of this, and she's not sure that Eleanor would listen because she is barely pausing for breath.

'It's tough love but things will only get worse if I bail him out. He'd think me a bottomless money pit – just like Aiysha! Would keep on doing it and there'd be absolutely no incentive to change.'

'But we'll lose the house. We won't have a home. The kids will have to leave their friends and school . . .'

'You and the children will always have a home with me, you know that, if you need it, but I can't do this. *He* – not *you* – will have to find another way.'

And even though she had expected it, Rachel feels a toxic mix of shame and anger. Fear, too, which colours everything, and frustration that they've never spoken sufficiently honestly about money – not as far as Rachel's concerned. Of course, as Eleanor's accountant, she couldn't be more aware of her mother's turnover and royalties; knows exactly how much she takes in dividends and places in trusts. (Her grandchildren, thank goodness, will be accounted for at twenty-one.) But having given her elder daughters that generous £100,000 bequest, her mother is uninterested in how they manage financially, and averse to ever discussing a raise. And yes, their salaries are good five-figure ones, Rachel knows she's scraping at the world's tiniest violin, but they're not comparable to what they could earn in the City and, with two young children requiring childcare and a hefty mortgage in London, they haven't allowed her to save for difficulties. Now, they're in trouble. And, it might be self-inflicted, but that's irrelevant: Tom has made this problem theirs.

Her mother clearly expects a response.

'Yes, um, OK. I completely understand,' she mutters, careful not to sound begrudging. 'Of course. That makes perfect sense.' But it doesn't, not entirely. Because what she wants to say is that her mother's fear of spoiling her daughters, or being thrust back into poverty, or the financial power imbalance she experienced with her ex-husband, are all irrelevant here.

There is a man who is harassing Tom; who is threatening to expose him to his hospital trust or to get him struck off; and who now appears to know of his connection to Eleanor – that she has a birthday, and, quite possibly, the fact there's a celebration this weekend. And Rachel reckons there'll be some mileage in an allegation that the son-in-law of the country's bestselling children's novelist peddles drugs, is a gambling addict, and is hundreds of thousands of pounds in debt.

Eleanor isn't going to help, she sees that now, and that's absolutely fine: there is no earthly reason why she should do so.

But Rachel can't take a risk on the idleness of these threats.

Does your mother-in-law know? Nice birthday present for her.

If her mother won't help them, she will have to do something underhand.

Twenty-two

Eleanor

Eleanor is furious. And hurt, if she is entirely honest: she's hurt.

All anyone wants from her these days is money. An open cheque book (or rather, bank transfer). That's how she is perceived.

Aiysha's disgruntlement is fair enough, though she resents the girl's insinuation she wrote part of the book: the odd line here or there, a plot thread hammered out does *not* equal ownership. There was another young woman who made similar claims and more, years ago, and she stamped that *right out*.

But Rachel's request? Well, it's left her rather dumbfounded. Didn't she know she would never give in? How could she forget her mother's principles so completely? All those values she tried to instil: of never relying on others; of making your own way; of not living beyond your means. OK, so she accepts it's not Rachel who has done this but her husband, and that's surprising. (She had always liked Tom;

thought him dynamic and reliable – a good combination.) Then again, all the apparently good men disappoint in the end.

Tom must have set Rachel up to this. That's the only explanation. The worm was willing to use her daughter and grandchildren as emotional collateral. He clearly has absolutely no idea. Not the slightest sense of how her life's been tainted by others' addictions, not just Delia's or Michael's but her father's. It takes a particular level of self-absorption to drink despite your children being hungry; to waste every last shilling, and they were shillings then, on beer or gin; and to continue, even though you were an ugly drunk who took out your rage and self-loathing on your children and wife.

Tom's behaviour reminds her of Michael, too. Not that her ex-husband squandered her money, but money tainted their relationship; tarnished it like a once-bright penny. It had been an issue right from the start. From that moment when Mr Justice Kingman and his elegant wife, Penelope, pressurised her into signing a pre-nup before marrying their darling son, so mistrustful were they of this girl with a northern accent, no credentials or, apparently, family, let alone any sort of hinterland that they could get a handle on.

The contract had stipulated that, in the event of a divorce, Michael and her earnings would be distinct. Well, that backfired spectacularly and had led to bitterness whenever anything felt transactional: childcare; domestic work; time to write; eventually and inevitably, sex. 'It's the root of all evil,'

Michael once said, when they'd gone to bed after a particularly bad row during the period when they were adjusting to her earning substantially more than him. And she had traced the whorls of hair on his chest and refrained from saying that only someone who was brought up to take money for granted could possibly say this.

But this won't do: this obsessing about Michael. It's those emails, which she's pored over this afternoon, that have done it – but he couldn't have written them. His love letters were exquisite. These emails with their goading, and venom, hold no trace of his voice. But someone who very well might have penned them is Peter, with whom she's arranged to have a pre-dinner drink. He's still as waspish – but is he as wily, as intellectually dexterous, as he was before?

She watches as he makes his way towards her, liver-spotted hands dancing along the back of the sofa, perhaps testing the quality of the furnishings: getting a true sense of her worth.

If he is her emailer, if he really *is* that embittered, then she's going to do her damnedest to find out.

His is a double gin. A single tonic; plenty of crushed ice, rosemary, a couple of black peppercorns. He is still exacting, he tells her, about his aromatics.

Funny the things one fails to remember. She doesn't recall him drinking gin before. Coffee, yes. Thick, strong espressos from Bar Italia on Frith Street. Whisky on the rocks; a glass of good red wine. Their early meetings were as likely to take place in a wine bar as they were in his Soho Square office.

Until he suggested she would work better with Carole. Then, his bonhomie, his obvious enjoyment in helping a young woman, disappeared as swiftly as if he'd flicked a light switch. From having basked in the full glare of his sunshine, she was cast out into the dark.

She has a single glass of champagne and barely sips it. It's not that she doesn't drink: she hasn't inherited a predisposition towards alcoholism, but she doesn't trust him and she needs to stay alert.

Peter appears oblivious, giving a contented little sigh as he admires the view. 'I never had you down as a country mouse, but I can see this all suits you very well,' he says, and turns to check her reaction. 'Very well indeed.'

'Well, Cornwall has a long literary tradition. Hardy, Du Maurier, Le Carré. It's always been a source of inspiration for writers.'

'No need to be defensive!' He's amused, and she reminds herself not to react. 'I can see that it would be hugely inspiring. I was just remarking that, though people can change a great deal, one would never have anticipated this, when we first met all those years ago.'

And there they are. The ghosts of their former selves are circling their conversation. Better to take the initiative.

'It's funny you should say that because I've been thinking about the past.'

'I rather thought you might . . .'

'And I was regretting never having retrieved that first manuscript from you. I'd like it for my records; would like to bequeath it to the British Library as part of the archive of my work.'

He looks at her blankly, giving nothing away. She stifles her irritation. No doubt the British Library would like it, but that's not the reason. She waits, but reasonable persuasion isn't working, and it's time to cut to the chase.

'Look, this is all terribly tiresome, and I know you maintained, during all our legal correspondence, that you no longer had the manuscript, but I wondered if you might have been mistaken. If, because I know your office wasn't the tidiest, you might have mislaid it and then stumbled across it at some point in the intervening years?'

Peter massages his forehead with tobacco-stained fingers, perhaps hoping to coax a recollection.

'A manuscript?' As if it's an alien thing.

'Yes, of my first novel. The adult one. The one you said was unpublishable.'

His brow furrows, the wrinkles deepening into canyon-like crevices. 'My memory isn't what it was, I'm afraid. Thoughts come and go.' *Great*, she thinks. *Absolutely tremendous*. 'No. I don't believe I have it, no.'

She watches; waits; tries to read a face that's inscrutable. Can she believe him? If the manuscript doesn't exist, he has nothing that hints at what happened because she dressed it up as fiction, aware of the importance of deniability, even then. But does that mean he has no memory of its contents, or of what he once said? That forensic résumé which cut to the heart of the matter, and his acid response.

'I mean, obviously the thing can't be published,' he had said, as he wafted the manuscript as if it were a fan. 'It's verbose. Self-indulgent. A baggy mess of pretension. I can't understand why you're not leaning into your working-class roots rather than writing about a world you know nothing about?' As he warmed to his theme, his voice dripped with disdain. 'Aristocrats. A baronet and his daughter: you've made them far too affected, and you've got their dialogue all wrong: you just don't understand the cadences of their speech or quite what's *infra dig*.

'There is one thing that rings true, though: the daughter's extreme hatred and resentment. That, and, of course, her fear. There's one particularly visceral part, a scene that stands out as inherently true.' He had given her an especially perspicacious look, making sure she was taking this in. 'I would imagine that those few pages might raise certain questions.' Another pause. 'I rather suspect you've written about something you shouldn't admit to.'

She had felt herself go hot, then chill; had concentrated on looking stolidly defiant. 'I don't know what you mean. I've just got a good imagination.'

He had raised an eyebrow, not believing a word she said. 'Well, submitting this would be professional and personal suicide. Would be *very* problematic,' he had concluded. 'Besides, no one would pick it up.'

They hadn't, of course. It hadn't been submitted. Had been left festering in a pile of discarded manuscripts on a bookcase, only to be recycled some years later, or so he'd persistently claimed.

'I don't suppose you remember anything about it?' she says now, keeping her tone studiedly off-hand. There was no reason he would recollect either her manuscript or his response: he wasn't known for his sugar-coated feedback and there would have been thousands of manuscripts he had rejected throughout his career.

'As I said, memories come and go,' he says, in an equally off-hand way. 'Some days, the distant past is more vivid than the present; on others I'll have no recollection at all.'

He's been looking at the horizon but now he turns and looks at her in a way that is far from vague.

'I'm afraid I'm rather mercurial.' He gives a small chuckle as if he's to be indulged. 'Wasn't there something in it about whisky? Paracetamol? An act that was far from benign?' He watches as she refuses to react; waits a beat, then another, then one more again.

'Ah well. As I said, much of the time, it's as if the past has been wiped completely, but on others? Well, occasionally, I have such a good recollection of conversations it's as if I can remember every word.'

Twenty-three

Delia

'So, I'm going to a family dinner. Not a birthday party for my ma, but a pre-birthday meal, and I've got to say, I'm nervous.' Delia pauses and chews her bottom lip in a way she knows is winsome, then looks back at the camera on her phone.

She's sitting cross-legged on the lawn; the sea behind her; no glimpse of her mother's home because she's mindful of Eleanor's privacy, and, besides, nature's a better canvas. Towards the house, a marquee has been erected complete with fairy lights and a wooden floor, but all work's stopped for the night. The air shimmers with possibility – though of fun or high drama, Delia doesn't yet know. That's one of the things her sisters always accuse her of: turning an atmosphere toxic, just for the fun of it. But it often happens on the off-chance. She doesn't intend to stir things up: she just can't help provoking reactions, then watching the fireworks fly.

She straightens her back, restless as ever. Forget about it. There's work to do. It's nearing golden hour, and the light is perfect, and Delia's looking pretty perfect, too. She sits even higher, the silk of her vintage slip dress straining against her chest; her bare nipples showing through. Too much? Well, it worked for Kate Moss, though Delia has a more toned physique than those Nineties babes. Holding her arms out to the sides, she luxuriates in the stretch, then leans forwards, one spaghetti strap slipping and a breast popping out. 'Oops,' she laughs as she rights herself. 'Nothing like a good stretch to calm my nerves,' she explains, as she performs a reverse prayer stretch, her chest pushed up and out in a move that sings of self-confidence. Her smile is serene; her tone, assured. Those watching will be intrigued: does she know she's so hot, or is this just how upper-middle-class Influencers behave? 'That's better – and breathe.' And she demonstrates: in for four; out for eight; holding that smile; looking steadily at the camera before blowing a kiss.

She switches the camera off and sits with her arms hugging her knees, more foetal position, now, than any Buddha pose. No Calling the Earth to Witness. Despite the physiological benefits of stretching and breathing and meditating and all the things she advocates and believes in, and yes, she really does, she can't get rid of the acid churning in her stomach; that creeping sense of dread. The Awful Incident happened over eighteen months ago. And although everyone's terribly careful not to mention it, still the memory persists. It's the tequila of her memories: something she initially thought fun but which she never wants to revisit.

She still can't remember what she said to her sisters: she hopes there was nothing specific; just a general haughtiness about being their mother's favourite, something the others acknowledge, half-jokingly but with an edge, and which she generally tries not to mention. Still, it left a bad taste in her mouth. She wrote to apologise from the clinic; received a nice reply from Gilly; a brief but polite one from Rachel. Her sisters are nothing if not well brought up. Things aren't right, though, and she dislikes remaining in the wrong. It's enough to make her play up her maverick, spoiled little sister act. Hard to break away from consigned roles in a family. No doubt they expect it. As she makes her way into dinner, she wonders if she will ever revert from playing to type.

'Not for me, thanks.'

Delia puts her hand over the top of her wine glass and shakes her head vigorously as a waitress tries to pour Sancerre.

Christ. Doesn't everyone know not to place a wine glass in front of her? She shoves her chair back grabbing the glasses in one hand and strops off towards an unsuspecting waiter – Josh, the lad she'd considered inviting in the night before, who has clearly commandeered all the jobs around here.

'Here you go,' she says, thrusting the glasses towards him. 'I won't be needing these.'

God it is hard, though. Coping with her family was just about bearable when she drank, but now that she is sober, it is torture. There is nothing to soften the possibly imagined barbs or the edges of her anger: to smooth over those past difficult conversations or neuter her resentment towards her lucky older sisters, who resent her in turn.

In general, Delia was a happy drunk. A bit manic, perhaps, and sometimes, it's true, it made her more argumentative, but definitely happier, on a superficial level, than she is now. Not that that's her narrative. No, now it's all *calm and clear; strong and sober; focused and free.*

Bla-de-fucking-blah.

She is so tired of alliterative mantras, but she will make her way through the entire alphabet if it prevents her from reaching for the bottle the waitress is now placing by Gilly – *bad marks, there; she really should have told the Cornish staff that she has an alcoholic sister; what's with Eleanor's normally uber-organised eldest daughter?* – and gulping it straight down.

'I think you should take this, too.' She grabs the bottle and thrusts it at Josh, then sits back in her appointed seat, between Peter and Gilly, at one end of the large Georgian walnut table; begins fiddling with the cutlery, tapping the blade of the knife against the polished wood with a dull, repetitive sound.

'Can you stop doing that.' Gilly quivers with irritation.

This is about Delia's interview with Ned. The fact she dared to state the obvious. Because why on earth not? She'd been open about it online; Ned knew she would do this; and Gilly, as her mother's publicist, should have predicted it. Her sister's annoyed because she knows she slipped up.

Delia puts the knife down, and picks up her fork, tapping it less rhythmically this time.

'For god's sake,' Gilly mutters.

She refrains from uttering a bolshy *What?* but lays the

fork down after a disproportionate length of time; gauging it perfectly to make Gilly wince.

Tired of this game, she turns to Peter, wondering if there's some mileage to be had there. But he's talking to Carole, and their conversation has undercurrents she can't get a handle on, born of a history she will never understand. Tom sits opposite her with Rachel to his right. The two of them are usually effortlessly relaxed in each other's company and yet her sister's body language is off: her shoulders are taut, and her mouth is doing a weird little twitch. Something is going on.

And suddenly, Delia is hot with fury. Her brand, such as it is, is all about openness and truth and confronting past trauma, but while she's trying her best, everyone else is doing precisely the opposite, being peak pass ag as they shove their petty, and perhaps not so petty, grievances down.

She is so tired of this shit, and the need to be an agitator, a disruptor, an anarchist, surges as a starter is placed in front of her: scallops on a cauliflower purée, garnished with micro herbs; a confection of coral, cream and green. She spears a scallop. To her right, Gilly starts to cough: a delicate catch in the throat at first, then a dry rasp that's repeated until Delia realises she's in trouble: that her eyes are bulging as she gesticulates wildly towards her face.

'OK?' asks Tom, sitting the other side of her sister, and apparently primed to come round and give her a good whack on the back.

'No – oh,' Gilly gasps, her face going red.

Is she choking to death? It sounds bizarre. One moment,

Delia's goading her; the next, Gilly's fighting for breath – but this seems to be happening, she recognises, as Tom hits his sister-in-law between the shoulder blades.

'Better?'

'No,' she rasps.

Rachel pushes back her chair to help, and the conversation stops as the sound of Gilly's gasping fills the air. A sharper thud as Tom delivers a heavier blow, then moves as if preparing for a Heimlich manoeuvre to force the micro leaf out of her chest.

The air stills and Delia is caught between the mundanity of the drama – what a way to die! – and the increasing realisation that no one else is finding this even mildly comic, as Gilly clutches the table, and Tom springs into action, hands locked beneath Gilly's breasts.

He pulls up sharply and there's a strangled gasp as Gilly coughs up the offending twirl of green, and it lands on the table in front of her.

'Thank you,' she croaks, reaching for her water and gulping too fast.

'OK, darling?' At the other end of the table, Eleanor sits, knife and fork suspended in the air. Her hands are trembling, and her dark eyes, anxious as they flit from Gilly to Rachel and then to her. *So, she does love us*, she thinks, and in that moment, she realises that everyone else – Carole, Peter, Aiysha, Tom and those turning up tomorrow – is irrelevant.

Her mother's world is here.

'Fine, thank you,' Gilly manages with a watery smile as she wipes tears from her eyes.

The others resume eating as if nothing has happened, and there are little contented murmurs as they polish off the purée and the scallops, and gently push the tiny leaves to one side.

'Well done, Tom,' Rachel says, sufficiently loudly for everyone to hear.

'Always good to have a doctor in the house,' Carole adds.

'Excellent choice of brother-in-law,' Gilly chips in with a watery smile.

'Good to see you in action.' Delia might as well add to the praise. 'The old adrenalin kicking in . . .'

She gives him a smile because she likes Tom. The one member of the family who has never lectured her about her drinking but baldly told her she had a problem and came up with a solution. (Not a solution, he admitted as he provided details of the Swiss clinic, available to most.) But he doesn't like her reference to adrenalin, and neither does Rachel. *Interesting.* Her middle sister shoots her a look that signals that she should keep quiet.

What's also interesting is that her mother remains resolutely silent. No praise from her end of the table: her lips are pursed as if she is stopping herself from saying something. Delia knows that look only too well. When her mother lavishes you with her warmth, it feels golden; but when she withdraws – as happened eighteen months ago, after Delia racked up £5,000 on her stolen credit card and disappeared without a trace, refusing to answer her phone or any messages for three days, a period she can only hazily remember – the whole world turns dark.

'Tell me, have you ever been to Cornwall before?'

Eleanor has turned her attention to Aiysha, to her left, but the question is asked out of politeness, rather than any genuine interest. Delia glances at Aiysha who has been studiedly concentrating on cutting each scallop into quarters but who now almost flinches under the attention, her shoulders inching towards her ears.

'I'm afraid not,' she says as her knife slips on the plate, sending a spot of purée onto the white linen tablecloth in front of her host. 'I'm so sorry,' she says, as she starts to dab it and turns it into a smear that is infinitely worse.

'Not to worry.' Eleanor is typically charming, but Aiysha seems fixated by the small beige mark – an obvious rebuke – and by the time she looks up, Eleanor has turned from her and is chatting to Carole on her right. And Delia knows, as she watches Aiysha smarting from Eleanor's indifference, that she is doing the right thing.

Because she's been having doubts, ever since receiving that text earlier and realising that something she initiated is finally going to happen. That what has long felt like a theoretical possibility is about to become real. The immediacy of it was shocking. *Just arrived. See you tomorrow night.* There is no rowing back, and that has made her nervous because, for all Eleanor's faults, she isn't a monster. Delia has seen – when she arrived and moments ago, at this meal – that her mother loves her, and Delia responds to, and craves, that love and attention, too.

But Aiysha's nervousness makes her more resolute because it's hard not to see, in the illustrator's desire to please, a glimmer of little Delia. That eight-year-old who contorted herself to please her mother, and who, as an adolescent, was conscious of being too old, too rebellious, too sexual.

Too much, and never enough.

She pokes the last remaining bit of scallop in her mouth. Not bad, though she's still not a fan of cauliflower and, given what happened to Gilly, those micro herbs could be fatal. Any therapist would tell her she was doing the right thing. *Honest and happy*, she tells herself, though the gnawing pain in her stomach undermines this idea. Her eyes flit towards the wine glasses opposite, which glitter like Christmas decorations. Red and white and sparkling gold jewels.

Very deliberately, she picks up her tumbler of San Pellegrino and swigs hard, enduring the burn of the bubbles; no, *enjoying* the brief thud of pain.

Twenty-four hours until this party gets started, and things will look entirely different then.

Twenty-four

Rachel

Would your mother-in-law enjoy a birthday surprise?
A visit from uninvited guests?
The more the merrier?
The deadline's nearing.
Tick tock. Tick tock, Tommy boy.

'OK. OK, I'll do it.'

In the privacy of their bedroom, Rachel faces her husband. They have sat through dinner, and after-dinner coffee and drinks, both aware of the midnight deadline hurtling towards them. It can take two hours for bank transactions to clear and it's now ten past ten.

Tom is chalky pale. Throughout the meal, he has simmered with anxiety: his knee jiggling beneath the table, a rigidness around his mouth, a reluctance to meet her eye. He was all too aware of the threats piling up in his pocket, but Eleanor's coldness has exacerbated his despair. And it was her mother's failure to acknowledge his help in saving Delia, and that chill air of disapproval from her end of the table, that has softened Rachel. Tom is not a bad man. He is weak, and he's behaved appallingly, but he hasn't been malicious. He didn't intend to bring this level of jeopardy to her family. And she can't cast him out.

Now, he looks thrown, as if he can't believe a word she is saying.

'What do you mean, you'll do it? Your mother wouldn't lend us the money. You told me she was adamant. There's nothing you *can* do.'

'Yes, there is. I can just take it.'

'Take it?'

'From her account.'

He looks at her as if she's insane.

'I know all the internet banking details. I can transfer fifty thousand pounds to her current account and make the payment without her noticing, then repeat that over and over the next few days. I'll explain it away by the time I do the tax return. And we'll pay her back eventually. I mean, I know that technically it's fraud,' she gives an odd laugh; there's no technical about it, 'but we'll pay her back, we'll work out a schedule for that, and we'll just be countering the immediate risk of you being exposed, or of someone coming here, someone causing havoc and ruining the party, and this sum doubling to over half a million.' She sounds joyful, albeit a little manic. Why hadn't she done this immediately? It's all so obvious.

'And we'll be keeping Edith safe.'

'Yeah, that too.' Because maybe there *is* something going on with the man he met on the cliff.

'Well, that's a very elegant way of justifying it,' Tom says, smiling for the first time in three days. No, for the first time in months. It's as if the tension he's so clearly been holding in his body is finally being allowed to ease. 'God, I love you,' he says, putting his arms around her and pulling her into a deep hug.

And as she breathes in his familiar smell and feels the breadth of his shoulders and the way in which their bodies meld together, she holds him tight. It is not like her – it is not like *them* – to be angry, and although she will never be able to fully understand how he could be this duplicitous, it's a relief to relinquish some of her rage. She kisses his shoulder, and then, when he looks at her enquiringly, his wide, warm mouth. His lips are dry, and though it's not exactly a moment of passion – there's too much to do, and there are residual traces of her anger – still, it confirms what they've decided. Like a stamp validating a ticket, the kiss seals the deal.

'I'll do it now,' she says, breaking away, though she wants to linger; to feel his hands on her waist; the certainty of him, when that constancy has been lacking. 'It can sometimes take up to two hours, and he'll be checking, won't he?'

On cue, Tom's phone vibrates. Another message. *Tick tock. Tick tock.*

'I'll do it in Eleanor's study. And I'll round the full amount up to three hundred thousand, so we can bung him an extra twenty thousand if he gets difficult. It will literally take a couple of minutes.'

'Shall I go back and distract them?'

But she sees how tired he looks. He had left the dinner early, claiming to be shattered by the drive down, and his grey pallor confirms this.

'Won't it look odd, given that we've just come up?'

'Yeah. Good point.' He's grateful for the reprieve.

'There'll be no reason for anyone to look in the study.' She tries to reassure them both. 'Eleanor will be in her element. I'll be no time.'

The study is dark. All the lights are off, but she's guided by the moonlight filtering through the French windows. It spills onto the carpet; shrouds the walls.

She fumbles her way to the desk and the vast iMac that sits like the control deck of a ship from which her mother will drive her fortune, grateful that Eleanor is technologically inept and always leaves it in sleep mode. Grateful, too, that she never changes her password; that her older daughters know it; and – despite Rachel urging her countless times not to do this – that it's the same she uses for her online banking, too.

The website's homepage fills the screen. Despite being confident the others will remain chatting in the dining room at the other end of the house, she is hyper-alert to the noise of her fingers on the keyboard; aware of the need to act quickly – so quickly that she miscalculates the required letters of the password and inserts the 11th not the 12th. *Try again*, the website suggests. She counts on her fingers, striking each on the surface of the desk before double-checking, anxious she shouldn't be locked out of the account. Success! At some point, Rachel has removed the dual verification option – no need for a confirmatory text – and so she navigates her way to her business account, clicks on 'transfer money between accounts', and enters £300,000, from which she'll make several £50,000 payments over the next few days. Ensuring she's inserted the correct amount, she clicks, and, with a satisfying whoosh, the money wends its way from her mother's business account to the current account.

Nearly there, she tells herself, and then: *Nothing illegal yet*. All she has done is transfer a sum of money between her mother's accounts; nothing untoward, if you ignore the fact this hasn't been authorised; nothing that, as her mother's accountant, she might not enact. But who is she kidding? Rachel isn't the sort of accountant who is creative at interpreting HMRC's rules. She's never even failed to pay for something at a self-service checkout, and just swiped it through, like those new middle-class shoplifters she's read about in *The Times*.

And yet I'm going to defraud her, she thinks as she picks up her phone with the bank details that Tom typed in, whispering them to herself as she inserts them and realises that she's got a digit wrong. *Bit late for scruples*. But she is doing it partly for her mother, who would be utterly humiliated if her party was gatecrashed and her son-in-law exposed; she is doing it for her children, and of course she is doing it for herself and for Tom. She tells herself this as she corrects the sort code. And she is still reminding herself of this as she is interrupted by the creak of the study door being pushed open and the click of a switch as light floods the room.

Twenty-five

Gilly

Gilly slips from the dining room soon after Tom and Rachel.

'So much to do,' she pleads, but in truth she needs a moment to herself.

It has scared her, the choking episode. Her throat feels raw with coughing, but it's the tightness in her chest that preoccupies her because her body knows it has only just escaped danger, and her heart is reeling: an odd syncopation, a stuttering jump, then a flurry of beats that come too fast.

What a way to die. Mundane. Domestic. Tragic. A tragic accident. But a little pathetic? Forty years of a perfectly ordinary life, and then to die in such a ridiculous way.

And if it happened, she suspects it would be the most interesting thing anyone would say about her. *She died tragically young in a freak accident. A one in a million eventuality. What rotten luck.* As if her four decades of trying to be a good daughter, sister and friend, a conscientious worker and a decent person counted for nothing. All those memories of her true self erased by the randomness of her death.

She considers all this as she sits at the end of the table straight after it happens, while Rachel squeezes her hand in sympathy and Tom glances over to check if she is OK. Because although she appreciates their warmth and her mother's concern – Eleanor's anxiety glimpsed in that moment when the room turned silent, and she asked if she was OK – she wonders if anyone would really miss her. If anyone would truly *care*. To her left, Delia barely seems to notice, and her mother's guests have moved on as if it were no more than a diverting hiccup and certainly not something to provoke an existential crisis.

And yet this is precisely what it has done. She needs to get out into the fresh night air, *right now*, she realises, as she pushes her chair back abruptly. To do something reckless. Something that will make her feel alive, bold and free. The sort of thing that no one would expect of sensible, organised Gilly Kingman. Something red in tooth and claw, as her mother might say. Raw; almost animal. Something that's the very antithesis of death.

And so, she makes her apologies and walks from the dining room, across the slate flagstones of the hall and, briefly, up to her bedroom, pulling out her phone as she does so, and texting with furious urgency.

Gilly, the most diligent daughter. The one who has subsumed all her needs into those of others – being a surrogate mother to her little sister; a general dogsbody for her mother – is going to attend to her needs for once. The ultimate self-care. Isn't that how Delia would put it?

Can we meet? I need to see you. The summer house. Now.

The summer house, or writer's hut, hunkers in the distance. The night is partially cloudy; a meagre light, which gilds the slate roof silver, spills from the half-hidden moon.

The air is warm. Scented with tamarisk, thyme, chamomile: a heady herbal cocktail. Freshly honed pine. The salt of the sea. It smells of freedom, she thinks, as she feels her breath ease. Freedom. Possibility. Excitement. Straining to peer ahead, she can't see a thing. The insides of the hut, empty except for the shelves and an old desk placed to give a sense of dimension, remain an opaque, velvety black.

She steps closer, the hypnotic thud of the waves filling her ears because this is far closer to the wildness of the cliffs and the beach than the house, where the lights are shrouded by shutters; just the one lamp glowing golden in the hall. A liminal space, more of the cliffs than the house. It even smells of the woods: of the bookshelves only just built, and the rich oak of the floor. A transformative place, as well, where Gilly can explore a different version of herself. Bolder, braver; decidedly darker. Undoubtedly more selfish. Unperturbed by what her family might think.

She reaches the door, pushes down on the solid brass handle, enjoying the weight of the frame and the ease with which it swings open. Steps forwards, listening intently for the sound of another's breathing; the evidence of anyone there.

Charcoal shades into impenetrable black, but she can make out the edge of the desk through a shard of watery light filtered through a window. She listens to the heavy silence; trying to gauge quite where he is, because she hopes – no, she is sure she is not alone.

It's as if the air has emptied from her lungs.

Two hands are over her eyes: large; firm; slightly callused. A warm breath on her neck. The knowledge that someone far stronger than her is behind her; has caught her tight; that they are moving closer. Then a delicious frisson of anticipation before a mouth nips her softly on the neck.

She turns and the hands lift off, are on her waist now, and sliding past the base of her spine to cup her bottom, and she is reaching up towards him, her movements frantic, as if she is desperate to shed her usual self and become this new one who meets her lover, here, in this secret space. The Gilly that fears being obliterated; that is embracing the opposite; that is crying out, with every shiver of desire, that yes, she knows how to live. Wood, and sea, and darkness; and flesh and limbs that jigsaw, sometimes cackhandedly, so that they stumble around the room and bang against the desk, but then somehow fit together in a forgiving mesh. A union that works without the need for words, or explanations, because she deals with far too many of these each day.

Outside, the hedgerows rustle as a field mouse scuttles from a hovering owl, and a vixen cries, urgent and anguished. For a moment, Gilly stops and listens to the call of an animal that has been so important a part of her mother's life, and whose cry captures Gilly's earlier distress.

'Come here.'

A whisper, throaty, intent, and she is distracted.

The vixen continues its mating call – visceral, eerie – and drowns out any sounds inside.

Twenty-six

Rachel

'Hello?'

Delia stands in the doorway of their mother's study, peering down at her sister.

'What are you doing in here? I thought you'd gone to bed.'

Her tone is amused but there's an edge to it: the youngest sister catching an older one doing something she shouldn't. Rachel is ambushed by a memory of Delia discovering her trying on a coveted top of Gilly's; posing in front of her mirror; then her embarrassment at having this thrilling, private moment observed. Delia had been more biddable then: bribed with a spritz of Body Shop White Musk fragrance or a handful of stickers. That's hardly going to work now.

'I just remembered something I needed to do.'

'On Eleanor's computer?'

They both know that their mother's study, and in particular her devices, are sacrosanct. Rachel and Gilly might access information, if Eleanor asks them to do so, but both are unlikely to use them on their own.

'I forgot to transfer a payment for the party.' *If you have to lie, stay as close as possible to the truth*: from somewhere in her subconscious, Rachel dredges up this advice. 'I needed to pay Josh and his friends from the village for checking the invites.'

'That boy seems to have sewn up all the jobs round here.' A pause. 'Wouldn't you usually pay them after the job?'

'What are you doing? Checking up on me?' Rachel yelps in concern.

And suddenly Delia is next to her, and Rachel reaches for the mouse to close the window, but she isn't quick enough. The page incriminates her: banking transfer from Eleanor Kingman current account to – and the payee is empty, but the amount isn't: £50,000.

'You're giving Josh fifty thousand pounds?'

Rachel clicks and the window disappears. 'It's complicated. Just leave it, OK?'

'What are you doing transferring fifty thousand pounds from Eleanor's current account to Josh?' Delia's voice rises with incredulity. 'Is he blackmailing her or something?'

'Keep your voice down.'

'Why are you paying him?' Delia persists, eyes sparkling with glee. 'I mean, that's what you're doing, isn't it? Or – omigod! – is he blackmailing you and you're defrauding Eleanor? Stealing from her account?'

'Don't be ridiculous,' Rachel says. '*You're* the one who stole from her. Who took her wallet in front of us all.'

'I was ill. It was an addiction. But this is a different level.

Oh my god, you are! You were about to take fifty grand from her account.'

And Rachel has another flashback. They had recently moved into the house by the Thames, and she had an unrequited crush on the gardener's seventeen-year-old son; was painfully tongue-tied in his presence, and Delia, with uncanny percipience, just knew. 'You like Ben, don't you? You're in love with him. I'm going to tell him you're in love with him,' she had taunted, while Rachel flushed a deep puce. She had stormed off, confirming her little sister's suspicions; praying her threat would never be enacted; dreading that this first, intense love, as she was sure it was then, would be exposed to him, to his father, to her mother. The situation feels horribly similar now.

'I was *not* about to take fifty thousand pounds from her,' she says, but she's a rubbish liar, she always has been, and they both know this: her cheeks go pink and her voice, shrill. 'If you'll excuse me, I'm going to bed.' She pushes back the chair so aggressively it gives a loud screech against the slate – a nails-on-the-blackboard moment – and stands there.

And still she waits, vainly hoping that Delia will leave and let her complete the transaction – or perhaps that she will surprise her; will drop the spiky, spoiled younger sister act and, for once in her life, show some concern. What would happen if she asked Rachel why she was doing this? Could Rachel confide in her? And might their relationship shift, Delia not just flattered by her sister choosing her as a confidante, but recognising this olive branch and grasping it for all its worth? Perhaps Delia was genuine in her letter from the clinic in Montreux and *does* want a better relationship: one that's matured beyond childish envy and resentment and would let them be each other's allies? Delia, after all, would understand Tom's addiction; might even be willing to offer some advice . . .

And yet, as she considers making this plea for help, she takes in her sister's body language: hand on her hip, nostrils that don't quite flare but look as if they might. Everything signals her enjoyment of the situation, the fact she might use it for some leverage. Leopards don't change their spots, and Rachel is stupid to think that they might.

'Aren't you going to log out?'

'Yep, of course.' Not looking at her, Rachel sits back down, clicks on the relevant part of the screen, then goes to the Apple menu and scrolls down to 'sleep'. To think she was *this close* to being honest. 'Sleep for me, too.' She yawns theatrically. 'You coming up?'

'Yeah. Big day tomorrow.' Cat-like, Delia sidles to the door, where she waits for Rachel; she's clearly not going anywhere until she's seen her older sister out.

Making no effort to disguise the fact she finds this intensely petty, Rachel stalks past, all hope that she could sneak down and log back in extinguished as Delia waits for her to go ahead up the stairs. How quickly can she return? The money must be transferred by midnight and proof sent. And what's Delia going to do now? Will she tell Eleanor? If not now, then tomorrow? She might be intensely self-centred, but surely even *she* won't ruin their mother's party?

At the top of the staircase, Rachel turns and whispers, 'I can't explain properly, but it's not what it looks like.'

'And what does it look like?' Delia asks, all faux innocence.

'You know,' she hisses. 'Like I'm defrauding her.'

'*Like* you're defrauding her?' Delia echoes, widening her preternaturally blue eyes.

There's a squeak and the door to the children's bedroom opens.

'Mum-my.' Maisie, red-faced, sleep-creased, bemused, sways in the doorway. She blinks at the light, and the fact her mother and aunt have materialised. 'Mum-my, I can't sleep.'

'It's all right, sweetheart.' Never has she been so relieved to be interrupted by a child. 'It's all right. Come here, darling. Let's get you to bed.'

'Mum-my.' Her daughter's face folds in on itself in shame. 'My bed's wet.'

'Oh, OK, sweetheart, we'll sort it.' Her heart sinks a little: she'll have to find fresh linen from the staff, clean and reassure her daughter; won't be able to get back down to make the payment for a while.

But at least Delia is satisfied that she'll be preoccupied.

'Sleep tight, Maisie. See you both in the morning,' she says. And then she gives Rachel a look. It's one Rachel remembers from their childhood but that she hasn't seen for years: that clearly conveys she will retain this information and use it at the optimum moment.

That says: *I'm going to tell on you.*

SATURDAY

Twenty-seven

GILLY

Dawn comes earlier to the coach house than the manor house.

Or so it seems to Gilly, as she watches the curtains grow lighter, sunlight stealing around their chinks to turn the newly whitewashed bedroom a soft golden by five thirty a.m.

She must arrange blackout blinds; and then, as she stretches out across the sheets – high thread count Egyptian cotton; a good choice – she realises that she won't need to. That won't be her job. She won't be here.

Gilly hadn't intended sleeping in the coach house. (Not that she's done much sleeping.) But after her summer house assignation, there seemed no reason to return to the manor house alone.

The clouds had lifted, and they'd walked along the heath at the edge of her mother's land, pointing out the different constellations – the Plough; Orion's Belt – because the sky, free of any light pollution, was clear in a way she had rarely seen.

She had eked out that walk, and as they reached the gravel driveway, he'd nodded in the direction of the former outbuildings: a clear invitation in the jut of his jaw, the glint in his eye. She'd been quiet: tiptoeing to his room; suppressing a bubble of laughter – the illicit nature of what they were doing making her excitement more heightened, her desire so pin-sharp she had to tell herself to calm down and stop reaching for him constantly.

They'd made love fiercely; then, at around three or four, more tenderly. Now, the sensible part of her questions how she will survive on so little sleep. Then she wonders if it matters. She had felt so alive last night. And it's not that he's *awakened* her – though the sex is unlike any she's experienced before – but more that she has finally recognised a part of herself that has long lain dormant; that she has long suppressed.

She, Gilly Kingman, is not just sensible, practical, responsible; the eldest daughter who has shrunk herself to fit around the needs of her mother and her sisters; kind, supportive, dutiful, and more than a little dull. She is fierce, and she is fire. Every cell in her body capable of experiencing intense sensations; every part of her – or so it felt last night and two short, sweet hours ago – capable of evoking desire.

She looks across at the broad back of the man lying on his front next to her. A younger man: in his early thirties, sweet Jesus. His back, honed from carrying equipment; his buttocks, like something Michelangelo might sculpt. (And here she smiles at herself, knowing she is being ridiculous;

that this way of thinking is the stuff of fiction; that she needs to rein it all in.)

Who would have thought it. The dating apps she'd joined after her disastrous fortieth birthday brought only embarrassment: all those middle-aged men who read desperation into her conversation and for whom she had felt not a flicker of interest – and yet, in a way, they had helped.

'Maybe I need a younger man,' she'd lamented, poking fun at herself as they'd chatted at the end of a meeting to discuss the parameters of filming in Cornwall. They were at the Thames-side house, where he'd been capturing some footage, and perhaps it was the late May sunshine – that sense of spring burgeoning; of delicious possibility – that had made her reckless. 'Maybe you do,' he'd said and then, as they'd moved out of earshot of the others, 'So, do you fancy a drink?'

An hour later, they were in a riverside pub; an hour after *that*, they'd abandoned the conceit of a pub altogether, improbable, and deeply unprofessional, though it seemed. And they probably have no sort of future: neither has suggested this is anything but casual, and she is under no illusions that a younger, globe-trotting documentary maker would have any desire to settle down. But perhaps that needn't matter. This has been so uncomplicated. So refreshing. So joyful. As he held her in the early hours, she had felt as if she understood something seismic: that she needn't remain the Gilly Kingman of the past four decades; that the experience has taught her to be bolder than she ever thought she could be.

The world will be stirring soon. Twenty to six. She is sated. Aching. What she needs is a hot shower; plenty of strong coffee; another couple of hours' sleep.

The temptation to kiss the nape of his neck; to trail her fingers down that beautiful back; to nudge him over and taste him is strong.

But the need for sleep is stronger. Quietly, she slips from the room.

Twenty-eight

Eleanor

'No, not like that.'

Eleanor bats her hands at the hair and make-up girl who is no doubt doing her best, though her best isn't good enough. They can never get her hair quite right. Too bouncy; too inane-looking, as if all women in late middle-age (she refuses to use the word O.L.D.) want an identikit version of a specific blow-dry: a US newscaster crossed with Jane Fonda at the turn of the millennium.

She fiddles with the strands of her fringe; kisses a tissue to transfer her lipstick-y gunk. Her thoughts feel sluggish. A double espresso, that's what she needs. She'll get Gilly, who's looking rather exhausted, to go and fetch one. Until that has happened, the filming can wait.

'All set?'

Ned is beaming as she settles into the chair which he directs her to, five minutes later. The lighting is brutal: a globe of white heat positioned to the right of the camera so intense, it's as if she's being interrogated. Her forehead prickles. She can't risk a hint of sweat.

'Could you alter that? It's in my eyes.'

'Adam, would you mind?'

The globe is shifted a little to the right.

She blinks. The fact it is just out of sight is almost as distracting. 'I'm sorry. Could you move it more *that* way?'

'It's a pay-off. You won't be well lit,' says the cameraman, a lovely-looking young man who's usually charm itself but he's unusually emphatic about this. He is standing, legs apart, arms folded across his chest. Wagons circled. Pistols at dawn.

'But I won't be as uncomfortable,' she insists.

Because, while there is no point in being distracted by minutiae, they should want to put their interviewees at ease. She glances at Ned. Is he going to let his colleagues speak to her like this? Ned turns to his cameraman and shrugs, as if to say: you heard what she said.

'Let's find an alternative,' Ned says smoothly, while they fiddle with the lighting and adjust the set to take better advantage of the natural light. After a few minutes, the globe is gone, and she feels sufficiently in control to indicate that they can begin.

'So, we've talked previously about your writing process but let's recap for continuity's sake,' Ned begins.

And as soon as she starts, she realises that of course she can do this. The words will flow, just as they always do. This is no different from holding forth at any literary festival, though without the discomfort of a damp tent, or the discombobulating sense of looking out at a sea of unknown faces or an auditorium of black. Befuddled brain or not, words are her currency, and this is a script she knows by heart. Like a mechanical toy, Ned just needs to wind her up and watch her go.

'You didn't start writing until you met your former husband, Michael Kingman,' he is saying now. 'Was that relationship creatively fruitful?'

Her eyes fix on him; it is very hard not to glare. They have established that she won't say much about her marriage; have agreed on a pat answer, designed to shut down extensive questions. There'll be nothing to indicate quite how much she loved him, nothing about his numerous betrayals, and she'll do her very best not to sound bitter as they touch on the start of her writing career.

'Well, it resulted in three daughters, so, in that respect, it was creative! And the element of competition helped. I was twenty, and a final-year student working in the Goodge Street bookshop, when we met. He was a couple of years older than me, doing an MPhil, and immensely beautiful, so I wanted to impress him. That gave me an added impetus to get better, to hone my style.'

'And was he supportive?'

'In those early days, incredibly so, yes.' She has a flash of him reading a second draft, and looking up, stunned at the strength of her writing. 'We would read each other's work. I edited early versions of his debut, which was rather successful, but that aspect of our relationship became one-sided, as you might imagine.' She arches an eyebrow, despite herself. 'I helped him, but after he was published and became relatively successful, he was rather less inclined to help me. And then, of course, the children came along, and while he had his time to write, I was significantly distracted.'

'But then you started writing the *Fox Hole* series.'

'Indeed.'

'Inspired, I believe, by spotting a vixen one night near your home in Chiswick?'

'Hardly the most romantic jumping-off point,' she says, getting into her stride: this is regular festival fodder, and she barely has to think. 'It was late at night. Ten or eleven. I'd gone for a walk. The pram in the hall was getting to me, I remember. It was claustrophobic in that little house, which was always filled with damp washing and the needs of tiny children, and it felt particularly so in the deep midwinter – this was just before Christmas – when it was dark by four.

'Michael was writing at his desk in the lounge, and I'd been trying to at the kitchen table, but it felt particularly oppressive: I'd cooked a stew, and I needed to get away from the smell of fried onions, the saucepans on the draining board – I'd probably made mashed potato – the condensation dripping down the walls. It was freezing, there had been a frost and it had started snowing, and I went for a walk, down to the park and the swings where I always took the girls: a bit of urban scrubland, by the railway track. And there she was in the snow: a vixen, ripping apart a bin bag. Her coat mangy; her ribs visible; a chicken carcass in her mouth. She gave me a look, calm but brutally realistic, from one desperate female to another. And I imagined the lengths to which she would go to feed her cubs. The lengths I was prepared to go to, as well, to protect my sanity and my girls.'

'That's quite a tale.' Ned smiles.

'It's also the truth.'

'I meant, quite a point of inspiration, and the series quickly became hugely successful.'

'Twenty million copies sold to date.'

'There were ten books in the series. How did you keep coming up with your inventive plots?'

Oh really. What sort of infantile question was that?

'It's no different from writing adult fiction.' She is bored of this now. 'You start with character, ask "what if", and several different scenarios emerge.'

'After the second book was published, you started employing young women who would work as a sort of cross between an au pair and a PA, didn't you?'

'Yes,' she says, crisply, and, like that vixen, her ears prick up.

'There was a run of them, none lasting longer than a year?'

'Well, I suppose that I was a little too exacting.' She shifts in her chair. 'I was a busy working mother, and, with hindsight, I probably expected too much. They were young girls, straight out of university, who were hoping for a gentle route into publishing. Sometimes they hoped I'd mentor them, but I hadn't the time. I felt under immense pressure: to prove myself; and to provide financially, too, because by this stage Michael was struggling with his second novel. I had short amounts of time away from my daughters when I needed to achieve a lot, and I expected my PAs to be as engaged as me.'

'Did you expect them to act as sounding boards for your ideas?'

'Well, very occasionally that might occur . . .'

'Did they help with plot threads?'

'No.' The denial's perhaps a little too emphatic.

'There are a few NDAs relating to some of them: why was that?'

'Oh, I expect they knew too many secrets!' she jokes, keeping her expression amused and her tone light. These are *her* books and no one else deserves any credit: certainly not the young woman who claimed she'd come up with the ideas for books six to eight, not to mention her *other* swiftly rebuffed claim. 'No, but being serious, I was concerned they didn't steal my ideas. Intellectual copyright is everything in writing and I didn't want anyone who had worked for me copying – no, pinching – what they'd seen. And to be frank, I hadn't worked out how to manage my publicity. I didn't have a publicist in those early days, and I didn't want anyone to reveal anything about me or my family.'

'You were shaping your own story, so to speak?'

'I was protecting my family, and I had every right to do so.' She takes a couple of deep breaths. She needs to calm right down. Ned gives her a reassuring smile: he has noted her discomfort and has pushed her as far as she will go – and further than she intended. If he persists, she will have to suggest a break before they move on.

'Let's go back to the beginning,' Ned says smoothly. 'It's the most incredible story: your success from really very humble beginnings . . .'

'I was lucky. Born at a good time. A loathed Baby Boomer. Bright, so I benefitted from a grammar school education and one particularly inspiring teacher who encouraged me to apply to university. A full grant, of course, which made everything possible. So yes, through education I managed to escape.'

Ned smiles. 'But it must have taken real drive to get there?'

She shrugs. She has that in spades. You don't create the wealth she has without it.

'I mean, you didn't have the easiest start in life?'

She takes her time. He has agreed to deal with this very lightly. She didn't, she told him in their preliminary conversations, feel it was especially relevant.

'There was nothing all that noteworthy about it. An alcoholic father; a depressive mother. Perfect ingredients, perhaps, to write about familial dysfunction, but I chose not to. I chose to create happier endings.'

'Although your fox cubs suggest you know all about sibling rivalry . . .'

'Well, I have three daughters . . .'

'But no siblings yourself?'

She shakes her head. It's automatic, this denial; so automatic that it has stopped feeling like a deception. He waits, head tilted to one side, perhaps expecting her to elaborate, but what more can she say?

'Actually, do you know what, I could do with another coffee,' she says, 'and a little break. I'm sure you've got enough for the moment, haven't you?'

Without waiting for an answer, she disentangles the tiny microphone attached to the edge of her silk shirt, gives him a brisk nod, and gets up to walk away.

And, as she does, her ears fill with the sound of her heightened breathing, one question flooding her head; pulsating in time to her heart, which beats a tattoo against her chest.

What does he know? What does he know? What does he know? What does he know?

What on earth does he know?

Twenty-nine

Delia

It's a good job no one was planning to get married in Trecarrow's parish chapel of St Morwenna this Saturday, thinks Delia, as she walks down the oak-lined valley towards it.

She'd checked when searching for a spot for their meeting, knowing that secrecy was key. The beach was obviously out – too many people virtuously wild swimming – as was the garden of the Blue Bell Inn, where many of her mother's friends are staying. But a chapel, however picturesque, that was barely attended? Priceless. Not much chance, early on the last Saturday of August, of anyone venturing a mile beyond the coast path towards this.

And so, here she is.

And so, she very much hopes, he will soon be.

She pushes open the bleached oak door, studded with rusted nails, and steps into the cool of the building. It's so quiet! Who knew medieval stonemasons were so skilled at soundproofing, because the birdsong has been silenced, leaving her alone to think. The air is cool and slightly musty: scented with incense and an arrangement of star jasmine, lilies and roses with an undertone of fetid water. The floor is scattered with petals, and several browning rosebuds droop.

She walks up the aisle, focusing on the tap of her shoes on the worn flags and the light streaming through the stained-glass window, motes of dust dancing like fireflies. For a moment, she considers whipping out her phone because the light is *so* flattering, she could make a lovely reel. It really *is* excellent, and she could lean into the spiritualism. But she doesn't do God; knows any mistaken hint of Christianity would be toxic for her brand.

She takes a pew on the left-hand side towards the front, and stares at the stained-glass window: Christ on a cross; Mary weeping at his feet, lots of cobalt and red and gold; all fine if you like that sort of thing. What she wants isn't a spiritual epiphany. It's just some quiet. Some clarity.

Is she doing the right thing?

It's a question that has tormented her ever since the meal last night, when she'd felt an uncharacteristic stab of guilt at seeing her mother's nerviness. Eleanor's mothering, various therapists have reassured her, has been damaging in the extreme. To take her childhood and refashion it for commercial gain; to set her apart from her siblings all while denying her contact with her father went beyond mindless damage. Her mother has been psychologically destructive, and she needs to be called out for this.

And so, the plan has been to challenge her: to present her

with evidence – tangible, physical evidence – of the pain she has inflicted; to show that *her* story – the story of Eleanor Kingman, the doting mother inspired by her daughter – doesn't quite stack up.

Only, it's hard to hold on to this belief when she sees that Eleanor loves her, after all; that her mother seems newly vulnerable; and when her sisters, not having experienced the same childhood, can't back up her account. Rachel has made her feel weirdly protective, too. Fleecing Eleanor of £50,000 while working as her accountant? Delia may have put stuff on her credit card, but she did it while off her head. Rachel's premeditation, and this amount, is in a very different league.

But it's difficult to backtrack because she's been so consistently angry with her mother for appropriating her childhood. Sometimes, after a particularly gruelling therapy session, she has felt so *heard*, she wanted to scream. Instead, she would create an Insta reel about forgiveness meaning abandoning all hope of a better past. Recently, Gilly had liked a similar post. Delia didn't DM her to say: 'You get this?' But the recognition – which stirred memories of all the times her eldest sister had hugged her, or reassured her – had felt like a private code.

But then Delia saw her mother, and the doubt started to creep in. Love and hate coexisted, as they always did. With every act of rebellion, she was still performing. *Fuck you*, she was saying, but also: *please notice me*.

Well, she is about to grab her attention now. Not just

through her interview with Ned but by doing something far, far worse. And so, before she hurls the final grenade into her mother's world and watches the sky burst into flames, she needs to know she is doing the right thing.

He is late, though. Only fifteen minutes. She won't give up on him yet, but she needs to leave by ten.

And then she hears the footsteps. Slow. Deliberate – as if their owner is also having their doubts and is walking with a degree of caution. She won't turn around. She has coped for twenty-two years without him, and she can't be doing with any sentimental schtick.

The footsteps stop at the end of her pew, and she turns her head, assessing him coolly, calmly.

'Hello,' he says.

Because there he is.

Michael Kingman.

Her father.

Of course, he looks pretty bloody awful.

It is still a shock. Even though she's met him several times over the last six months, she can't get used to him being so gaunt. Her father was never hefty but had cheerfully inhabited his broad, six-foot-four frame. Now, it's as if he has shrunk, and, as she has grown upwards – now a willowy five foot ten – he has started to bend, as if ashamed of taking up so much space.

'Fancy giving me a hug?' He gives her a rueful smile, craving connection though knowing it's more than he should expect after two decades away from her. There's a weariness to his movements: he's resigned to this last act of his life being played.

'Of course,' she says, and they perform a slightly odd embrace, Delia standing on the edge of the pew, and so taller than usual; feeling as if she's doing the parenting, perhaps apt since he hasn't done so for years.

'Let's sit,' she says, and they lower themselves, side by side. He's too warmly dressed for the heat: a navy blazer with a white shirt underneath; faded terracotta chinos. The clothes of a man who has always passed through the world easily, or who, perhaps, now feels the cold.

It's cancer that has done this to him, of course. That has speeded up their reconciliation. Little point in playing games. The ticking of the clock, the realisation that he has so little time and that they have wasted so much already, means she hasn't considered being off-hand, or guarded, as she would otherwise have been.

But still. There are arguments they retrace, and things left unsaid.

'Why didn't you want to see us?' she can't help repeating now, her voice that of a little girl.

'Oh, Delia.' He lets out a long sigh. 'We've been through all this several times. Your mother exerted considerable emotional pressure for me to stay away. I'd hurt her so much; she wanted to protect you. And I regret it, of course I regret it, but it seemed easier not to fight. I was preoccupied, too,' he continues, more sheepishly. 'And besides, I was like a kid in a sweetshop. I'm sorry that you seem to have inherited that from me.'

Delia fidgets in her seat. She doesn't want to get into the affairs he's alluding to, and she resents his assumption she's like him. Fellow addicts normally provoke compassion, but she doesn't buy into sex being addictive: a previous boyfriend claimed it and it seemed far too easy an excuse. And she knows, although he doesn't know that she does, and she is testing him still, that there was another, more compelling reason.

'But what about later? You could have made contact once I'd grown up?'

'Yes, I know. That's on me. But Eleanor has such a powerful way with words that I truly believed I wouldn't be welcome.' He shakes his head, clinging to this fictitious version of events.

She shrugs like the small child he left behind and picks up one of the ancient kneelers lined up on the pew front, tracing its design with her index finger: the colours faded, the thread tough. If she confronts him with the other reason – her knowledge that Eleanor gave him a substantial pay-off in return for an NDA and the promise he stay away – she will frighten him off completely, and she can't bear that. She still craves this contact with her long-absent parent. Besides, in confronting Eleanor and telling her how much he regrets not seeing his children, he is part of her plan.

Because Michael is fully on board with the idea of challenging her mother. 'An opportunity to say my piece. To write a better ending. She'll understand that,' he said when Delia casually mooted the idea when they first met. But his failure to be honest bothers her, and feeds into her fear about doing this. And then there's the question of how she'll feel afterwards. Elated – or momentarily triumphant? As if she's drunk with abandon, and is then left with the most horrific hangover?

Best to think of logistics.

'So, if you come along the cliff path for nine p.m., I'll persuade her to come near enough to see you and orchestrate your conversation.'

Because, while she can hardly prevent her father from meeting her mother, now that she has set all this in motion, she can try to mitigate the damage she will cause.

Exposure is what Delia has always wanted. But, in the cool of this church and conscious of her mother's vulnerability, she realises a melodramatic exposé might not work best. That it would be enough for her mother to acknowledge the pain of keeping her daughters from their father in private. On the beach perhaps, or at her writer's hut.

Far from the party, and the cameras.

Thirty

Aiysha

Just the next twenty-four hours, Aiysha tells herself, as she pounds the coast path, trying to put some distance between herself and Dame Eleanor. That's all she needs to get through. This time tomorrow, she'll be on a train back to London, leaving her creative collaborator far, far behind.

All she has to do is to keep a low profile. The memory of trying to extract money is going to take quite some time to fade, but, if she's looking at the hedgerows, or the seabirds, or the beach (it's low tide and she's fascinated by how the dips and craters have turned it into a moonscape), then at least she's not spilling gravy, or picking up the wrong bit of cutlery, or breaking a form of etiquette she didn't even know existed. At least she can breathe without feeling choked with a vicious anger – or absolutely mortified.

'Hello, there!'

A short, round figure is barrelling towards her, her wide face wreathed in a beam. It's Carole, Dame Eleanor's agent;

an automatic enemy because she perhaps suggested – and certainly didn't reject – the flat fee idea.

'Hi, there,' she responds, because it's too late to pretend she hasn't seen her. 'How're you doing?'

'Better for seeing you. Can I join you for a bit on the beach?'

It's a suggestion, not a question, and Aiysha finds herself nodding then following her down the sheer path, which Carole navigates with surprising ease. They talk about the weather and how exciting the party will be – *yeah, right* – and then after Carole clambers down the rocks at the end and jumps, somewhat heavily, onto the sand, she turns to Aiysha, and says, conspiratorially, 'I wanted to chat to you about something specific, actually.'

'Oh, yes,' Aiysha says, while internally she screams, *uh-oh*, because this is *just* what she needs. Eleanor's closest ally terrifies her, with her sharp eyes and her five decades in the business, and she senses a reprimand coming. Except, she is no longer putting up with it. Because *Tyler* would be *nothing* without her drawings. 'A few efficient lines that are all the more affecting for it,' according to *The Times*. 'It's the illustrations that lift this picture book head and shoulders above the rest,' said the *Guardian*. The praise spools like a mantra through her head. And, though Eleanor never acknowledges this, she helped in other ways: it was *her* idea that Jess be captured by the thieves, and Tyler solve the riddle that saves her – a pretty integral part of the plot. And then there were the lines of copy she added. *Little, but fierce. Sharper than everyone thinks. Who wants to be ordinary?* Only yesterday someone DM'd her with a photo of a dinner service they'd created with *What is Normal?* hand-painted around each plate's rim. Not that Carole would want to hear any of this.

'So as I was saying,' the agent continues, as they walk towards the sea spread slick across the sand like melted butter, 'and I hope this doesn't come across as patronising, Aiysha, because you're clearly a bright young woman, it would be very much in your best interests not to make Eleanor your enemy, but to keep her as your friend.'

She peers up at her from beneath that bird's nest of hair. Her eyes, so heavily outlined with kohl it's as if a child has taken a crayon to them, don't leave the younger woman's face and Aiysha is reminded that the agent is far shrewder than her bohemian persona might suggest.

'I don't want to make her my enemy,' Aiysha manages to get out. 'I really don't. It's hardly great for creative collaboration. I just want to be valued and properly compensated for my skill.'

'And you will be. Don't you worry about that. But you're only just starting out, and with a talent like yours – no, don't thank me; I love the pictures and can *quite* imagine how useful you've been – you can afford to play the long game.'

They resume walking, and Carole keeps her tone conversational and light, as if to take the sting out of what she says next, though it bites, as she intends.

'Eleanor – and I say this with the greatest respect for her and on the understanding that this will remain confidential' – she waits for Aiysha to nod – 'has been to places, and experienced things, that neither of us has, or, at least, I very much hope you haven't. And because of this, she has an inner strength you probably have some idea of, but, again, can't possibly guess.'

She pauses while Aiysha tries to work out this riddle. 'Why are you telling me this?' The illustrator frowns. 'Is this some sort of threat?'

'Oh, dear me, no.' Carole pats her arm. 'I wouldn't dream of doing that, my dear. Think of it as a piece of friendly advice.' She bends and picks up a long strand of red seaweed. 'Look! Isn't that pretty.' She does such a good impression of being easily distracted. 'Or, if you like, a warning,' she says, looking up and checking that Aiysha has got the message loud and clear.

'OK, I hear you,' she says, standing still and trying not to glower because little flames of anger are shooting up inside her. 'I completely understand.'

Carole gives her another long, scrutinising look, then smiles as if to say: *I'm glad that's sorted.* 'I'm off for a paddle. My own form of mindfulness, isn't that how Delia would describe it? What would she say?' She gives Aiysha a wink, all friendliness now, '"*And breathe . . .*"'

Aiysha nods, incapable of saying anything to counter the sense of being put firmly in her place. She is too humiliated to make small talk about Dame Eleanor's daughter, either. 'I'll let you have your walk . . .'

'Lovely!' Carole beams at her for taking the hint.

Aiysha watches her potter off towards the shore. Might as well set off in the direction of the cliffs. After all, she prefers the sensation of walking on grass to sand, with its pockets of quicksand and rivulets you have to navigate, and she needs to burn off her anger because her embarrassment has sharpened into this. These bloody Boomers have no *idea* how expensive life is; of how charmed their lives have been; of the white privilege they exude as they drip their condescension. Shit, she's angry, and she uses this to push her, glutes burning, up the cliff.

She climbs it in one, not allowing herself to stop and look down until she's reached the very top, from where Carole is a dot in the distance, and the only figure on the private bit of beach. It would do her head in to live somewhere this remote – she needs to be around other people – but for a moment she can see its appeal. It stills her mind, or it does until Carole's warning, her piece of friendly advice, forces its way back in.

'Quite the climb, isn't it!'

An old bloke – fat, bald, very red-faced – calls out to her as he stands perilously close to the edge of the cliff. She starts with surprise: he must have been clambering up some way behind her or joined the path from the public footpath that feeds into the top of it. He mops his forehead with a large, white handkerchief and smears perspiration over his lips.

She catches a whiff of his BO. Not the best time for someone this unfit to be walking. Late morning, and the sun is high. He's breathing very fast, too. Oh god, she really hopes he's not about to have a heart attack. Some old guy had one when she was waitressing at Pizza Express and they only got him back with a defibrillator, hardly something you find on a cliff.

'Are you OK there?'

Aiysha snaps out of her catastrophising because the man is calling down to someone else, a woman, even larger than him and equally pink-cheeked, who is heaving herself up the coast path.

'Shan't ... be ... a ... minute.' Each word is punctuated by a gasp of breath.

'Easier if you don't talk,' says the man, as he assesses the steps. He turns back to Aiysha. 'Well, this is worth it for the view, isn't it?'

'Er, yeah.' What is it with people in the country feeling they need to chat to strangers? Now that she sees that the man isn't alone, her instinct is to get away as soon as possible, except that she isn't a stone-cold bitch. She's a kind young woman; the sort who's concerned when another woman is a peculiar, she wants to say *vermillion*, red.

'Are you OK? Do you have some water?' she asks, as the woman reaches them, though she has none to offer them. The woman shakes her head and clutches at the man's arm as she fights for breath.

'Well, I ought to get on,' Aiysha adds, though she hesitates because it is *slightly* strange that the two of them are walking on Eleanor's land, ignoring the private signs which, though discreet, are numerous. And the man, with his eagerness to talk and apparent intention of continuing up towards the house, seems unaware that they're trespassing. Eleanor will hate this and perhaps it will endear Aiysha to her if she points this out.

'You do know, don't you, that this area's private? A private part of the coast path, leading to a private estate and from a private beach?'

'Oh, yes.' The man grins broadly.

'So this bit just leads to the house at the top. The manor house, up there.'

'That's where we're going to, yes.'

'Oh, so you know Eleanor, do you?' Perhaps they're former colleagues and she is being horribly snobbish.

'You could say that,' says the woman with a sardonic roll of her eyes.

'We've been invited to the party,' the man explains.

'Oh, OK!' Then everything's fine.

'But we didn't want to just turn up. After all, it's been quite a while.' He puffs out his cheeks. 'We thought we'd try to catch her first. Only, I'm not sure we feel that comfortable doing that, do we?' As he turns to his companion, his bumptiousness disappears. 'She might not want us just turning up – what with her becoming so famous. A *Dame* and all that.' He gives a wry little smile, apparently bemused by her level of success. 'Perhaps it would be better to come as planned, like we were told?' he continues, his tone now decidedly hesitant. He looks to Aiysha for guidance. 'What do you think?'

'Well, she'd probably prefer that,' says Aiysha, because she knows Eleanor hates being taken by surprise: just look how she reacted when Aiysha turned up early. 'I know everyone's quite busy, preparing for the party. And I think Dame Eleanor's being interviewed, so she isn't around.'

'Well, we should do that, then.' The woman looks concerned; all eye-rolling bravado gone. 'We don't want to put her on the spot. And Katie was quite specific about our coming later . . .'

'Katie?'

'Katie from the TV company,' the woman continues because Aiysha is clearly looking blank. 'She told us this was happening and invited us down. But we'll come back later, Bill, won't we? I think that would be the best idea.'

This all sounds very weird: the TV company inviting people. Why would Katie do that? Perhaps she should check with Gilly, or even with Eleanor herself? Aiysha's a great one for believing in your gut and her gut is telling her that something about this is very wrong indeed.

'Well, this path doesn't go anywhere apart from on private land,' she repeats, somewhat bossily. 'If you turn around and continue straight along the path but don't go down to the beach, that takes you to the public footpath. And if you continue, you'll get to Trecarrow.'

'That's right,' says the man. 'We're staying in a cottage in that direction and that's the way we came.'

'Oh.' Of course. 'Well, that's great.'

There's an uneasy stand-off, during which both wait for

the other to leave. It starts to become uncomfortable, and she is just about to probe some more: to ask precisely why they seem surprised that Eleanor's so famous – 'a *Dame* and all that' – and when they last saw her, when Bill turns and ushers his companion back down the cliff.

Aiysha waits and watches, torn between feeling she should have questioned them more, and knowing that it isn't her place.

All she can do is stare after them until she can no longer see the two heads bobbing between the hedgerows, and she is satisfied they have disappeared.

Thirty-one

Eleanor

Well, that's just what she needs.

In the sanctity of her study, Eleanor logs onto her computer, hoping to find the original email in which Ned pitched the retrospective. How had he proposed it? Had it been his idea, or, as she remembers, had it originated from the BBC?

She'd been hugely flattered, of course, and perhaps in the flurry of excitement, she hadn't picked up on the precise angle he was proposing, though that feels *most* unlikely.

But she never gets to his email because, six hours before her party, she's blindsided by yet another from her tormenter. There it sits at the top of her inbox, daring her to read! She pauses, wondering what it will contain. More pretension; more of that grating mock-chumminess? But, as she reads, her stomach twists.

Well, it's brief, thank god, but it's brutal. More literary pretension, and then what amounts to a threat. *Breathe*;

words signifying nothing – though she doesn't believe that for a second, she of all people who knows the power of language. Reading more critically, she makes herself go through the email again:

From: ineverythingillegitimate@yahoo.com
To: freida@eleanorkingman.co.uk

I've been thinking about Lear.

'*I will have such revenges on you both.*'

It's such a fantastic line, isn't it? Lear to Goneril and Regan, of course, though I like to think it could be applied more widely.

'*No, I'll not weep.*'

That's excellent, too. Say what you like about Shakespeare (and bar the odd, bittersweet soliloquy, the comedies leave me cold), he wrote some cracking one-liners. And he was *so* good at threats.

'Revenge is a dish best served cold.' That's not him, of course; the proverb's translated from a nineteenth-century French novel. Far less effective, though it has its merits. Revenge meted out after being considered for a while . . .

Well, I won't take up any more of your time – but I'll leave you to ponder.

And I'll see you tonight.

She is shaking, now. Despite her determination to view this flippantly, she can't buy into this faux humour, because *I'll see you tonight* is an explicit threat – her tormenter is coming to her party – and a declaration of intent. There's a mania, too, and an insistent malice. Someone has been harbouring their resentment; stoking this desire for revenge. But though Peter may well feel vengeful, this voice just isn't his. He'd never refer to Shakespeare's *cracking one-liners*. That adjective just isn't in his lexicon. He couldn't bring himself to do it. He'd as soon as refer to Romeo's rizz.

If it's not from Peter, or from Michael – though could it be? she's swithering – might it be from one of the ghosts from her past? And she thinks of the couple she saw the day before, who sent her scurrying when she set out for the cliffs. She's not sure she can bear that, so perhaps it was just her mind playing tricks. Because after more than fifty years, what can she deduce from the shape of a head seen from some distance, or a particular gait?

She needs to get out of here; she needs to escape whenever she receives these emails. Sunshine, sea, exercise, the sense of being proactive: main character energy, as Delia would say. She doesn't want to be anywhere where she can access such messages, because she was quite wrong: ignorance is bliss.

It would be far better to bury this, to delete it, and to never have to read this, or the six that preceded it, ever again.

Yes, that's what she'll do; she'll get out of here, without her phone or any means of anyone – not least this emailer – getting in contact, and she'll go for a long walk with the dog. That's what she does when she's searching for a solution to a plot hole, and just like then, her subconscious will start working and the answer to this particularly knotty problem will magically appear. And if it doesn't, and if she still feels this jittery – she's not *scared*; she's been scared before and this isn't it – then she'll do what she should have done long ago, and confide in her daughters, or, at least, Gilly. Not everything. Of course, not *everything.* The thought of launching into a decades-overdue confession is *bizarre*. But this threat can no longer be contained. *I'll see you tonight.* If she can't fathom who sent it and neutralise them on her own, she'll need to confess to receiving these hideous emails.

Grabbing her sunglasses, she puts her computer to sleep and sets off through the house towards the kitchen where Edith is likely to be lingering. Just the thought of the welcome she'll receive – all exuberant tail wagging and general excitability – is reassuring: a silky-haired spaniel trotting at her heels, that's just what she needs!

Because this is all very unpleasant. It's *deeply* unpleasant. If the emails *are* from them – and, despite her moments ago insistence, she fears it was them – and if they turn up, that will be emotionally traumatic, but perhaps, to be brutally frank, she can pay them off? Because it must be *money* they're after. Why else would they seek her out after all these years?

For a second, she stands in the hallway, ambushed by the weight of an unfamiliar emotion, but she mustn't give in to the ache that's clawing at her chest and have a good old weep. Dame Eleanor Kingman doesn't cry. Of course, she did when she sent Delia off to that clinic (her admission that her daughter was ill); and she did over Michael. Not every time, but the first, and then the worst: the time there were clear consequences and she ended up giving him an ultimatum. But, in general, she's learned to compartmentalise unpleasant emotions, and loss, because that's what's clamouring for her attention now, and regret are the types of sorrow she just can't allow herself to feel.

'Edith?' She calls out to the dog in that peculiarly warm-hearted, slightly high-pitched way she always does, expecting a scurry of paws and a waving of her gorgeous flag of a tail. 'Eeed-ith?' The spaniel tends to lie outside her study door when Eleanor's working, but she's not there, nor in the drawing or dining rooms, where she often lolls in front of the windows in a rhombus of sun. 'Eeed-ith?' she repeats, picking up her pace as she moves to the back of the house and the kitchen, where Rachel and Delia are huddled around the marble-topped island, deep in chat.

'Have you seen the dog?' she interrupts, because there's no scurry of paws; no enthusiastic snuffling and that's rather *weird*. Her dog needs to be around humans. 'Have the children got her? It's just I'm off for a walk and I'd like to take her now.'

Rachel goes red. She's looked embarrassed ever since asking Eleanor to bail out her husband, and Eleanor would like to admit that she knows it's not her fault; to reiterate that, of course, she'll always provide for her and the children, but she can't do this in front of Delia. Besides, she hasn't the time.

'I think Tom's taken her for another run. She loved it so much yesterday we thought it would be good to tire her out. I assumed that would be OK?'

'*Another* one?' She feels rather put out. Edith's *her* dog, and she hasn't walked her since Tom arrived. 'Not to worry. I'll walk towards Trecarrow. Perhaps I'll meet them on the way?' Her voice quavers a little: she really does want the comfort of her dog. Rachel shrugs but Delia is glowering at her sister: perhaps it was an argument she interrupted and not some sort of cosy tête-à-tête? Well, they'll just have to sort it out; she has far more pressing things on her mind.

I'll see you tonight.

Giving an involuntary shiver, she sets off for the cliffs.

Thirty-two

Rachel

'Well, that was close. Being interrupted by Mum.'

Delia rolls her eyes theatrically, but when she stops her expression is just as critical as it was before Eleanor's arrival. 'So, are you going to tell me why you were transferring fifty thousand pounds from her account in the middle of the night?'

'It wasn't the middle of the night.'

Her younger sister arches an eyebrow. She might as well stamp her foot, she's doing such a good imitation of being a stroppy teenager. For a moment Rachel wonders if she can appeal to her sense of humour. She risks a smile, but Delia merely glowers then turns her head aside.

The air feels very still; the silence between them, loaded.

'Are you going to tell her?'

'I think I'm going to have to.' Delia looks back at her and tilts her chin.

'Oh, for god's sake!' She's not going to beg, she's really not. 'Please don't. You really don't have to. You know I wouldn't be doing this without a good reason, and she'll hate being bothered just before the party. It's really *not* a great time.'

Delia leans back against the vast, white marble-topped island in the middle of the kitchen, arms crossed over her chest. *She is loving this,* thinks Rachel. Is revelling in no longer being the difficult daughter, but the one with some information that would lead to Rachel being sacked, disowned and pushed out of the familial nest. Information that could see her being stripped of her professional qualifications and means of livelihood, too, because Eleanor can be ruthless. Does Delia know quite how much power she holds? She gives Rachel a smirk. So that's a categoric yes.

'Please. I can't explain, but Tom's in some trouble. Eleanor knows.'

'That's *interesting.*'

'I can't go into it.' If only she could, but Rachel doesn't trust her younger sister. Besides, the slim possibility she might understand and show some compassion is outweighed by Rachel's sense of overpowering shame.

'Did you go back downstairs and transfer it? After Maisie went to sleep?'

She looks down, reluctant to lie.

'You did, didn't you?'

Irritation jostles with guilt. Of course, she did, though it was nearly midnight by the time Maisie fell back to sleep and she was able to extricate herself from her sticky grip.

'Oh my god, you did.' Delia gives a low whistle. 'And

to think you were so self-righteous when I took Eleanor's credit card.'

'It is *not* the same.' Rachel's voice is tight.

'No. I was an *addict*. I was mentally ill. But you don't have that excuse, do you? This was theft because of what? Greed?'

Rachel shakes her head.

'And this is for tens of thousands of pounds,' Delia continues. 'Oh my god! That's the maximum you can take out in one day online. You could be funnelling it away each day! You were?' Her hands fly to her mouth, as if to keep this thought in, and when she speaks, it's in a conspiratorial whisper. 'How much have you nicked altogether?'

'It's not stealing. It's a loan and it was just the once.' Rachel sticks to this story. No need for her little sister to know that she made a second payment of £50,000 – bringing the repayment to £100,000 – in the early hours of the morning; or that she'll keep doing so over the next four days.

'And it's a loan Eleanor's agreed to?'

Rachel shrugs.

'She hasn't, has she?'

'Not exactly. Not yet.'

'Rachel! You've been *stealing* from Eleanor's account. Stealing tens – hundreds?' – she pauses but Rachel refuses to nod – 'of thousands of pounds.' She blows air from her cheeks. 'How could you do that to her? Be so *bent*. You could be struck off for this—'

'Only if you tell—' Her voice quivers.

'Perhaps I should! You're a *bent accountant*!'

'No, I am *not*.' She is *not* having this.

'Yes. Yes, you are. This is fraud, Rach.' Delia whistles, and Rachel can see that underneath her apparently gleeful fascination, she is shocked. 'It's not even a sophisticated fraud that's pretending to be creative accountancy. I caught you transferring money from her account without her permission. You're *fleecing* her. It's fraud, embezzlement, theft.'

'I am *not* fleecing her, and there's a very good reason.'

'What possible reason could there be to steal fifty thousand pounds – no, let's be honest, *more* – from our mother?'

'I have to help Tom.'

'Not your problem. His.'

'Well, yes and no.' Frustration creeps into her voice. Because for the second time in twenty-four hours, a member of her family has failed to understand that she can't just cast her husband aside because he's become a liability. Of course, he *is*. But he's also a man who saved Gilly; who's concerned about Eleanor; who knows he's fucked up terribly in the grip of a compulsion (and he hasn't promised to get help, but she trusts he will: he's been sufficiently terrified by this). She has to help because his actions will have dramatic repercussions: the loss of their home; new schools for the kids. And because, despite everything, she loves him.

'It's not as easy as just casting him aside.'

'Well, perhaps it should be. Did he make you do it? Coerce you into stealing? Oh, Rachel.'

And she has had enough, because for all his faults, Tom hasn't suggested she do this. It was *her* brainwave, and he would never force her into anything, let alone something as devious as this. *But he tried to swindle you. To trick you into a remortgage.* But there is a distinction, she tells herself, a little shakily: he must have known on some level that she would find out about it, and part of that was his money. She was the one who suggested this theft.

'I've had it with you,' she says because Delia is never going to understand. 'For Eleanor's sake, please don't tell her until tomorrow. Let her have her party.'

'As if that's important.'

'It is to her, you know that. It clearly is.'

Delia tilts her head to one side as if considering the suggestion. 'I'll think about it,' she says.

She starts shaking after Delia leaves; her knee jiggling involuntarily; fear coursing through her veins.

Her sister's new, supposedly Zen persona has never fooled her. The girl's an incendiary device just waiting to go off. And while she hopes she will keep her secret quiet until tomorrow, for the sake of their mother, there are absolutely no guarantees. Whatever Delightfully Delia might claim about the need for calm, her creator thrives on chaos. That's what makes her so potentially exciting – and such a nightmare.

She could do with talking to Gilly. Where is she? She wasn't around at breakfast, and Rachel only saw her fleetingly just before ten, when she collected a double espresso for their mother. 'Busy?' she'd called, and Gilly had started; no doubt preoccupied by her never-ending to-do list. She'd looked knackered, too: once this is over, she will talk to Eleanor about not running her into the ground. But now she could do with some advice on how to handle their younger sister. Gilly's always been far better at dealing with Delia, acting like a surrogate mother, when their parents raged or loved.

She's anxious about Tom, of course, who has texted Ralph to suggest a payment plan they can meet: six £50,000 instalments over six days. And she is worried about Eleanor. Recently, she's caught glimpses of the old lady she will become (a concept her mother can't abide). She saw it earlier in her mother's enquiry about Edith: that momentary wobble of confidence; that reliance on her dog, something she would never have admitted to six months ago. She checks her phone. Neither her mother nor her older sister have replied to texts she's sent, and so she sets off to find them, heading to the front of the house and past the marquee, towards the cliffs.

The sun is high; the sky a startling, hard blue; and she squints as she sees a figure running from the direction of Trecarrow. Shielding her eyes, she sees that it's Tom, the dog bounding by his side. He looks terrible: not just red-faced, but frantic, his movements panicky and uncoordinated, as if he's pushing himself so hard he's forgotten how to run, and his limbs are rebelling.

She rushes to meet him. 'You OK?'

'He's not buying it.' He thrusts his mobile into her hand and nods at her to check it, then bends down, his hands on his knees, to catch his breath. 'Won't accept less than the five hundred and sixty thousand pounds.'

She looks at his phone, and the WhatsApp notification.

And there it is. Brief and to the point.

The full £560k, nothing less.

With £50k by midnight.

Tick tock. Tick tock.

Thirty-three

Gilly

'Gilly? Could I have a word?' Ned Simpson raises his hand in greeting as their paths cross on the driveway.

'Of course.' Gilly flashes him her most charming smile. For a moment, she wonders if he's cottoned on. Before last night, they'd been so discreet, but the coach house stairs had creaked and perhaps he knows his cameraman sufficiently well to decipher any extra jauntiness in his manner.

Mad, really, that it was Ned who'd first caught her attention. That she'd been briefly distracted by his relative youth – he's thirty-four – and infamous beauty, her stomach lurching the moment she opened the front door. But his Alpha self-confidence – the way in which he so comfortably inhabited his space, one leg slung idly over the other, an arm draped over the back of the chair – began to grate once he started to ask increasingly searching questions. It was excitement at their collaboration she'd felt, she quickly realised, rather than anything like lust.

Anyway, there's no vestige of that feeling now, only a

concern that he views her professionally – one of the main reasons she has been concerned about discretion – and that her mother's interview has gone swimmingly well. Only, it's immediately clear that's not happened because Ned's expression suggests he's the bearer of bad news.

'I'm just a bit concerned about Eleanor,' he says. 'We had a slightly *robust* exchange and I've a feeling she might have found some of the questions a little probing.'

'Oh, Ned.' She needs to rectify this, and fast.

'I'd love to get some more of the interview in the can before tonight, but she asked for a break. That was a couple of hours ago. I assumed she meant a few minutes, but I've not seen her since, and she's not in the house.'

'OK. OK, thank you.' She tries to think of where her mother might have gone. 'I'll look for her and ask her to come back straightaway. And I've got my phone, though reception's a bit erratic on the cliffs, so I'll call or text you?'

'Fine, fine. Great. Perfect.' He gives her the thumbs up and backs away. Gilly starts walking hurriedly in the direction of Trecarrow, telling herself not to panic; to ignore the tightness in her chest. Hopefully this will be a wrinkle soon ironed out, but she doesn't believe this for a second and is running through arguments she hopes will persuade her mother to return to the interview when someone else calls after her.

'Hi, Gilly. Can I ask you something?'

She turns and sees Aiysha, half-running behind her.

'Can we walk? I've lost my mother!' she says, in a tone that she hopes sounds light-hearted, while making clear she has no intention of stopping.

'Oh, right.'

'And come to think of it, I haven't seen Delia for a while. I don't suppose you've seen either of them?'

'No, sorry.' Aiysha catches her up. She's naturally athletic in a way that Gilly will never be, and her manner is easy: a blithely unconcerned twentysomething who has no idea that Delia can be problematic, though she clearly has experience of Eleanor. 'They weren't on the beach. I've just come back from there, but I'm sure they'll be OK.'

Gilly smiles tightly. Aiysha's a perfectly pleasant young woman, but her platitude's just that: she can't know this with any certainty. She ups her pace, conscious that the bliss she experienced, in the early hours of this morning, has been short-lived. For a moment, she remembers how she felt then: strong, desired, and capable of achieving anything she wanted. A snapshot of images flicker through her mind – things she would like to write about; and the thought makes her hot – but she is pulled back to the present by Aiysha's voice.

'I just wanted to check,' the illustrator repeats, and Gilly realises this is the second time Aiysha has said something.

'Sorry, Aiysha. I was distracted.' She shakes her head. 'Check what?'

'That you'd asked Katie to send the invitations?'

'Katie?' Her mind is blank.

'From the production company?'

'Katie, who works with Ned?' She thinks of the young woman with her candy floss pink hair; a colleague of Adam's who seems smitten with Ned, who in turn seems oblivious. What does she have to do with the party? Aiysha's question doesn't make sense.

But the illustrator is insistent. 'Yes. Was she, or they, in charge of any of the invites? If so, then that's fine.'

'No.' She stops on the path: this is quite odd. 'Where did you get that impression? Why on earth would I involve her?'

'Oh, OK.' Aiysha chews her bottom lip. 'That's what I thought . . .'

'Sorry. Can you start again? Why would you think that? That Katie would be issuing invitations. She's Ned's runner. She doesn't work for me.'

Aiysha plays with a bracelet around her wrist, turning the beads as if they are worry beads and Gilly almost snaps at her to stop.

'Because I met a couple on the cliff who claimed they were coming to the party – and that Katie had invited them to it. But maybe I got the wrong end of the stick . . . Look, forget I said anything. I can see you're really busy . . .'

'I am a bit.' Gilly tries to curb the irritation creeping into her voice. Could Eleanor have instructed Katie? It's possible, though hardly likely. Why on earth would she circumvent her? If she looks at Eleanor's emails she might find out. 'Sorry, I need to go,' she says, because the potential for this party to spiral into a catastrophe is escalating dramatically. 'I'll try to speak to Katie, but I need to find my mother now.'

Thirty-four

Eleanor

There is nothing like anger, thinks Eleanor, to galvanise you into action. Powered by this, she is speeding along the coast path on the hunt for Tom and Edith, and, of course, for *them*.

I will have such revenges on you both. Who on earth sends an email like that? she wonders, as she strides along, and also: *That's better, now stoke it.* Because rage is something she can cope with; is more familiar, and desirable, than fear.

She's hungry, too, she realises. It's nearly two p.m. and she would normally have had lunch by now, but, today, nothing feels normal. The heat, where the path is sandwiched by hedgerows, is oppressive, filled with the stench of rotting bracken and the incessant buzz of bees. She misses Edith, too. Her shadow: loyal, intuitive, supportive. With her dog at her heels, she is very rarely on edge. Which is more than can be said for now when there's a tall, thick-set man striding towards her, and she feels just the *tiniest* bit trepidatious, her heart jumping, her throat tightening with fear. He's too young to be *him*, but there's something that makes her skin creep: that tattooed tentacle crawling up his neck or the shaved head, perhaps; the too-pumped muscles; or the assured smirk that, as he looms closer, remains fixed on his too-smooth face.

'Afternoon!' he calls out as he sails past, and she feels ridiculous for being such a silly old woman. Her heart does a little hop, and she concentrates on trying to breathe deeply, filling her diaphragm as a voice coach once taught her (because it took some time to eradicate those flat As). Once he's breezed past, she risks looking at his departing back. Oddly overdressed for a day like this: Barbour jacket, smart jeans, box-fresh green Hunters as if he's trying too hard to play the part of someone in the country. Well, she knows all about putting on a role. But at least he's no ghost from her past; is unconnected to the emails. Despite his looks, he's clearly no threat – or not to her, at least.

Do they know what you're capable of doing? Do they know what you did?

Think of something more positive. Something mundane. Imagine resting in your room before the party; no, don't think about the party. Imagine what you'd really like now: a chilled glass of water; a crisp shortbread biscuit; a pot of Earl Grey tea. But she has so much to do before everyone arrives in five hours, and she needs to perfect her story, both the one she's clung to for so long; and a still-sanitised version that's nearer to the truth – that's based on her true story – in case what happened that night is something that, given the threat of her emailer turning up, others are about to hear.

Perhaps it's time, though, that the truth came out . . . A party would be a great time for that to happen.

Oh god. For over fifty years she has done her damnedest not to think about it, and now the memories are cascading, as if her brain has sprung a leak. Here, under the hot late summer's sun, she stands with her hands pressed to either side of her head, trying to stem the flood, and failing. She has woven such a credible, compelling narrative – and she isn't prepared to accept an alternative.

Because the human capacity for self-deception is immense. Tell a story often enough and not only will you learn it by heart, but you'll almost believe it. Others will, too, if you do it sufficiently well. And why shouldn't she rewrite her past? You only have one life, as Delia is so fond of telling her followers, and since she hated the first eighteen years of hers, why not edit them into something she prefers? After all, to whom does she owe a strictly truthful version of those years? Everyone's memory is subjective. Look at how Delia sees her childhood. She is just taking this to extremes.

And, though she is jumping through semantic hoops, she has never felt the need to justify doing so. It was something that evolved: this rewriting through omission and one tiny white lie. Perhaps it was psychologically necessary. To cope with what she did, and to become Dame Eleanor Kingman, to have the innate self-confidence to believe her stories were worth telling, she had to reinvent herself.

Only, it's clear that at least one person knows the truth behind the reinvention. And if they reveal it, then that's the end of her life as she knows it – and the immediate devastation of her career.

Her eyes are burning now, but she picks up her pace, barely knowing where she is walking, but desperate for it to be in the direction of Edith, because she needs her dog to help restore her: it's been quite a while since she's felt this bleak. *Oh, this won't do,* she thinks, not least because there is a couple making their way towards her, fast approaching a kissing gate, and she needs to pull herself together before they see she is on the brink of losing all self-control.

Or she could avoid them by making for a bench, just before the gate, which overlooks the sea? She races, reaching it in time and sits while they tramp past, their heads down, perhaps suffering from the heat. Thank god, they don't acknowledge her, or so she assumes because she keeps her head turned away from them, and inches along the bench, inordinately fascinated by the sea. Blood gallops through her head as she listens for the click of the gate; straining until she can no longer hear the man's breathing, and it's only then that she allows herself to look at their backs.

It's the woman who seems the most familiar: the studiedly downbeat trudge of her and a familiar lack of carefulness, as if she hasn't the time to look after herself, or the inclination to care. She's wearing a sleeveless top and alongside the indentation from her bra strap, there's an angry pink streak against the tender white of her skin.

The man, well, the man is just another badly dressed Brit in late middle-age: shorts, wiry legs, and a stomach thrust against a Hawaiian shirt. And yet he's the one who causes Eleanor to go cold. It's the set of him: the breadth of his shoulders, and that little duck's tail that would never lie flat at the back of his neck.

And with that, a kaleidoscope of memories shifts, confounding her vision, like black spots forming while looking at the sun. Below her the waves rise and crash on the shore, their dull, percussive thud recalling footsteps leading her back to a time and a place she once fled.

But which, it's clear, remains inescapable.

Thirty-five

Eleanor

Leeds
20 December 1969

The cobbled streets glint with rain, and Lea nearly slips as she stumbles towards her childhood home with her suitcase.

There's a metaphor there somewhere, but she's too weary to try to work it out. It's after nine p.m. The train from London was delayed by three hours, and she's walked the two miles from the station, dawdling, despite the cold seeping into her bones and the mizzle dew-dropping her hair. The closer she gets, the more apprehensive she becomes. Torn between excitement at seeing her mother, and little brother and sister; and fear of a man who can change the atmosphere with one sour look, and whose behaviour, she realises after three months away, isn't how every father behaves.

The feeling deepens the closer she gets to their red-brick back-to-back. It's London that's done this, and more specifically Bloomsbury. For the past three months, she's lived in a place of vast squares and beautiful, Georgian houses; with the British Museum within spitting distance, and the green expanse of Regent's Park. She's discovered galleries and theatres; roamed Soho: seedy, glamorous, intriguing; been infused with a restless sense of revolution, the spirit of '68 still strong. Here, it's all so tired and *familiar*, when what she wants is a life that's shiny and new. Across the city, slums have been cleared, but hers still stand: these tiny terraces, with their shared privies, their sole windows to the front of the house, their doors opening out onto the street.

In July, a man walked on the moon.

One giant step for mankind.

And yet her family remains in this dense triangle of bricks; trapped in a volatile home.

Her father is simmering with rage from the moment she enters the house. Bill and Joanne have gone to bed, up in their attic room, and William seems to think she's chosen to arrive this late on purpose. 'Nice of you to turn up,' he says, his tone a sneer, calculated to wound. It's a Friday night, and he has left the pub early to greet his eldest. Perhaps that explains the mockery, she thinks, years later when she has teenagers herself, on the rare occasion the memory of that night takes her by surprise. Beneath the bluster and the chippiness, the ambivalence at his daughter moving away, geographically, socially and intellectually, perhaps he was genuinely hurt? Could it be that his sense of self was so paper-thin, her being late felt like a personal affront? Or perhaps he was just hankering after another pint?

'Has he got worse?' she whispers to her mother, as they do the dishes together in the scullery, hunkered shoulder to shoulder like seasoned conspirators.

It's the first time she has addressed the fact of her father's mercurial temper so explicitly. The first time she has spoken to Grace as a clear-sighted adult, and not as her child.

'Is the drinking always this bad?' she goes on.

Her mother ducks her head in a nod, eyes firmly on the saucepan she is scrubbing in the sink. She pulls it from the dirty water, rinsing it sparingly, and places it on the wooden draining board, a streak of grainy starch still smeared to the outside.

'And does he still hurt you?'

There is a pause, during which she is surprised that she has dared to ask this, and half-hopes her mother will make excuses or lie. But perhaps Grace has grown tired of lying, or maybe it's the relief of having her eldest daughter home. Perhaps she simply has a premonition they haven't much time together. Whatever the reason, she decides to open up.

And so, she rolls up her left sleeve and nods at an angry pink burn on her forearm; a branding caused by an iron or a scalding saucepan. An everyday domestic injury, except that Grace Savage is deft and careful as she moves to and from the hearth and navigates the tiny scullery; ever alert to the presence of her bear of a husband; ever conscious of not making a wrong move. Her mother turns her head, and Lea sees the faint green trace of a fading bruise to the left of her cheekbone: he's getting sloppy; he usually beats her where it's hidden. Her chest aches, a physical pain in her heart, a weariness that this *keeps on happening.* 'Oh, Mam,' is all she can say.

But Grace shakes her head and puts one finger to her lips. She can't bear pity, and she is scared of her husband hearing them.

'He's not listening,' Lea says, gesturing towards the next-door room where William is slumped in his armchair, all his attention on the bottle of beer in his hand.

Her mother double-checks, then, returning to the dishes, speaks even more quietly. 'His liver's bad, but the doctor said he can't have too many painkillers. Sometimes I think of grinding a few up – five or six – and slipping them in his drink.'

Lea's not quite sure if she's heard right: it's so unexpected, her mother suggesting this, and yet the thought is thrilling. It's like something out of the Grimms' Fairy Tales she read her when small. Red Riding Hood, Snow White, Hansel and Gretel all overcame extreme danger before their happy endings. Could Lea help? Crush up the pills and add them to his drink? If anyone suspects, they could say he was confused. William Savage was a drunk, and he'd been in pain, and the old fool had fumbled his way to his paracetamol and gulped too many down . . . Only, the questions might continue: *Where was his wife, when this happened, and his kids? Asleep. The poor woman was worn down. But what about his eldest, just arrived from London? Wasn't it the tiniest bit suspicious her turning up that day?*

'I could do it – but would they know it was me?' Lea says.

'Not if you're not here. Not if we do it now, and you leave straightaway. Not if no one has seen you.'

Lea looks at her, stunned. How has this escalated so swiftly? It's almost as if her mother has been plotting it, not least because she is right. It is just after ten p.m. on a wet midwinter's night. Most people will be huddled at home, and those in the pub won't yet have spilled out onto the street. If they work fast, it is *just* possible they could get away with it.

Lea looks at her mother and sees a feverishness she's never glimpsed before: the ember of a spark that's been reignited. A desperation, a ruthlessness, or a realisation that if they don't act now, they never will. Her face then shutters as if she can't bear the thought of sending her eldest away. But it wouldn't be forever. Just until they knew they were all safe. Until this blew over. If they had known what would happen, that these would be the last few minutes they'd spend together, Lea later wonders, would they have gone ahead?

Without speaking, Grace reaches for the brown pill bottle and shakes six out into her hand. Her palm quivers as she stares at them, but this isn't the time for indecision. Tipping the pills into a bowl, Lea breaks them into shards and grinds them down. This could be it. His brutal bullying, the temper that once saw him pound Grace's head into the table over a late dinner, could be gone. Excitement rises in her chest and she's so immersed, she doesn't hear him get up from his chair and come in. It's the smell that alerts her: beer and smoke and damp woollen clothes, and a peculiarly male tang of sweat.

'What you talking about? You talking about me?' He's belligerent, his eyes bloodshot and unfocused as they roam in her direction before homing in on his wife's pale face.

Grace shakes her head rapidly.

'I said, are you talking about me?' he enunciates, pushing his face into hers until he's an inch away.

His wife yelps, and he gives a bark of a laugh. Sardonic, arrogant, grim. A laugh that says he's in control even though he moves his head away. Then, just in case there's any doubt, he grabs the back of her head.

'Owwww,' she cries as he pulls her up by a hank of her hair.

'What are you gassing about? Badmouthing me, are you?' His top lip curls in derision and, though she's a couple of feet away, Lea can smell his foul breath.

'Leave her alone!' she screams, with a force she didn't know she had, and which surprises them both. 'Get *off* her. *Now.*' Her hands grip the edge of the wooden draining board behind her, because if she doesn't hold on to something solid, she fears she will push him – and who knows what that will unleash.

William releases his wife, and laughs. A merciless sound that's completely joyless.

'Oh hello, Miss High-and-Mighty, Miss Thinks-She's-Better-Than-Anyone-Else. You're a piece of work, aren't you? Since when can *you* tell *me* what to do?'

Since never, she thinks, *but I should have. We all should have.* Not that she says this because he's not interested in an answer;

he's too preoccupied with shoving her against the sink and slapping her across the face with the flat of his hand.

'Not so full of yourself now, are you?' he says, as she stands absorbing the sting of pain, sharp as a whip, and the shock, because he stopped hitting her at thirteen when she threatened to tell a teacher. She tries to think of a worthy response. What can she say to calm him down? But there's nothing any of them can do when he behaves like this. Still, the room's too cramped, the three of them squashed together. If he left the scullery, the atmosphere might ease. And it's this, just as much as her sudden desire to retaliate, that makes her do the previously unthinkable and push hard against his strong arms, to get him away.

He staggers, but he doesn't fall, of course he doesn't fall, he merely totters. And then he comes at her. She feels a second slap, more biting than the first, and crouches over, anticipating more. But he's had his fun with her for the moment and now he reaches for Grace.

Later, she tells herself she isn't quite sure of the order of events. She knows she blocks out certain details. Her mother is a rag doll, to be picked up and manhandled because it's his undisputed right; something he's been doing for years. But, as Lea gets her breath back, she realises she can't watch this anymore. She needs to stop these scenes being played, because this is far darker than any story, let alone any life, should be.

The saucepan is on the draining board. The heavy iron pan that her mother uses to boil potatoes, that trace of starchy graininess still on the outside; and as he and her mother continue their fighting dance into the main room, where he has more space to shove her about, Lea grabs it, lunges forwards, and strikes him on the back of his head.

He falls, of course he falls. Like a cartoon villain. Down on his front, with a heavy thud and a cry of rage. Somehow, she is still gripping the pan, her knuckles white, her entire body quivering as she sees that it has made a dent in his skull from which blood is now seeping and running down the side of his face and the back of his head, soaking that greasy duck's tail of hair.

'Go.' Her mother's whisper is as savage as their name. 'Get out of here. Now.'

Lea blinks. Is she angry? Wasn't this what she, what *they*, all wanted?

'Mam . . .'

'Get *out*. Now. Before anyone sees you. And don't come back. You can't come back, don't you see?'

And there it is: the faintest quiver in her voice; a detail Lea will obsess over for weeks to come as she tries to convince herself that Grace misses her and loves her. A detail she will cling to in the absence of a hug or a kiss.

'But I haven't seen the others.'

'You can't.'

'And what about you?'

Grace is speechless as she stares at her husband. 'I'll say it was a burglary,' she says, at last. 'Take his wallet.' And she nods to the small table by the side of his chair where he'd placed it as usual. 'It's payday: take the money, then get rid of it far away.'

'They'll think it was you.' She starts crying at the horror of what she's done, at the prospect of her mother being suspected, and her reluctance to leave her. 'And how will I know what happens?'

'How do *I* know?' Grace fizzes with fear. 'For god's sake, take your suitcase and get out of here. Scram.'

'But—'

'Just go. And don't come back. Now. Get out, why won't you?' Her tone is harsh, and her eyes cold. There's no trace of their solidarity at the kitchen sink, no sense that they are in this together. Grace might not be bending to help her husband, but neither is she offering any comfort to her child. Her gaze – bewildered; hurt; then angry, or that's how her daughter reads it – continues as Lea backs out of the room, as she shoves on her coat and picks up her suitcase, and as she pulls the front door closed behind her.

And so, she runs through the dark, wet streets, suitcase battering against her legs, her head down. *Just go*, her mother's order rings through her head as she ducks down alleys or into doorways when she spies someone coming. *Just go and don't come back.*

Just go and don't come back. The command continues as Lea spends the night awake, shivering, and terrified of being spotted, in a boarded-up shop near the station; as she takes the earliest, five a.m. train to London; as she returns to her hall of residence, where a few other girls, with their own dysfunctional families, have remained. And all the time, she is reframing the night; rewriting what happened; creating an alternative narrative; praying that none of the neighbours, who are sure to have heard the fight but might hope William Savage has finally got his comeuppance, noticed her coming and going; or that Bill and Joanne – keeping quiet in their attic bedroom – peered from the small window of their end of terrace house, or questioned their mother's lie that a burglar, or one of his drinking cronies, struck their father as they slept.

When the police eventually contact her, to inform her of his death, she sticks to her story that she was in London all along; that a bout of severe food poisoning meant, sadly, she never returned for Christmas. Lack of technology probably saved her, she realises years later, and their neighbours' suspicion of the police.

Oh, and being able to tell a good story. Sticking to it, making it credible and endearing her audience. Grace, never charged with his murder, was evidently good at this, too.

But something fractured inside her that night, or perhaps froze: the 'splinter of ice' Greene identified as necessary for a writer. A part of her recognised that to survive the trauma she would have to renounce her mother and siblings. *Just go and don't come back.* How could she return when her mother was clearly furious about what she'd done? When Grace looked at her so coldly? How could she risk not only nudging a memory of that night but a second rejection?

It is only years later, when her own daughters leave home,

and her mother is long dead, that she understands Grace's behaviour. That apparent disdain as her husband bled to death.

Without showing such coldness towards her eldest daughter, such detachment, how could she possibly send her away?

Thirty-six

Present day
Saturday afternoon

Eleanor

On her bench on the coast path, Eleanor slowly raises her head from between her knees to see if the ghosts from her past, now very definitely alive, have vanished.

They'll either take the path to the beach, or to a rental cottage on the cliffs, or continue to her manor house. Perhaps she should accept the inevitable. A showdown. An explanation of why she behaved as she did.

Not just then, of course, but ever since. Because she could have gone back. Not immediately. But five years on, when memories might not be jolted; or eight, when she learned through an aunt, with whom she was in sporadic contact, that Grace had died, but that Bill and Joanne, then seventeen and eighteen, were doing OK.

There are a few turning points in our lives, she thinks, as she concentrates on breathing deeply. Her leaving, that bitter

December night, the most critical of all. Not merely pulling the front door shut, or boarding that train, or returning to her near-empty hall of residence, but choosing this bright, new life.

The days immediately afterwards were a blur of fearing she or Grace would be arrested: she'd spent them pacing central London, as if clocking up miles between them and imprinting her new world on her brain. But on Christmas Eve, a Met detective informed her of her father's death, without appearing the least suspicious, and she realised she could get away with it if she just stuck to her story. On Christmas Day, she attended mass at the magnificent St George's church and had an epiphany as the sharp winter's sun filtered through the stained-glass. Having escaped, she would not just survive but *thrive*.

It came at the cost of shutting herself off completely; of telling herself it was far easier to close that chapter of her life; that the others would manage; that it would be more disruptive if she returned. And her mother hardly encouraged it. In the following months, Grace sent only three letters: sparse statements of fact. *The police haven't arrested anyone; they've dropped their investigation; the weather is bad.* Never *I miss you, I love you.* Still less, *can you sleep at night?* Nothing indicating what would now be termed emotional intelligence. For Lea's own sanity, she needed a clean break.

And life soon became brighter, and busier. She began writing, refashioning her story, which, much reworked, would become the manuscript she showed Peter. A rich and autocratic father killed in his library by his beautiful daughter, who ground paracetamol into his drink.

Then, in her third year, she met Michael and fell deeply in love. Dangerously, too, because the splinter of ice melted a little and she became tender and unguarded, albeit only slipping up the once. 'You never see your parents?' he asked, in the early days, just before he set off to Suffolk for a weekend of healthy walks and board games, and claret and roast lamb. They had just made love, and she was unusually relaxed. 'Oh, we had a row,' she said airily, trailing her fingers along his forearm, enjoying the different textures of their skin. 'When was that?' 'Christmas of my first year.' She turned aside, biting her lip, cursing herself and her foolish heart, now hiccupping a little. *Damn, damn, damn.* 'And your dad's dead. You told me that.' 'Yes?' She turned around to scrutinise his face, but his expression was warm and trusting. Still, it would be better to distract him. 'Why are we talking about parents when we're both naked?' she asked – and wriggled down the bed.

And then life became busier. Work, writing, marriage and the girls followed. Lea Savage became Lea Kingman and then *Eleanor* Kingman, and she laughed at and leaned into the coincidental play on Shakespeare's tragic hero because tragedy need have no place in her life. The richer life became, the less frequently she thought of Bill and Joanne, until eventually, she almost believed her own story. She didn't have a family, she repeated; she didn't have siblings. She stuck to this narrative so doggedly, she almost forgot they might exist.

Well, they evidently do, and she must get back. It's after four p.m. and she needs to get on, she realises, as she starts tramping back down the coast path, keeping a wary eye out for them, though they seem to have vanished. Perhaps they *are* renting that cottage on the cliffs. The hedgerows have come to a stop, and soon she's passing the steps running down to her private beach and is on her land, and how she *loves* saying that; she's just fifty metres from the point where her lawn meets the top of the cliff. And her chest aches because the relief is so intense, it's like physical release. She is home. She is safe. She hasn't found Edith, but at least she knows who has been sending these emails, because it can't be a coincidence that her long-lost siblings just happen to be holidaying so close to her home, to coincide with her party.

And part of her is intrigued, and secretly relieved, that either Bill or Joanne has had an education; is versed in Shakespeare, even if the tone of the emails is sly and menacing, because perhaps there is some common ground? *Who would have thought the old man to have had so much blood in him*, the second email had said – a clear reference to their father. *I do enjoy our literary chats*, and could that be a form of wish fulfilment? Perhaps these emails, despite fizzing with malice, were a conflicted way of reaching out?

She has been out in the heat for far too long; feels weak with hunger; but it's a relief to finally know who she's up against and to prepare for this. There are little more than three hours before the party, but she still has time.

Time to think, but first to rest, to shower, to dress, to reassemble herself, with hair, make-up, fine jewellery, exquisite clothes. To reconstruct Dame Eleanor Kingman.

To leave the person known as Lea Savage far, far behind.

Thirty-seven

Tom

'But Dad, you promised!'

Charlie's football has been kicked right underneath Tom's car, at some point in the early afternoon when Tom was freaking out about the new messages, and his son has been banging on about him retrieving it ever since.

'OK, OK . . .' He kneels, gravel prickling his knees, the back of his thighs burning from all the running he's been doing, and peers under the chassis. The ball has skittered right into the centre of the covered ground. Tom lies down on his stomach and shoves his arm underneath, but he still can't reach.

'We'll need to get a stick,' Charlie says, lying down next to him, half-forlorn, half-intrigued by this puzzle they can fix together.

'Or a broom . . . Can you run and fetch one from Marta?'

His son nods and races back to the kitchen while Tom fruitlessly tries to reach it, and succeeds in banging his shoulder on the underside of the car. The jolt sends a spasm of pain down his upper arm, and he feels disproportionately distressed. If only every problem was as simple as retrieving a lost ball. If only Charlie's concerns could stay this minimal. A vibration in his pocket heralding the arrival of the latest WhatsApp reminds him that's impossible: that his children will soon discover what he's done. Wriggling out from under the car, he reads the message. *Looking forward to the party?* It's as if the guy is spying on him as he plays his mind games. Watching his every move. How does Ralph even *know* about the party? Gilly's stressed the need for confidentiality among guests, and he's pretty sure he's never let slip that he was on his way down: he only communicates with Ralph to grovel about not making payments. Perhaps there's something online, or it's just a lucky guess.

He's considering all the potential threats – the thug with Edith; the owner of the black Range Rover Sport – when Charlie hurtles from the house, a large broom in his hand.

'Dad. Dad, I've got one.'

He forces a smile on his face.

'Brilliant, mate. Do you want to have a go?'

His son lies on his stomach and prods the handle of the broom beneath the car, but he's so little he still can't reach.

'You try it, Dad.'

And at least he can be a hero in this way, Tom thinks, as he thrusts the end of the pole forwards, the broom's bristles close to his face. He thrusts once, twice, and the ball shoots out, the pole striking the underside of the car as he withdraws it and knocking against something within arm's reach. A circular object, as small as a pendant or a key ring, swings. *Great. That's all he needs.* Tom doesn't know much about cars but he's pretty sure he shouldn't be dislodging bits of the chassis. Is it important? It's white, not blackened metal, which it would be if integral to the vehicle, wouldn't it? As Charlie kicks the football away, Tom stays on the ground, peering at the object: trying to marry what it looks like with its immediate surroundings; experiencing a strong sense of discombobulation because this doesn't make sense. He nudges it with the pole again, more gently this time, wondering if he is actually going insane because this can't be what he thinks it is, can it?, and manages to unhook it.

'Charlie!' he calls, and his son comes running over. He'll fit, like a child up a chimney. 'Can you do me a favour, matey, and wriggle underneath the car for me? Something's dropped down. Can you see that white thing? Reckon you can get it for me?'

'Sure, Dad.' The boy's all smiles as he stretches underneath. 'Got it!' he says, triumphantly, then wriggles back, the spoils in his hand. He opens his small, grubby palm – and Tom feels as if the bottom of his stomach is falling out.

'It's an AirTag.' Charlie's face is a picture of bemusement. 'Why have you got one of those on your car?'

It's a good question. One his ten-year-old son shouldn't have to ask, and one Tom doesn't want to answer. He goes very cold, as if he has been plunged into an ice bath. *How the hell did this happen? Has it been attached for weeks? Ever since he took out the first loan? Or before he left London – which would explain the Range Rover following him down; the fact that, as he feared, he has literally led someone – the guy on the cliffs? – here, and how the guy must have been laughing at him for thinking he'd thrown them off . . .*

His mind's reeling with questions. *Breathe. And start to fucking think.*

'Good spot, Charlie. It *is* an AirTag. I think the garage must have put it there when it had its MOT so I didn't lose it.'

The boy looks unconvinced; so much so that, for a moment, he resembles Eleanor. But if Charlie's sceptical, he knows it's in his interests to believe this lie.

'You haven't seen anyone hanging around here: around the car – or on Eleanor's land who seems a bit unusual, though, have you?' *Mustn't scare him, but still: worth gaining any information.*

Charlie wrinkles his nose and shrugs. 'Not really. Only the man we met when we were playing by the cliffs.'

'The man you met by the cliffs?' He concentrates on keeping his voice calm.

'Well, the heath bit.' Charlie immediately backtracks. He and Maisie aren't allowed on the cliffs on their own, nor on the heath.

'You're not meant to go on the heath,' he reminds him.

'But Edith ran off there.'

He had asked the kids to keep a close eye on the dog while he and Rachel discussed the latest WhatsApp messages and the need to come up with the full payment. They were supposed to stay in the house for those twenty minutes but, of course, they ran out and let the dog off the lead. No point reprimanding him over this. Charlie will only clam up and he needs some answers fast. He glances over at Maisie, making Edith perform tricks – *down; roll over* – just outside the kitchen door. *Keep calm*, he reminds himself. *Don't let them see you're so incredibly freaked.*

'And this man: what happened with him?' He keeps his tone casual.

'Well, Edith ran straight over. Made a big fuss of him. And he bent down; said something like "Hello again, princess". Maisie didn't like it. Told the man we weren't allowed to talk to strangers.'

'Good. Brilliant. Fantastic girl.'

'And the man said, "It's OK, I know your gran," which I knew wasn't right because no one calls Eleanor "gran". So, we called Edith and put her on her lead and then we ran back. Can I go and play now?'

'Yeah, yeah, thanks, Charlie,' he just about manages, putting his arm around his shoulders and dropping a kiss on the top of his head. 'Don't go far, though: dinner's soon.'

'OK.'

And his son hurtles off, no doubt bemused by the intensity of his father's emotion because that fucker has been here, and whether or not he's connected to the AirTag, he's been talking to his kids. He looks at Maisie, then at Charlie racing across the lawn, and he knows that he doesn't want them out of his sight.

'Charlie!'

'What?' His son stops in his tracks.

'On second thoughts, just come back and stay with me, OK, until dinner?'

'Aw, Dad.'

'No, really. I mean it.'

And there is obviously something in his voice that makes Charlie run straight back.

'Thanks, mate. Let's go and find Mum, hey? Come on, Maisie.' She looks up. 'We all need to go and find Mummy, now. Bring Edith with you.'

Because he can't leave any of them out here, in case *he's* still lurking. He needs to find Rachel, and then they need to call the police.

Of course, Eleanor will hate it. Will never forgive them for ruining her bloody party, but more than that, for bringing shame on her and her family – because everyone will be aware of it; there'll be police combing the grounds, hopefully swarming all over the place. She could have avoided all this had she lent them the money in the first place, he briefly thinks – but this isn't the time for bitterness or recriminations. He's faced with no choice: he brought jeopardy, in the form of Ralph or a sidekick, to Eleanor's party and now he can't contain this threat.

As they troop into the kitchen, a young woman, dressed in jeans and a sweatshirt with hair in a sensible ponytail and an open smile, wends her way towards them. Edith dances around her legs and rolls onto her back as she bends to stroke her.

'Oh, you're pleased to see me,' she addresses the dog, then smiles up at him. 'I'm Nikki. Edith's dog-sitter – here to take her off your hands.'

Relief floods through him: Rachel had mentioned something about this, and Edith clearly knows her. At least the dog will be safe.

Now, he just needs to keep an eye on the kids. With them traipsing behind him, he goes upstairs to find his wife.

Thirty-eight

Rachel

'We can't tell the police. Absolutely not.'

Rachel, dressed for the party, is agonising over Ralph's impossible demand for another £50,000 by midnight, when Tom bursts in to tell her about his discovery.

'Rach,' he repeats, frantically. 'He's attached an AirTag to my car.'

'OK.' This is pretty bloody scary but she's more frightened by his revelation that SOMEONE HAS APPROACHED THE KIDS! They mustn't panic, though. They really mustn't panic. She needs to calm down and she needs him to calm the fuck down and understand that hours after she's defrauded her mother of £100,000 – with more instalments planned! – they *really* shouldn't be calling the police.

'Look, OK,' she repeats. 'I agree this is horrific. It's absolutely horrendous' – she lowers her voice as she forces herself to be logical – 'but he already knows you're here, and he still hasn't turned up. Why *is* that?'

'I don't know, Rach.' He throws his hands upwards. 'Maybe he's biding his time?'

'Or perhaps he gets more mileage by intimidating you by text? What if we gamble on him not coming? Call his bluff?' The idea takes hold, and she can see this could be the solution. 'Think about it. Ringing the police an hour before Eleanor's party is going to be highly detrimental for us – and ruin things for her. It's probably *exactly* what he wants.'

'Yeah.' He doesn't sound so sure. 'Yeah, I guess.'

'OK, so what if we sit tight, and get through tonight – then leave, tomorrow, without him knowing. Have you checked the number connected to the AirTag and disabled it, so he can't keep tabs on us? You know you can do that?'

'God, no. I haven't a clue.'

She starts scrolling on her phone, dredging up some distant knowledge. 'Look.' She finds the Apple support page and reads out the instructions to discover the final four digits of the connected number. 'Now. Is that his?'

He double-checks his WhatsApp messages. 'No. But perhaps someone could have done it for him?'

'Yes, that'll be it.' She's reading ahead, working out how to disable it; then takes his phone and goes through the process. 'Right, so there are no electronic eyes on us. I'll just screenshot the connected number so that, if necessary, we can show it to the police.'

From the chaise longue, Charlie, with his intuition for things becoming interesting, removes his headphones and scrutinises his parents.

'What are you talking about?'

'Nothing,' they chorus. 'Won't be a minute,' Rachel adds, as she gestures for Tom to follow her into the bathroom, half-closing the door.

'If we call them now,' she says, feeling calmer now that some sort of plan has emerged, 'then even if they do take this seriously, we're so cut off they'll only arrive once the party's started. And I know Eleanor. She will *never* forgive us if we show her up like this, and she'll be even more furious about the loan—'

'The loan.' He shakes his head, sardonically, and she feels a spurt of irritation because they wouldn't be in this situation if it weren't for him.

'Yes, the *loan* . . .' She dares him to defy her. 'Trust me on this. We can call them first thing tomorrow if Ralph hasn't backed off.'

'And what about the guy with Edith and the kids?'

She feels sick: it's a clear reason to ring 999 right now, and only the fear of a fraud conviction and lengthy prison sentence, and the impact that would have on them all, stops her. 'Couldn't he just be a local weirdo? Someone a bit odd?' She clings to this explanation, though she's unconvincing, and unconvinced. 'Thank god the children did exactly the right thing. Look, I'm not trying to minimise it, but I've paid the babysitter triple the usual rate to mind them tonight. I'll give her strict instructions, and we'll both be there. I'm not going to let them out of my sight.'

'I just . . . I feel it's got too big.'

He looks broken. Crushed by the impact of what he's done to their family.

'I know,' she says, because she feels this, too. 'There's another thing,' she says, even more gently. 'Delia knows.' Quickly, she fills him in on her sister interrupting her the previous night, and her refusal to back down earlier today. 'She's got this febrile look, like she had at that disastrous family dinner in London. I wouldn't put anything past her. I guess that's my real fear. That she'll throw in some reference to my "creative accountancy" if the police turn up. Pretend it's a joke or be cavalier: not necessarily do it deliberately – but not care if she blows everything apart.'

'Fuck.'

'Exactly.' Her eyes start to burn, and she rubs them hard, refusing to cry. If they have to call the police – because they will, of course they will, if Ralph or his crony turn up – might her mother be persuaded to lie? Could Eleanor claim she authorised the amount; that it's a forgotten gift? Rachel doubts it, particularly if Delia stirs things up and remains as outraged and vindictive as she has been.

Silently, Tom pulls her towards him, and she allows herself to be held; to take the briefest of comfort from his warmth and the reassurance of his brisk heartbeat. Then she steps back because she really hasn't the time.

'Look. I'm obsessing about today's sum not having gone through. I'll double-check the account then come straight back up. Can you stay with the kids?'

He nods as they head back into the bedroom, where the

two children are immersed in Clash of Clans, having lost interest in their parents' conversation.

'Don't worry. I'm not letting them out of my sight.'

Less than an hour to go. She rushes down the stairs and into the study, not thinking to pause and enter it slowly.

'Oh, hello!' The greeting flies from her automatically. 'What are you doing here?'

Gilly is sitting at the desk.

Ohshitshitshitshitshit. Has she somehow discovered what Rachel's done? Can she see that she's made the two transfers? The colour has drained from Gilly's face, and she is staring at her as if she is unrecognisable.

'Come round here. I need to show you something.' Gilly gestures to the screen, her voice tight.

I can explain. I can explain. I can explain. But there's no story in the world that Gilly will believe. When they were children, she always knew when Rachel was lying – that tell-tale flush of her cheeks; her voice rising too high – and so she gave up trying. As an adult, there has never been the need.

'What is it?' she asks, trying not to leap to conclusions, as she moves to Gilly's side of the desk.

But her sister's not looking at a list of bank transactions and those two incriminating payments from her mother's account to hers for £50,000 each, but at an email from some pretentious address, ineverythingillegitimate@yahoo.com, sent this morning. Addressed to her mother, it seems particularly cruel.

'Look!' Gilly has highlighted a section – the cursor's flashing at the end – with the phrase *I will have such revenges on you both.*

'Who wrote this?'

'I don't know. She clearly has a stalker. There are more of them . . .'

'How many?'

'Six, including this, starting six months ago. One last night and another on Wednesday morning, then three before.'

'And this is the latest?'

'Yes.'

'But why didn't you know about them at all?'

'Because it's her personal email.' Gilly is defensive. 'I don't screen them, although, clearly, I very much should. But you know her: she likes to be on top of everything; hates delegating; guards her privacy. And she's never going to admit she's vulnerable.'

'Maybe she's not bothered by it, then?'

'Oh, come on, Rachel. This is nasty stuff.' Gilly pulls up the email sent the day before and highlights a line: *Do they know what you're capable of doing? Do they know what you did?* 'It looks like some sort of attempt at blackmail from someone who knows something about her past. Something incriminating; maybe – probably – criminal.'

'"*Do they know what you did? Perhaps it's time they found out.*" It *sounds* like they're threatening to expose her.'

'Yes – and there's this bit from today's email: "*I'll leave you to ponder. And I'll see you tonight.*"'

'Has she replied?'

'Not by email.' Gilly double-checks. 'And look at this: it's threatening exposure again, here.' She highlights a passage from the third email, sent a month ago: *It's not the sort of thing one expects of the nation's storyteller. Of someone who writes books for children. I wonder how those children's parents – the ones buying the books; funding your lifestyle; paying for your beautiful homes and keeping you in the bestseller charts – would feel if they knew quite what you had done.*

'Should we call the police?' Rachel doesn't want to, and the irony of her suggesting this minutes after dissuading her husband from doing so doesn't escape her; but later she will remind herself that at least she offered; that she wasn't so selfish as to jeopardise Eleanor's safety at the expense of her own. Still, the WhatsApps to Tom; the AirTag; the man on the cliffs approaching the kids; and now these emails: there's so much *menace* – from so many sources. Perhaps it's time to accept they're all out of their depth?

And then she looks at the clock on the computer. Six ten. The guests will be arriving in just over an hour.

'We haven't the time, have we?' says Gilly.

'Not really.' She tries to think logically. '"*I'll see you tonight*": that means they're going to turn up. But if it's someone from her past, how old are they likely to be? Maybe we could enlist Ned and his crew to help Josh turn them away?' She is struck by how amateur they've been in their preparations; how very naïve. It's as if they've bought into the myth of Dame Eleanor Kingman with her formidable Paddington

Bear stare so entirely that they have failed to anticipate she could ever be under threat.

'I'll ask Adam.'

'Adam?' Rachel can't think of who she's referring to at first.

'Yes, Adam. Ned's cameraman.' And there is something about the way Gilly mentions him, self-consciously but with an easy familiarity, that snags at Rachel's attention. So much to unpack in those two syllables, so much to quiz her about or tease her over, but this isn't the time.

'I would have thought the last thing you'd want is for a TV crew to be involved in this,' Rachel says instead, because Ned is a journalist who won't necessarily be creating the glowing piece Gilly seems to have assumed he is concocting, particularly if he stumbles upon a good news line.

'There's something else.' Gilly runs her hands through her hair, her expression increasingly stricken. 'Aiysha bumped into a couple on the cliffs who claimed to have been invited by Katie. That's why I was checking the emails: to see if Eleanor was liaising with Katie about this for some reason, but there's nothing there.'

'And do you think this couple are connected to these threats?'

'The emails refer to her as Lea Savage. Not many people knew her as that: Dad; Carole and Peter when she was in her twenties; and then, I guess, people from her childhood. Perhaps this couple know her from then?'

'"*Do remember . . . that some of us know the truth,*"' Rachel reads from the screen, and shivers. 'I don't know. But we do need to tell her we've found this. That we'll muster some sort of support; that she doesn't need to face this alone.'

'I'm not sure. She'll hate our prying; she'll hate feeling exposed.'

'But she can't deal with this all herself.' Tenderness isn't a feeling her mother evokes, but Rachel is overwhelmed by a wave as she considers Eleanor reading these vicious emails. She must have felt so affronted, opening them amid her clutter, the silver Mont Blanc pen, the screwed-up Post-its and scraps of paper on which she scribbles. It would have felt like an invasion of her sacred place.

Rachel's eyes dart to the clock. *Six eighteen.*

'Are we going to do this? Tell her?' They need to crack on if they're going to do so.

'OK,' Gilly says, but she still sounds unsure. It's an equivocal agreement. One uttered without much conviction at all.

Thirty-nine

Rachel

'Gilly?' Eleanor says, when they appear at her bedroom door, moments later, still undecided about how to broach this. 'Why haven't you got ready?'

Their mother looks unsettled: her make-up's applied but her hair is damp and her skin, flushed, as if she's been racing around all day. The plan had been for her to have a leisurely afternoon: time to wash and style her hair (she hates others doing it); to take tea and rest; to run through her speech. Now, it's clear she's had a lengthier walk than anticipated and is playing catch up, not having managed any of this.

'Well?' she says, the lines between her eyebrows deepening as she scrutinises her eldest daughter. 'Rachel's changed and you need to do so. I'd better get on. I've got to finish drying my hair.'

'I'm off to do so now.' Gilly bows her head, and shoots Rachel an apologetic look at leaving her to explain what they've discovered, the coward. 'And there are some last-minute details I need to check.'

'Well, you'd better get on!' Eleanor says, as Gilly hurries off in the direction of her bedroom. 'Rachel, darling, if you don't mind, I really must finish my hair.' She goes to close the door, and her middle daughter feels stymied: incapable of blurting out her support when Eleanor is so resistant to conversation, but equally incapable of leaving without any attempt to connect.

'Rachel?' her mother repeats, her voice sharp and more than a little querulous, because her daughter is standing on the landing, staring at her blankly. 'Was there something you wanted to ask me?'

And this is it, except that Rachel can't think of quite what to say. 'Are you OK?' she manages, at last, but her tone is off: as if her mother is infirm or deaf.

'Quite all right, thank you,' Eleanor says, briskly. 'But you really *must* let me get on.'

And all Rachel wants to ask is: *Why didn't you tell us about the emails? How can we help? Do you have any idea who sent them? I'm so sorry – for this, and for Tom potentially luring someone down, and for what he and I have done, too. I was so scared – for him, for me and the kids – but you must have been as well. 'I'll see you tonight', the emails said. Are you frightened? Please forgive me. Mum, be careful. Please. I love you.*

All these opportunities to speak from the heart and we don't take them in this family. Why is that? Words are her mother's currency and yet the ones that Rachel has always craved – demonstrating love or pride in her elder daughters – are used too sparingly, her mother's frugality extending to affection and praise.

'I mean, how are you feeling about the party?' she manages.

'Well, you know. Gearing myself up for it. Now, this hair won't dry itself: I must be getting on.'

She gives her daughter a quick smile and straightens up, shoulders back, chin tilted, and with the change in posture becomes Dame Eleanor Kingman. Someone who would never admit to being perturbed by unsettling emails. A trooper who understands that the show must go on.

And then her smile, brittle and somewhat crystalline, softens to reveal a glimpse of the woman behind the brand: the woman her daughters are occasionally allowed to see.

'I'm a little apprehensive, perhaps, but I often feel like that before a big event.' She leans forwards, and to Rachel's surprise, plants a gentle kiss on her left cheek. She smells of sandalwood, and her cheek is soft, the skin thin. 'Now. You let me finish up and then I'll meet you downstairs for a glass of champagne, and then, let's get this bloody party started, shall we?'

Forty

Gilly

Gilly is never, ever organising a milestone birthday again, she vows as she fastens her gold platform heels and smooths down her green silk jumpsuit. She is just not up to it. As out of depth as if she'd been caught in a rip tide, only with far less chance of floating free.

Why didn't she monitor Eleanor's personal email account, when she takes such care to shut down criticism in print or on social media? And why on *earth* didn't she organise proper security? True, Eleanor had insisted this would be discourteous to her guests and quite at odds with the vibe of the event, but it's Gilly who is having to deal with the consequences and, at the very last minute, cobbling together some sort of amateur security team.

She has fucked up so badly, she thinks, as she texts Josh for a second time, while weaving her way through the house to find him. *Message not delivered*, her phone informs her, and she's reminded of the unreliable mobile reception; how difficult it would be to access immediate help if someone had an accident on the beach or on the cliffs. The truth is she's been distracted these past three months, ever since she decided to resign; or ever since she became involved with Adam and discovered the exhilaration of a new relationship and the intoxicating joy of good sex. Even now, when she has half an hour in which to put together a motley crew, she is thrown by the memory of his tenderness last night, as she'd pointed out a constellation, and then that moment when his look had sharpened to become warmer, sexier, more intentional, as he'd said something filthy and then silenced her with a kiss.

There's no time to think of that now, though, while her guilt weighs down her shoulders like a lead jacket. It barely matters that she's ticked off all the last-minute concerns: greeting the caterers and the musicians, overseeing the flares being lit, double-checking that the waitresses have aligned the champagne glasses (something she should have delegated but it's one of her mother's pet peeves). This is window-dressing at best. Because while she's been attending to these, she's failed to notice the bigger issue: that her mother is being threatened by someone who will turn up tonight – and that she's understandably unsettled: not yet dressed or ready; irascible and spiky; possibly even *frightened*, rather than excited for this night.

She has reached the kitchen garden now, where the air is scented with not just thyme and jasmine but the sickly-sweet smell of weed. So that's where Josh and his mate are lurking. Two strong twenty-year-olds who will have to pass as bouncer material, because that's exactly what she needs.

'Is that what I think it is?' she says with a reproving nod, as she surprises them behind the green beans.

'All right?' Josh juts out his chin but swiftly drops and stubs out the rollie. 'This is Ross,' he gestures to a shorter, stockier youth of around his age. Both are wearing black trousers and white shirts, the uniform for silver service, so at least they've got that right, but the weed and laidback manner – they're not giggly, but are clearly relaxed – are hardly reassuring.

She must look as if she's about to reprimand them, though, because he straightens up.

'Ross's going to help with checking invites. Like you said: no invite and no name on the guest list means no entry?'

'Yes, although some will have RSVP'd by email so if they can show you an email from me on their phones, then that's OK.'

'Sorted,' Ross says. The young man looks like a rugby prop although his face is pimpled with acne. Still, you wouldn't want to cross him. There's a quiet surety to him, as if he would step in if there was the risk of a fight.

Perhaps it's best to prepare them for the worst.

'I'm anticipating gatecrashers, I'm afraid, though they will claim to have been invited. A couple. Middle-aged. I realise that doesn't narrow it down much,' she says with a wryness that she hopes belies her anxiety. 'There's a possibility they may become difficult. Let me know if they turn up – and come and find me if a text doesn't send.'

'Gotcha,' Josh says while she wonders if she's conveyed the severity of the risk. Ross is clearly suppressing a smirk.

No doubt he thinks she's being neurotic. Perhaps she is, but those emails felt nasty. *I wonder how those children's parents would feel if they knew quite what you had done.* She shivers because her gut tells her this is no hoaxer. There's some unacknowledged darkness – a secret that's driven her – in her mother's past.

Which brings her to the TV documentary, with its pre-occupation with mining this despite Gilly's best attempts at gatekeeping, and the crew who are making it. Should she involve Adam? He's a decent man, but in asking for his help, she's alerting a journalist to the fact that there's so much more to find. She needs to get to the bottom of the invites with Katie, though, a good enough reason to crunch over the gravel to the renovated coach house, her emotions so different from her giddy excitement last night.

Rapping on each of the bedroom doors, she discovers Ned's, Katie's and Glen's are locked. Little surprise because the light is glorious: no threatening storm clouds, despite the forecast; the sky, a picture-perfect blue. No doubt they're out, getting footage of the guests, but, just as she turns to check this, Adam's door swings wide open.

'Hey!' he says, his face wreathed in a smile of surprise. 'Couldn't stay away?' He was clearly about to leave as she knocked, and she's struck by his energy; the way he moves as if seizing all life has to offer. He leans against the door frame, and she can't help noticing the blond hairs on his tanned forearm, the casual flex of a bicep. 'Everything OK?'

And a combination of pride and a sharper sense that

perhaps she shouldn't be semaphoring a secret from her mother's past stops her from asking for his support.

'Just looking for Ned. I needed to check something, and just wondered if you'd seen him?'

He smiles. There's no reason to doubt her lie. 'Think he was hoping to chat to the first of the guests. I'm just off to join him, but I'm glad you caught me.'

'Oh yes?'

'Yeah.' He looks momentarily less confident. 'Look, it's probably not the best time, but I've been thinking things through . . .' And this brings her up short because this is a Dear John phrase, isn't it, and the part of her that's been hurt in the past assumes she's misread the signals: that he's about to let her down gently. 'I meant to say: thanks for texting me last night . . .'

'Oh, no problem,' she says, politely. 'I mean, I had a good time . . .' The words belong to a different woman. The Gilly of her fortieth birthday, who was defensive, had forgotten how to flirt, and who is speaking in a clipped, stilted manner because what the hell is she doing hanging around, waiting to be rejected, when she should be trying to counter her mother's stalker?

'Well, yeah,' he says, 'so did I.' And there's a warmth to his voice, a secret gurgle that reminds her of quite what they did last night, as do his eyes, which crease with amusement. She very much wants to reach up and grab him, but she can't mix work and pleasure, nor be vulnerable in this way. 'But I was pleased, not just for the obvious reasons' – and there's a pause which tells her he is thinking along the same lines – 'but because it often feels like you keep me at arm's length, and you don't need to. Not if you don't want to, that is.' He pauses, while she wonders if she's misread the situation: if she's assumed that he wants a no-strings, purely sexual relationship – a situationship – when what he wants is something different. 'When we've finished the filming, perhaps we could see a bit more of each other? If you'd like to, that is?'

And Gilly can't quite take this on board. 'Yeah, yeah. Great.' Despite her smiling, she senses the words are inadequate. 'But I've got to find Ned?'

'Yeah.' He gives her a smile that's less sexually charged as if to say, *I get it: we need to focus on the job in hand*, or perhaps: *OK, I'll back off. I've misread you. I've got the wrong vibe.* All these missed opportunities, she thinks, these moments of miscommunication. 'Yeah, yeah, sure. OK, well, I might see you later . . .'

'I'd like that,' she says.

Six forty-five. Despite Adam's words, and his apparent suggestion that he really likes her, her stomach roils with acid. Talk about the wrong priorities. What the *hell* is she doing? She ducks into the marquee, empty except for a couple of waitresses and the string quartet tuning up, although, as she quickly reminds them, Eleanor had requested they play on the lawn as the guests arrive. Her mother had been resistant to having either a marquee or a sit-down meal – 'It's a party, not a wedding' – but there are trestle tables draped in white linen cloths and laden with drinks, and later there will be cheese boards and a variety of puddings. A few round tables, crowned with bowls of cornflowers and Michaelmas daisies, have been set up as a concession to those odd individuals who might want to eat, but Eleanor doesn't want to encourage them. As she put it, 'I didn't spend over four million for my friends to sit in a tent.'

Oh, but there's no point looking here! A camera has been set up. Adam needs to take it down; she has stipulated that there should only be general shots and none of people eating, but she can't deal with that at the moment. There is just too much to check. Rushing from the tent, she almost bumps into Natalie. 'Sorry – sorry.' Her heart is flickering, and she presses her chest as if to stop it speeding.

'Are you OK?'

'Yes. You haven't seen Ned, the TV presenter, or his assistant Katie have you?'

Natalie wrinkles her nose. 'I saw him about an hour ago, with your sister.'

'My sister?'

'With Delia.'

Gilly's scalp prickles. 'What were they doing?'

The girl shrugs. 'I dunno, chatting? I only noticed because it looked a bit intense.'

'A bit intense?'

'She just looked a bit . . . flushed?'

'*Flushed?*' Did she mean sexually? Is it possible that two Kingman daughters are involved with members of the documentary team? Her mother would hate that; would think it most unprofessional. Or could Delia have suspected her involvement with Adam, and be stirring things up?

'Never mind,' she calls, as she heads back towards the coach house, hoping Katie or Ned will have returned. It would be so typical of Delia to seduce someone at her mother's party, though far better than her falling off the wagon. But perhaps she's being unfair. What if her youngest sister is flushed for some other reason? Is it possible that Natalie has misread intensity, or attraction, for fear?

She mustn't predict the worst, a tendency of hers because she has always felt acutely responsible for Delia: a legacy of looking after her as a teenager when she understood their parents were so egocentric that she needed to provide some consistency. Of course, she had failed in this, escaping to university when Delia was nine, shortly after *Jess the Detective* was published and Delia's childhood became public property; then spending a year in France, the most wonderful year except that it occurred as her little sister transitioned from adored youngest child to resentful, pubescent teen.

So, she let Delia down and she should have been more vigilant. That was her firm belief, as Delia rebelled spectacularly in her later teens and through her twenties; and that's her feeling now as she's assailed by all the tiny doubts that she suddenly realises she has been harbouring about Ned. About some of the questions he'd posed: about Eleanor's childhood; about how she was viewed as an employer. All queries Gilly told herself were valid; that she had no power to veto, but that, if she hadn't been smitten with his colleague, she might have questioned far more closely.

And there Ned is now: walking purposefully towards the house from the direction of his accommodation. Could he have been avoiding her? Conscious of appearing suspicious of him, she is overenthusiastic in her greeting. 'Ned. How are you doing? Are we all set?'

'Gilly.' He smiles pleasantly, and she is struck yet again by how comfortable he is in his own skin. Perhaps being beautiful engenders that self-belief? The Cornish sun has burnished his face, and his white tailored shirt, rolled casually at the wrists, skims his torso and gives just a hint of his chest. He's too pretty for Gilly's tastes – or too aware of his good looks – but if you could design a man who would appeal to elderly female writers, and younger ones too, he would be perfect. 'Did you want me?' he asks now, and his expression is so affable she wonders how she could have doubted him.

'Yes,' she says. 'I wanted to check that Katie hasn't been offering invites for tonight. I know it sounds ludicrous, but Aiysha came across a couple of people, trespassing on the cliffs, who claimed that she did.'

'I mean it's possible,' he laughs. 'You'll have to check.'

It isn't the response she expected, and she rapidly tries to a recall a conversation when she intimated that something like this would be OK. This is her mother's *birthday party*, at which the crew had been permitted to film some 'colour': not an opportunity for them to invite strangers, and certainly not those they deem interesting for the documentary.

'I'm sorry. I don't understand.' She blinks rapidly. 'We didn't agree that you could invite anyone, did we?' *That's bizarre*, she wants to say, except that hurling allegations minutes before an event is hardly ideal. But being direct *is*. 'Look, I'm just worried something's up. That you're going to pull some sort of stunt,' she adds, as she feels blood rushing to her face.

'My brief was to create a documentary about the real Eleanor Kingman,' Ned said, and his tone is equally direct, with all superfluous charm shorn. '*Eleanor Kingman at Seventy*, or *Eleanor Kingman: The True Story* as we're thinking of renaming it, is a profile. Not a hagiography. A study of your mother as the necessarily complicated and inevitably flawed individual she is.' He holds out his hands, palms up, as if to suggest that she can't blame him for trying. 'Look. I'm just doing my job, and as the consummate professional, I'm certain your mother would expect nothing less.'

There is an awkward silence, during which she notices a vein pulsing at his right temple and a certain tension around his mouth: his top lip is tightening. His beauty is cruel, she realises in the couple of seconds while they stand in an apparent showdown and before he remembers to switch his smile on again.

'I'd better get on,' he says, and then, as if to appease her, 'Try not to worry. I'll do a good job.'

But as he tramps back over the gravel drive, one hand raised as if in a cheerful farewell, cold creeps into her bowels. *Eleanor Kingman: The True Story* as he's thinking of renaming it? He has revealed more of himself than he may have intended, and she doesn't like what she's seen.

What does she know of him beyond the professional TV persona? Very little.

But she does know that she doesn't trust him.

Forty-one

Delia

Say what you like about Eleanor Kingman, and in private Delia has said many an unmentionable thing, but she knows how to throw a good party.

At least, by her genteel standards.

An hour in, and no one's drunk, or doing coke, or getting naked, or disappearing to the loos or a discreet part of the garden with someone else's partner, though perhaps it's only a matter of time.

The great and the good are mingling on the lawn, and knocking back champagne like it's book launch Prosecco. The air hums with the fluting laughter of women in chiffon and the fruity tones of gents in crumpled linen suits. In the background, the string quartet plays Mozart, while the guests coo over the decorations: Celtic flares marking out the lawn, fire pits offering warmth, and fairy lights strung around the vast marquee. But, as ever, it's the west-facing view, the sea and the sky, which will turn salmon-tinged before the storm clouds gather, that demands attention. Every now and again, one of the guests will break off their conversation to stare. 'Hasn't she done well?' they'll say to the chink of champagne flutes. 'Of course, it's no less than she deserves,' they'll hurriedly add in case anyone suspects them of envy.

'I'll have one of those, thanks!'

Delia swipes a glass of champagne from the tray proffered by one of the young waitresses gliding past. Holding it to the light, she admires its buttery colour and the speed of the bubbles swimming to the surface; brings it to her nose and has a quick sniff.

God, it is gorgeous. She can almost taste it. Veuve Clicquot – her mother pulling out all the stops for these first, favoured guests. The temptation to have a sip, and then one more, and then to quickly down the glass – just the one – is so acute, she holds the flute to her lips. Because doesn't she deserve it? God knows how she is going to get through the evening without some Dutch courage.

'You're not seriously going to do that, are you?'

Rachel stands in front of her, like the good angel she clearly thinks she is, or should be, on her shoulder.

'Oh, don't be such a killjoy!' She takes another, lingering sniff.

'Put it down, Delia. You'll only regret it.'

Her sister's voice is preternaturally calm, just like it is when she's disciplining her kids.

'Mmm ... mmmm,' Delia goads her, though it's all performative. If she is going to undo eighteen months of sobriety, she doesn't want Rachel to witness her shame. 'Keep your hair on!' she adds, rolling her eyes. 'You're hardly in a position to lecture me.'

'Shut up,' Rachel hisses. 'I mean it, Delia. Don't go there.'

'Or else?' Rachel has always been easy to wind up, and it's so refreshing not to be the bad sister for a change.

But Rachel's fire has left her, and she's deflated by her empty threat.

'Yeah, I didn't think so,' says Delia. 'You have nothing on me. In fact, given that I know your little secret, you should be being particularly nice.

'How *is* Tom, by the way?' she continues. 'He's looking a bit jumpy. Must be quite some trouble he's got into if you're defrauding Eleanor of hundreds of thousands of pounds. Oh, sorry? Was that a bit loud?' Because Rachel looks pained. She's trying to shush her, and Delia supposes that, in her excitement, her voice has risen a little high. She lowers it, conscious that she's being nasty, yet unable to stop. 'You don't have the *right* to tell me how to behave. How's your glass house?' She thinks of the Crittal doors on Rachel's recent extension and starts laughing manically: the hysteria that has been building since late afternoon, ever since she realised the terrible thing she has set in motion, finally gaining some release. Rachel shrinks back as if frightened, but Delia is unrepentant. 'I can do whatever the *fuck* I like.'

She slams the glass down on a side table, so forcefully the drink slops over the top, and she wonders at the stem not snapping. *Happy, now?* she wants to say, because she hasn't drunk anything, she *still* hasn't drunk anything, and she deserves some recognition for this! The hubbub of conversation dies as several of her mother's oldest colleagues look up at the sound. Well, let them. It's not as if they don't already know that she's a complete nightmare.

Rachel is showing no sign of moving, but her expression has shifted from fear to fury. That jibe about Tom clearly stung. Throughout their conversation, her eyes have been darting behind Delia as if checking on the whereabouts of Tom or her kids – she's ridiculously overprotective – but now they harden to convey her contempt.

'Oh, just grow up,' Rachel says. 'Please try not to ruin Eleanor's party. For once in your life try not to be so completely self-centred. Try not to make everything about you!'

Delia stands there, at a loss at how to retaliate. *That's just charming*, she thinks, though, obviously, her sister has a point: she *is* behaving like a complete child, and she wishes she wasn't but that's the role she's been assigned. Unable to conjure up a sufficiently pithy response, she stalks across the lawn to mingle with the newly arrived guests.

And they're having such a wonderful time!

'Isn't it idyllic?' they ask each other as they look across the sea, and back towards the house, which glows in the light as if confident of its beauty and historic significance. They are smart, these guests, and, just like the manor, exude affluence, privilege, good taste. Lots of elegant gowns for the older women and black jumpsuits for the younger ones. A notable lack of floral prints. The odd flash of orange, and Aiysha is wearing the most fabulous gold lamé, and, since she keeps tugging it down, looking as if she regrets it.

In their tasteful taupe, white and blue, her mother's friends blend with the sky, which will soon turn golden as the sun becomes molten and dips into the sea. The temperature is dropping, too. Shouldn't summer be over? Because, god, how Delia longs for a break in the weather: a gunshot of lightning, and unapologetic, cleansing rain. Anything to break this meteorological apathy and her own restlessness; her need for something to happen quick . . .

She pulls at the knot of her halter-neck dress, freeing a tendril of hair sticking to the back of her neck, and enjoying the sensation of the silk settling just above the cleft of her bottom. ('Veeeeery sexy,' Gilly had noted. An odd sort of comment from the sister who has always seemed so strait-laced.) And though she tries to curb the cortisol racing through her, she thrums with nervous energy; wants to sprint across the grass, flipping and tumbling. *Strong and serene* doesn't cut it, but *anarchic and disruptive and disturbing* does – none of which fit her usual statements of intent.

Her father will turn up at nine, he promised, and has agreed that they all meet somewhere private. The summer house would allow him to approach from the coast path unnoticed and is sufficiently far from the party to ensure any meeting's discreet.

She glances at her phone. Ten past eight. Far too late to halt this.

The confrontation she had thought she wanted is now less than an hour away.

Forty-two

Tom

From his spot on the terrace, where he's been pretending to listen to Peter Jamieson, Tom sees Rachel rowing with her younger sister.

Is Delia threatening to expose them? he wonders, and then: *What on earth am I doing here?*

It's a question that preoccupies him whenever the sisters bicker, but tonight it has a white-hot urgency. *What the actual fuck am I doing here? When someone has tagged my car and followed me down, and – because this can't be a coincidence – when someone has approached my children? Why the hell am I making idle chatter with someone about whom I don't care?*

It's not that he doesn't understand his wife's point that, if the police are called, Delia is likely to betray them and they'd be struck off, charged and convicted of theft. And yet doing *nothing* doesn't make sense. How can he stand here, necking champagne and nodding along to an insanely convoluted story – something about Eleanor and paracetamol, perhaps he should be listening – when Ralph has not only failed to acknowledge the second payment but has placed an electronic tracker on him, and has probably sent a heavy – the guy who fed Edith; who has the Range Rover Sport that he's sure tailed him – to spy on him on the cliffs?

A buzz in his pocket.

'Would you excuse me a moment?' he says, and without waiting for an answer, half-turns to check the WhatsApp.

Do remember: failure to pay in full equals double trouble.

£560k – and the next £50k by midnight.

He takes his time in turning back to the old man. He doesn't need this reminder of the threat he received earlier today, with a sum that's impossible. If he can't pay £280,000, how the hell can he pay double? Over half a million pounds. Nor can they logistically transfer another £50,000 tonight: the bank won't allow it. His chest tightens and his vision swims so that the scene of the celebration takes on an appropriately mirage-like quality.

'Everything all right?' asks Peter, his head cocked to one side.

'Absolutely fine,' he manages. 'Just work not understanding I might have a social life.'

Another buzz, and yet another.

'Someone's popular!'

'Sorry.' Tom grimaces as he retrieves it. 'I'll just switch it off.'

'No, no. You must answer if it's the *hospital*!' Peter clutches Tom's forearm, enjoying the melodrama. 'Someone's life might *depend* on it.'

With a crushing sense of inevitability, Tom turns to the messages again.

How's the mother-in-law's party?

And then: *I love a good party.*

Bile rises into his mouth. What the hell does that mean? Is Ralph here – or the guy on the cliffs? Could either have swanned into the grounds? Both would have the chutzpah to talk their way around Gilly's lads, and, if that failed, the requisite air of menace to muscle their way in.

His eyes flick to his children, weaving around the lawn to some of the guests' consternation. At least *they're* safe, he reassures himself, as Peter returns to his theme of how Eleanor should have leaned into her working-class roots. Rachel has hired a babysitter from an agency, and the young woman, Lisa, is watching the children intently as they hurtle around. Tom has barely taken his eyes off them, and nor has his wife, though she is making her way towards him, he hopes with a view to rescuing him now.

'Can I borrow my husband for a minute? You don't mind, do you, Peter?'

'Of course not, my dear.'

'Pleasure, Peter.'

'A pleasure, too, dear Tom. You tell your employers to leave you alone, I say!'

'What was that about?' she asks, as they walk quickly away, then before he can tell her, 'You look as if you're going to do something drastic. Why don't you get away for a bit? Go and have a break?'

'Yeah, great.' His palms are damp with sweat and his armpits are pricking. 'Yeah, I might do that. Thank you. Great.'

She gives him a brief, dry peck on the lips, and looks at him quizzically. 'You're not thinking of doing anything stupid, are you?'

'Like what?'

'I'm not spelling it out here.'

'Don't worry. I don't have a death wish,' he says, because he can't repeat his fear that Ralph is about to turn up to the party and his need to do anything he possibly can to prevent it. Besides, from now on, he is trying not to lie.

Love a party – especially one when things don't go to plan.

When someone turns up uninvited.

An uninvited guest.

That's when the fireworks kick off. When things get properly spicy.

Bet your mother-in-law would love that too. Because she loves a plot twist, doesn't she? A bit of drama. A good story.

But you? You prefer the quiet life.

And you can have that. You can have that, Tommy.

When you clear your debt.

'*I don't have the money tonight, but I can get it. But not if you turn up. Please don't do that . . .*' Tom's fingers fly over his phone screen as he races to reply. In the relative quiet of the kitchen garden, he rereads his message then immediately deletes it. He sounds utterly *pathetic*. Why is he pleading, putting himself in a position where Ralph can air him and leave him dangling by a thread? This isn't a conversation for WhatsApp but over the phone or in person – because he's nearby, Tom knows it: Ralph, or his man. He can *smell* him here.

He sniffs but fails to detect excessive testosterone amid the fresh runner beans and honeyed sweet peas. Still, Ralph is near: he can sense it. After all, he's threatening to turn up. *Love it when someone turns up uninvited. An uninvited guest.* Jesus fucking *Christ.* His loan shark is going to gatecrash Eleanor's party, and he can just see him sauntering in. He'd do it so well: late thirties, charming, urbane, in his open-necked white shirt and well-cut navy suit, he'd make slightly risqué small talk with the guests, who might take him for an up-market estate agent, or an unspecified business contact: his mother-in-law's friends are too polite to enquire about such things. And all the time, he'd be shooting Tom the odd dark look or raising a glass in his direction; intimating that they go back a long way; that they wouldn't *believe* the stories he could tell about Eleanor's son-in-law; no, *really.* But by this stage, Tom would have fled the party: frantic, desperate, utterly unable to cope.

There's only one thing for it: he needs to find the *fucker.* And so, five minutes later, he is back on the coast path, without the dog now but for the second time that day. Fear makes you run faster, he soon discovers, but brogues and suit trousers slow you up: the ground is hard through the soles of his shoes, and where it's parched, he slips. Still, he races on, scanning the path ahead, pausing to check as it dips down to the beach. Where *are* they? One of them *has* to be here. But the cliffs are typically empty for this time of night. The wind is picking up, though, and causing flurries out on the water. He shivers, then glances behind him, the hairs pricking at the nape of his neck.

He deserves all this, he thinks, as his calves burn and his throat rasps. It's his penance, or at least the start of it, because how can he atone for luring this *shit* here? Thanks to him, Ralph's heavy has invaded Eleanor's grounds; stroked her dog; approached his kids. What if the *bastard* had touched Maisie or Charlie? The idea of him putting a meaty hand on their shoulders, picking them up, carrying them away – no, he can't go there. He vomits noisily behind a bush and feels strangely better as if he's physically expelled the idea.

Tom is not a violent man, but he wants to pummel that guy for speaking to his children; to wipe that smile off his face. It's obviously a fantasy, because violence isn't the answer, and, more practically, the guy would beat him hands down. But he uses his anger to drive him on, and to consider how he'll argue forensically. He's bright: he'll reason that Ralph will receive an extra £20,000 over the initial £280,000, within four days. That the debt will be cleared then, at around 7 per cent interest. No point being greedy. Surely that will be enough?

He starts to slow. He's nearing the mobile homes now; leaving the cliffs with their palette of sandy red and sage green and mustard gorse, and the deep, deep blue of the sea. The static caravans are a clotted cream and faded white: neat cuboids interspersed with cars, some four-by-fours, most gleaming granite, or black and red. It's a world away from his mother-in-law's house, from where he imagines the chink of champagne flutes and the murmur of amused conversation, lightly carried on the breeze.

There's none of this here. Just a rustle. He turns to check but it's only a rabbit, or a field mouse in the hedgerow, or the breeze ruffling the leaves of a gnarled hawthorn tree. At the kissing gate that opens to the field before the site, he stops. Despite viewing Eleanor's world as self-absorbed and privileged – far removed from the daily grind of the hospital – he'd far rather be talking to those publishing types.

He walks through the field. No point exhausting himself any more than necessary: he might need to conserve his energy. And no point doing anything that will make him laughably puce. He has absolutely no strategy, except for pointing out that the second payment's been made, outlining his plan, and appealing to the man's better nature.

Does he have a better nature? Seems unlikely, on past form.

It's eerily quiet as he approaches the mobile homes: no children out playing; far fewer cars than he'd expected; the unlit windows of many of the units draped with curtains or shielded with slatted blinds. It's the Saturday at the end of the summer holidays. Changeover day and the date most families head back for school. The black Range Rover Sport's nowhere to be seen, and Tom's legs go weak with relief. Thank god he can run back to the party, knowing that he's tried to confront him and been unable to do so, through no fault of his own. They'll keep making the payments; keep defrauding Eleanor because, apart from Delia discovering, it's been so horribly easy; and he'll stop the gambling. Yes. Really, truly, because this has been the most brutal wake-up call.

He starts to slow. Nope. Absolutely no black Range Rover Sport so he's safe to turn back, and he's now walking, ridiculously fast. Just a couple of homes to pass, and then he'll break into a run. The weather's changing: the wind picking up; there's a cloud bringing rain to the west, which will chase him all the way home. But as he anticipates flying along the cliff, a figure steps out from behind the last home and casually blocks his path.

'Looking for me?'

And even though he'd anticipated seeing him, it still comes as a shock; his chest tightens as if he's been thumped.

'I . . . err . . .'

'Not got the dog with you, this time?'

Tom glances to either side of him, then shrugs in apology, apparently surprised that Edith's not there.

'Such a little princess. She with your mother-in-law – or did you get a dog-sitter?' The man pauses and his tone, so unnervingly conversational, becomes conspiratorial as he almost whispers, 'Hope you got someone you trust.'

'What do you mean?' The question – clunky, unnecessarily aggressive – takes Tom by surprise.

'Oh, you know. You're never quite sure who you're getting to look after them, do you? And she's such a flirty little bitch, she'd probably go after anyone who made a fuss of her. Anyone who offered her a sausage.' He pauses. 'I'd hate her to come to any harm . . .'

The threat hangs while Tom stands there ineptly, hands by his sides, though he clenches and unclenches his fists. He's conscious of the nip in the air and of the light fading. The odd mobile home is lit but, if he manages to get back to Trecarrow Manor, it will be getting black when he runs along the cliffs.

'But enough small talk,' the man says, and Tom is simultaneously relieved that he hasn't been imagining this man's malevolence and so terrified, he fears he might piss himself. 'I think you owe a friend of mine some money?'

Tom swallows, his throat closing tight.

'Nearly half a mill left. Four hundred and sixty thousand pounds. Not the sort of sum I'd imagine you'd forget?'

'No,' he manages. 'No. No, I haven't forgotten.'

'And yet,' and the guy's tone is delicate, almost refined with none of the rough bonhomie of earlier, 'you haven't paid him back?'

'I can do so. I *am* doing so. I've paid a hundred k, and I can get you another two hundred over the next four days. It's coming, I promise,' he gabbles. 'That'll be three hundred grand. Twenty grand more than I owed.'

The man gives a laboured sigh.

'I know it's not the full "double trouble" amount.' Tom can't bring himself to say £560,000; can't bear to even think about it. 'But it's still more than the sum I owed yesterday, and you'll have it all within four days. You'll have it by Wednesday,' he ploughs on, aware that he sounds quite pitiful. 'I'm so sorry – but, as I explained in my message, it's the very best I can do.'

The guy isn't even listening. Has pulled a silver iPhone from his pocket. Is he scrolling? Behaving like a teenage boy who's bored. Only now, he's not: he's shoving the phone in Tom's face, so close that Tom has to take a step back, and showing him a photo that makes the contents of his bowels turn cold.

'Nice gaff,' the guy says, watching Tom's reaction before he pockets the phone. 'I mean, obviously overpriced, but that's West London for you. Crap security, too, with that decoy alarm. You really want to get that looked at, but then again, security's not something you or your wife's family are particularly hot on.'

Tom nods mutely. *His house. The guy's just shown him a photo of his house.*

'Anyway, we know where you live,' the guy states the obvious. 'So, we'll be paying you a visit if the full amount isn't transferred by, let's say, midday tomorrow, and we'll be taking back what we're owed.'

'You can't do that. You can't just come to my house and break in.'

'Can't we?' the man asks, and, at first, he seems wryly amused but then his smirk turns sour and he's stepping closer. 'Can't we?' he repeats, and suddenly he's gripping Tom's shoulders through his suit jacket and hauling him up so that he can smell the guy's breath: lager masked with mint, not entirely unpleasant, but they're so close, they could kiss. Then Tom wonders if he's going to headbutt him and is just anticipating the pain when the guy shoots him a look of utter disdain as if an addict in hock to a loan shark is not worth the risk of a headache, or a charge of GBH. And instead, he lets him go, shoving him away with a laugh and a sneer that Tom will obsess over for nights to come. He flinches, expecting a gobbet of phlegm spat in his face, as has happened in A&E, but the guy doesn't need to stoop to that level (and is certainly not going to deposit his DNA), and as Tom flounders, staggering backwards, stumbling and swaying, his tormenter abruptly turns and starts striding away.

And that's it. Tom's off, and he's running all the way back towards the cliff, his heart thudding against his ribs, his stupid shoes slipping and sliding, and he's tripping now and falling like a cartoon character, only there's nothing the least bit funny about this – not the shock, nor the pain, the burning that brands his ankle as it twists and he falls; and that, as he lands, sears through and burnishes his wrists.

He might have escaped, but he can barely contemplate the fact because, if he has experienced pain before, it is nothing compared to this. There's a different quality: a pureness, a sharpness, an intensity that obliterates everything as he lies on the cool, hard ground. Thoughts of Ralph, and of his men turning up at their home, and how the hell he'll repay the debt. Thoughts of Rachel, too, and the kids, and the brief, transitory thrill of gambling – a thrill that provided an escape from life's mundanity; and that he knows he'll never feel again.

His vision fades, white lights blinking at him, then merging: their edges tessellating and smudging.

And then, nothing.

Forty-three

ELEANOR

'Eleanor.' Carole greets her on the terrace and envelops her in a silk kaftan she is sure she remembers from the Seventies. 'I hope you're deservedly proud of yourself, darling?'

Eleanor smiles thinly while her eyes dart to scan the grounds. Nothing. No glimpse of Bill and Joanne. As the string quartet plays a little Haydn, it's only the people who make up her current life – editors and publicists; fellow authors she has known for decades and counts as friends – who are milling around.

'All these people who have trekked all this way to celebrate you. Some I haven't seen for *years*. Some I thought were *dead*.' Carole's incredulity swirls, but Eleanor barely listens. 'Eleanor?' Her agent demands attention. 'I'm not sure you've heard a word that I've said?'

'Sorry.' She shakes her head. 'You're right. Too preoccupied. Lots going on.'

Carole gives her the same sly, appraising look as on Thursday. '*There aren't any skeletons in your closet, are there?*

Any secrets you're not telling me?' Has she underestimated her agent of forty years?

'Talking of the past,' Carole continues, and now she has her attention. 'Peter seems rather taken with Ned Simpson.' She jerks her chin in the direction of the marquee.

Eleanor turns to see the older man speaking to the younger intensely and leaning a little too closely. 'You don't mean?'

'Oh no,' Carole laughs. 'The old goat may have a huge ego, but even he can't imagine that someone that young and beautiful would be interested. But I do wonder if Peter knows he has something that will interest Ned?'

'Are you telling me that Peter has my old manuscript?' Eleanor asks, very quietly, because she is tired of playing games, and her agent should be too loyal to play them.

Carole gives her a shrewd look: an acknowledgement that now is the time to get to the heart of the issue. 'I'm not a hundred per cent sure but I'd say so, yes. I know how he operates, remember, and I've been noting how assiduous he's been in cornering Ned. And, despite what he claimed, I was never convinced he lost the manuscript, because retaining it made sense as some sort of insurance. It might explain why he's here.'

And Eleanor, far from feeling confused, is suddenly clear-sighted. Despite the uncharacteristic idioms, it must be Peter, rather than either of her siblings, who has been sending the emails and is intent on exposure. And she can deal with that because she can outwit him.

'Besides,' Carole says and, once again, her ability to read

Eleanor's mind is uncanny, 'if I were him, still bitter about the money he knows you could have made him, it's exactly what I would do.'

She'll speak to him. That's what she'll do. Confront him properly because she's never been one to shun difficult conversations. But it's impossible to navigate her way through her own party at speed. All these people who want to wish her a happy birthday, who insist on going through the whole publishing malarkey of copious air kisses, who want to *chat*, for goodness' sake. She tries not to appear perfunctory but by the time she's extricated herself from a lengthy conversation with her former editor, Rebecca, both Ned and Peter have disappeared.

And now Aiysha is moving towards her, an empty glass of Veuve in her hand. She looks incredible in a short shift of shimmering gold, though she's wobbling on her platform heels.

'Dame Eleanor!' The young woman holds up her hands as if to put them either side of her arms and bestow a kiss before thinking better of it. She is more than slightly drunk. 'I'm really sorry. So very sorry—'

'Oh, tush.' She can't deal with this now. 'There's really no need.'

'No. Sorry. *Sorry.*' The younger woman gives a grimace. 'I won't waste your time. *Sorry.*' She makes as if to leave. 'Oh,' she adds, as she backs away, 'but did Gilly get to the bottom of the uninvited guests?'

'The uninvited guests?'

'Don't worry. I'm sure she's got everything in hand.'

'What on earth are you talking about?' Her senses are on high alert. A whooping laugh; the chink of glasses; the ingratiating tone of a conversation: all these catch at her attention, but she is back to scanning the grounds.

'Just a man and a woman I met on the cliffs, who said they knew you . . . that they'd been invited by the TV people; by Katie—'

'By Katie?' And as she speaks, Eleanor's scalp prickles with unease. They were apprehensive about meeting her, Aiysha goes on; and here Eleanor's sternum aches with a pain so intense, she has to stand quite still and wait for the sensation to pass. Aiysha had told them to leave; she hopes she did the right thing? But Eleanor can barely take this in. Everything's too heightened: the chatter, louder; the colours, more vivid; the mock orange, more heavily scented. Her senses are being barraged – and she wants to scream.

And then she sees them. Delia might call it manifesting; *she* calls it a bloody disaster. Nearly fifty-two years she has spent denying their existence, and they have chosen her seventieth birthday to threaten everything she has become.

'Is that them?' she asks Aiysha, nodding towards the two of them, who have come through the house and are standing at the other end of the terrace, looking diffident.

'Yes,' Aiysha says, as if she wishes this wasn't the case.

They are dressed for a garden fête: she, in a floral sundress, paired with a pink cardigan; he, in navy shorts, with a smartly ironed linen shirt. He rubs at the back of one calf with his toe, while she plucks a perhaps imaginary piece of lint from his shoulders. *There*, Eleanor imagines her saying, *we scrub up OK*.

A waitress offers them a glass of champagne and they hesitate, as if not sure whether they ought to; and here Eleanor's anger fuses with a disconcerting tenderness and a fierce self-loathing; emotions she can barely express. She forces herself to breathe, to pull back her shoulders: to prepare as she would before giving a reading or appearing on TV – and yet she remains rooted to the spot.

'Do you want me to talk to them?' asks Aiysha, sounding suddenly sober. There is a tangible shift in the air.

'No,' Eleanor says, her voice low and controlled as she bows to the inevitable. 'It's my party. I should deal with it.'

And yet, she pauses, teetering on the edge of another of those moments that will define her; that will shape her story.

'Do you want me to find Gilly?'

'Yes, yes, perhaps you'd better. Thank you.' Though does she really want her girls to witness this? To understand what their mother has done? 'No, perhaps not,' she prevaricates before pulling herself together: shoulders back; head high; tone, decidedly bright.

'Well! I suppose I'd better find out what they want.'

Forty-four

Eleanor

Dame Eleanor Kingman is no stranger to adrenalin-inducing situations.

A traumatic childhood tends to make you vigilant, while living off your imagination is hardly a career for someone who shirks risk.

And yet, as she walks across the grass, towards the two figures, peering around as if they're at a stately home, Eleanor's legs are shaking. How should she deal with this situation? Deny all knowledge of them? Suggest they discuss this at another time? Or acknowledge them, as she probably ought, before telling them to get the hell out of here?

It takes an age to make the fifty-metre journey, the air so solid she feels as if she has to force her way through it. Sufficient time for her to run through her options; insufficient to work out what on earth to do. There is something so unnecessarily *public* about them being here. Why couldn't they have asked to meet in private? Perhaps the documentary crew, who no doubt coaxed them down here by flagging up her wealth, were keen to maximise her humiliation?

The suspicion, however spurious, that greed has something to do with this hardens her. That must be it. Ned and his team have told them about her multiple bestsellers, about her homes. They'll have Googled her net worth and made assumptions. She knows what money does to people: look what it did to Aiysha; look what it did to Tom. It makes them believe they have a right to a share.

She arranges her face as the woman turns around and she sees how she might have looked if she'd had a different life: less affluent, with different stresses. *He* has her eyes – playful, astute – and she can see that his instinct is still to be warm. Both are more cushioned in flesh. They all have that genetic predisposition, inherited from their father, and she's fought against it: the broad shoulders, and tendency to put on weight around the belly and jowls. 'Three peas in a pod' was how a neighbour once described them when they were two, three and ten, and she'd resented their physical similarity as she grew older, as if it tethered her and made it even more difficult to leave.

'Hello there,' says Bill, his expression an uneasy mix of delight and reservation.

'All right,' his sister adds.

Joanne was always more combative. The same gender, and a bit of a sulker, whereas Bill didn't have the capacity to be sullen.

'Joanne, Bill.' She inclines her head. But it's difficult to get the words out: her throat constricts as if it is closing over. The ground rears up, and where are her girls? She doesn't want them to meet her siblings, but still she searches for one of her daughters to anchor her. Is this what growing old does? Makes you dependent on your children. Reverses the usual order of things.

'Mum?'

And she has never been more grateful to see Gilly, now running towards her in her hideous jumpsuit.

'I'm so sorry.' Her daughter is talking to them. 'I'm not sure who you are?'

'Well, we're family,' Bill says.

'She doesn't have any family, apart from us,' Gilly replies, but even as she says it, Eleanor sees her expression shift and hears the lack of conviction in her words.

'Yes, she does,' Joanne, fifteen months older than Bill, has clearly had enough. 'I'm her sister, and Bill's her brother. And *you*' – she jabs at Gilly with her gel-manicured nail, a watermelon pink – 'must be one of her daughters?' Gilly nods. 'Which makes you my niece.'

'Get them away,' Eleanor just about manages. She can't bear to look at them; to note Bill's disappointed reproach or Joanne's disdain. 'I don't know what they want but I am *not* doing this. Not here, not at my party.' The words, petulant and irrational, flood in an unseemly rush.

'Would you mind coming this way?' Gilly is solicitous. Her lovely, naïve daughter is talking about offering them a cool drink, but then she would call them a cab, if they haven't driven, OK? And perhaps they could meet tomorrow when things are a little quieter? She hopes they understood that their arrival is a shock: it's been quite a surprise for her mother and, as they can see, she's a little shaken, but Gilly knows she'd love to catch up with them. She hopes they understand?

But Joanne isn't budging.

'Must say, she's behaving true to type.' She glowers in Eleanor's direction. 'She was like this when we were little. Always thought she was better than us. The reason she left. That she never came back once she got to London. Just washed her hands of us. Couldn't wait to move on.'

'Now, now, Jo. I'm sure it's not that. She'll have had her reasons. We've just caught her on the hop.' Bill is trying to make everything better, just as he always did, and Eleanor sees the little boy who would hug her fiercely: who was their mother's little sunbeam; a force for good trying valiantly to flourish despite his father's snarls. She turns, hoping to latch on to someone who will prove reassuring, and Carole is just behind her; has clearly heard the whole thing, and has possibly always known.

'Gilly, can you handle this?' her agent directs her daughter, and Eleanor is so grateful, though she can just imagine Joanne's response to being told she should be 'handled'.

'I can't discuss this now,' she says, compelled to get away. 'Excuse me.' And she bends her head and starts striding off towards the sea and the coast path, craving space and solitude and never feeling so alone.

'Fabulous party, Eleanor!' 'Ellie! Stay and chat?' her guests call out to her as she sweeps past, and she throws smiles in their direction, and watches as their expressions slip and fade.

'She looks a little fraught.' 'I wonder what is going on there?' And there's a general craning of heads, a turning in the direction from where she's come, but she doesn't stop because, while she might not be able to halt what will happen next – the dismantling of herself by everyone; the discovery of the real Eleanor, so very different from the fiction she's spun – she doesn't need to witness it.

But for now, she just needs to concentrate on not crying because *that* would be the ultimate humiliation. She swipes at her cheek with the heel of her hand. Delia would tell her to touch her breastbone; to ground herself, because of course she watches her 'reels', every single one of them, whatever her youngest daughter might think. But her heart is racing, and the view that never fails to calm her isn't working its magic.

And all the time, her chest roars with pain.

Forty-five

Eleanor

'Eleanor, wait a moment!' Carole calls after her as she powers along, fighting her emotions.

'I just need a minute,' she shouts back, as she reaches the scrubland bordering the coast path, the area the estate agent described as the heath. The ground is thick with purple bell heather and western gorse, with pink thrift and the delicate white of sea carrot, but its beauty is deceptive: roots trip and insects sting. Something claws at her ankle – a jagged twig; an unseen creature – and, looking down, she sees it's been slashed a vivid red.

'Why is this happening to me?' she rages into the dusk. 'Why – and how did the TV people find them?'

Carole keeps a judicious silence. No need for her to remind Eleanor that a retrospective of her life means examining just that.

No need to mention, either, that the sort of research Ned and his team will have done, using her birth certificate as a springboard to those of her parents and from these to any possible siblings, is pretty rudimentary: easily accomplished by anyone who's watched a genealogy programme or played around on an ancestry site.

No need, either, for Carole to remind her of her warning. '*Are you sure there are no skeletons in your closet?*' she had asked, not just on Thursday but when the idea was first pitched, over a year ago. Eleanor recognises all of this as she stares at her agent, and as Carole stares implacably back. The silence swells between them until Eleanor turns her gaze to the sea, trying to regulate her emotions and to work out where to go from here.

'Did you know about them?' she asks, eventually.

'No.'

'Did Peter tell you anything?'

Carole blows out her cheeks. 'He couldn't understand why you weren't exploiting your working-class roots creatively. He guessed there was something you were hiding. Your manuscript, which I read by the way, confirmed it. The aristocratic setting was deeply unconvincing, but the abusive father, and the murderous daughter, sprang from the page. I assumed you had a pretty turbulent childhood. That first draft of *The Fox Hole* was rather dark. Do you remember the cubs eating the weakest sibling before I told you to scrap it?'

Eleanor nods. Cubs occasionally ate the runt of the litter. Survival of the fittest. Perhaps an apt metaphor for her abandoning her siblings? Like any author, she was recycling, and trying to make sense of, her life.

'I figured you'd tell me if you needed to, but you never

did. It clearly wasn't a story you needed me to hear.' Carole pauses, before adding pointedly, 'Presumably it's not a story you want others to hear?'

'No, very much not.' She shakes her head.

'I don't need to know how accurate the patricide passage was' – Carole gives her a sharp look – 'but we need to work out how we'll act. We'll obviously try to get the whole documentary pulled, but first we need to shut down filming. Ned's bang out of order: has no right to invite them to a private party and to spring this surprise.' She pauses again, then asks, in a softer tone, 'Is there anyone else I should know about? Now is the time.'

And Eleanor thinks. Because this is the moment at which to tell her agent about the threatening emails, which she can no longer imagine being written by her siblings. Could they be linked to the person who seems to be manipulating events: liaising with Bill and Joanne; speaking to Peter; pulling together all her past threads?

The answer is as clear as day.

And she feels calmer now. Well, not calm, but there will be no mad railing on the heath: there's no need. She has to focus. 'Aiysha mentioned that Katie had invited them to be part of the documentary: you know, the mousy girl with the pink hair? But Katie doesn't have the editorial control to decide they're part of the story. She's the runner: she just does what others ask of her.

'So the person driving this is Ned.'

Forty-six

Delia

'All right?'

Delia wanders up towards the end of her mother's lengthy drive, where Josh and his friend have been tasked with checking guests' invitations.

'Everything OK?' he adds, after glancing at a mobile phone being shown him through a car window.

'Everything's just fine,' she says with a slow smile.

Of course, it's very far from fine. Rachel's judgement has bothered her more than she wants to let on: those words – *For once in your life try not to be so completely self-centred* – have wheedled their way inside her, because although her sister's resentment is palpable, it doesn't mean this isn't true.

'Look, we're doing what Gilly said,' he indicates, as the car pulls away.

'Yeah, great,' she says, because who really cares? That's not why she's schlepped all the way from the house and is standing in front of him. He can't be completely clueless because there is *definitely* a touch of the Harry Styles to this boy. The luxuriant brown curls, the generous mouth, the lean but muscular body. (He did a bit of surfing, he told her, as he effortlessly hauled her bag to her room.) At thirty-one, she is still young, but he makes her nostalgic for being twenty. She craves some of his youth.

Still, he's a bit slow on the uptake.

'I'm not interested in that,' she clarifies.

'Was it about the weed?'

'What?'

'Your sister caught us with it in the kitchen garden.'

'No.' She shakes her head: despite her flirtation with the Veuve, she is not going there. 'I don't want anything illegal.' Now this is getting tedious. Maybe he just isn't that bright? From the corner of her eye, she catches his mate's wide smirk. He's not so slow, but he isn't her type. She speaks to the rugby prop directly. 'Are you OK to man the fort? Check the invites and turn the reprobates away?' She sounds every bit the entitled daughter of the manor she is. He gives her a nod – *I see you, cougar* – and she shudders with distaste.

'Come on, then,' she says to Josh, indicating with a nod that he should follow her through the overgrown grass towards a dense copse of trees that spreads along the perimeter of her mother's estate.

'Uh, your sister said we needed to check all the guests?' he says, though he ducks beneath the branches. The leaves filter the dying sun, and, like a Monet painting, he is dappled with pale glimmers of light.

'I'm sure Russ can manage.'

'Ross,' he corrects her. He glances in his friend's direction, clearly still uncertain. 'Oh, well. Yeah, I guess.'

'Come here,' she says, wrapping a slender arm around his neck and pressing her bra-less chest against him. (Three cheers for tit tape, and for small breasts.) 'I can think of something much more entertaining that we could be doing.'

'Uh – no, no, you're all right.' He backs away, trying to extricate himself politely, and becomes entangled in some twigs. She reaches forwards to help, but he puts his arms up – 'I'm OK. Honest!' – and she glimpses not just embarrassment but a flash of horror on his face.

What is *wrong* with him? As a fit twenty-year-old, shouldn't he be up for sex? Shouldn't he want an older woman? He isn't gay – her gaydar isn't that bad – and she's hardly proposing marriage. She just wants to do something risky. To distract herself with something more wholesome than drink.

'It's just . . . I mean, I'm flattered but I've got a girlfriend—'

'Jesus. I wasn't suggesting a relationship. But, you know, my bad!' She smooths down the satin of her dress, which moments before she'd imagined him yanking above her waist in a Lady Chatterley-style scenario.

'It's just . . . It's Natalie? She works for your mum. I don't know if you know her?'

Does he think she wanted to have a conversation?

'Not sure that I do,' she says, cutting him dead. 'Look, no hard feelings. I was just bored.' She sighs. All this explaining is so exhausting; she only wanted some mindless excitement. 'Forget it. And I presume you'll keep quiet about this?'

'Yeah, of course.' Despite the gloom, she can see that his cheeks are red. This clearly isn't something he'll brag about. 'You could always try Tinder, or something?'

She gives him a different kind of look. The one that says he-needs-to-shut-the-fuck-up-and-stop-dispensing-relationship-advice.

'Here's the plan,' she says. 'We'll forget this conversation ever happened. I'll head back to the party, and you go back to your job of checking invites.'

'OK.'

'And if you breathe a word of this, I'll tell Natalie you tried to jump me.'

'Yeah, right,' he rallies. 'But I'm not sure she'd believe you—'

'You'd be surprised,' she says. Then she pauses and gives a smile to indicate that she does have a sense of humour after all, and that, in five minutes, he'll be kicking himself for turning down her very generous offer. 'Normally, I can be very persuasive.'

She is glad of her mother's lengthy drive.

As she walks behind a couple of local taxis carrying guests, she uses the distance to try to curb her sense of self-loathing. *Jesus.* Straight after this bloody party, she'll have to do some more work on herself.

It's exhausting and distressing, but necessary unless she reverts to full-on emotional anarchy, which currently seems the easier option. Should she go there? She's lit the fuse – arranging for her father to confront her mother; speaking so honestly in her interview – but she can still row back. After all, if it isn't on the grid, has it even happened? She hasn't filmed a vlog or done an Insta Live.

There was something so masochistic about her flinging herself at that young lad. *Try not to make everything about you.* But she always does, and she misread him completely. Is it possible she has misread her mother, too? Rewriting the story of her childhood to make her the wicked witch who banished her father? But Michael took the money to stay away and only made contact with her once he knew he was dying. She knows so very little about her parents' marriage and yet she has lured him down.

She's been selfish in doing this, she can see that now. *Try not to be so completely self-centred.* Well yes, she was, she is and she'll carry on being so: it's the only way she knows to survive. Eight twenty-five p.m. Little more than half an hour before showdown, and, true to form, she's about to behave in a way which will cause distress – but that barely matters. All that matters is that she grabs hold of the one thing that will get her through this. Her coping mechanism.

Upping her pace, she heads for the house – and for the champagne.

Because it feels as if she has no choice but to slip off the wagon.

Five hundred and fifty-seven days she's been sober. Not a number to be dismissed lightly. Eighteen months and ten whole days. But it's just a number and she is only disappointing herself. (She has long since ditched her sponsor.) Flute in hand, she prevaricates, even as she's resigned to the inevitability; has always known it was coming. *Calm and clear. Sober and serene.* Looking towards the horizon, she sees Rachel trying to corral her kids, and it's this tiny trigger – this reminder of her sister's derision and of her expectation that she'll act to type – that pushes her to take the first sip.

The Veuve is glorious. Even more than she had imagined. God, how she has missed it. She drinks swiftly, too swiftly, committing to her decision, because if she is going to fall, she'll do so with gusto. No shilly shallying, as Eleanor would say.

She places her empty glass on a tray being passed by a waitress and swipes a second.

'Don't mind if I do!' She raises it in a toast.

The girl pauses and wrinkles her nose. Does she recognise her from Insta? Delia gives her a wink, making her complicit. 'Everyone needs to let their hair down occasionally, don't you think?'

The waitress smiles, a little equivocally. Perhaps she thinks she's insane. Well, frankly, who cares. She's a teenager from Cornwall. Not anyone who matters, and it's not as if Delia is getting drunk. This is her second glass and though it might be nectar – and god, it really is – her drinking is currently restrained (she's hardly doing shots), and medicinal. Because after the humiliation of rejection, and in anticipation of what is about to happen, she very much needs something.

Eight thirty-five. How many glasses can she down in the next twenty minutes, and still give the impression of being sober? She has her eye on the tent where she knows some of the more impressionable waitresses, too young to drink alcohol themselves, are working. Perhaps she should head off there?

On a mission, she weaves her way through her mother's friends, remembering to nod and smile, and noting that Gilly seems preoccupied with an older couple, apparently suggesting that they should be on their way. Perhaps Josh and Ross failed to do their job? As she ushers them out, she sees that her normally uber-organised sister is stressed. She loves Gilly, but there is something profoundly irritating about her lists, her spreadsheets, her obsession with getting everything just right; with making it perfect, when perfection – not least in their family – has always been an illusion. When Delia was three or four, and Gilly looked after her, she would spill a paint pot or knock a glass of milk just to provoke a reaction. All these years on, and Delia still itches to behave in this way.

Gilly hasn't yet spotted her, and she's keen to avoid Rachel. No sign of Tom. The kids are racing around, pretending to herd the guests like sheepdogs. 'Guys, try not to be too noisy,' Rachel calls, but Maisie ignores her, and Charlie just turns and laughs. And then her amusement curdles with envy, because Delia would have loved a sibling to chase her like that. She would have loved a *brother.* Perhaps her relationship with her sisters would have been easier if there'd had been a boy in the mix? A son to act as the lightning conductor for their mother's adoration; the protagonist for her books; to add some testosterone to an all-female household. Some much-needed boy energy.

She looks down at her glass. Oops! It's empty. Another drink. That's what she needs. She catches the eye of a waitress.

'Perfect! I'm going to take one of these and another for my sister.' With a flute in each hand, she sashays away.

Once outside, she strolls to the perimeter of the garden and begins to drink with a certain grim determination. Not savouring the taste but welcoming the effervescence of the bubbles; trying to ignore her apprehension about what lies ahead.

In less than ten minutes, Michael will meet her at the summer house, accessed via the private part of the coast path. He knows the route: they'd holidayed at Trecarrow as a family and Delia remembers tramping to the bottom of this garden, knowing to ignore the 'private' signs. Eight fifty-five. She needs to get on with this. To banish regret because this is what she signed up to; what she has promised she will do; what she has planned for quite some time. A spot of rain falls, a mere spit, and looking up, she sees that a cloud which was a mere anodyne wisp is now a washed charcoal grey: a splodge of dirty watercolour on a damp canvas of a sky.

'*Please* don't tell me you've been drinking?'

Her mother's voice carries across the lawn as Delia heads back to the marquee, the empty champagne glasses dangling like maracas between her fingers. Flanked by Carole and Gilly, she is storming towards her.

''fraid so. Guilty as charged.'

Her mother looks as if she's been tearing her hair, and her eyes are blotched with mascara. Delia is used to Eleanor looking composed and elegant: a woman who spends time and money on herself. Now she looks like a dotty lady novelist, not that there is anything wrong with that, but Eleanor is scathing of writers who embrace this trope. And, though she is clearly furious, she is also distracted: eyes scanning the crowd behind her, feverishly searching for someone, before they come to rest on her daughter.

'What a stupid, *stupid* waste,' she hisses. 'Give those to Carole – Carole, please take them.' She makes little shooing gestures at the flutes, and Delia, to her shame, does as she is told. 'For once in your life *please* could you refrain from being so wantonly self-destructive.' A flicker of sorrow jostles with the fury distorting her face.

'It's OK,' Gilly tries to hush her mother. 'Why don't we go somewhere more private? Can you give us five minutes, Carole? We need to get this under control.'

And if Delia wasn't enraged, she is now. Get this *under control*? She isn't an animal. She is merely a little pissed, and she is fallible, so very fallible. But she is only trying to be honest: to do something that would bring clarity and enable her to heal.

She glowers at her sister, and then at her mother, knowing that Eleanor's fury will only escalate. How could she be so very stupid? Eleanor has always got the better of her daughters; has always managed to come out on top.

And her mother is seething now: her look of contempt so extreme that Delia flinches beneath it until she realises it isn't directed at her, but at someone behind her.

She turns, expecting to see her father, and finds herself confronting a wryly amused Ned.

Forty-seven

Eleanor

'You!'

If Eleanor could distil her contempt more efficiently, she would do so, but one syllable is pretty emphatic.

'Who *are* you? And what the hell are you doing?'

'Me?' The man gives that infuriating grin: the one she initially thought so charming. 'You know who I am, Eleanor. I'm Ned Simpson. I'm creating the documentary and we're doing the final bits of filming. In fact, I was wondering if I could ask you a few more questions because there's quite a tale to be told. About your father's death, or should I say murder, and your decision, which seems to be linked, to cut all ties with your family. The family that you've given no indication ever existed, but who we've managed to track down.'

She goes very cold: ice trickling down her spine.

'That's not what I mean,' she says, hoping to distract her daughters from the reference to murder by spitting her words like pellets. 'This isn't an arts documentary that you're creating. The tone of this; what you're doing. You're on some sort of vendetta here. Bandying around accusations and springing lost siblings on me isn't responsible journalism; it's a malicious exposé. What's your motive? Why on earth are you doing this?'

His smile broadens. He is playing with her; teasing her; enjoying her reaction. Adam shoulders his camera and starts filming, and she holds her hands in front of her face.

'Just stop it!' Her voice isn't as authoritative as she wants. She sounds like a jangled old woman, but thankfully Gilly starts to remonstrate.

'Look, I'm not sure what's going on here, but whatever this is, could we do it off camera?' She is looking from Ned to his cameraman. 'Please. This is important.'

Adam lowers his camera, and Ned looks at him, perplexed. Tension flickers between the two men: irritation and incomprehension on Ned's part at Adam missing this scoop; a quiet determination on his colleague's.

'Adam?' Ned says, at last.

'You're all right. I'll give you a few minutes. Come and find me when you're finished.' He gives a nod to the presenter, and then, bizarrely, to Gilly. Something passes between them, and then her eldest is flushing and Eleanor just has time to think, *well, there's a plot twist I didn't see coming*, before the cameraman turns and strides back to the marquee.

'So?' she says, when she is sure he is out of earshot. That's better. The delay has given her some time to compose herself, while the possibility that Gilly, her dependable daughter, could surprise her has put some fire in her belly.

'You underestimate me, Eleanor. You've forgotten – or perhaps it never interested you enough to know – that my background is in investigative journalism. It's my job to root out a story, and wow,' he shakes his head, as if stunned by his findings, 'yours has real darkness at its heart. Your father dies following a brutal attack. A suspected *murder.* Oh yes, I've found the *Yorkshire Post* report. A burglary that went wrong, it said. William Savage was thought to have disturbed an intruder who bludgeoned him with a saucepan. The very definition of a domestic incident, but the senior investigating officer, now in his late eighties and long since retired, said there was no way of pinning it on your mother, Grace.

'There was no way of linking you, either. But it seems rather a coincidence that you sever all links with your family around this time – yes, I know you told everyone it was in the September, except you let slip to one person – Michael – that it was at Christmas, didn't you? And you then write what could be read as a confession – fictionalised, of course – but based on a true story and so vividly rendered that your then agent suspects it could raise questions about your guilt.

'And all the while, there are two children, ten and eleven at this time, who spend the remainder of their lives knowing that you have renounced them and their mother completely, and who, until now, never understood quite why.'

There is a sharp intake of breath. Gilly, Eleanor thinks, not daring to look around. Delia, for once in her life, is silenced, and she is so very relieved that Rachel, distracted by her children, and Carole are both somewhere near the house.

'Eleanor? Mum? What is he talking about? Do you understand what he's saying?' says Gilly. Then, to him, 'Please, can we stop this.'

But Eleanor ignores her eldest. Tries to ignore, too, the juddering of her heart, which is beating so loud the others must surely hear it; and her legs, quivering so violently, it's an effort not to sway. She has always fought her own battles, and she is the only one who can shut this down. Where to start, though? And how to do it cogently and emphatically because words have never mattered more than they do at this moment. *He's working on a hunch*, she thinks. *There is no concrete evidence. If the police couldn't pin it on me at the time, then he hasn't a hope.*

'That's a pretty big if!' she scoffs. 'It's a good story, but completely without foundation. I severed links with my family? So do millions of people. I wrote about a murder so I must have committed one? My goodness, does that make all crime writers serial killers?' She looks at her daughters with exaggerated incredulity as if to say, *how terribly naïve!* But her gaze catches on her eldest, who looks as if the ground has opened beneath her, and her youngest, who is freakishly pale. How to explain how terrified she was in that moment when she struck him, and how she realised that if she didn't defend Grace, he would go on and on and on . . .

'Perhaps I have some other sort of proof?' He dangles the surely empty threat, a smile on his lips. 'But my hunch is that even a sniff of this will prove hugely detrimental to your career. How will parents feel about reading stories by a potential murderer? It's hardly going to be *great* for sales.'

It's a line from one of the emails. She peers at Ned, scrutinising his features – the straight nose, the large, long-lashed eyes, the cheekbones slanting to a strong jaw – and taking his face apart. Beautiful men are dangerous, she knows that; it's the reason suave conmen succeed. Though she has never been beautiful herself, Eleanor thought she was alert to the leeway beauty provided. (She was, after all, married to Michael.) But it seems she was distracted and is now reaping the consequences of her mistake.

'Who *are* you?' she repeats, and Ned's eyes narrow as if he is calibrating what to divulge. Well, she is not going to be treated like this.

'Come on, girls,' she says, and starts walking past him. Gilly joins her but Delia remains transfixed. She rather hoped he would at least look surprised, but he still seems disarmingly unperturbed as if he has further cards held close to his chest.

'Wait a minute,' Ned calls when she can hardly bear his silence any longer. 'Do you remember a Louisa Simpson?'

The name sends a chill from her coccyx all the way up her spine. Of course, she remembers Louisa Simpson: the name instantly transports her to one of the most painful periods of her life. She thinks of her elfin former assistant: quick-witted, lively, keen, too keen, at least when it came to inserting herself into family life.

'Perhaps we should discuss this in private?' She turns towards him and tries to semaphore that her daughters shouldn't hear this.

But Ned clearly wants this audience.

'Louisa who helped you through books six to eight of the *Fox Hole series.* Who "acted as a sounding board for your ideas". Who "knew too many secrets" – I think that's how you put it – and who you sacked when she became pregnant.'

'I'm aware of who Louisa is, yes.' Her voice is ice. 'But I'm not sure why you've chosen to bring her up . . . Oh!' It hits her as he smiles. That charming smile: so generous; so expressive; so *calculating*; so familiar. Of course. Now that she sees it, the likeness is obvious. He has been hiding in plain sight.

'I was that baby,' Ned says, though she doesn't need to hear this, and she certainly doesn't want her daughters to. 'I was the reason she lost her job – or rather, *you* were. *You* were the reason she lost her career, her identity, her self-belief—'

'Oh, come on,' she remonstrates, because this is self-pitying *bilge.* She may not have given Louisa a *huge* pay-off – the young woman had taken quite enough from her by that stage – and she absolutely refuted her claim of co-authorship of those *Fox Hole* books, but she isn't going to be saddled with sparking any mental health issues. Louisa had one small baby, that was all, and she could quite easily have picked herself up again.

Besides, it doesn't look as if Ned has suffered, materially at least. An attractive young woman like Louisa would always find a new career, despite Eleanor's best efforts, and would, she was quite sure, have had the pick of the men.

But her son clearly has a victim mentality and is raging away.

'You don't think it impacted on her, and me? You made sure she was blacklisted from any marketing jobs in the industry. Until I was ten, and she married my stepfather, she brought me up as a single mother in poverty. Oh, you don't believe me? Well, it's easy enough to pass as upper middle class. Clothes can be bought; this vintage watch' – he gestures at his left wrist – 'was picked up from eBay for a song. My way of carrying myself? That confidence – well, it's paper-thin but I'm an observer, a chameleon, a shapeshifter and a social climber. A social grifter, just like you. And though it would be preferable to be a nepo baby, as Delia knows, it's still possible to succeed in the arts despite not being this.'

And there is something in this that rings so true. She should have seen, should have known, should have *realised* that that drive and desire to unearth a story came from someone who needed to prove themselves. She should have recognised his hunger and not assumed he had entered arts journalism through the well-worn public school and Oxbridge route. She, of all people, should have known that there were always outliers, and that sometimes, those who are the *hungriest* for a story are the ones with the most to prove.

Next to her, Gilly clears her throat as if she wants an explanation, but where should she start? With the murder accusation, or the disowned siblings, or this mention of a pregnant employee she is accused of treating so appallingly? Ned seems to believe this is the biggest issue, and perhaps it's the easiest for them to understand.

And yet there's a certain key fact she needs to keep quiet. Louisa's pay-off was conditional on her leaving the identity of Ned's father off her baby's birth certificate. Is it too much to hope she never told her son that truth? It seems unlikely, given his skills at persuasion, and this animus against Eleanor. *In everything illegitimate.* Of course. With his reference to his mother, he has betrayed the fact he's behind the emails. *I will have revenges on you both.* She is face to face with her stalker, at last.

Eleanor glances back at the house where the laughter is becoming a little hysterical, and the string quartet is playing jazz and improvising wildly. Carole is talking to Peter, though the two of them are glancing towards her. Her siblings have gone. There is no one else here to hear this. Just herself, two of her daughters, and Ned.

'Can we sort this out another way?' she says, as if the solution is simple. 'Is it compensation you want, because perhaps the sum your mother received was a little ungenerous compared to current redundancy packages. This should be easy to resolve, if that's the case.'

And if she thought that Ned has exhausted his capacity for contempt, she was wrong. His beautiful face turns ugly with a sneer.

'You can't buy your way out of this. There's no easy pay-off. I *know* you, Eleanor. The same ruthlessness you showed towards your father, you showed to my mum. She's dead, by the way. Cancer – though she was eaten up by bitterness at knowing she'd helped create your most successful story and was never acknowledged for it.'

'Oh, what rot!' She can't help herself: her fury spills out. What self-aggrandising behaviour on Louisa's part, and what judgement on his because how *dare* he pity her father. She was defending *her* mother, just as he is defending his.

'Mum!' Gilly implores her, and her voice catches as if she's trying not to sob. 'I'm sure my mother doesn't mean that,' she tells Ned, but her tone's doubtful as she tries to apply a forgiving spin.

'Yes, I bloody do,' she says, as she sees the angry burn on her mother's arm, the plum of the bruise by her cheek. 'My father was a violent drunk, who beat me and my siblings and tried to pulverise my mother, but let's get back to *your* parent and the suggestion that I used her idea?' She gives a laugh that can't come close to capturing her disbelief. 'Everyone knows the true skill is in how you not only spot the potential but *realise* an idea. It's not enough to have a good idea for a plot, otherwise everyone who claimed to have a book inside them – and oh my lord, everyone I meet seems to think that – would just get on and write the bloody thing!

'Anyway, I've had enough of this,' she says, because she needs to kick him out of here before he goes back to his accusation of murder. 'You accuse me of rewriting my past – well, big deal! I'm an author and writing stories is what I do. And you think your mother, about whom you're hardly objective, provided me with ideas? Well, good luck with that! You can't substantiate any of this. Nor can you substantiate the idea I was anywhere near my home when my father died. There's no one to back up your allegations. And there's no silver bullet.'

He gives a wolfish grin, and for the second time, she's horribly aware that this isn't necessarily true. It's perfectly possible that Bill or Joanne spied her leaving from their attic window, or that Grace told them what happened. They'd spent their entire lives living with his abuse and had no reason to tell the police. And then there's the manuscript he referred to and which Peter has no doubt passed on. A fiction, and everyone knows she has a superb imagination, but something Ned could gussy up as far too much of a coincidence; something he could suggest is based on fact.

And then her insides seem to fall away because a figure steps out from the cliff path and comes to stand by the summer house, as if playing a role in some closing scene of a Shakespearean comedy. He might be two stone lighter, his cheeks cavernous and his once thick hair now thinning, but there is no mistaking who he is.

'Dad?' Gilly's cry is disbelieving.

'Oh, for goodness' sake!' says Eleanor.

And then she turns to Ned, wild-eyed. 'How did you manage this? I paid him enough not to talk about our marriage.' She feels winded, as if her lungs are paper bags flattened shut.

Behind her, Delia gives a little whimper and Eleanor resists turning because she doesn't want to consider the possibility that feels as if it is about to become a certainty.

'Ah yes,' says Ned, his tone lilting and winsome; almost caressing, as if *he* is about to tell a story. 'Did you really think I could arrange this final reveal on my own?' He gives Delia an odd, cajoling smile, then turns back to her mother. 'Oh no. I needed some help for this.'

Forty-eight

Twelve months earlier

NED

It all started, as Eleanor's story did, with a father.

Or, in Ned's case, the lack of one.

For thirty-two years, he had no knowledge of his biological father, and that, he tried to persuade himself, was fine.

He had a perfectly decent stepfather, whose surname he had taken, and he accepted his mother's refusal to discuss the subject with only a little resentment. His defence against rejection, no doubt. Louisa *had* told him his father had another family; that he'd never shown any interest. *Well, fuck him*, he thought throughout his teens and twenties whenever his absence nudged at him. *I'm doing just fine.*

But then his mother was diagnosed with bowel cancer, and with a poor prognosis came a change of heart. Not only did she want her son to know his father's identity, but she needed him to know the circumstances in which she had met her lover, and why he'd played no part in his life.

Michael Kingman was a writer. He'd written one highly acclaimed literary novel; was, like his son, intensely charming. 'And I worked for Eleanor Kingman, his wife.'

'*The* Eleanor Kingman?' Ned asked, because by this point, he was working in arts journalism and, besides, he remembered Louisa choosing her books from the library. 'Author of the *Fox Hole* stories?'

'Yes,' she said drily. 'Those were partly mine.'

And while Ned treated this with some scepticism, his mother never having shown the slightest inclination to write, he didn't doubt the rest of the story. On discovering Louisa was pregnant, Eleanor had sacked her and stipulated that Michael would have no contact with his two small daughters unless he cut all ties. Marriage with Eleanor, with all the financial success she was starting to enjoy, or a fresh start with a penniless PA who had got herself pregnant during the briefest of flings? Louisa, though younger and far prettier, didn't stand a chance.

'And he's never seen me?'

'Once. By accident. I bumped into them on the King's Road. Refused to cross over. You were eighteen months and toddling, insisting on walking next to your buggy.'

'And what happened then?'

Her face had softened. 'He was intrigued. She looked furious, of course, and must have conceived Delia not long after. Your half-sister who manacled him to her, at least for a while.'

Grief lit a fire under Ned's desire to know more about him:

this stranger who'd given him half his DNA and who, fascinated all those years ago, would surely be *curious*? An only child, he craved connection but was wary of being rejected again.

And so, he came up with a ruse: contacting Michael, via a literary editor they both knew, on the pretext of researching a possible documentary into Dame Eleanor Kingman and choosing not to mention their genetic connection. Not even clear, initially, when, or *if*, he would come clean.

They met at the River Café one glorious lunchtime in May; sat outside, as the Thames shimmered beside them, which felt both discreet and wonderfully carefree.

Michael was hesitant, at first.

'It's all very hush-hush,' said his son, as he plied him with wild sea bass roasted with olives and Florentine fennel. 'I'm just at the research stage. Trying to determine if she even merits a documentary.'

'I'd have thought so,' Michael said, eventually. 'Not that I ever discuss her or our marriage. It's finally lapsed now, but there was a longstanding NDA.'

'So I understand,' Ned said smoothly, as he indicated to the sommelier that he should pour the rather nice 2016 Soave that was setting him back nearly £300 a bottle. 'As I said, nothing would be attributable. I'm talking to several people. It would just be deep background.'

'Well,' Michael said, as he took a sip of wine and visibly relaxed, 'of course, she's rather remarkable.'

Ned inclined his head as if to acknowledge this went without saying.

'But' – and here his father paused as if it pained him to say this but not setting the record straight would be dishonourable – 'she can be rather a difficult woman.'

'Funnily enough, you're not the only person to say that . . .' Ned looked at him over the rim of his glass.

Michael had given a joyful bark of a laugh, and his son could see why his mother had found him so appealing. Then he pulled a face to suggest there was much he *could* say, though he was reluctant to be drawn.

And maybe Michael was lonely, or perhaps Ned's charm worked on him as well as it would on Eleanor, but over three courses and coffee, he began to talk of the dark period after she divorced him. To tell of his deep regret, too, in allowing himself to be persuaded that it would be better for his daughters if he disappeared from their lives. 'I'd been a bit of a player. Profoundly selfish. I accepted her argument, only, well, with hindsight I can see I was foolish to do so. Her story was rather black and white.'

The portrait of a marriage continued over their second lunch, by which stage they were getting through two bottles of wine and Ned was opting for those nearer the £200 mark: still a bargain, given what he was learning.

'She used me, you know.'

'Oh, *really*?'

'Nicked my ideas. Of course you couldn't prove it. She would always claim we were just helping one another. That it was a symbiotic relationship. And I never wrote them down. They arose through storytelling, in conversation, or as we talked through plot holes. Just part of the process, as she saw it. But some of those that stuck were definitely mine.'

Ned, tackling his Scottish scallops, gave a gentle murmur to encourage him to continue.

'We'd tell the girls those early *Fox Hole* stories together. I'd take over if she was cooking, or we'd do one night on, one night off; picking up the baton of the story; leaving it on a cliffhanger for the other to go on. Gilly always wanted it to be me. I was better at plotting, you see, not that you'd know that from my adult fiction. Not that Eleanor ever acknowledged it.'

'Do you know, I've heard something similar elsewhere,' Ned murmured, because this chimed with his mother's claim.

'About my work?' Michael, ever eager for validation, visibly perked up at this.

'No, though I'm sure that's the case. About her magpieing stories.'

'From someone who worked for her?'

'What makes you say that?' For a few tantalising seconds, the air shimmered with possibility. Was this the point at which Michael mentioned Louisa, and the penny finally dropped that he was sitting opposite his son?

But his father was preoccupied with his chargrilled shoulder of lamb with borlotti beans and cavolo nero, and the moment slipped into the ether. 'Well – there were other NDAs,' he went on. 'And she had a habit of using people, then discarding them if needs be. The mistress of reinvention.' He took a swig of Pinot Noir and swallowed. 'I imagine you'll be digging around in her past?' Ned gave a nod. Michael appeared to be weighing up whether to tell him something. Ned waited. A large part of this job was listening. Often, you just needed to be patient. His quiet sympathy obviously worked because Michael leaned forwards, his voice quietly confidential. They were so close that Ned could feel his breath on his cheek.

'She fell out with her family. 1969. The first Christmas she was in London. I didn't know her then – we met two years later – and she never went into the details. To be honest, I didn't question it at all. They were up north,' he leaned back and gestured expansively as if this was a faraway continent, 'she was down here. She clearly felt they had nothing in common; that they held her back. Plenty of students reinvent themselves, so I didn't think it that big a deal, but since being estranged from my own daughters I've thought that's quite cold, isn't it? Quite ruthless. At eighteen, after your first term in London, to cut them off completely, and in all those years that we were together to never be in touch; to never try to make it up?'

He took another swig of wine, then circled the liquid around his glass, his expression increasingly contemplative.

'She used to joke about Lear once we were married. The coincidence of my surname and the abbreviation she used: Lea, never Ellie, and certainly not Eleanor. Lea Kingman. We even leaned into it when we realised we'd named our elder daughters Gilly and Rachel: Delia is Cordelia on her birth certificate. How clever we thought we were! Lear banishes Cordelia, but Lea – now Eleanor – banished herself. Estranged fathers, absent fathers. I don't know. No doubt it's my own preoccupation, or guilt transposed, but perhaps there's some sort of story there.'

Estranged fathers, absent fathers. Ned had sat, stunned by the irony of Michael discussing this with his unacknowledged son, and knowing that he couldn't reveal himself. He had left it too late: it wasn't the time. Besides, though the idea of a documentary had been a ruse, he felt that frisson of excitement that came with the sniff of a story. There was something here, wasn't there? A phenomenally successful writer whose brand was based on a true story that had been significantly rewritten? *Dame Eleanor Kingman: A Life (based on a true story).* He could just see the opening credits. Talk about meta. If he could truffle out this secret, he should pitch this documentary idea.

'You've never thought of contacting your daughters?'

'Of course.' His father was brisk. 'I'm not a monster.'

'And?'

'Christ. It's been too long. After the divorce, I think I was in denial. Went rather wild. And I took a pay-off to ensure I wasn't in contact until Delia was eighteen.' He looks shame-faced. 'Yep. I'm not proud of it but I wasn't earning much, and my parents got her to sign a pre-nup which ended up being hugely detrimental since she was the one with all the success. So.' A pause. 'I needed the cash.'

'And I assume it was a sizeable amount?'

'Not fifty pieces of silver.' Michael looked at him sharply; to be fair, it was an impertinent question. 'But seven figures, which, even today, let alone over twenty years ago, is not a sum that I could turn down. And then, when the period was up, I was conscious that none of them had ever shown any inclination to find *me*.

'I assumed she had poisoned them against me. She was always so good at telling stories and I knew she would be so persuasive: telling them they'd be happier without their old dad in their lives. A part of me believed that, too, but the larger part was too much of a coward. I couldn't bear to confirm that they didn't want to know. Better to remember those years when I'd read, and made up, bedtime stories. Before I proved to be so fallible. When I was in charge of the narrative, so to speak.'

He placed his knife and fork together, quite deliberately, then tore a piece of ciabatta and wiped it around his plate, mopping up the juices. As an illustration of the conflict that appeared to rage within him – between appetite and convention; not daring to rock the boat and being desperate to do so – it couldn't have been neater. Ned watched, fascinated, knowing he needed to see him again.

'You know that the youngest is quite high-profile in her own right? An Influencer. There are rumours of a book deal.'

'Oh, really?' That got Michael's attention. Chip off the old block. Never mind that it wasn't the least bit true.

'Are you on Instagram?'

''fraid not, no.'

'Well, let me show you. You could always follow her and then message her when she opens her DMs?'

But Michael, though intrigued by the photos of his youngest daughter, her reels and her vlog, was reluctant to do this. 'Not my style and she'd think me a creep.'

'Tell you what, if there's a story to be told – a documentary to be made, and it sounds as if there could be – I'd need to talk to her, and her sisters. If you're involved, then perhaps you can meet her that way?'

Because, of course, there was a story to be told.

Getting to know Michael might have been the original incentive, but Ned soon became immersed in the story of Lea Savage: what had happened before her near-reinvention (because no one reinvents themselves entirely: elements of Lea must have remained at her core). Her original agent proved particularly fruitful, and then came the hours spent in the newspaper records at Leeds Central Library; the thrilling discovery of an unsolved murder; and the interviews with Bill Savage and Joanne Outhwaite, so stunned to hear of their sister's success – and, in Joanne's case, so interested in her wealth – that they found themselves spilling out details of their early years.

And yet there was still no evidence linking Lea to William's murder. If they had heard or suspected their sister came back that Christmas, the Savage siblings weren't saying. Lea left in September 1969, they insisted, and she never returned.

The only person who had ever mentioned a row that Christmas was Michael, who remained emphatic that he wouldn't speak on camera; was clear he couldn't be persuaded, some chivalrous instinct, or fear of legal action, still at work.

And that was *fine.* A documentary could state the fact of an unsolved murder and encourage viewers to join the dots . . .

But how much better if a child of his could work on him? Ned couldn't do that; knew instinctively that if he mentioned his paternity, he would frighten Michael off.

But Delia, who'd told her followers about her ambivalence at being used as the muse for her mother's character, might help?

Yes, Eleanor's youngest daughter was the person on whom he now needed to work.

Forty-nine

Ned

'Hi!'

Ned wasn't quite sure of the etiquette of an AA meeting. Did you introduce yourself as you sat down, or did you wait until everyone did so formally?

He took his place in the circle next to Delia, first gesturing hesitantly to the empty wooden chair.

'I'm Ned,' he murmured, playing up his diffidence.

She gave him a quick nod but didn't offer her name. It hardly mattered. It wasn't as if he didn't know who she was.

It hadn't been hard to track Delia down. Her Insta followers knew her as someone who had battled alcoholism. It was part of her story: that she was coke-and-alcohol-dependent in her mid-twenties (she skirted over the fact it was more recent), before becoming a plant-based wellness guru with a zero-tolerance policy towards not just alcohol but wheat, dairy and, Ned assumed, joy.

These days, she downplayed her addiction. Recent followers would find few references amid the shots of salad bowls or the reels of yogic poses on empty beaches. But it didn't require much research to reveal she had gone through rehab at an exclusive clinic in Montreux. And though she only occasionally made references to 'checking in', it was enough for the more perceptive of her 689,000 followers, such as Ned, to understand she attended AA.

Of course, she didn't post where she went to meetings, and, given how regularly she travelled, it varied. But Ned was a journalist, and he was persistent. Having discovered she was living in Eleanor's Covent Garden flat, he searched for AA listings in the area, then put in a bit of surveillance, waiting outside each one and clocking who turned up. It only took four days before he spied a blonde figure duck from the bustle of St Martin's Lane and into the Quaker Meeting House. For a second, he prevaricated. Was it her? He had made a mistake last week and been stuck in a hall off Oxford Street for the entire session, but there was something about her posture – she clearly *did* do all that yoga – that made him follow her inside.

At the end of the meeting, during which he refrained from trotting out his practised spiel, he asked if she fancied the equivalent of a drink.

She looked at him in surprise. Maybe she didn't get asked out, or perhaps it wasn't an appropriate thing to do?

'I mean a Joe & the Juice or something. Or a coffee – if you do coffee?'

'I can always manage something green?'

'Perfect.' He beamed. 'I just' – he was good at playing this stumbling, socially awkward role; he'd spent his life feeling the outsider – 'I'd love to chat a bit more – perhaps somewhere less intense?'

They found a juice bar, and he paid for two large, lime green concoctions, each sporting a sea-foam-like froth. She curled up at a table in the most discreet corner and started tapping away on her phone. But when he approached her, she put it away and rewarded him with a smile so broad that he was struck by her physical similarity to Michael – the same high cheekbones, generous mouth and Scandi-blue eyes – and briefly wondered if it was meant for someone else.

'Here you go.' He placed the drinks in front of her. She was wearing a raw-edged, scoop-neck T shirt with 'Flow' embroidered across it, and when she moved, he could see the tender dip between her breasts and her bare, tanned skin.

She looked so vulnerable and slight that he felt a spasm of sympathy, which he dampened straight back down. Delia Kingman was a spoiled brat: one who was damaged, yes, but who had the resources and every opportunity in her charmed life – all the opportunities he hadn't experienced – to counter this.

'So, what do you do, *Ned*?' She paused a little before his name as if unconvinced it was his real one.

'I work in TV. I make arts documentaries.'

'Uh-huh.' A glimmer of interest. 'I can see that. You have a certain aura – don't worry, I'm not hitting on you . . .' She gave a growl of a laugh. 'Sex can be as addictive as the booze, can't it? So, I don't know about you, but I'm going through a self-imposed celibate period. My sponsor suggested it anyway. Thought I'd try a full year. Fun, right?' She sipped at the green froth, full lips carefully placed around the straw, and looked pensive. But there was nothing calculatedly sexual about what she was doing: she looked like a sad little girl.

'What about you? What do you do?' he said.

'Me?' She pulled a quizzical face. 'I'm an Influencer.' She made quotation marks in the air with her fingers. 'And before that, I was the inspiration for some children's books which is, yeah, where a lot of my problems began.'

'Oh, right.' He pulled a sorry-to-pry face. Say what you like about attending AA, but it was a swift way of cutting through the bullshit, because here she was, laying her life bare.

'Should I look you up now?' He pulled out his phone and smiled, enquiringly. 'What's your handle?'

'Delightfully Delia,' she said, with an eye-roll. 'Yeah. I should have given that more thought, but "deliciously" has been used. "Delightful" was something my mother used to say about me. "Delia's such a delight"' – she mimicked her perfectly. 'Unironically at first.'

'And then not?'

'Well, I don't suppose any parent wants a child who's an addict.'

'There is that.'

She sipped some more while he scrolled through her feed (all previously pored over) before settling on a shot of her holding her mother's *Jess* book: head tilted to one side, hair fastened in a messy bun. Her outfit – an oversized white shirt, stonewashed jeans and a neck-mess of gold chains – was on point, but her expression, so wholesome she could be presenting children's TV. He took his time, looking from the screen to her and back again, then delivering the line he had practised so carefully.

'You're not – looking at this book you're holding – you're not Delia *Kingman*, are you? Dame Eleanor's daughter?'

'The very same.'

'Christ.'

'Well, not quite. No Messianic aspirations.'

'I mean. Phew.' He exhaled, shaking his head. (He was close to overdoing it.) 'This is going to sound weird, but that's quite the coincidence.'

'The coincidence?' She looked at him with a raised eyebrow; not clear how to read this.

'You're not going to believe this, but I've been discussing filming a retrospective of your mother to be broadcast by the BBC around her seventieth birthday. I've been emailing your sister, Gilly, is it?'

'Yes, Gilly's my sister . . .'

'Yes, Gilly, discussing how Dame Eleanor might be involved.'

'And has my mother agreed to this?' She leaned against the banquette and looked at him intently.

'I think so,' he said. 'We're in the early stage of discussions, but I think she was quite . . . flattered. Does that make sense?'

'Very much so.'

He smiled but the atmosphere still felt a little tense. *Hold your nerve*, he reminded himself. *There's no reason for her to suspect you, let alone guess a personal connection. You reeled in Michael; and she is less of an unknown quantity. You're pushing at an open door here.*

But he needed to do this gently because he sensed she could startle. He needed to coax her, like a fawn. He flashed his most charming smile: the one that always worked with reluctant interviewees; that he would use to great effect on her mother and elder sister and that he had already used on her father.

'If she agrees, I think this could be quite something. Our greatest living children's author: a frank picture of what makes her so brilliant, so enduring – and, no doubt, so complex?'

'I can't cope with much more of this,' she said – but she meant the juice, not him. 'Come on,' she said, as she pushed the half-empty cup away and stood up, impatient. 'Let's go for a walk instead.'

It wasn't hard to get her to undermine her mother.

Of course, he didn't suggest she do this explicitly. Working in TV, he knew all about the need to put in the groundwork; to win over contacts; build trust, and once their defences were down, to persuade them to go that little bit further than they'd intended initially.

It helped that Delia was so desperate for someone to

confide in. God, she could be dull, though: not just needy but utterly self-absorbed. In some ways she was more like Eleanor than she would like to admit. Focused, driven, arrogant, and powered by an innate self-belief. The psychobabble of her grid, the whimsical alliterations, mantras and epigraphs, and the artfully shot reels of her performing her prayer stretches or holding a plank, all suggested an entitled young woman who believed her trite truisms and willingness to lay bare her vulnerabilities were actually *worth* something.

At first, Ned assumed she was completely cynical in monetising her past. That it was a pact she'd made. Grab every scrap of clothing, every free holiday, every beauty product, plus the added payment for endorsing them, but accept you'll need to exploit your fallibility. Recognise that that was the deal. But in time, he saw she had bought into the cult of herself, believing the pap she spouted, even as she knew that Delightfully Delia was a construct: distinct from the complicated, contrary, sometimes tearful individual who wasn't averse to sending him self-pitying texts at two a.m.

Spending time with her could be tedious, when she wasn't offering eye-opening vignettes about her mother, but at least there was no question of their relationship being sexual. He had been quite clear. It was easy to play the professional card. Hardly appropriate, he had said, when referencing a presenter of a TV programme who'd had an affair with a contestant, and nodding earnestly, she had agreed. Besides, she took the concept of abstention seriously, and then it just wasn't an issue. He was, she said at one point, almost like a brother. I haven't got one, she added, but if I had, I'd want him to be like you.

Of course, he toyed with coming clean. If he outed himself as a half-sibling, it could bond them tightly together, but, as with Michael, it felt too big a gamble by that stage. The last thing he wanted was for either to guess he was motivated for less than professional reasons. As *if.* And the longer he delayed telling them, the more impossible such a reveal became.

Playing up his hesitancy, he suggested that the Dame Eleanor who was emerging from his research was as deeply flawed as she was brilliant. Did that make sense? 'Oh, absolutely, abso*lute*ly.' After all, were it not for Eleanor's – he hated to use the term 'psychological damage': 'It's OK! She fucked me up,' – well, were it not for that, then Delia may have had an easier life?

'And then there's the question of your father . . .'

They were drinking green tea, and he circled the rim of the mug with his index finger, not meeting her gaze and apparently wary. 'You know I've met him?' he said, eventually.

'Noooo! No! You haven't? Omigod. Oh. My. God.'

'Well, to get a full picture, I kind of had to . . .'

'I'm not sure how I feel about that . . .'

He remained quiet for a while, then spoke particularly gently. 'Would you like me to put you in touch?'

'I don't know.' For the first time since they met, she looked stunned. 'I mean, at first, that was all I wanted, and then it wasn't. If he wasn't interested, then neither was I, if you know what I mean? I'll have to think about it.' She chewed her bottom lip, pensive. *How long did she mean: a couple of days? A week? He mustn't push, and yet he mustn't lose momentum.* Delia, he knew instinctively, would be able to influence their father in a way he couldn't: her involvement, her collaboration, and her skill in charming Michael were critical to the whole thing.

'Of course,' he said, soothingly. 'No one wants you to have to do anything difficult. Anything distressing. It's not as if he's really *that* important to the story. After all, he can't say that much because your mum paid him off . . .'

She froze before her eyes narrowed to slits.

'She. Paid. Him. Off?'

He waited a beat. Then another as he let the full weight of her incomprehension, hurt and then fury swirl around them.

'Oh god.' He winced. 'I'm so sorry. I thought you already knew?'

The pay-off worked against Michael, too, of course. At first, Delia was decidedly frosty with him. The fact he'd taken money to miss out on her childhood was difficult to stomach. But her father was as engaging as his daughter, and she wasn't immune to his charm.

Besides, with Eleanor cast as the evil parent, there had long been a vacancy for a good one. Ned almost felt sorry for Eleanor. Almost, but not quite.

'We all know how formidable my mother can be,' Delia reminded Ned. 'I'm not surprised he couldn't live with her.'

'And the continual infidelity?' Ned played devil's advocate.

'Obviously not *ideal*. But she made him feel stupid. I'm not excusing it, but yeah: he wasn't as good, or rather, as commercially successful, a writer. That fragile masculinity? She could have been more sensitive about it.'

'Should she?' No one could accuse Ned of not being fair, and he was surprised, and slightly appalled, by her take.

'I know her. She would have been quite matter of fact about it. That would have been painful. She couldn't have helped showing off.'

And then came Michael's bad news. Tragic for him, though fortuitous in terms of the project in that it helped his daughter forgive him. He had cancer: something he had suspected when Ned first approached him, and which explained why he'd been persuaded to meet in the first place because time was hurtling on. Death concentrated the mind, he told his daughter: he wanted to explain why he'd stayed away and he wanted to atone for his decision. A more satisfying sense of ending, in narrative terms, was what he required.

And she thought of telling her sisters about him then. With his prognosis, wasn't that fair? Ned advised firmly against it: the last thing he wanted was for Gilly to be aware of what he was up to and restrict access to Eleanor and her friends. Luckily for him, Rachel was barely speaking to Delia, and Gilly refused to discuss Michael, when her youngest sister tried to raise the subject. There was a tiny, unappealing part of Delia that was relieved. She loved keeping her daddy to herself. After all, he had left when her sisters were sixteen and eighteen; they had had him for most of their childhoods – whereas he had disappeared when she was only nine.

On Ned worked. There were still frustrating gaps in the story. Despite Michael's more cavalier attitude to risk, he refused to go on the record about the 'row at Christmas'. The link was tenuous but coupled with Peter Jamieson's recollections and a copy of the manuscript, which the agent promised to hand over at the party, Ned thought he could muddy the waters sufficiently to make the allegation stick. And then Delia suggested her father gatecrash the seventieth birthday party, and Ned detected an energy, an anarchy, as Michael agreed to this.

He was Delia's – and his – father, after all.

And by this stage, Ned saw himself as a scriptwriter setting up these characters and bringing them together in a charged situation, then stepping back and watching to see what caught light. And through it all, he remained stunned that both father and daughter had bought into the story that he was merely trying to create a rounded portrait. Perhaps that was the thing about egocentrics: they were so bound up in their own agendas, they didn't suspect others of having them at all?

But Ned had one. Of course he did. And it was no longer just about avenging Louisa, and gaining some recognition for her work, though that was a motivation. Ned had heard his mother's distress; had sensed her regret; a knotty fibre threading through her soul.

In a different world, Ned might have had a chance to love

his father and half-sisters. He would very much have liked the opportunity to do so.

And the person he blamed for denying him this – in forbidding Michael to have any contact with him; in paying Michael to stay away from his daughters; in curtailing this human connection – wasn't his father, but his father's wife.

Dame Eleanor Kingman.

Fifty

Present day
Saturday night

Eleanor

Eleanor stares at her former husband, standing alongside her youngest, most adored daughter. How could she? And how could *he*? *Why* has he come after all this time?

If she weren't so frightened, she might laugh. Isn't it enough to meet her siblings after over half a century without having to confront yet another ghost from her past?

She needs to get away. It's less a thought than a compulsion. Fight or flight – and flight is Eleanor's default option at times of crisis. She starts walking briskly, her eyes filming and her chest on fire. The fact that Delia has been somehow involved in this process slices through her like a shard of glass. *The stupid little girl.* She can't know what she has done, or at least she very much hopes she doesn't know what she has done. Unless she's been complicit in an elaborate unmasking – and here Eleanor can't help a sob bubbling up because how could her youngest hate her this spectacularly?

As she reaches the cliff, she turns to check to see if her daughters are following. Gilly and Delia are moving swiftly in her direction. She can't quite see the men. They'll catch her up soon, though, she realises, as she scurries down the sandy coast path, a spit of rain striking her face. Four seasons in an hour in Cornwall, isn't that what they say? The spits are turning into proper drops, a flurry that dampens her thin gown and makes her shiver so that she pulls her flimsy pashmina around her, clutching it with one hand as she steadies herself against the cliff.

A roll of thunder, and the sky is turning dark: the pathetic fallacy in full play, and it seems bizarre that she can acknowledge this, and the fact that everyone is coming together for a final act, while experiencing all the physiological tells of fear. Ned, who believes her life is a fiction, would no doubt think this is apt. But she is a different person from who he thinks she is. Lea Savage stopped existing in her early twenties, when she embraced her married name, and her author's name, and clung to it tightly. Dame Eleanor Kingman doesn't recognise the name – or the girl it belonged to – now.

And since her life's no fiction, she most certainly isn't going to be part of a dramatic showdown. Before the tide comes in, she'll make her way to the public beach and walk from there to Trecarrow, only returning late tonight once her guests have left. It's a somewhat eccentric move to miss her own party, but it's not the event she planned. Besides, she has a *great* excuse. It's not every day you're accused of murder; nor have to confront your ex-husband and long-lost siblings; nor discover that your favourite daughter has conspired to expose you.

Nearly there.

Just a few steps more and she'll be on the beach. The tide has turned – it's coming in – but if she gets a move on, she can skirt the rocks to the left, which are just visible, and walk entirely on the sand. It will be such a relief to be on firm ground, but as she's thinking this, she slips, her silly gold sandals skidding on the wet path so that she almost tumbles right down. *Ow, ow, ow, ow, ow!* Grabbing at a shrub, she manages to lean into the cliff as she rights herself but her wrist grazes on a piece of granite, and it stings, the skin ripped and her tender skin flayed and pricked with red. Sucking hard, she tastes mud and salt and perhaps the sweetness of a canapé – was that only earlier this evening? – as the rain soaks her torso, and pain shoots through her, and her toes become slippery and grimy with the earthy silt of the path.

She is scared. She can admit that as a jolt of lightning illuminates the sky, and she looks back up the cliff to see the others coming after her, Ned in the lead and covering the distance so quickly she knows there's no chance of escape. Kicking off her shoes, she scrambles to the bottom of the path, clutching at the sides of the cliff until her feet sink into the cool sand, then skitter through puddles of salt water which drench the hem of her gown. Her heart bites at her chest, but she won't give up; she'll do everything she can to resist him, and even as she senses him now sauntering behind her – because of course there's no need for him to race; he has her in his sights – she persists in her ludicrous, chest-burning stumbling until her body, far from as fit as she would wish, unceremoniously lets her down.

Darkness nudges the very edges of her vision as she fights a wave of dizziness.

'There's no point running.' His voice, amused, drifts towards her, as she tries to cope with the pain searing her chest.

'You!' she cries, and it's part battle cry, part hex; an attempt to ward off a bad spirit because he's malevolent, isn't he? A force of evil intent on corrupting Delia and destroying everything Eleanor's worked for: her reputation; her literary empire; her relationships with her daughters. 'Stay away from me.

'And stay away from everyone else,' she adds, as she catches sight of her ex-husband, who, flanked by Gilly and Delia, is making his way towards her.

'I'm assuming you were characteristically blinkered about this, Michael?' she calls, her tone more confident than she feels. She looks from Michael to Ned, and though the similarity isn't pronounced, Ned favouring Louisa with those remarkable green eyes, now that she sees them together it is obvious: evident in the breadth of the shoulders; their high cheekbones; the shape of their heads.

'Blinkered about what?' And it seems incredible that he has to ask. She didn't see it, but why didn't *he*?

'About Louisa's child. That you didn't even realise this was *him*?' She sees from his reaction that she is right. Oh, this is priceless! 'You didn't?' And she turns in time to catch a flicker of disgust – or is it distress? – on Ned's face.

'And what about Delia?' She glances from Michael to her youngest, her troubled, damaged baby, who she can see herself forgiving if, as seems likely, she was hoodwinked. 'Did you know about Ned's hidden agenda? No, I can see you knew nothing about it . . .'

'Knew nothing about what?' Delia says.

And Eleanor stares at her because she seems to need it made explicit. Well, it is rather a lot to take in. Still, she makes them wait for the pay-off to this story. A twist worth savouring, as she looks from Michael to Ned.

From father to son.

'That Ned is your half-brother,' she says.

Fifty-one

Delia

Her mother isn't making any sense. For a split second, Delia wonders if she's given birth to a son that somehow none of them knew about.

Then she looks at her father and, like a twist of a Rubik's Cube, the pieces slot into place.

She feels herself turning red, blood pumping to her cheeks as she's consumed with a rage so intense she doesn't know what to do with it. Then she retches, once, twice, acid filling her mouth and compounding her self-loathing at falling off the wagon. Her bitter shame.

Ned must think she is so stupid.

'You used me!' she screams, though this doesn't come close to encapsulating his betrayal. 'You manipulated me. You didn't want to create a "rounded portrait" of my mother, you just wanted to get to my – your – father.'

'And you wanted me to create a "rounded portrait"?' his voice rings with disbelief. 'You wanted me to expose the pain she caused. To paint her as someone who'd exploited your childhood; and who paid your father to stay away.'

'I didn't, no,' she insists, though of course she did. She wanted some sort of comeuppance, although compared to the other crimes being levelled at Eleanor – murdering a father; abandoning siblings – exploiting her daughter is peanuts. Her brain aches and she feels hot with humiliation at being tricked. All she wanted was for Eleanor to hear her pain. She'd hardly planned on discovering a vengeful half-brother who has played both her and her father in the process.

God, he makes her skin crawl because, yes, she had felt an immediate attraction when they met; a giddiness, a sense of connection as if he *knew* her and understood. Didn't that happen with siblings separated at birth? That they felt intoxicated on meeting. Those thrilling first few months had felt a little like falling in love.

A bolt of lightning. Ned's face is spectral in the light: his cheekbones more pronounced, the hollows of his cheeks disappearing into the darkness.

'Don't pretend you were taken in by me,' he says, and his tone is brutal. 'You were complicit. You never doubted what I was up to or questioned why I wanted Michael on board.'

And that's it: the look on his face; his tone of complacency; the assumption he can understand the complexity of her emotions – and of course he can't. She hasn't come close to understanding them herself until this weekend when she began to recognise Eleanor's vulnerability. She wants to wipe that expression off his face.

'You!' she screams as she runs at him and gives him a fierce shove.

'Woah!' He staggers back, stumbling over a rock, and putting his hands up as if to steady or protect himself; surprised at having been caught off-guard. Later, it will transpire that there is seaweed, slimy and wet on the rock, and that this is enough for him to slip. That, and Delia's force, because though she is slender, she is strong, and, fired by adrenalin and cortisol, and fury at what he has done, and at herself, because the drinking was so bloody self-destructive, she is powerful. A second shove, her hands flat against his broad chest, and he is down with a dull, percussive thud.

She brushes her hands and starts walking back towards the cliffs, expecting him to be winded; to get up any second. The exhilaration of flooring him carries her forwards, and the desire to get out of the pissing rain. She isn't worried about him following; it was a fair old whack, and he should be cowed. The thunder is grumbling properly now: a full timpani-roll, and there is a second crack of lightning. It feels operatic, just right for a fight during which she avenges her mother and vanquishes her opponent, and she almost expects her mother and sister to cheer.

She half-turns: she isn't interested in unpacking any of this evening with her father, but she's surprised that Gilly and Eleanor aren't following. Perhaps she should go back and help her mother at least? But as she dithers, she sees that her parents, bizarrely, are standing together and her sister is crouched over Ned. She wipes the rain from her eyes. Another roll of thunder. Despite every instinct telling her to get back to the brightness and light of the party, she is drawn to them.

'What's going on?' Her voice is swallowed by the wind as she runs back and sees that Gilly has her fingers around Ned's wrist. She can't see his face, shielded by her sister's body, but she doesn't like his stillness.

'He's not conscious,' Gilly says.

'Can you feel a pulse?'

'Very faint. Only a whisper.'

Delia bends down so that she is on the other side of him.

'Ned? Ned? Can you hear me?'

His breath is almost imperceptible and there's no response. She peers closer, steadying herself by putting a hand near his head on the granite, and finds that her fingers are sticky with a ferric substance, and that the back of his head feels matted with it.

'Is he still breathing?' she asks because she can't hear anything above the wind. Bending nearer, she can't feel his breath either. 'Is there a pulse?' she repeats, avoiding Ned's name, making him anonymous, his body a thing.

'I can't feel it.' Gilly's voice is tight as she leans over his chest and starts counting compressions and working fast.

'Shouldn't we . . . I mean, aren't we meant to stem the blood or something? To stop all the blood?'

'We can't move him,' Eleanor says, her tone crisp despite her exertions. 'He might have damaged his spine.'

'But this isn't working.' Delia's voice rises in a wail, fear clawing at her throat. 'Is it working? It isn't, is it?'

Her sister continues counting compressions to an ironic, desperate soundtrack – *One, two, three, four; staying alive; staying alive* – and gives a grim shake of her head.

Later, Delia will wonder if they might have continued for longer had the weather been better; had it not been dark and wet and thunderous; had they not been conscious of the difficulty of getting help, their mobile signals not working and the distance from the house, at which to try the landline or secure a signal, too great.

Perhaps the truth is they would have continued for far longer if Ned hadn't posed a threat.

But two or three minutes in, as her father's teeth chatter audibly with the cold, and her parents remain rooted to the spot, her mother tells Gilly to stop. 'Time to end it now, darling.' And it's the *darling*, her quiet tenderness, that catches their attention.

'I can't.' But there's a sliver of doubt in her voice.

'We need to cut our losses,' her mother insists, and she looks out towards the sea, where the white horses are crashing on the shore and rolling in with alarming speed. 'Because look: the tide's coming in.'

Fifty-two

Gilly

As plot twists go, it's a good one.

The tide is coming in, and so they should give up trying to save a man's life. Abandon his body and let the ocean wash the evidence away.

Her mother is emphatic. Eleanor at her most clear-sighted and calm. She is so authoritative that Gilly knows, with utter certainty, that this is not the first time she's been in the aftermath of a murder. The thought's so arresting that she briefly stops the CPR.

'We need to leave *now*.'

'But what do we say?' Delia is frantic.

'We don't say anything,' Eleanor shouts into the wind.

'But Adam saw you arguing – and maybe Carole – and there'll be guests who notice we disappeared,' sobs Delia as Gilly resumes her chest compressions. 'He'll know . . . he'll guess . . . oh my god! . . . he'll guess it was me.'

'Adam didn't see *me*,' their father says, his tone that of a parent reassuring a small child. 'He was heading back to the house when I met you on the cliff. I'll say I saw the three of you leave Ned.'

'Don't worry about Adam,' Gilly says. 'Leave him to me.' Because he'll believe her, won't he? *You don't need to keep me at arm's length*, he had said. You don't share what they've shared without building some trust. It's just unfortunate that, so early in their relationship, she'll be abusing it.

Still, this is no time for scruples. There's no pulse; there is still no pulse. She strains to detect one; bends to sense a breath. And all the time, her parents discuss the logistics of how to get away with murder, and the sea growls like a Rottweiler, barely ten metres away.

Delia is hysterical; her wails a descant over the riff of the waves until Michael puts his arms around her. *Bit late for that*, because Gilly remembers the pain their father caused – and here she is thwarted by a memory: herself aged six, which must have been her age when Ned was conceived, and her mother, uncharacteristically, in tears.

'I could say he and I had a row,' Michael offers. 'I told him I'd changed my mind; he lunged – then slipped. It gives you an alibi.'

'It's a good story,' his ex-wife says.

'And credible?'

'Absolutely, yes.'

Perhaps it's the ending her father needs. A grand gesture; a sacrifice; some narrative closure that atones and is emotionally satisfying.

'An estranged father and son arguing?' he elaborates.

'Yes,' says her mother, through the rain. 'If that arises, then yes.'

They stand in silence, perhaps contemplating so much that will never be said. That Michael was always good at plot: it was the discipline of getting the words down that was the issue; that, before their marriage turned sour, they worked well together, each editing the other's work. And all the while, Gilly continues with the chest compressions, though her arms feel as if they're made of lead and she's building up a sweat, and she knows, as she's known for the last couple of minutes, that this is all a complete waste of time.

'You go back,' she says at last. There's no breath. No pulse, and she can't continue as the tide overtakes them. 'I'll keep going a little longer. You go back and call the emergency services.'

Her father nods, but Eleanor steps in.

'No calls. We leave that to his team.'

We can't just leave him here, Gilly wants to object, but she's surprised by a roar as the tide crashes then slithers forwards as if to drive them in.

'Don't be long!' Her mother turns away from Ned and starts back up the beach, moving at a pace that conveys her determination. Their father follows, and their survival instinct, or perhaps his generosity, means they walk together. Though Michael will leave Eleanor once they near the house, he will help her up.

'Come on!' Gilly screams at Delia, a couple of minutes later. 'Wash your hands!'

Delia crouches by a pool in the hardened sand and scrubs frantically at her fingers.

'Now run – and when you get in, go straight up and shower. Scrub under your fingernails; get rid of any trace of him. I'll come and find you. And if anyone asks, we spoke to him, but he stormed off. We got caught in the rain; then came back and showered because we needed to warm up.'

They start off up the beach, the tide chasing their heels, Ned's body left to the elements. The rain makes her skin slick and she's shivering: the chill creeping into her bones. As they race towards the house, she thinks through anything she might not have covered because as the eldest daughter that's her job, even if she's failed in not screening emails or adequately performing background checks. Did Adam know about Michael and the planned showdown? Did anyone else know that Michael was Ned's father? Is there a record of their emails? And what about the manuscript?

So many loose ends and strands to this story but her parents are adept storytellers: perhaps they can fix this, she tells herself, as a figure hurtles down the beach.

And Gilly's heart clutches. All the narrative skill in the world can't counter what's about to happen.

Because someone is racing in the direction of Ned.

Fifty-three

Rachel

To say that Rachel is intensely stressed is an understatement. For the entire evening, as she's made polite conversation with her mother's editor and publishing director, with people from the BBC, and with old family friends, her mind has been haring in three directions: checking on her children; fretting over her mother, last seen arguing with a late middle-aged couple – could one of them be her stalker? – and agonising over where her husband might be.

He slipped away some time after eight thirty. After she'd argued with Delia, but before her sister started drinking. At first, she assumed he was chatting in the drawing room or hanging around the kitchen, checking on Edith. Perhaps he was still heeding her advice, having taken himself off to calm down. But, half an hour in, there was no response to her texts. The erratic mobile signal, she kept telling herself: you had to virtually stand next to the router to receive anything, though she knows, deep in her bones, that she's deluded. Knows, as she declines another glass of champagne, as she gathers Maisie for an impromptu hug, as she plays the role of the dutiful daughter, chattering away to anyone who looks a little lost while constantly noting the presence of her children, that something is horribly wrong.

Because Tom is a doer. A fixer. Someone intent on improving situations (his rationale for placing one more bet, despite all evidence suggesting this would only make things worse). Rachel might have vetoed the idea of calling the police, but he looked distraught when talking to Peter. Did he receive a particularly menacing WhatsApp? Some sort of ultimatum? Might he have decided to take things into his own hands?

It's hard to imagine another explanation, and as she engages her mother's friends in conversation, her head fills with monstrous images: her husband being beaten to a pulp, or stamped on, or stabbed; him bleeding out on the coast path after a fatal slash to his heart.

'Yes, we're all terribly excited about the programme,' she hears herself say. 'Yes, it's been quite something, watching the documentary team. Being interviewed. Now, would you excuse me? There's something I need to check.' And she goes back inside to see if Tom has read or received her text, and when she discovers he hasn't, retreats to the bathroom to quietly scream.

On her return, her mother is having what looks like an animated conversation with Delia at the far edge of the garden and it's clear her sister has been drinking heavily: defiance cloaks her as she stands with her hands on her hips. The children are safe with the babysitter – she checks again – and Gilly is making her way towards her sister. But Tom? She runs through the house; around the walled garden; out to the tennis court – but he is nowhere to be seen.

She shivers with apprehension, and perhaps because the temperature's dropped: the air, earlier so oppressive, has a distinct chill to it; the edge of a tablecloth flaps against a table leg and she's struck by a fat drop of rain. More follow, and soon there's a flurry of them driving diagonally, chasing several guests inside. With squeals of surprise, they scatter, running into the marquee or seeking shelter in the drawing room, the hall and the snug.

'Maisie! Charlie! Come in the warm!'

She shepherds her children, Charlie trembling as his shirt turns translucent and clings to his ribs; Maisie shrieking with excitement, before she and Lisa slam shut the French windows. But she can't stay here, in the dry, as a storm starts to build. There's a crack of lightning and she thinks of Tom – that image of him bleeding out – then of Eleanor, and those horrific emails. *Do they know what you're capable of doing? Do they know what you did?* Then: *I will have revenges on you. I'll see you tonight.* What if she is out in the storm on her own; or worse, is being confronted by her nemesis?

Another crack and the lights flicker off, so that the room is only lit by the warm white of a pool of Diptique candles.

'Could we get some lights on?' calls a man, in a tone that suggests he is used to delegating and to being heard.

And just as swiftly, they flicker back on. Rachel takes in

the packed room, the shiny faces of her mother's friends, now smiling with relief at their adventure, and the rain flurrying against the panes like a tantruming child. She can't be here while Eleanor is in danger out there. 'You'll stay with them at all times, yes?' she checks with Lisa, kisses her children, and slips outside.

Perhaps they'll all be in the marquee, she thinks, as she runs over grass that squeaks with moisture and skids, nearly loses her footing. But it's full of guests drinking raucously and tucking into puddings, while the string quartet plays valiantly despite the sides of the tent being blown inwards by the wind.

No signal. Still no signal. The lightning's stopped, and a cheese-paring crescent of a moon silvers the clifftop and sea, but her family – Eleanor, but also Gilly, Delia, Tom – seems to have vanished, or at least she can't see them, as the wind whips around her, howling in distress.

Where would Eleanor be? Sheltering in the summer house, perhaps, the place where she is going to write? But her mother's never been one to hide from confrontation. In moments of high drama, she needs to be at the heart of the action: where Cornwall is at its most wild and intense.

There is nothing for it; and she starts to race towards the cliff – and the beach.

The cry comes as she sprints across the wet sand and stops her in her tracks.

'Muu-um?' she calls into an air filled with the keening of

the wind and the churn of the sea. No answer. There's no answer. *Please don't let it be Tom; please don't let it be Tom*, she mutters, under her breath, as she resumes her dogged running in its direction. *Please don't let it be Eleanor*, she prays.

Is there someone out there, in the darkness? Or a group that seems to shift? It's just an intuition. Her visibility's marred, not just by the blackness but by this mizzle which cloys and smudges everything. A torch might help. She fumbles with the clutch bag; retrieves her phone; and finds the torch setting. A pale white light puddles on the sand, and then she sees it: a mound, just lying there.

She slows and creeps the last few metres, the tide not just lapping her toes but swilling around her ankles, her trepidation growing with every step. The sea is swirling over a jagged outcrop of granite rocks, and the mound – the awful, unmoving mound – is part of and seems to extend from this.

Sometimes, as she later tells her sisters, though not the police, you can recognise something and refuse to accept it. That's how she feels when she sees Ned. His head smashed against the rocks, his clothes sodden with salt water, his eyes tight shut. His face – and here she shines the torch beam over it – the look on his beautiful face.

She reaches for his wrist. His skin is warm, still warm, and she puts her ear to his mouth, hoping to detect the faintest flicker of a breath.

Nothing. There is nothing.

Just a smell of iron that sticks in her nostrils; that comes from his hair. *It's not Tom, it's not Eleanor.* She's filled with relief, but, still, this is brutal. *Focus*, she tells herself as her breath comes too fast and shallow. *Concentrate. On the howl of the wind, the rush of the sea.*

And then, despite the churn of the waves and the roar of the elements, she senses something. The back of her neck prickles and her vision sharpens: she is hyper-alert because there is someone else, and possibly more than one other person, near.

She twists and stands abruptly, heart hammering so loudly she is sure it can be heard, but knowing she has to confront whoever is lurking behind her.

'Mum?'

'Rach?' the voice, as familiar as her own, says.

And then her big sister's arms are tight around her, and Rachel can feel her shivering. She's soaking wet, her clothes clinging, her hair plastered off her face.

'Where's Eleanor?'

'Back at the house. She's safe,' says Gilly. Then, 'Ned sent the emails.'

'What happened?' Because her sister's avoiding the obvious issue, and none of this is making sense. She pulls away to look her in the eye. 'Gilly. What happened to Ned?'

'There was an accident.' And Delia is there, too, moving out of the darkness.

'*An accident?*'

Delia looks at her squarely, and in that moment, a silent transaction takes place. Delia won't be telling anyone about Rachel pilfering her mother's funds. And Rachel will accept their claim. Will do nothing to undermine her sisters when they inevitably speak to the police.

The three of them stand in a tight circle, not saying anything, just watching, their eye contact, deliberate and intense. Rachel notes their trepidation, their fear, her own revulsion – because there is a dead body lying here and whatever happened, he didn't deserve this – before giving a slight nod of her head.

Besides, there's no time for discussion. A roar and a wet, silky slither as the tide circles their ankles.

'Come on. Let's go.' She gestures at her handset. 'I've no signal. We'll have to call an ambulance back at the house.'

'No, we just let the tide take him,' says Gilly, standing by the body. 'The story: it's all been sorted. I'll fill you in.'

And as Rachel realises that others may have been involved, she starts running across the sand with her sisters, the wind at their backs, heading for the cliffs. By keeping quiet, she has bound herself tighter to her family, but now she needs to find Tom and organise a search party for him – even if that involves calling the police.

They haul themselves up the cliff, and just as the path meets the border of her mother's heath, she stops and turns to her younger sister.

'We're OK,' she says. A statement, not a question. She gives Delia a firm hug; watches Gilly's strained features soften with relief.

And then they stumble through the scrubland towards

the garden of their mother's Cornish manor, the fire pits still burning valiantly, the fairy lights twinkling, the string quartet playing the blues – as if the players are fed up with being unappreciated and will do whatever they damn well please.

The first violinist improvises. A sweetly mournful ribbon of sound that brings Rachel to the brink of tears, because too much has happened tonight, and is still to happen – Tom is out there in the darkness – and it won't take much to tip her over; to express the sorrow and fear she's been trying to suppress.

'Come on,' says Gilly, and there's a steeliness to her tone that tells Rachel they can see this through; that they'll walk quietly past the guests, before re-emerging, showered and newly dressed – and in Rachel's case, calling the police to hunt for her husband. That they'll cope with the latter stages of this party. 'Come on. We've got this.'

EPILOGUE

Drafts

From: ineverythingillegitimate@yahoo.com
To: freida@eleanorkingman.co.uk

Now, gods, stand up for bastards!

Act 1, scene ii. *Lear* – Edmund, as you might expect. My favourite character, and probably my favourite line.

Why brand they us / With 'base'? with 'baseness'? 'bastardy'?

Same soliloquy, and another stinger. When it comes to juicy quotes, the tragedies just keep them coming, don't they?

Oh, one final one: *Edmund the base / Shall top the legitimate. I grow. I prosper!*

Vaulting ambition? Well, perhaps. I'm a realist, but I can't help hoping.

After all, as you of all people know, those with sufficient grit and talent can claw their way up.

So why shouldn't that happen to me?

New Year

Four months later

Eleanor, Gilly, Delia

'Let's have a bonfire,' Eleanor suggests.

'A bonfire?' asks Rachel.

'To go with the fireworks? The children will love it. There's all that old wood from the summer house the builders still haven't got rid of, and besides, there's something I need to burn.'

Her daughter looks at her quizzically.

'I'm sure I don't need to elaborate.'

'Well, no.' Rachel shakes her head as if righting an idea. 'I just assumed you'd got rid of it?'

'Not until the inquest was over. Not until the coroner ruled, quite rightly, it was all an accident.' She sticks to pronouns. *The. It.* Not Ned's name. Nothing that would give him an identity.

'And not until the police indicated they were closing their inquiry?'

Eleanor folds her lips on top of each other as if to restrain herself from saying any more, and gives a quick, sharp nod.

To be fair, it's no wonder her daughter seems bemused. There has been rather a lot for them to adjust to. The body disappeared, just as Eleanor had predicted: picked up by the tide and carried miles down the coast towards Sennen. Spotted after ten days at sea.

Beached on some rocks, it was unrecognisable. Bloated. Broken. Pummelled. All forensics lost. Any blows from a backward fall confused by lacerations from the cliffs and general decomposition. The latter made it easier for everyone not to think of it as a person. As Ned.

An accidental death, the coroner ruled. When questioned, the day after the party, Michael provided his ex-wife and daughters with the alibi he suggested. He'd seen them chatting to the TV presenter, as Adam had noted, but then had watched them leave. Michael had subsequently argued with the man, himself – but then he tweaked his original story. (No point risking sounding murderous, even if it made him less heroic.) On telling him he no longer wanted to be part of the documentary, there was no fight, no shove, no lunge: Ned had merely stormed away.

Devon and Cornwall police tried their best to pinpoint foul play, but there were no eyewitnesses to discount Michael's story. The guests were sheltering from the storm; their hangovers persisted for days. The discovery of malicious emails – including one in Ned's drafts folder, claiming 'Now, gods, stand up for bastards!' – only consolidated the idea that the dead man was not only a vexatious stalker, but the melodramatic sort who might race along a beach in a storm. With the coroner's ruling, the police dropped their investigation. Since the death was accidental, there was no need for a murder inquiry.

The ruling came just before Christmas, but there is still the issue of the manuscript which Eleanor needs to get rid of. The one which Gilly found, in the hours after the tragic accident, in a leather man-bag in Ned's room.

Despite having claimed the contrary to Eleanor, Peter kept banging on to the police about its existence, but Carole swiftly put an end to this idea. 'There *was* no manuscript,' she told detectives. 'I can provide you with legal documents he signed *years* ago attesting to the fact he binned it. You might have noticed my former colleague is in the early stages of dementia? Confuses the past with the present. Has a hazy grip on thc truth.'

Anyway, the script is now in Eleanor's locked bottom drawer: the one for which only she has the key. Rather belatedly, she has realised she is lax about security. And yes, she did eventually notice that Rachel was transferring money; that she had siphoned off £560,000.

'Why did you do it?' she asked, incredulous that her most financially cautious daughter could do such a thing.

There had followed what she is now framing as a constructive exchange, certainly the most honest she has ever had with any of her children, during which she learned the depths of Rachel's anguish and fear.

'You were willing for us to lose our home, for our family to be split up, for Tom to be terrorised and badly hurt, though you could easily have afforded to help us. And for what? A determination to stick to your principles? To teach me to stand on my own feet? I fucked up.

'I made a mistake. We all make mistakes. We've all done stupid, terrible, *criminal* things. Not Gilly – but Tom, me, Delia – and *you*.'

And there it had hung: the fact of Eleanor's fallibility and guilt. She had taken Rachel in her arms, not something she initially found comfortable, but then the old muscle memory kicked in and she remembered having done this, and loved it, when Rachel and Gilly were small. 'I'm sorry,' she said, not something that she ever found easy to say. And yet, to her surprise, she found that she was. She still didn't quite see why she was expected to pay for her son-in-law's addiction, but she saw that she could afford to show this kindness to her daughter. It was complicated, but then so much of life was.

Easier to discuss practicalities of rates of pay and how she could show her generosity moving forward.

'Perhaps I *should* have been paying you more. I'll make up the difference to Gilly, too.' Neither was so cynical as to suggest that Eleanor was buying Rachel's discretion, but there was no harm in covering all eventualities. Fraud or murder? (One of two murders.) Which was the worst? Well, they both knew the answer to that.

And now? Well, now is the time to obliterate this document.

'So, a bonfire, yes? Lit before the fireworks? Edith will hate those, but I'd have thought the children will love them.'

'Absolutely, though Tom might keep the dog company.'

'Ah, of course.' Her poor son-in-law, who is still recovering from his broken ankle, and who, these days, is more nervous of sudden noises after spending several hours lying injured on the cliffs. Adam had found him, cowering and near hypothermic, in the early hours of the morning. There's been no more online gambling since then. Of course, the therapy has helped; and it was a massive shock to discover men emptying their London home; for him to see the distress this caused Rachel and the children. Yes, it's fair to say the whole experience has quite curbed his appetite for risk.

'And the others are still coming?'

'Oh yes.' Gilly, and Adam, dear Adam, who has been quite the revelation; and Delia, with whom she has become closer, her daughter realising that her mother isn't malicious even if she is, inevitably, flawed. Dysfunction breeds dysfunction. *You try having my childhood*, Eleanor has wanted to say, though she manages to resist. Talking of which, 'Jo and Bill will be coming, too.'

'You've prised them from the Devon cottage?' Rachel looks surprised.

'I was wondering if I should sign it over to Jo? She loves it so much, and you're right: maybe I needn't be so anxious about money.'

Her daughter looks as if she's trying to stifle a smile.

'You quite like her, really.'

'Not as much as Bill.' Eleanor softens at the thought of her little brother, with whom she is now rather close. The siblings have discussed that long-ago night. 'I *knew* you wouldn't leave for no reason,' said Bill; 'I *knew* you were there,' added Jo. 'I heard the door bang and I *saw* you run away, from our top window. Don't worry, I didn't tell Ned.'

'Sisters can be tricky,' Eleanor says now. 'But when they're loyal, they are absolutely priceless.' A pause, while she considers how Rachel's relationship with Delia has improved.

Her middle daughter stands up, clearly having had quite enough of this sentimentality. She's more like her than Eleanor thought.

'Are we going to do this then? Get rid of this old story?' Rachel asks.

'Absolutely,' says Eleanor. 'Let's get the children to help with building this fire.'

'All right?'

Gilly arrives at Trecarrow Manor in a very different state from when she helped her mother move in, seven months earlier.

Crucially, she is no longer on her payroll. Ned's death meant she delayed her announcement, but in late September, she managed to resign.

She is writing. Not as Gillian Kingman but under a pseudonym because she writes erotica. Turns out she is rather good at it. All those years of failing to commit to her writing; of doubting she had a voice. Who knew a sexual awakening would lead to such creative and commercial success?

Perhaps being flooded with oestrogen helps? For a while she had blamed her tight nipples and swelling breasts on her work: maybe feeling semi-aroused was an occupational hazard if you wrote what her mother persists in describing as 'filth', and her publishers as 'stories of female-centred desire'? Then she wondered if Adam was the cause because, since the night of the party when he had chosen to believe her alibi, when he bought into their story and he rescued Tom, he has become a permanent part of her life.

And then she joined the dots. It turned out that if you have lots of spontaneous, unprotected sex then something might happen, even at forty. She is fourteen weeks' pregnant, and the sex is like *nothing* she has experienced before. She hopes she has a daughter. Dysfunction breeds dysfunction, except that it needn't. As Delightfully Delia, and a whole raft of Instagrammers might say, she chooses to break the cycle.

She turns to her lover, who may very well doubt Michael's story but is sufficiently canny not to admit to this; and who she sent to search for Tom while she ransacked Ned's bedroom, and she knows that she is more than all right.

'Absolutely,' she says, as she plants a kiss on his open lips and lingers for longer than is perhaps polite. He squeezes her bum as she knocks on her mother's door.

She will tell her family about the baby tonight.

*

'OK, Daddy. I'm going to have to go now, but I love you. I love you.'

Delia watches the image of her father on her iPhone as he waves. As ever, she doesn't want to end the call. *What if this is it?* she wonders, as she always does. *The last time we say goodbye?* He is too frail to come to Cornwall for this ceremonial burning of the manuscript. To see in a new and better year. But his generosity – lying on all their behalf; claiming he was the last to see Ned Simpson alive; volunteering that, yes, Ned was his long-lost, illegitimate son, and he could quite see why the Detective Sergeant was suspicious, but he had never touched him in his life, she would just have to take his word for it (and she was convinced by the crack in his voice, the tear in his eye) – all this justifies his presence. Her mother had asked him to come; will visit him next week in Chiswick. 'Bye, Daddy, bye,' she says to an empty screen.

Delia has been doing the work, she really has. But it's amazing how the possibility of a murder charge focuses the mind. Far more than therapy! She got away with it – but she owes her parents, and her sisters, *quiiiiite* a lot. Delightfully Delia's account has gone rather quiet. 'Taking some time for my mental health. Sending love to my wellness girlies!' was her last post, in November, captioning a snap of her smiling and making the peace sign on the beach. 'Was that where he died?' 'OMG it was where that presenter died!' There were a few negative comments amid a wealth of 'Sending love xxx', 'You take your time, babe', 'Love a digital detox' – but there were enough. *For my mental health*, she whispers, powering off her phone and placing it in a drawer. (These days, she practises good phone hygiene.) Pulling on one of Michael's old cashmere jumpers, she prepares to go outside.

Aiysha's fashionably late. She's now learned that if Dame Eleanor tells you to arrive at six thirty, she means seven. Unless it's a publishing meeting, of which there have been several. They are working on *Tyler 2*: everything crossed, it will be out next October and should be topping the Christmas charts. And yes, her terms have been completely renegotiated and it's most definitely a true, properly compensated partnership. A 40/60 split. Unprecedented, according to Charlotte. Aiysha had been stunned.

That's part of the reason she's down here, in Cornwall. *Tyler 2* will be Eleanor's final book for children, and she wants it written *right now.* And Aiysha wants to capitalise on this enthusiasm. For them to brainstorm ideas efficiently, and for her to learn as much as she can from the woman she views as her mentor, before pitching the first of several projects of her own.

But Aiysha's not stupid, and as Marta opens the ancient oak door and ushers her into the candlelit hall, she allows herself a small smile. It's all so different from when she came down, four months ago. By inviting her to this select New Year's Eve party, Dame Eleanor has confirmed that, if not part of the inner sanctum, Aiysha is important to her. Significant in some way. All she did was keep quiet about having met Bill and Joanne on the cliffs. It was better if no one suspected there'd been prior knowledge of Ned's manipulations, explained Gilly, and Aiysha, with one eye on her new draft contract, was happy to oblige.

After all, it's small acts of kindness like this which the *Jess* and *Tyler* books celebrate, and which make Aiysha feel so much better about herself. That moment of madness on the cliffs when she'd imagined pushing Dame Eleanor down? C'mon. She's already rewritten that.

They build the bonfire at the edge of the heath, perhaps on the same spot where Eleanor confronted Ned and his plot started to unravel. It's a substantial pyre, made of dried-out hawthorn, the old floorboards of the summer house, and several yellowing A4 pages screwed into individual balls and tucked in between. The children swiftly lose interest, but Eleanor's daughters take the job seriously: each concerned that the pages properly catch light, and that the edifice acts as a sort of beacon. Once the flames get going, it should be seen from the headlands up and down the coast.

Her girls dress for the part, too. *They could be the three weird sisters*, thinks Eleanor, the hoods of their Canada Goose parkas pulled around their faces as they stare into the fire like Macbeth's witches. *When will we three meet again?* Well, they're here now, and she savours the moment, as the wood catches and crackles, and sparks fly from the dry tinder, the odd piece of ash sailing up into the night.

The children are excited, too. Caught up in the hysteria that causes their mother to take their hands and dance around in a circle, a few metres away from the flames. Maisie is giddy, her laughter spiralling like the orange dots fizzing and spraying from the pyre and showering down on the crushed heather and thyme. 'Faster, faster. All fall down!' Except no. A flash of Grace, felled by William's fist; and of William – the way he'd fallen; then Ned, shoved backwards by Delia. Eleanor catches Jo's eye, and then Bill's, who smiles. Are they thinking of their father? She sees him; sees Ned. But there'll be no more falling. There'll be no one else harmed.

'Come on, *dance*,' her granddaughter insists.

From the recesses of the past, she remembers doing so. Perhaps whirling with Jo, or playing skipping games, after all, in the street outside their home. Her sister takes one of Maisie's hands and she takes the other and swings it as she shuffles from foot to foot. But she's too self-conscious to do so for long and she lets Jo take over, with a smile she hopes conveys it's *her* problem, not her granddaughter's. 'Let's do this instead.'

Because there are other ways to feel free, she thinks, as she hands the little girl one of the few remaining sheets of the document, held back for this ceremonial burning, and watches her throw it at the fire. The flames lick its edges then gobble it up, insatiable, ravenous, and she offers others to her daughters and Charlie.

'Careful now,' she tells her grandson, but he is more reverential than reckless, recognising the fire's power.

And as she watches them feed her words to the flames, and the fire gulp them down, she knows there are plenty more where they came from. She is only seventy, and she has so much more to say. Unlike Peter, her mind is as sharp as ever, and her plotting as good. Plus, there's an obvious outlet. Plundering Tom's experiences of the criminal underworld – everything is copy – she is going to start writing crime.

Of course, she had considered writing her autobiography with certain criminal elements excised. *The Official Eleanor Kingman Story.* Rich, potent, honest. Or honest to a degree.

The documentary has been scrapped, of course, Ned Simpson no longer a tragic but problematic figure once news leaked of his malicious emails. She and Gilly had debated long and hard about whether to destroy his laptop and phone, but realised that would only implicate them since the emails from ineverythingillegitimate would be discovered by the police.

So, there was room for an autobiography, but she would far rather rewrite her past and pass it off as fiction. Because isn't that what every writer tried to do? Make sense of their life while aiming for a happy ending or at least a more emotionally satisfying resolution? Based on a true story – but made more gripping, more affecting, with increased jeopardy.

There's no collaboration. No one to bounce ideas off. No one to accuse her of stealing their ideas, either (though Tom *has* been useful). But she is enjoying knowing she has sole responsibility for these stories: that she alone is authoring this book. Though she still maintains she only ever breathed creative life into others' ideas, it is a relief to know this is her creation entirely, and that no one will be able to claim otherwise. And it is such a thrill to be writing for adults. All those deeply flawed characters, and not a precocious tween or anthropomorphised animal in sight!

For the first time since she bent over her typewriter in that cold Chiswick kitchen, she is fired by the sheer pleasure of writing – and she is *flying*, driven by the innate knowledge that she is crafting something really rather good. Reams of words tumble from her as she shapes her narrative and tells *her* story. Or at least this version.

She reckons she has a bestseller on her hands.

Acknowledgements

Like all the coolest guests, *Based on a True Story* is somewhat late to the party. My heartfelt thanks to my publishers, Simon & Schuster UK, and in particular, my editor Clare Hey, for putting up with such borderline Delia behaviour. I so appreciate your patience and compassion, and sincerely hope you've a better book, as a result.

Massive thanks, as ever, to Lizzy Kremer, agent and friend, for her unwavering support, sharp eye and sixth sense for when I might need to hear from her; to DHA's Maddalena Cavaciuti, who gave astute notes on an early draft; and to Orli Vogt-Vincent, who is unfailingly patient and kind. A chat with DHA's Christabel McKinley proved invaluable in the early stages of writing, as did one with Rosie Walsh, another of Lizzy's authors. The DHA rights team continue to hustle on my behalf as does Georgie Smith, my film and TV agent in the UK. In the US, I am so grateful to Sylvie Rabineau, at WME, and to Stacy Testa, at Writers House, also in the US.

Huge thanks, too, to everyone at S&S UK: executive publisher Phoebe Morgan; my dream team of Jess Barratt and Hayley McMullan; Louise Davies and John Sugar;

Tamsin Shelton for the copy-edit and Federica Leonardis for the proofread. My gratitude to Olivia Allen, Jade Unwin, Heather Hogan, Katie Sormaz, Madeline Allan and Rich Hawton for selling the book so that it can be read.

In the US, I'm thrilled to be published by Sarah Stein at Harper, and am grateful for her light but perceptive notes, and for believing in this so strongly.

Based on a True Story has required the least research of any of my novels, but I still benefitted from the expertise of Graham Bartlett, retired detective, crime fiction consultant and bestselling author; of Sally-Anne Youll and Cath Wohlers, of The England Illegal Money Lending Team; and of Olivia Dwyer, at the NatWest media team, for letting me check details of banking. The remainder of my research involved visits to North Cornwall, where I've holidayed for the past forty plus years; and studying my dog and constant writing companion, Olive, without whom Edith wouldn't exist.

Polly Chase (Eve Chase) has helped immeasurably as my writing buddy: the friend who will always understand if I send a slightly despairing text. I honestly do not know where I would be, writing-wise, without her support.

And my husband and children, Ella and Jack, as ever remind me of the important things in life – as do my parents: relationships and, at the risk of sounding like a sentimental card, family.

Which leads me to my sister, Laura Tennant, to whom *Based on a True Story* is dedicated. I doubt I could have written this without experiencing the ultimately unconditional love of a sister, or that of Bobby Hall, our strong and inspiring mother.

Finally, thank you to my readers, who have given up asking me when the next book will be published, but who will hopefully pick this up. There would be no point in writing were it not for you.

About the Author

SARAH VAUGHAN read English at Oxford and spent eleven years at the *Guardian* as a news reporter and political correspondent, before leaving to write fiction. Her first two novels were followed by her first psychological thriller, *Anatomy of a Scandal*: a *Sunday Times* top five bestseller, Richard & Judy pick of the decade, and the TV adaptation was a global number one on Netflix. Her fourth novel, *Little Disasters*, was a Waterstones thriller of the month and developed as a number one Paramount Plus show. Her fifth novel, *Reputation*, was a *Sunday Times* thriller of the month and is currently in development by the team who made *Anatomy of a Scandal*. *Based on a True Story* is her sixth novel.

A million-copy international bestselling author, her books have been published in twenty-seven countries.

Reading Group Questions

1. The three sisters have very different characters. Which one did you most relate to, and why?

2. Which characters did you dislike or distrust? Did this change as the novel went on?

3. What was the meaning of the fox metaphor that ran through the novel? And how effective did you find this?

4. There are literary allusions throughout the novel, especially to Shakespeare. What do these allusions say about the characters and their actions?

5. If you have read any of Sarah Vaughan's other novels, are there any similar themes you recognised? Compare and contrast how these are explored in the different novels.

6. *'You make everything up.'* The process of writing fiction is examined throughout the novel. Discuss how that informs and reflects the ways in which the characters construct stories and outward personas in their lives.

7. *'Dysfunction breeds dysfunction, except that it needn't.'* There is a strong sense of history repeating, or echoing

through the generations. To what extent do you believe people are able to break these cycles?

8. *'After all, every female writer of any stature experienced abuse.'* Consider the forms of abuse explored in this novel. How have they influenced the characters and affected the plot?

9. In what ways does class have an impact on the characters and their roles in this story?

10. *'She would far rather rewrite her past and pass it off as fiction. Because isn't that what every writer tried to do? Make sense of their life while aiming for a happy ending or at least a more emotionally satisfying resolution?'* Were you surprised by the revelations of Eleanor's past, and did you better understand her character after those were revealed?

11. Did you feel the setting of the novel in Cornwall was effective, and in what ways did it influence or strengthen the plot?

12. What were the most memorable scenes or passages in the novel, and why did they stand out to you?

13. How well do you feel the title of the book and the cover design reflect the story?

14. How do you feel about the ending? Was it satisfying? Was it surprising? Was it the ending you were hoping for?